ONE CONSCIOUS BREATH

A WILD TALE OF AN ADVENTURE INTO PEACE

PATRICK JOHNSON

KNOWING YOURSELF
IS THE BEGINNING OF ALL WISDOM.

–ARISTOTLE

THE MORE YOU DO, THE LESS YOU'LL BE.
THE MORE YOU KNOW, THE LESS YOU'LL SEE.

–CHRISTOPHER CROMPTON

THERE IS NO SUCH THING AS
'GETTING TO HEAVEN'.
THERE IS ONLY THE KNOWING
THAT YOU'RE ALREADY THERE.

–NEALE DONALD WALSH; CONVERSATIONS WITH GOD

I AM A HOLE IN A FLUTE THAT
THE CHRIST'S BREATH FLOWS THROUGH.
LISTEN TO THIS MUSIC.

–HAFFIZ

SEE DIFFERENTLY
AND ENTER THE KINGDOM.

–JESUS

**JUST REMIND THE PEOPLE
OF WHAT A FREE MIND CAN DO.**

–NEO; THE MATRIX RESURRECTIONS

YOUR SIMPLE BREATHING MODELS YOUR ENTIRE VOCATION AS A HUMAN BEING. YOU ARE AN INCARNATION, LIKE CHRIST, OF MATTER AND SPIRIT OPERATING AS ONE. THIS, MORE THAN ANYTHING WE BELIEVE OR ACCOMPLISH, IS HOW ALL OF US CONTINUE THE MYSTERY OF INCARNATION IN SPACE AND TIME – EITHER KNOWINGLY AND JOYFULLY, OR NOT.

–RICHARD ROHR; THE UNIVERSAL CHRIST

FOLLOW THE YELLOW BRICK ROAD.

–THE WIZARD OF OZ

CASTLE WALLS LEAD ME TO DESPAIR.

–BOB MCLEAN

**ONCE IN A WHILE YOU GET SHOWN
THE LIGHT IN THE STRANGEST OF PLACES
IF YOU LOOK AT IT RIGHT.**

–ROBERT HUNTER, GRATEFUL DEAD

ISBN: 978-1-68489-657-8
Cover Art: Mackenzie Schmidt
Cover Design: Faisal Habibi
Interior Design: Dino Marino
Interior Artwork: Ellen Black

TABLE OF CONTENTS

PREFACE

I am so pleased OCB has found its way to you. I hope you enjoy it, and while enjoying the story for what it is, also read it as a metaphor for the journey we are all on. After all, the undercurrent of this novel is one we are all in the flow of. And fundamentally, that's what this book is all about – the flow of our individual and collective journeys into 'The More', and the deepening of relationship with the God of one's understanding.

In the summer of 2020, when the world was in the throes of the COVID-19 pandemic, it seemed fear, uncertainty, and division had become the cultural norms… and I wanted with all my heart to play a role in reversing that tide.

So, I offered up a prayer asking how I could extend any positive influence that might want to flow through me. One morning, before a whitewater kayak run while on the bank of the Arkansas River in Brown's Canyon in Colorado, my prayer was met with a simple inspiration:

Tell your story.

Well, that felt a bit vulnerable! I immediately began dealing with all sorts of limiting beliefs and came up with many excuses for why I should not. Even so, I ruminated on the notion during the months that followed, and I couldn't escape the fact that friends and clients have consistently said my life experience offers a lot of hope and inspiration. I believe that's true, and further, that if that is the case, then I don't have any right to keep something like that to myself.

Indeed, it's true the story I've lived thus far does submit conviction about, and evidence for, a paradigm of peace and love that transcends understanding and undergirds everything. So, if only one person is nudged even a little more into a fulfilling life with less struggle and more contentment, wouldn't all the considerable effort and vulnerability of writing a book be worth it?

I don't see myself as a teacher, except to the extent that any of you would be the same to me, should I have the privilege of hearing your story. We all have something to teach and learn from one another. Wisdom in all her beauty seems to show up in profound ways if we simply slow down, hold space, and *really* listen to what she has to offer as we engage with others and with life.

There are a lot of phenomenal teachers who bring powerful insights to arenas which this book doesn't touch on. There are also many teachers who speak to the concepts in this book far better than I do. What specifically, then, does *this* book offer, and who would benefit most?

I hope it offers the reader timeless insights and truths in a fun, relatable story… and all in the spirit of 'show, don't tell.' OCB does not fit nicely into a specific genre, and I don't want to guess at who might benefit most. It is one of those rare, idiosyncratic works that is best qualified by what it has hints of, but which it is not. It is not: memoir; clear spiritual teaching; self-help; religious; autobiography; pure fiction. It is a spiritual fiction novel based on a true story that has a heavy memoir feel.

The facts of my story are unique, while the theme is not. We are all on a hero's journey home… even though, in a very real sense, we never left. That is the lesson Sophia, wisdom herself, will ultimately teach each of us, and I am grateful and humbled if she chooses to use One . Conscious . Breath to that end for you.

Namaste,

FOREWORD

I "met" Patrick Johnson on a sunny, June afternoon, although for him it was morning. At his home in Colorado, he was a mere 7500 kilometers away from my home across the pond in England when his message arrived in my inbox, asking if I would be interested in editing his spiritual fiction novel. I would indeed be interested, although I had no idea then just how much.

It's not commonplace for an editor to write a book's foreword. And of the many manuscripts I have edited, this is the first time I've been asked to do so. But then very little about this book or my experience of working on it has been commonplace. On the contrary, it has been a remarkable ride.

My own spiritual journey, if you could call it that, has been very different to Pappy's story that you are about to hear through this book. While the Christian tradition is still pervasive enough in modern British society that I was aware of it, had read the Bible and even been to Bible studies out of curiosity, I've never considered myself a religious person. I've mused with broad strokes and an open mind on questions and themes that span across many spiritual traditions - along the way taking meditation classes from a Buddhist monk, and even living for a while in an intentional community following Sufi teachings, although admittedly as a curious sceptic.

While none of these traditions felt right to me in totality, there were things that did feel right about all of them. There were threads of warmth and wisdom that wove through the many paths that might lead to that which is beyond us. And pretty much all those positive threads converge in this book - through the challenges, questions and revelations that make up Pappy's personal journey.

Most of us like to think of ourselves as essentially good people, doing the right thing by ourselves, our families, perhaps by society at large or our religions. And we want to feel we are getting through life with some measure of success doing the best with what we've been given. We also want others to view us that way and to judge us positively. The problem so often is that the constant struggle to achieve and maintain all of that creates a lot of anxiety. We might doubt our decisions, feel uncertain about our futures, or just wonder if we're doing enough with our lives. Are we living authentically and realizing our potential? All the while, we worry about outside judgement - earthly or divine. Without noticing it, we become driven and guided by fear. The irony is that this leads us to be anything but our best selves.

Pappy started out just like this in the story he begins to recount. While everything looked calm and rosy on the outside, his internal world was one of uncertainty and dissatisfaction. As is often the case, it took him a long time even to acknowledge this default state of fear, let alone to figure out what he could do about it. At its core, this story is about Pappy's struggle to find that peace that all of us need to feel. It also has a lot to say besides: about setting values to live by; about social and technological progress; about human compassion and empathy; and, about faith. Each 'wisdom nugget' feels hard earned and carefully observed, raising questions without being too domineering. And the story strongly rejects the suggestion of dogmatic doctrine - the idea that there is only one true way of going about things.

It was a great surprise and delight to me as it became apparent that Patrick and I found ourselves on the same frequency of awareness and understanding about so much, despite arriving here on very different roads. Through the course of our discussions and work together, we quickly became friends and I know we each consider it a great privilege to have convened through the story told here. It gives me hope that all readers arriving at this book can draw something from it, regardless of the road they have walked.

One. Conscious. Breath is a tale of adventure. It tells of a quest of vast possibility, aspiration and yearning with more than its fair share of doubt and heartache. But ultimately, it is greatly uplifting. The story offers not just hope, but a vision for our future as individuals and as a collective. It tells one man's story, but it carries the universal in it – traces of fear, uncertainty, hope and love that resonate on some level with each of us. And ultimately, there is wisdom here for those who are open to seeing and feeling differently… one conscious breath at a time.

I wish you very well on your own path.

— Christopher Crompton, Editor

ACKNOWLEDGEMENTS

To the God of my ever evolving understanding. For choosing me to live this story… what a ride it has been!

To Jenny. My soul's mate, and the best partner for the journey that anyone could ask for or imagine.

To Lauren and Luke. My inspiration, and my friends. Having the opportunity to be your father is one of the greatest joys of my life.

To my extended family. You have offered so much support and love along the way. Thank you for trusting me to tell this story faithfully.

To my 3am crew. You folks who have been with me through the highs and lows of my journey thus far. I know you would be there for me, no matter what, if I called on you at any time. And I for you. I cherish that knowing.

To those I might have hurt as I've fumbled along. The lessons you have taught me through my awareness of the pain I have caused you have been powerful. Thank you for your sacrifice, and I am so very sorry.

Colorado Parks and Recreation | Arkansas Headwaters Recreation Area (AHRA). Thank you for your faithful commitment to conservation and management. This novel was inspired by the natural resources you steward.

And, last but certainly not least, to Christopher Crompton, my editor and dear friend, whose encouragement, generosity, and professionalism is largely responsible for this book coming to fruition.

PROLOGUE

When I 'died the first death', it was a profoundly personal experience. And, frankly, I am a bit shocked the story has become a novel! But, as you will soon see, I've been nothing if not faithful to promptings; and, as you might have read in the Preface, a prompting is why this book exists.

I debated how to best lay out the story, and I decided on a standard format which you will likely be familiar with, but which I feel compelled to point out. There are effectively three parts to the novel: Introduction; Context; Crux.

You will identify the natural breakpoints between these sections as you move through the novel, and I hope you enjoy the full arc. I will offer that this is a story to settle into and enjoy, more than it is a work to approach with an agenda of learning anything.

I just hope you enjoy reading it as much as I've enjoyed living it.

With love,

FAMILY TREE

TO HELP THE READER KNOW THE FAMILY BY AGE AND RELATIONSHIP

Cecil (7)
McLean (5)
Sam (7)
Susie (6)
Kell (5)
John (30)/Polly (30)
Lou (30)/Susan (30)
Mike (28)/Andrea (28)
Betty (28)
Mack (24)
Sid (53)/Becky (53)
Lauren (55)/Greg (55)
Betsey (85)/George (86)
Nana (118)
Grampy/Gran

CHAPTER ONE

INTO THE FLOW

The deep black of the Colorado night sky was awash with stars, and the cool early summer air was laced with the smell of pine. The sound of the rushing Arkansas River was a powerful reminder of continuous flow of life – appropriate, considering the events of the week. It was the summer solstice of 2093, and that year marked a significant turning for our family.

I was staying in one of the four guest cabins on Pappy's and Nana's Buena Vista riverside property with a very pregnant Naomi and my four-year-old daughter, Jenny. The evening had been a late one, with everyone finally leaving the firepit a little after three in the morning, much to the delight of the few exhausted kids who had somehow managed to stay awake. As I watched our large family disperse to their rooms, I privately indulged in the fond memories of my many experiences with Pappy. He had invested so much of his life's energy in us, and we were better for it. That was true even for those of us high in the branches of the family tree - like me, his great grandson.

"Don..." he would sometimes say while holding my gaze for a long moment with his lively blue eyes, "... *family!*" A whole lesson in one word.

Earlier in the week, the daughter of Pappy's old buddy, Dean, had brewed Pappy's longtime favorite using her dad's recipe. She wanted to give some to Pappy for his 120th and had dropped off a few growlers on a recent trip to the valley with her family. True to form, Pappy had been generous and shared freely. The beer had paired with the evening perfectly, so I ended up a couple of pints deeper than intended and still had a healthy buzz when everyone else went to sleep.

Since I dislike going to bed feeling at all loopy, I decided to sit on the porch and ruminate on all we heard from our patriarch that night – the incredible narrative I will relay with this story. Over the years, I had gleaned bits and pieces about Pappy's and Nana's life together, but never many of the details. And I'd heard nothing of his profound personal transformation. Pappy and Nana had always just seemed more interested in listening to us than talking about themselves.

But that night he had shared a lot, and in response to the most unlikely of catalysts. Pappy delivered a wild tale of his adventure from existential pain and fear into deep personal peace. He spoke of whitewater kayaking adventures in South America, intimate conversations with God, crazy neighbors who blew up houses, visions and modern-day prophets, and even mini unicorns. He shared how he and Nana had followed their hearts and left their comfortable suburban life in search of a more grounded experience on a homestead which they built together from raw land. We learned of their suffering and fortitude, of family and faith. Most important, he offered a grand story of hope that inspired and empowered. The time together listening to Pappy around the firepit had perfectly closed out a fantastic week of reunion for our family.

Until everything went haywire.

The heads-up display on my eye-lens said the time was 3:03 a.m. Pappy's two dogs, Frankie and Leela, were lying with me while I rocked gently in a custom walnut and cedar chair. Pappy and Nana had two identical rockers commissioned more than eight decades ago by a carpenter who told Pappy at one point that he made every piece to last because he never knew 'when the Master would have a use for it'. That story has always touched me. And indeed, those chairs had seen much use over many years.

My bare feet were enjoying the contrast of the cool flagstone underfoot and the warmth of Leela's thick coat on top. I had turned the porch light off so Naomi and Jenny wouldn't be disturbed and so I could better appreciate the sky packed full of stars. The cats hunting near the chicken coop were barely discernable, every shadowy movement laden with intentional precision. My rocking had settled into a rhythm that matched the pace of my slow and listless thoughts.

The familiar sound of heavy metal sliding on a track suddenly interrupted the silence. Pappy and Nana had purchased and developed this property in the Arkansas River Valley many years ago, and I had spent so much of my childhood there. Almost every door on the property was a slider, and to this day that sound feels like home.

With my thoughts distracted, I scanned the property to determine where the noise had come from, and eventually saw it had been the door that led from Pappy's and Nana's room on the back of the house out to the lawn. I was surprised to see Pappy's lean, six-foot frame silhouetted against the soft yellow glow from his bedroom. He never liked the white of LEDs, so all the lights on the property were tinted to offer the old 'soft glow' he and Nana preferred.

He didn't appear to be wearing anything but his old river shorts, and looking back, perhaps I should have thought more of that. But he lived in them during the summer months, so I just watched without making any effort to get his attention. His shoulders lifted slightly and dropped gently on an exhale. Then he walked with a purposeful stride from his room, across the patio, and onto the lawn. Our little cabin was situated toward the river from the main house, about twenty-five yards downstream of the huge firepit where we had all been gathered earlier.

He walked between the firepit and me without a glance and seemed to be headed for the boatshed near the river. Frankie and Leela got up and sauntered toward him, likely wondering what sort of adventure they could possibly be getting into at that hour. Pappy knelt to greet them both and whispered something in their ears. They leaned into him hard, one furry neck on each of his shoulders. The three heads drooped together in an embrace, and the line between dog and man blurred. Pappy wore Nana's wedding ring around his neck on a leather strap, along with a silver medallion she had made for him years before by a local artist. Engraved on either side were Pappy's favorite admonishments from the Stoics: "Momento Mori" – *Remember You Must Die* and "Momento Vivere – R*emember to Live*. As he stood, I could faintly hear the ring and medallion clank together. The significance was not lost on me.

He finished the short walk to the shed with the dogs at his heels. Then he told the lights to turn on, slid the door open, and walked in. He disappeared after quickly moving past the rafts, kayaks, and paddle-barrel. The dogs knew to stay outside, so they laid down on the flagstone under the overhang of the shed. A wrought-iron chandelier hung from a piece of climbing rope that had some story behind it that I can't remember, and the light from the fixture exposed the cats as they scampered up the rough-hewn logs that trimmed the sides of the stacked-stone structure. They scurried into the shed, nimbly navigating the timber eaves that held the weight of the earthen roof. I heard some rummaging around, and then some barely audible *shhhh... shhhh... shhhh* sounds that went on for a while.

Pappy emerged from the shed and slid the door shut behind him. What I witnessed was so ludicrous and out of context that I have wondered many times if my vision was influenced by the beer. Or perhaps if I had fallen asleep and was having a bizarre and vivid dream. If it had been anyone other than Pappy, I would have concluded that was likely the case.

There he stood on the patio of the boatshed wearing only his river shorts and sun-faded life vest. But it was the enormous, inflatable unicorn around his waist that made the scene decidedly bizarre. The huge waist-tube of the floatie transitioned into a long neck supporting a large rainbow-colored mane with grab handles on either side. A small head with sparkly eyes and a very prominent horn capped it off. I rubbed my eyes.

The dogs, who would normally have been pacing in anticipation of an adventure, stood beside him with their bodies touching his legs, seeming to lend faithful support. Their postures created a sense of gravitas in a scene that otherwise could only have been described as a silly. The cats had slipped out of the shed as the door shut, and they sat beside each other holding regal postures. Their tails were wrapped around to their forepaws and their eyes focused on Pappy. Suddenly, he looked at me and winked with a playful smile. Then his lips moved briefly with the 'off' command, and all went dark.

I was frozen with surprise as I tried to process the scene, and so I didn't get up or call out to him right away. I also wanted to respect that it all seemed to be some sort of planned exercise. Maybe this was one of the strange rituals Pappy was rumored to have practiced privately? Perhaps. I also didn't want to make a noise that might wake up Naomi or Jenny. Whatever the reason for my inaction, I sat there for a second or two wondering what he was up to.

I remember being amused that the behavior seemed so in character for the man we all loved, even while we didn't really understand him. The night vision application in my eye lens was weak due to little ambient light, so I could barely see him walking toward the river with Frankie and Leela on either side. Something finally fired in my alcohol-laden pre-frontal cortex. A strong and visceral instinct to intervene rose within me and I sprang upright. As I called out, "*Pappy!*" and took my first stride toward him, he confidently stepped into the deep black where river met sky and was swept away.

I moved quickly to cover the distance between my cabin's patio and the riverbank. *What was happening?* I lengthened my stride to run, but immediately tripped and fell where the patio sloped sharply as it transitioned to grass. I rolled down the small bank, used the momentum to launch myself back up, and continued to run toward the river, yelling,

"Pappy… *Pappy*… P-AAAA-PY!"

I was sure nobody in the main house or guest houses could hear me, and I didn't have time to wake anyone. I stared out over the river, trying to gain sight of him. Powerful emotions surged through me, and I convulsed forward, then stood back upright, kicked the grass, and shouted, *'What the ----!'* My head was now spinning, and from far more than the alcohol. I noticed with some frustration that the dogs had settled calmly where he had entered the river. They didn't budge, nor did they move their gaze from the rushing water. It seemed they were offering homage.

No! I couldn't accept that. I snapped back into action, trying to spot him while sprinting downstream along the grassy bank. My eyes darted between the river and hasty assessments for foot placement. *There he is!* In one of those quick glances, I could barely make out the profile of the absurd bobbing unicorn about fifty yards away and moving downriver fast. *This is insane!* I yelled and ran and yelled some more.

I was fast approaching the edge of the property where a timber fence cut a stark transition between irrigated lawn and the rocky Bureau of Land Management property on the other side. Having been a decent track athlete years before, and thinking those old skills might still be intact, I leapt the hurdle. My left heel cleared the rough-hewn top log perfectly, and a split-second later my right foot clipped it. As I pitched toward the ground, I glimpsed a large boulder to the left of my intended landing zone. I tried to get my hands in position to deflect the impact, and that is the last thing I remember.

CHAPTER TWO

CHAOS

I woke at the base of the fence with my face pressed against the rough boulder and with my left leg perched awkwardly on the bottom rail of the fence. The headache was excruciating, and my mouth was as dry as the high-desert dirt I was lying in. The sirens of Chaffe County's Search and Rescue vehicles arriving to the property brought me back to consciousness.

Pappy!

I worked my way up to a seated position, did a quick systems-check, and was pleased to find that nothing seemed broken. I put a hand to my brow to shield my eyes from the bright sun, the position of which indicated late morning. As the knuckle of my forefinger touched my blood-clotted forehead, a sharp pain shot down the left side of my face and neck and manifested in my shoulder as what felt like many hornet stings. I tried to ignore the pain as I surveyed the scene unfolding around the house.

The first responders were setting up a command center while random people milled around the property close to the house. Family members were standing together in clusters and the looks on their faces ranged from concern, to fear, to shock. Andy and Betsey were huddled around the picnic table closest to the garden with a crew of first responders. They seemed to be looking intently over a holographic map of what I assumed would be the search area. I was some distance away and wasn't easily visible to anyone since the earth tones of my clothes camouflaged well.

I worked my way to my feet with some difficulty and climbed back over the fence onto our property. Then I stood and stared across the lawn to the heaving mass of water at its edge. The dark ribbon that had carried Pappy into the night was now a dazzling flow of dancing light, the morning sun sown out in burning gold as the flow rushed towards the distant sea. I stood there, awed and blinking. *All that power, unrelenting.* I traced it out of sight, shook my head, and looked away.

Not wanting to be seen yet, I walked behind the tall hedge along the fence toward the huge rock formations on the eastern edge of the Ruby Recreation Area and away from the river and all the activity. The remaining dew on the lawn felt good on my bare feet, even while the rest of my body ached and throbbed. Once the fence ended at the rocks, I turned to walk along the base of the towering boulders, part of me hoping that any one of them might break from an awkward perch and relieve me of my profound sense of failure and shame.

I got to the frost-free spigot where I had filled water bottles so many times before while hiking in that area, and I suddenly noticed the heat made my flannel shirt unnecessary. I stripped it off, turned the spigot on, and held the shirt under the water. I was careful to only take the minimum amount needed, a holdover from Pappy's and Nana's instruction before desalination and meaningful conservation had finally tempered the water crisis. Once sufficiently soaked, I used it as a towel to clear the blood and dirt off my face. Though the wound to my head had clotted, my hair was matted with enough blood that I had to turn the spigot on again and lower my head into the stream to help get it off. The cold water brought me more fully into the morning. I hung my shirt on one of the lower branches of a pinyon pine and knocked the dirt off my jeans and t-shirt. Then I walked toward the house.

The people on the front lawn were talking amongst themselves with muted voices, only briefly acknowledging my presence with quick glances as I walked by. If they cared at all, they likely and rightly assumed I was a part of the family in town for the reunion and Pappy's birthday. I only recognized a handful of Pappy's closest friends, several from his cycling group in Denver. Their faces were familiar only because I had seen them on Pappy's memory wall in his garage. Over the years, he had pinned up thousands of pictures of people and events he wanted to recall quickly during what he called his 'good-vibes meditations'.

When I was about twenty yards from the house, I saw Susie dart from the kitchen door and run across the lawn toward the guest house where she and her family were staying. Her bare feet moved quickly in short strides, and her tie dye dress bounced around her in a colorful dance that was completely out of sync with her distraught face. She was sobbing and clinging to her beloved stuffed-toy mouse, Squeeners. I shifted direction and followed her, as much because I wanted to comfort her as because I welcomed the distraction from having to immediately face the rest of the family.

When I entered the cabin, Susie's little head was barely visible below the back of one of the large leather chairs that faced the enormous river-rock fireplace. The ashes of previous evenings' fires formed a grey heap around the heavy iron log-rack. I walked across the room, and her muted sobs stopped as she heard the creak of the boards under my weight. I noticed a cap hanging on a hook, grabbed it, and put it on to hide the wound on my head. She didn't turn around, and I saw her shoulders heaving as she tried to quiet her crying. I walked around the chair, entered her peripheral vision, and said, "Susie, can I sit with you?" Her head pulled away from Squeeners and turned. Her beautiful, green, water-filled eyes looked up at me and released two enormous tears in rapid succession.

Susie and I had a special relationship. She was one of the kindest, most imaginative, and big-hearted children Naomi and I had ever encountered. She was my cousin Andrea's first child, and was a significant reason Naomi and I had decided to have kids. Susie laid Squeeners on the floor and scooched over to make room for me. There wasn't quite enough room for both of us, so she shifted into my lap, pulled her dress around her legs, and tucked her little toes between the worn leather of the armrest and the seat cushion. We were both dealing with the events of the last few hours, and I held her small frame in silence. After several minutes, the crying returned and then steadily grew into soul-wrenching sobs. I suppressed the same urge welling up inside me.

She eventually said, "I'm glad you're here. I was worried about you."

I didn't know how to respond except to hug her in tighter. After a few minutes, she calmed a bit and I ventured, "Can you tell me what's wrong?" I wondered what people knew, if anyone else had seen anything, or if Pappy had said anything to anyone that might offer some insight.

Susie pulled her face away from the crook of my shoulder and started to speak, "Pappy is m-mm-miss…." and she broke down again. She couldn't control her voice, but between sobs and sniffles she managed to blurt out, "Pappy is *missing*!" That was all she could say before diving back into me while shaking her head. She continued to sob and pushed deeper into my chest. The energy of a distraught six-year-old is powerful, and I recognized it as sacred.

I hugged her in closer to affirm her desire for peace. When the time felt right to try again, I asked, "What do you mean by missing? Can you tell me what you know?"

Susie managed to put together a rather good explanation of what she knew, and it seemed offering details was cathartic for her. She said the family had all slept in since we had stayed up so late the night before - the delight of which flashed briefly on her face as she remembered the late-night departure from the firepit. She said the adults had gotten their coffee while the kids started to wake, and that someone had said it was strange Pappy wasn't already up making breakfast.

A few people had gone out to look for him in the yoga and meditation cabin. And some of the kids had noticed Frankie and Leela were down by the river, which meant he couldn't have been on a hike. Susie noted that

Naomi was asking around about whether anyone had seen me, and that she seemed really concerned since I hadn't come to bed that night. But Susie explained that nobody was too upset about any of it at that point, and that the adults had started putting breakfast together. Pappy and I had a history of heading off into crazy adventures on a lark late at night, and the family very likely had just assumed we were out together. So, while there was a heightened awareness about us not being around, and some level of understandable concern since neither of us had left any messages, Susie's recounting made it sound like it was still a rather typical morning. The girls let the chickens out to free range and the boys picked up the game of lawn-darts Pappy had started the night before. Nobody had thought to look in his bedroom since he was such an early riser.

Susie grew quiet for a while. She shifted in my lap, moved her head away from my chest, laid it on the padded armrest, and turned pensive. She didn't seem finished, and so I waited for her to continue.

"But I just felt something wasn't right. I knew it wasn't ok and I was scared for both of you. After I helped with the chickens, I went into Pappy's room. It was still pretty dark since the curtains hadn't been opened. The bed was made and that lamp with the stained-glass hummingbird was on. And on the table was one of those old-fashioned envelopes like he used to send Mommy and Daddy letters in. It was propped up against that picture of him and Nana in that big, silver frame."

I knew the one. It was a picture of them in their late twenties, newly married. They were both laughing hard and obviously delighting in being with one another.

Susie continued, "On the front was: *For whoever finds this first.* There was also a really big, fat envelope lying on the table with that picture of our whole family from our trip to Africa taped to it."

Susie stopped talking and drifted off again, seemingly not interested in explaining any further. I asked her if she had opened the letter. She shook her head, reached to pick up Squeeners, and hugged the worn stuffed animal tight. I pressed and asked her if anyone else had read the letter. She pulled away from my shoulder. She seemed reluctant but wanted to respect my question. She looked up at me and said, "Well, when I came out of his room, I saw Andy in the great room reading one of those old books with paper pages, and I took the letter over to him."

"Did he read it?" I asked.

She shook her head again and said, "No… not really… I mean, I don't know. He looked at it real quick and then he got up and went to the kitchen calling really loud for Betsey. Then I went over and sat in the chair where Andy had been and just watched. I was scared."

"What happened then?" I encouraged.

Her sweet tone suddenly carried even more sadness as she continued, "Betsey came out and I saw him hand the letter to her and she read it more slowly. Then it seemed like her legs gave out and she slouched into that big chair next to the kitchen door and she put her hands over her face. Then Lauren and Mommy walked over and they read it too. Andy and some of the other adults talked for a few minutes, and then Andy suddenly told Albert to start calling the emergency people. I've never seen Al's display flash so much. He must have talked with them all at the same time!" Indeed, the android had been a faithful servant to Pappy and Nana for many years.

"Then the adults went into the kitchen and slid the door shut, and that's all I saw. I sat there for a long time, and then tons of people started showing up and coming into the house. And they were all so serious! Naomi was crying really hard, and even Sheriff Charles didn't say hi to me when he came in!" She started crying again, though a little less despondently. I held her closer and told her that everything was going to be alright.

She looked back up at me and said, "Do you think so, Uncle Don? Do you really think so?"

I felt sadness surge up from deep within me and tears filled my eyes. Susie's heart and mine were in coherence, awash in the emotions that only grief grounded in mystery can elicit. I looked away and didn't say anything. Even if I could have found any, words would have failed.

It didn't feel right to leave her quite yet, so we sat together in silence and listened to the commotion outside. Engines whined to life, doors slammed shut and vehicles could be heard heading down the driveway back toward CR 305. I heard a helicopter flying low, the sound coming from the south and getting louder. It must have been coming in from Salida to participate in the search. Several people came into the cabin to get dressed, grab gear, and join. I squeezed Susie, then lifted her up and shifted out from under her deadweight. She settled back into the chair by herself, seemingly without any interest in moving except to hug Squeeners in even tighter. I wrapped one of the large quilts around her while she put her head back down against the arm of the chair and stared with lazy, distant eyes into a world that only a six-year-old can comprehend. She was completely cried out.

When I walked outside, I saw Mike and Betsey gathering the adults to explain what was known up to that point. Andy had most of the children gathered around him in front of the boatshed, and I walked toward the patio outside of Pappy's bedroom where the adults were congregating. Naomi saw me and a look of relief washed over her face which quickly turned to anger. She approached, pulled me aside, and we had an intense few seconds of conversation. She could see in my eyes and demeanor that accepting my plea to talk later was wise. I noticed some glances as we joined the group, but before anyone could ask if my disappearance had anything to do with Pappy's, Betsey spoke up.

"Pappy is missing, and he left us all a letter. It was brief. It said he loves us all, and that he was excited to head out on a new adventure." She fought back a wave of emotion and continued, "He said we very well might not see him again." She paused again, fighting to hold her composure. "He apologized for any suffering his disappearance might cause, and that he knew we likely would not understand. He wrote that while he recognized it was a significant request, he didn't want any of us to worry about him or look for him." Betsey paused for a moment and took a deep breath.

"He did mention specifically that he didn't want to be remembered as an invalid in a hospital bed hooked up to a bunch of tubes and machines." She wiped tears away from her eyes and then held the note against her chest as she looked around at us and continued.

"Those of us who read the note first reacted out of fear and without much thought. And we regret that. Someone commanded Albert to call emergency services and report Pappy missing. We didn't necessarily intend to put a search into motion, but that's what has happened."

"This is a tight community and word has spread fast. That's obviously why all these people are here. We showed the letter to the authorities when they arrived and asked about honoring his request to not look for him… as hard as that was for us. They said protocol didn't allow them to not deploy a search once a report was filed. So, the wheels have been set in motion and a search has begun. Search and Rescue will keep everyone posted with updates on our family GenLove page." Then Betsey turned toward the house and walked away swiftly.

While the adults generally understood the situation, the looks on each face indicated a collective shock after hearing all Betsey had relayed. The children were still gathered around Andy, and he appeared to be answering their questions. I was surprised there were no tears on the kids' faces, so he must have been handling the conversation well. That was no small task and was a testimony to the gentle and straightforward essence he was known and loved for.

Knowing Pappy like the family did, a bizarre acceptance of the situation seemed to settle amongst us. It wasn't an enthusiastic acceptance, or a depressed one; the mood seemed confused, and yet not particularly sad. There were of course some tears, but they were nothing like Susie's.

Mike came back from the house as the adults were mingling and said there was more to share. He cryptically added that it involved an important message Pappy had left. He wanted to wait for Andy to join before saying anything, and suggested we not wander off too far. Some of the adults stayed in a cluster, while my dad, Jesse, and I walked to the house in silence. We entered the large messy kitchen, and I walked over to the wall where Pappy and Nana had displayed an array of beautiful artisan pottery mugs on custom iron hooks. I chose a dark green and brown one, noting how the muted colors matched my mood. I swirled the carafe and was pleased to find there were still a few cups left. Dad had taken a seat at the center island and was resting his forehead in his palms, rubbing his eyes with the pads of his hands. He looked up briefly and I held the carafe out toward him. He silently shook his head. I poured a half cup, then started putting together a bacon and egg sandwich from the remnants of the partially prepared breakfast. I wasn't all that hungry; my hangover just needed some grease.

Then I suddenly felt an overwhelming urge to tell someone all I had seen. I had to share… and right then! "Dad…" I ventured. He looked up with tired eyes, and I was surprised to see moistness in them. The shock of that observation interrupted my sense of urgency since I had never known Dad to show emotion.

Even I don't know the whole story since it happened before I was born. Mom says that ever since his brother had died tragically during the Defi|Climate War, he had dealt with life differently. Not necessarily 'good different' or 'bad different' - just different from who he had been when they had met. Perhaps that was why I had felt safe sharing with him; I trusted he would receive the news without emotional reactivity. "Yes, Don? What is it?" I had looked away for my private reflection, and just as my eyes met his again and I started to speak, we heard the call from Mike.

"Jesse, Don… the adults are gathered. Join us, please."

Dad looked at me. "Can it wait?"

"Sure." I said.

We walked out to the patio, and I noticed the children were all down by the river, sitting quietly together and staring out over the water. Some of the girls were leaning into each other and a few of the boys were picking absentmindedly at the grass. Frankie and Leela were still lying where I had last seen them the night before. They had not moved, even with the busyness of the morning.

Once the adults were gathered, Andy explained that the large envelope Susie had found contained estate planning documents. Adding to that, during the acute stage of the chaos, Pappy's and Nana's attorney, Catherine, had messaged him and Betsey asking them to meet her for a brief conference. They had done so in private from Pappy's office without telling anyone.

Catherine had exuded compassion and had explained she was aware of the situation. She had acknowledged how challenging the events must be for the family, and that being contacted by her was undoubtedly causing even greater concern. She had said she wanted to lift the burden of concern as best she could, and that was why she had requested a meeting in such difficult circumstances and on such short notice. She explained it was important she deliver a message Pappy and Nana had created for Andy and Betsey. She suggested that after they watched the message a meeting should be held to review the estate planning documents Pappy had left in the large envelope Susie had found.

The fact that the documents were left, and that Catherine had known about the situation, said everything we needed to know - and yet nothing. Pappy and Nana had built an enormous estate by anyone's measure. And as we had learned from Pappy the night before, they had built it together brick by brick after a season of devastating financial challenges during their early forties.

They both had enjoyed successful careers, but it was their progressive investments that had really catapulted their net worth: carbon sequestration; alternative energy; water; crypto and blockchain technologies; and regenerative agriculture. Everyone knew that one day there would be some type of distribution, though no one in the family knew any details. Even with the window suddenly open to discuss such a potential windfall, nobody broached the subject. Concerns about Pappy took center stage.

Looking back with the benefit of much hindsight, I still don't have a good explanation for why I didn't take any number of opportunities to speak up about what I had seen. Of course, I was embarrassed that I had watched him enter the river and had failed to prevent it from happening - deeply ashamed, actually. I even had a niggling and unfounded concern the family wouldn't trust that I had tried to intervene. After that moment in the kitchen with Dad, I hadn't felt the urge to share again. It almost seemed like the interruption of my attempt was meant to be. And even if I had felt the urge, it would have been hard to know the right time since news of estate planning had sharpened the emotional knife-edge everyone was perched on.

I also just wasn't sure Pappy would have wanted me to say anything. In my mind, his smile and wink that night just before he disappeared had become a playful Pappy way of saying, "Don, this is between us for now." Adding to that, the family had all settled into an understanding that the search efforts were against his clearly stated wishes. The information I could have offered would almost certainly be actionable and would narrow the search.

Naomi and I had a chance to discuss it all thoroughly the first evening of Pappy's disappearance, and we weighed the pros and cons of gathering the family and telling them about what I had seen. But she admitted the complexity of the situation and some nuances of family dynamics made it hard to clearly determine what was best. Considering all that, and because of the busyness of the remaining time together, the opportunity to say something ultimately felt closed to me, and I believed inserting an attempt to do so would achieve nothing except to offload my burden.

Or maybe my silence was simply rooted in my cowardice and pain.

The search for Pappy went on for about a month and was finally called off in late July. The Search and Rescue teams and local law enforcement were completely perplexed. Rarely were they unable to locate a missing person with the technological resources available to them. And Pappy's case was especially confounding considering the manpower deployed by professionals and volunteers alike. Pappy had been a part of the Search and Rescue community years before, and so extra efforts had been made since he was 'one of their own'. He had simply vanished. Word spread about the letter he had left, so friends who were volunteering with the search efforts had chosen to honor his wishes and stand down. And ultimately those friends persuaded the professionals to do the same.

The only additional attempt to find him was made in the late fall. It was an extremely-low-flow (ELF) kayak trip from the Ruby put-in just upstream from Pappy's and Nana's property. A large group of volunteers had gathered for the somber mission early one Saturday morning. But the somberness was offset meaningfully by the group's decision to make the float a tribute to Pappy on behalf of the Arkansas Valley boating community. Pappy had always delighted in ELF boating, and this run would certainly be that. So, it seemed a fitting opportunity to honor his legacy by wearing Pappyesque floral shirts over dry-tops, play music, and offer positive remembrances during the trip. The idea was to honor the positive energy he let flow through him so consistently – energy he would say was not his, but was … *just the flow, man!*

The working assumption at the time was that he must have used the river to set out. No vehicles or bikes had been taken from the property, and no shred of evidence of him was picked up anywhere within a thirty-mile radius. All the rafts, kayaks and paddleboards were still in the boatshed. But it was noticed that his life vest was not hanging in its place next to his old blue and silver glitter helmet. The assumption was that for some bizarre reason he must have tried to swim. It was difficult for us to know the helmet still hung in its place. Since the river had been particularly high and cold that night, the mission for the late season flotilla was to find his body, which was assumed to have lodged at the base of one of the many thousands of large boulders on the river's bed.

The antiquated and grisly rope-and-hook method had been used without success that summer after water levels had come down, and after the thermal imaging searches had proven fruitless. The even lower water coupled with the size of the search party would allow a thorough visual search as a final effort. The group of over a hundred people scoured the river from their kayaks all the way past Canon City without success.

The case was closed. Pappy had disappeared. And to this day, his disappearance remains shrouded in mystery.

CHAPTER THREE

HONORING THE LEGACY

The family gathered the next June for another reunion, and with a stated intention to honor Pappy's and Nana's legacies during it. Naomi and I discussed several times throughout the interim year about sharing what I had seen, but we were never able to determine the best way to go about it, or when. We finally decided telling the whole family at one time at the next reunion would be best. And when it was agreed the focus of the 2094 reunion would be on Pappy's and Nana's legacies, it was obvious that would be our best opportunity.

Their estate had settled quickly and much to everyone's satisfaction. And because Pappy had offered so much insight into the challenges he and Nana had overcome to build their net worth during our fireside visit the night he disappeared, there was a tremendous appreciation for the designations made with their planning.

The expansive acreage of the Arkansas River property had been placed in a conservation trust, with much of the land dedicated to training farmers in regenerative agriculture. Because of the competitiveness for farming programs at top universities, the program Pappy and Nana had designed was for anyone who wanted to enter the lucrative profession of farming, but who did not have the funding to attend the expensive university programs. Some RegAg professors had even left prestigious tenured posts to join the mission and teach there. In conjunction with the RegAg initiative, Pappy and Nana's home, cabins, and outbuildings were to be used as a retreat center dedicated to the development of personal spirituality and the evolution of human consciousness. All costs associated with both offerings were completely paid for by a trust, the assets of which were managed by the wealth management firm Pappy had helped to start many years before.

Their planning had also provided full funding in perpetuity for all the expenses related to the family's annual gatherings, a generous gesture which they had established many years before and which the entire family accepted with much gratitude. For the reunion of 2094, we reserved a week on the Arkansas River property where we had been in 2093, and which had already been converted to the retreat center.

We enjoyed a few great days of catching up and happily participating in some of Pappy's and Nana's favorite activities like rafting, hiking, gardening, and yoga. In Pappy's honor, we even endured most starts to our days with what he called 'Polar Power'.

This was something he did daily without fail in all seasons. Even while traveling, he would decide where to stay based on how cold the showers were. This ritual involved walking calmly – and calmly was an important part of this – into a stone-walled pool filled with frigid river water. The pool was an eddy he had carved into the bank of the river near the boatshed, and the challenge was to stay immersed in the snowmelt for as long as one could endure. And that typically wasn't very long for any of us, but it was a fun way to feel connected to him.

The time together at the reunion had been deeply restorative for us all and we agreed that Pappy's and Nana's presence could be felt. On the final night, we congregated again around the firepit. We cozied up together in an assortment of Adirondack and camp chairs, and on the ground under and on blankets. Even Frankie, Leela, and the cats were there and seemed pleased to be back on the property after being taken in by Andrea and Polly on their small farms in Tennessee. That night, the dogs took a break from the riverbank where they had spent much of the week and joined us around the fire.

As the evening went on, the mood was increasingly fed by the beautiful emotion that comes from awareness of deep contentment. While gazes were fixed on dancing flames and embers mutating elegantly from black to orange, I spoke up.

"I have something I would like to share with everyone."

All eyes drifted lazily toward me. I observed a hint of surprise in some since I was Jesse's son and had inherited his quiet disposition. I took a deep breath. This was it. I tried my best to hold a strong tone and said,

"I saw Pappy late the night he went missing. I saw him out here at 3:00 a.m. I was sitting on the porch over there, and I saw him come out of his room and…" Suddenly, a lifetime of suppressed emotion consolidated into sentiment about a singular event and overwhelmed me. I sobbed uncontrollably and the experience was a beautiful gift.

As I allowed the emotions to run their course, the silence of the family was deafening and I remember thinking my sobbing was harder than Susie's the year before. I noted the refreshing taste of salt while I felt the pressure of blood surging in waves throughout my head. I eventually looked up. Through my tears I saw blurry figures shifting in their seats, sitting up and leaning in, their faces and bodies illuminated by the flames. A small figure stood up from the lawn on the other side of the fire, walked over to me, and crawled into my lap. I recognized the figure as Susie and noticed how she had grown so much in just one year. After a minute or two, or perhaps ten, she said,

"It's ok, Uncle Don. Will you please tell us about it?"

I tried to gather my emotions and regain composure.

Dad slowly walked over, stood behind me, and put his huge hands on my shoulders with a gentle touch. After a respectful moment, he said,

"Don, please do tell us."

Naomi was sitting beside me. She shifted her hold on our sleeping six-month-old, Hazel, and reached over and touched my arm as if to say, *Don, this is the right time.*

It has often been said that God can always be seen if we will simply pause and look. As I cleared the tears from my vision, I saw the Divine that night on the faces of my family, and even in the deep wells of Frankie's eyes as he gazed up at me from the edge of the firepit. I could only see and feel love.

I went on to share the bizarre scene that had unfolded that fateful night. I told about my efforts to call him back to shore. I tried to relay the confusion, shock, and my flustered internal debate about whether to get help or give chase. I explained I had chosen the latter and that I had been knocked unconscious in the effort. I explained how hard it had been to say anything the next day, and that I had tried with Dad but that the circumstances ultimately hadn't allowed. I tried to explain my sense of shame.

They knew I was offering explanation, not excuse. I've learned over the years that fewer words are usually better than more, and suddenly it was done. I had been consumed with thoughts and emotions for the last twelve months about all I had seen, and it felt so refreshing to let it go. I felt a lightness in my being. I felt in tune with the energy of the moment in a way that I had never felt before, and thoughts were not able to interrupt the experience. It felt so right.

There was a period of silence as everyone digested the story, and no requests for clarification or expansion were made. Silence enveloped our group as gazes returned to the fire and bodies collapsed back into chairs and onto blankets. Soon after I finished, I heard something that sounded like a muted laugh. But because that seemed almost irreverent, my mind wouldn't allow me to interpret it that way. Then everyone heard it and started looking around. All eyes finally rested on Betsey, who was sitting in her chair next to Andy's.

She held an embroidered pillow against her face and her blanket was wrapped around her. She was laughing so hard that the shaking of her shoulders eventually made the blanket slide over the back of her chair. Andy was laughing too, though he was trying to be more discreet by looking down toward his lap. Betsey could feel the stares, and she lifted her head slightly to risk a glance. Her tear-soaked blue eyes peeked over the edge of the pillow, and it was immediately clear hers were not tears of grief. She pulled the pillow away from her face just long enough to squeak out with a huge smile, "Well, isn't that just *perfect?*"

Then Andy, knowing Betsey and Pappy so well, fell into fits of laughter and he alternated between holding his belly and wiping tears from his eyes. Then Dad started laughing. The laughter of Andy, Betsey, and even my stoic father, had a permissive and purging quality to it. Then the whole family, who just seconds before had been shocked by Betsey's and Andy's behavior, were laughing, crying, and looking around at each other with smiles. Heads shook and some got up to walk around, while others slumped further back into chairs. Others hugged.

As the slight breeze of the evening carried our mixed emotions down-valley, we gathered back around the fire and settled in for a bit longer. Little Jenny had just started to meaningfully find her voice, and she suddenly spoke up with more emphasis than was necessary.

"I miss Pappy and I hope he is having a great adventure!"

The explanation Andy had offered the kids by the boatshed twelve months before had generally satisfied, and their vivid imaginations undoubtedly pictured him getting into all manners of far-fetched adventures. McLean said she was sure he was, and then she offered that her favorite memory of Pappy and Nana was how they would just sit together holding hands in silence, so obviously enjoying one another's company. Then she said,

"I wonder if they are together now."

We all held space for the notion for a few moments, the mystery of his disappearance never fully satisfied in any of our hearts. Then a cascade of memories about Pappy and Nana started to flow. Many comments were made about the incredible story Pappy had shared with us. It was a tale full of wild adventures, highs and lows, joys and sorrows, transformations from fear to love. And ultimately, it was one of great inspiration. As family shared what was on their hearts, I was struck by how powerfully Pappy's recounting had impacted us all. That evening ended up being another unplanned free-flow, and it was a perfect way to wrap up the week.

I was touched by the beauty of how we engaged with one another as we packed and said our farewells the next day. Pappy and Nana had indeed left a beautiful legacy, one being lived through many people who enjoyed profound and multi-faceted wellbeing throughout long lifespans.

It has now been several months since that memorial reunion. The family has held no grudge against me for my withholding, and many have even taken time to express compassion and understanding about how hard the lonely knowing must have been for me.

Pappy's smile and wink that fateful night over a year ago bonded me to him in a way I still can't explain, but which I want to honor with all my heart. Recounting all he shared before he confidently stepped into the flow seems to be an appropriate effort to that end.

I remember it all so vividly, the memories seared into my consciousness by the charged emotions I carried for the long twelve months that followed. And so, with this recounting, I have written the stories as they were relayed. I hope any readers to whom these stories might find their way will benefit from them as much as I and our family have.

To all who knew him, Pappy was a remarkable man, though he never considered himself as such. He was a beacon of kindness, faith, and hope who made it his life's mission to help others enjoy deeply fulfilling lives. He was engaging and relatable, and always shared his wisdom humbly through his example more than his words. And he firmly believed the same truths he had discovered about himself and the world - truths that had transformed and inspired his full life - are truths that are readily available to us all.

But he had not always been that man. He evolved into who he was the hard way. His was a long journey, weighed down by uncertainty along a road beset with obstacles. He would often say his was a story of constant evolution and expansion throughout his long life, with much change happening after the dramatic transformation he experienced in his mid-forties. And that was the story he finally shared in his 120th year during his last reunion with us. It is the story which, in turn, I will share with you now.

And first, I will set the stage. I believe some of my personal reflections during the drive to the property for that pivotal reunion, the property itself, and even some of the activity of the week, will all help to offer insights that will be of benefit to you as you experience this incredible story.

CHAPTER FOUR

SETTING THE STAGE

Plans for the reunion had started in our family's typical manner about six months before. While there had been some chatter that 2093's reunion would be in April over spring break, Naomi had suggested it might be fun to gather over the summer solstice somewhere stateside. Everyone appreciated the opportunity to 'hit the easy-button' with summer dates and limited travel. So, we had all shifted away from the spring break idea and decided on June 15-22, with the solstice falling on the 21st. Someone had commented that the proposed dates would be ideal since we were celebrating Pappy's 120th that year and we could celebrate him on a day that had always been special to him, even if his actual birthday was in September. The dates were settled, and as the dialogue started shifting toward location, Pappy chimed in with a note:

Hi all:

I'm so excited to visit with you again this year, and the dates sound great. 120... wow! It has been quite a ride – and for a long time!

As to location... how about our property in BV? I have some firm plans that necessitate me being here in the valley over the solstice.

Thoughts?

Love, Pappy

That settled it. We were headed to Buena Vista, Colorado in June for some family time in the Arkansas River valley, and I was thrilled about it. Tickets were booked, a vehicle rented, and the anticipation began.

The day arrived and travel to Colorado Springs was easy, as was the rental pickup and the drive through the large city. As we passed the beautiful Garden of the Gods area, I was struck by the vibrance of the red rocks and green of the pinyon and ponderosa pines. As Highway 24 transitioned into Ute Pass, I was awed yet again by the towering Pikes Peak to the left. The looming presence of the massive mountain always had a way of humbling me.

The snow season that year had been a good one for Colorado. This was now a more consistent occurrence than when Pappy and Nana had moved to the area many years before, when weather patterns were still seeing increasing heat and decreasing snowfall in the area. It had taken several years to implement all that had been fought for during the D|C War, and then many more years before the benefits of the changes had started to manifest. A decade had passed since I had last been in the area, then for my twentieth birthday. The effervescent feeling was familiar though. Perhaps that feeling was simply rooted in my many memories there. Or, perhaps I was feeling the vitality of the land as it benefitted from less harmful human impact and settled into homeostasis.

As open road transitioned to twisty canyon, Fountain Creek rushed toward Colorado Springs between the four lanes of highway 24, nourishing the bright green leaves and gnarled trunks of cottonwood trees along the way. The canyon released, and as we got closer to Woodland Park, I looked over at the massif of Pikes Peak. The ski lines were still holding snow, and I was reminded of the many times I had boot-packed up Little Italy couloir and skied down the steep line with Pappy. After those outings, we would usually head back to their home across the valley in Woodland Park for lunch. We would make something together in the kitchen with its big sliding doors that opened onto a huge deck with a sweeping south-facing view. Often Nana would join us, and we would sit out on that deck for hours enjoying our meal and one another's company. As that view of the peak brought those memories to mind, it struck me just how much fondness I felt for those years and my time with Pappy and Nana.

We arrived in Woodland Park and Naomi said she needed a break from the travel. So, we decided to stop at Joannie's to get something to eat. Joannie's had been a local's favorite since Pappy and Nana had moved there in 2016. We ate slowly, Naomi enjoying her Greek salad while I savored every bite of my turkey melt. As our lunch settled, we sat talking while Jenny played with her marbles beside us on the patio. The conversation drifted toward excitement about seeing everyone and the fun things we would do in the valley, and Naomi specifically wondered if the family flotilla would be prudent this year with the river flowing at about 5,000 cubic feet per second.

"Likely not." I said, "But then, it is Pappy's 120th and you know how important getting on water is to him. We'll see." She looked at me with a familiar look, her eyes questioning her husband's family's penchant for risk-taking yet again.

We finished the remaining drive over Wilkerson Pass to 285, then headed south for the final leg of the trip into the valley. In about twenty minutes we rounded a corner and the valley floor unfolded in front of us. The Collegiate Peaks stood as sentinels on the west side, and the enormous Mount Princeton still presented as formidably as ever.

"It's so lush this year!" Naomi said.

I agreed. The precipitation of the year had been good to Colorado's banana-belt, a region that enjoyed warmer and more consistent temperatures than the rest of the state. Pappy called the area his spiritual birthplace, and indeed one would have to be callous not to experience awe and a sense of restoration when in the area.

After crossing the Arkansas River in Johnson's Village, Naomi and I both commented on the robust activity in the now well-established THRIVE community. It was one of Pappy's and Nana's projects, one which

Nana had been the primary developer and promoter of. The development was established on a site that was once a single facility in a sprawling network of large federal correctional complexes. The buildings had been repurposed after the Streeter administration had successfully reduced prison populations and, with Nana's help, had simultaneously promoted awareness of the importance of indoor air quality. The award-winning and stunningly beautiful development was dedicated to holistic wellbeing and offered all sorts of amenities for residents and visitors. It also served as a place of healing for people suffering from biotoxin illness and Chronic Inflammatory Response Syndrome. Before Pappy shared all he did with us that night, I had no idea the suffering he, Nana, Andy, and Betsey had all endured from those illnesses. And with that insight, their motivation to take on such an incredible project made perfect sense.

We eventually turned right onto the driveway of their property which took us to the turn-court in front of the main house. It was a sprawling, 3,000-square-foot, ranch-style home with a metal roof and board and batten siding accented by stacked stone. It sat about one hundred yards from the river, with Mounts Princeton, Antero, Wasatch, and Shavano all visible above the green bank of the far shore. The place was simply idyllic.

A few of the kids ran out to greet us as we pulled up. Jenny saw them and piped up,

"Daddy, let me out!"

I stopped the car and unlocked the door. Jenny jumped out quickly to join the gleeful kids, who by then had caught up to us. It deeply warmed Naomi's and my heart to see Jenny so happy to be with her extended family, and that moment was a vivid reminder of a primary reason we made the effort every year to join the reunions.

The main house was flanked by several smaller cabins on each side, all built many years before when Pappy and Nana were hosting wellness retreats there. Spread over the rest of the property were a yoga and meditation studio, several outbuildings, a large garden, and a chicken coop. The stone and log style of the buildings was uniform, and they were connected by flagstone walking paths. The beautiful paths occasionally bulged into small patio areas, each intended as a place for guests to pause and be still or practice qigong, yoga, prayer, or whatever stillness and connection practice they were inclined toward. I chuckled to myself as I noticed the colorful yard art accenting the setting. While Nana was never a fan of the random art, she did delight in Pappy's happiness about it and had allowed at least a modest sampling around the property.

Most of the family had arrived before us, so we were greeted by a welcome round of smiles, hellos, and hugs. Several years before, and as multiple generations were increasingly represented at our reunions, we had decided to dismiss with quasi-formal prefixes like "Grandma", "Grandpa", "Aunt" and Uncle" – not to mention "Great" or "Great, Great" or now, "Great, Great, Great". So, everyone was addressed on a first-name basis, and it felt wonderful to reconnect. After saying hellos, I unloaded our bags with Dad. Then, Naomi, Jenny and I headed over to get settled into our cabin for the week.

When we emerged, I saw Pappy down by the river with all the kids having what I assumed was his typical safety speech and explaining the boundaries on the property. Apparently, he had been with them for a long time just hanging out, playing tag, joking around, and throwing rocks into the river. But when I saw him, he was all business. And the tone was appropriate and appreciated considering how fast the river was flowing. Every parent had likely had the same talk with their own children. And if there had been any disobedient temperaments in the mix, the property would not have been a sensible place for the reunion.

I observed how Pappy delighted in watching the children run off when he was done talking with them. Then I noticed how the patina of sadness he had been carrying for the last two years seemed to settle back into his countenance. Ever since Nana had passed, we were all a bit concerned for him. He called her 'Sunshine', a holdover from her days at Duke University where she brought so much light to her cohort of friends that the nickname had been given and had stuck. Pappy never missed an opportunity to let people know he considered himself the most fortunate man on the planet to have been able to partner with his soulmate for most of his life.

They had married in their late twenties, and they were rarely apart since. They had done so much together: raised a family; traveled extensively; built businesses that had positively impacted many lives; were successful activists for environmental projects important to them; among much else. And, notably, that list would not be complete without mentioning they had also endured considerable hardship together. They had lived truly remarkable lives as a couple, and as two independent individuals.

Nana had lived a healthy life right up until her death. She had passed peacefully in her sleep at their winter home on Lake Atitlan in Guatemala, shortly after returning home from a special family reunion in Africa. We all traveled to Guatemala to attend her beautiful celebration of life, as did so many people from around the world. In Pappy's and Nana's typical style, people had simply gathered at the ordained time and without much formality. The ceremony was held on the huge lawn of their lakefront property, which looked over the massive crater-lake to volcanos San Pedro and Atitlan in the distance. Guatemala is known as 'the land of eternal spring', and that day the weather was an excellent example of why. The sun was shining from a partly cloudy sky, and the air was a perfect seventy-two degrees with low humidity. A steady, gentle breeze drifted in off the lake.

Some brought blankets to sit on and others brought chairs, while still others stood. There was a long row of tables set up on the lawn behind the crowd with an abundance of Guatemalan foods and juices available for guests to enjoy. The ceremony had lasted most of the day as person after person had shared stories of Nana and her impact on their lives. At one point, about a hundred locals who had graduated from Nana's orphanage-school in Panajachel stood together in solidarity with the lake as a backdrop, and they cast the petals of native flowers into the air. The petals drifted in the breeze above the audience and then rained down gently amongst us. While the meaning of the gesture was left to interpretation, the reverence and intention with which each of the young adults released the petals was deeply moving. Pappy spoke first, offering a succinct eulogy while admitting words ultimately failed him. As he took his seat, those near him could see his shoulders shaking as he quietly wept. Betsey and Andy were on either side of him, and they hugged him and held his hands for the remainder of the ceremony.

From that day on, Pappy's spirit just wasn't the same as before Nana's passing. He was still happily engaged in his various projects and was always keenly interested in anyone he was talking with. But the consensus opinion was that when not talking with another person, Pappy was in some very real sense somewhere else.

Each structure on their Buena Vista property had been built on a raised earthen pad to stay dry in the event of a flood. I walked from the porch of our cabin down the grassy pitch toward the riverbank where Pappy was standing barefoot wearing boardshorts, a t-shirt, and a worn trucker's cap. He was looking out over the rushing current with an intentional gaze.

"Hi Pappy!" I said. As he turned and saw me walking toward him, a big smile broke out on his face. I smiled back, genuinely excited to see him. My smile turned to muted laughter as I noticed the glitter on his toenails. This was something he had taken a fair amount of ribbing for over the years, but he didn't care. He had painted them once a year right before boating season because, as he would say, "It just makes me happy, man!" But he was a softie. Those who knew him best understood it was a feel-good ritualistic holdover from when Betsey was a little girl and had painted them for him during one of their special 'Daddy-Daughter Date Days' early one summer.

"Well, hi Don! Man, it's great to see you!" I noted how his sincerity made me feel fantastic. "Thanks for making effort to be here… how does it feel to be back?"

"It feels great, Pappy. The whole drive I was thinking of memories with you and Nana, and I'm really excited to spend the week with you. Naomi and I so appreciate you hosting."

Pappy smiled even bigger and strode toward me, his bare feet quickly covering the short remaining distance between us. Once he was within range, he reached out with his long arms, pulled me in, and gave me a paternal version of a bro-hug, which I eagerly offered back. We made some small talk by way of catching up a bit, and then walked toward the main house where most of the family had gathered in the kitchen to start preparing supper.

That night was a lot of fun and kicked off what was to be a week filled with a perfect balance of activities. Some days required early wakeups for big adventures, and other days we slept in and just relaxed on the property. One day we rented ATVs and drove up Mt. Princeton to where the clearing for the ancient cell-towers still allowed for decent parking around the crumbling concrete footers that remained. We plugged in our vehicles at the solar charging station Pappy and Nana had funded years before, then hiked the remaining distance to the old stone backpacker hut perched on the saddle below the summit. Pappy coordinated a meal to be ready for us, and we had enjoyed a delightful lunch together overlooking Buena Vista and the sprawling valley.

Other days, we soaked and played at the local hot springs, knocked around Buena Vista and Salida, played at the whitewater parks with the dogs, and went to feed the chipmunks up in St. Elmo. To the relief of Naomi and a few others, our typical family-flotilla raft trip was, in fact, not on the cards that year. But Pappy and a few of the other kayakers in the family did make a run down Brown's Canyon while Lauren oared a raft for those who were feeling adventurous. It was a tremendous week full of laughs, meals, outings, and evening firepit visits. We all noticed Pappy made a special effort to have a meaningful visit with each of us. And over the years that followed, many in the family commented on just how much they had enjoyed that last time with him.

For the final day together, we enjoyed a big lunch celebration for Pappy's birthday. Betsey, Lauren, Sid, and their crews were on duty for that night's supper. And since nobody was particularly hungry after the big celebration lunch, they planned to offer a smorgasbord of leftovers. While they prepared the meal, many of the adults lingered around the kitchen helping, while others moved to the great room to visit. A few of us went outside to enjoy a cocktail. Pappy joined those of us on the patio for a while, and then rounded up a group of kids to play lawn darts until supper was served.

Our meal that evening was enjoyed by all, and even included another prolonged s'more making competition. After the contest, the fire was burning hot enough to start introducing hardwood in anticipation of a long visit, so Andy pulled a few large pieces of oak from the stack and tossed them in the pit. The oak took some time to catch, and it was about seven when the fire was casting off meaningful warmth.

Pappy had missed the s'more event and was late to join the group, but his seat had been left open for him. His was an Adirondack chair draped with a heavy blanket Nana had commissioned for him by a Guatemalan craftswoman for their thirtieth wedding anniversary. He was barefoot, as usual, and had donned jeans and one of his old, lined flannel shirts. When asked why he loved those particular shirts so much, he would usually wink and say, 'Well, it's the only shirt I ever found that has purpose-built pockets for a bottle of beer and my tobacky'. A jacket was tucked under his left arm, and he carried a thermal mug in his right hand which was a Christmas gift from the family many years before. We had 'Pappy's Sippy Cup' etched into the plastic casing and he carried it with him often, its contents always a mystery. Pappy sat down quietly while we were all staring at the fire, making small talk, and enjoying each other's company.

Once he had settled in, the dogs took their places near him, with Frankie close to the firepit and Leela draped across his feet. His favorite cat, Piccolo, walked elegantly to him, made a few passes against his leg, then jumped nimbly into his lap. Piccolo turned a slow circle and then burrowed in, clearly satisfied with his nest. While we all continued chatting, Pappy sat contentedly looking at the fire, sipping slowly from his mug, and gently scratching Piccolo behind his ears. He seemed deeply fulfilled and very much at peace.

Little McLean was sitting about ten feet away and was watching him intently. Her auburn hair was flowing down her back from underneath a blue and white knitted cap Mack had brought her from a recent trip to South America. She suddenly spoke up in her typical sweet and precocious way, her voice elevating above the drone of our chatter and laughter.

"Pappy?" Conversation paused and all eyes turned toward her with curious attention.

"Yes, McLean?" Pappy asked with a tender amusement in his voice.

"Did you actually, *really*, shoot one of your favorite pets when you and Nana were farmers… *just* because you were a little upset?"

Pappy paused for a few moments before answering. "Yes, I did, sweetie… and I'm not proud of it." He didn't elaborate, though his face expressed deep sadness.

McLean's eyes welled up with tears as she tried to make sense of his admission. Her demeanor expressed so well what many of us were thinking and feeling, and a heaviness fell on our gathering as we looked uncomfortably at one another or down at our laps.

It was obvious Betsey was deeply saddened by her memory of the event, and she filled the moment with grace.

"Daddy, that just isn't at all like the man we know now. It makes me think… Nana passed without us knowing some of the more important stories from her life, and I don't want to let that happen with you. I know you changed so much during the season when we were on the farm. I'm wondering… will you tell us about it tonight?"

Pappy looked up and around at us, and we noticed the usual energetic playfulness in his eyes had given way completely to a profound gentleness. He let Betsey's request float amongst the family, the silence serving as a sincere question. Voices around the fire answered with enthusiastic *yes, pleases*. A faint smile stretched across his lips, one which matched the softness of his eyes.

"Thank you, Betsey. All of you. I believe I'd like to share about that." He acknowledged some of the nodding around the campfire. "That time was responsible for most of what has flowed during these eighty years since… and it certainly changed the course of this family forever." Pappy continued to look around at his gathered family, seeming to absorb the moment deeply. Then he said very intentionally, "I really do appreciate your interest… it means more to me tonight than you could possibly know." It wasn't until the next morning that we would understand just how sincere that statement was.

Pappy gathered his thoughts for a long moment. "Ok. Well, I need to know something… how much do y'all want to hear? There's a lot to this story and I could probably sketch it for you in about fifteen minutes. Or we can go on a ride for a few hours, and I'll give you the color." Pappy sat up in his chair, his posture expressing a sincere openness with no attachment to one version or the other. He slowly looked around at his gathered family. The answer was unspoken but obvious: we wanted the ride.

The twinkle in his eye returned. "Alright then. Now, y'all know I like to tell a good story… and this is one. But if I'm going to tell it, then it's worth taking the time to tell it right… and that'll take a minute." Pappy winked at each of us, and nobody particular. There were a few snickers and raised eyebrows amongst the family; we all knew what 'a minute' meant. Understanding everyone had been gathered for some time between supper and the s'more event, Pappy said,

"Y'all have been sitting for a while. Why don't we take a break, stretch a bit, and get some extra layers? That'll also allow me to gather my thoughts."

That seemed like a good idea, and we got up to do that, refresh drinks, and make hot cocoa for the kids. I asked Pappy if I could enjoy some of the beer his friend's daughter had brewed for him, and he generously said, "Sure, Don. In fact, just bring up the growlers from the beer fridge… I'm sure others will want some too." I said thanks and got up to walk down to the cold-plunge eddy where he kept his beer cache chilled behind a small rock formation within it. As I got up to head toward the river he said,

"Do you mind also running up to the house and filling my mug with some warm water and a teaspoon of honey?"

I received the heirloom from him with a smile. "Not at all, Pappy." I said, as I walked away. A few minutes later I happened to notice him set Piccolo on the ground, get up, and walk over to one of the nearby storage buildings.

We all returned before long and the mood around the firepit was one of excited anticipation. Next to Pappy was a stack of old composition books, the edges of their pages turned yellow from age. We focused expectantly on him as we settled deeper into our places. Pappy returned each of our gazes briefly, and then reached down to the large stack. He grabbed the one on top of the pile and brought it to his lap. As he opened the old journal carefully, I noticed *April 2009-August 2009* was written in faded ink on the cover.

Beyond our silence, the river flowed swiftly, and the tall pines swayed gently as a breeze weaved along the valley. Pappy pulled the colorful blanket off the back of his chair and over his shoulders. Then a log on the fire crackled, split, and threw sparks high into the air. Pappy stared at the fire for a moment. Then he looked up, glanced around at us again, and began.

For an image gallery to go along with the story, please follow this link:

CHAPTER FIVE

SEEKER

It was widely known Pappy was a gifted storyteller, and he had a seemingly endless inventory available on any moment's notice. When this observation was made, he would often respond with something like, "I am a Southern boy, after all." We were in for a healthy dose of his talent that night.

"Well, there's a lot to that long season. It's tough to remember details from that far back, so I've dusted off some old journals." Pappy lifted the composition book in his lap slightly, then reached down and touched the stack of at least twenty others. "I used to journal faithfully, and these contain a lot of my musings. I haven't held onto many journals from over the years, but these are special."

Pappy paused and reflected. "I need to say here at the outset that I've always believed this story isn't really about me. I've lived it, sure… but it's bigger than me. Much bigger. This is all ultimately about God's love and overwhelming presence, and the opportunity we *all* have to recognize and enjoy that ocean. And I believe that's true no matter how you relate to God, or Source, or whatever you call It. But I know telling you all that falls flat." Pappy smiled. "So, I hope this story shows you." He smiled and shrugged.

He continued his preface. "I believe my transformation is, in a very real sense, the story of everyone. Of course, the specifics of my life are unique. But I hope that as we move along, you'll relate to this story more as a metaphor for your lives rather than focus on the details of mine." He paused and reflected for another long moment, then smiled. "I hope that makes sense."

Pappy noticed me turn on my recording unit and set it on the arm of my chair. He caught my eye, smiled at me, then at the rest of his attentive audience. He looked down and flipped slowly through about half of the first journal. One of the pages prompted a thought, and he used it as a launch point.

"When I was in my early thirties and things were going well on almost every front, I was asked by a mentor to describe myself using only one word. Luke was a wise, older man, and we had a standing visit once every two weeks when we'd grab a bite or beer, or both, and just chat about life. Seeing as I couldn't come up with something on the spot, he told me to think about it and have one for him the next time we got together. It was a simple enough task, but it sure wasn't easy! I liked the challenge though, and I put in a good effort. After a few days, I ended up satisfied with the word 'seeker'. So, I'll start there."

"Seeker fit because wanting more defined so much of my life back then. I wasn't particularly clear about what I was after, though I know now it was basically just peace… and I mean of the deep, soul satisfying kind." Pappy paused. "And no matter how good the circumstances, I just didn't have it… and that *really* bothered me."

"It's like I just *knew* life could offer a more beautiful experience. But I felt…" Pappy stalled as he searched for the right word. "…*stuck*. Just stuck in the 'isness' of it all… or something like that." Pappy let go of a little laugh and shook his head. "This might be a long night for me. It's hard to put words on some of this stuff." He sighed and shrugged, then continued with a smile.

"But somehow, at the same time, I knew I *wasn't* stuck. And knowing that was one of the greatest gifts – and burdens – of my life... I had to do something about it. Looking back, I believe God was gently calling me... and also nudging me... into a crux part of my journey. And I guess it was time to get on with it in earnest." He took a sip from his mug while he peered at us over the lip. Then he set the mug down on the arm of his chair, flipped a page, and continued.

"Backing up a bit, it's important to know I grew up in what some used to call the 'Bible-Belt'. My culture was a conservative Christian one, and it was generally accepted that religion was the best solution for things like the existential angst I carried. And as a kid I had no reason to doubt it since I was surrounded by what seemed like good folks, living generally good lives. My parents and whole extended family were always loving and supportive and they never put pressure on me along these lines. I mean, it was clear they had strong convictions which they willingly shared and that certainly influenced me, but I ended up deeply immersed in religion more through cultural osmosis than anything else. It's hard to put a finger on it. Even so, over all the years of childhood and young adulthood, I committed more and more to that path... specific beliefs, youth groups, Bible studies, Christian community, and all that."

"But, for me, it was like the more I tried to find satisfaction on that path, the more frustrated I became." Pappy was about to continue, but paused and reflected. "My grandmother would roll in her grave if I left it at that... so I should clarify a bit. What I understood folks to teach, and what I chose to believe, was that I'd be granted peace and joy and all sorts of other 'fruit of the spirit' - not to mention 'eternal life' - if I just believed a very specific narrative about Jesus. I was taught these gifts were given as a grace once I believed in that story, and that there was no room for any effort of mine in that equation."

"Well, I certainly believed everything I was told to, and was ready to receive as much grace as God wanted to give. But when honest with myself, I had to admit my life didn't seem to have any authentic beauty in it. I struggled constantly with all the things I believed a 'saved' person shouldn't struggle with. I mean, I could act a good game, and I took some comfort in believing I was rescued from hell and that I'd go to heaven when I died." Then he paused, and shook his head slowly, seemingly saddened by the memories.

"But I knew there was more. I held onto a deep conviction that if I somehow 'got it right' with God then I'd find that elusive soul satisfaction... peace, love, joy, and all that. And that I could experience it all during *this* lifetime. It certainly wasn't any set of circumstances that I thought would fulfill my yearning. It was something that transcended and undergirded any circumstances... I'll just call it *The More.* I believe Jesus called it The Kingdom of God, though nobody who followed him while he was preaching really seemed to know what he was talking about." Pappy chuckled.

"And I should say that an amazing part of all this is that I don't remember being *acutely* aware of the yearning. I was generally happy and well-adjusted growing up. It evolved over time... but this powerful subconscious force ended up driving so much of my mental and physical energy. And I spent many years like that. It's so obvious looking back on it with the benefit of hindsight. It's surprising how immersed we can be in such formative life experiences lasting over many years, and yet not be consciously experiencing it for what it really is."

"And it's important to go back and emphasize what I said earlier about this being everyone's story. I've come to learn that more folks identify with this stuff than you might think, even if they aren't religious at all. For me, I was hoping to find fulfillment in a relationship with God. But many folks are aware of this same yearning and try to satisfy it with work, relationships, money, hobbies... and all sorts of concoctions that numb pain. And that's just because that's what *their* communities and cultures suggested would bring fulfillment. So, this knowing there's more... then trying to satisfy it one way or another... well, it's just sort of the human condition, and my experience with religion is more of a metaphor for it than anything."

"But I'm still grateful I ended up on the religious path with all this. It was a generally healthy one that I'm pretty sure kept me out of a lot of trouble. I wouldn't trade the experience… and that's saying something considering the wounding I got from it." Pappy paused and stared into the fire again, this time for a very long moment. He was seemed to be struggling about whether to share an important piece. Pappy needed a distraction, and Piccolo knew it. He stood and pressed his head into Pappy's chest, begging for more attention. The effort brought Pappy out of his ruminations, and he continued while scratching the delighted cat's ears.

"Because of my soul's absolute commitment to finding The More, my commitment to God through Christianity became my bedrock. It became my core identity and my life's very purpose. Just like a professional identity, or money, or relationships, or whatever, can become a foundational identity for other folks. And every day over lots of years that bedrock grew deeper and stronger."

"I spent countless hours reading religious books and having quiet times and studying the Bible… always seeking. In my late twenties, before I met your Nana, I'd even attended seminary to study philosophical apologetics, hoping theologians and professors might have the answers. They had lots of theories, ideas, systems of theology, and all that sort of stuff. And I listened to them and absorbed it all. But there weren't any answers that really satisfied me." Pappy paused, thought for a moment, and continued. "My head knowledge grew a lot… and so did my yearning. I just sort of fell into a sad state of accepting the disconnect between what I longed for and what it seemed Christianity was able to offer. And it pained me."

"I should probably add here that over the years I was tempted in all the typical ways boys and men are in our culture. And in college when I was spreading my wings a bit, I thought maybe some of the fulfillment I was searching for might lie somewhere along those lines. Afterall, there were plenty of folks having a lot of fun who weren't worried at all about religious stuff… and they seemed happy. I don't know if they were deep down… I mean, I seemed happy on the surface too. Regardless, I played with some of those temptations but always ended up feeling emptier. And I'm glad to say that my heart was always right as I fumbled along. The tripping and falling and getting back up was all just a part of the pursuit for me. And I just kept committing again and again to what my community, pastors, and friends told me would eventually yield fruit." Pappy paused. "What's that definition of insanity?" He smiled and let the question go unanswered. "And to be sure, along the way I'd occasionally have what folks would call 'mountain top experiences' when I'd feel something special spiritually… a taste of what I was after. But those experiences never lasted the way I just knew deep down was possible."

"Anyhow, fast forward to when I was about thirty-five years old. And let's see… Andy was about four, and Betsey was two." He winked quickly at his two elderly children. "We had moved from the heart of Cherry Creek in Denver to a suburban neighborhood in the foothills. That new lifestyle allowed for easy access to most anything we could want or need… from recreation to grocery stores to doctors' offices, and everything in between. Nana and I were dedicated parents who were very committed to the type of Christianity we'd been exposed to growing up… and mostly from our broader communities than anything we'd specifically learned in our own homes."

Pappy seemed to be enjoying that part of the reminiscing, though a sadness came over him as he continued, "While that time was beautiful in so many ways, it was also a really challenging season for me and Nana. The demands were so hard on both of us… each in our own ways. I think those are tough times for most - trying to raise your kids well and making every effort to do right by them… plus trying to balance careers, society's expectations, and some sort of personal life."

I smiled, knowing the same season was an imminent reality for me and Naomi.

"For many years before, I'd taken a lot of risks and had worked hard to grow a business in a tough environment. So when we got to that point with young kids, I had a thriving wealth management practice and some real professional tenure. I was enjoying both and was really starting to soar with my work."

"But the way I went about things back then wasn't good. Even though I'd claim faith in God and say He was in control, I know now I really believed it was all up to me. I'd see walls, and rather than look for a way around or over, I'd just run right through... especially with work. When there was a challenge, I'd just charge right into it and wrestle it to the ground rather than simply pausing and letting what would have likely been better solutions simply reveal themselves. And I thought that was a good way to go about things. Back then our culture indoctrinated men to believe that kind of testosterone laden drive was good. And I have to add that I'm ashamed to this day that I handled my roles as a father and husband that way too."

"I knew that even after all those years of earnest seeking, my success was rooted in the behaviors of a man driven by something other than God. I certainly wasn't as soft, kind, and loving as I believed I should have been... and I mercilessly judged myself for that, even while believing God forgave me. It's a weird head-and-heart space. Looking back on it all years later, I realized a primary driver was a fear that because I wasn't at peace I must have failed God somehow... " Pappy smiled. "... that I'd even failed to just receive grace."

He paused and collected his thoughts. "And as to what I mentioned a moment ago, I never really heard your Nana when she'd try to explain the challenges of being a stay-at-home mom with two toddlers. I'd listen a lot... but I never *heard* her. So, I charged through all that too – seeming to care on the surface, but really just pressing on with my self-imposed and self-aggrandized agenda. I mean, I think I was a good dad and provider in those days. But I definitely could have paid more attention to what was happening at home and with Nana's heart."

Pappy's eyes filled with tears. "I apologized to her many times for all that over the years, but it still hurts to remember. All she wanted was to be seen, and to have me *in* her experiences with her. And all I did was hire her a nanny." Pappy shook his head and paused, as if considering whether something more should be said. He only volunteered brief insight to where his mind was.

"I wish Nana was here so we could unpack a lot of this together with you. But she's not, and I don't feel right speaking to all I could that might make this even more impactful – especially for some of you married folks. Let's just say this story is not just a story of God's love – it's a story of Nana's and my love. We really hung in there together through some tough times – both during that season, and even more so in the challenges I'm about to share with you that were in store for us. Your Nana always had such a great perspective and way with words, and I so wish she was with us now and we could tell this story together. It'd be so much richer with her input. But she isn't, and so my perspective will have to do." Pappy stalled and let memories of Nana flow elegantly amongst us. Then his energy suddenly shifted.

"I don't mean to suggest that season was only hard times and frustrations! It was a such a great chapter in our lives, and I have so many fond memories of those years. I'm just pointing out that it was tough in a lot of unique ways too, and the way I handled those challenges reflected a lot about me back then: I was a hard man."

Betsey chimed in, "I have great memories of that time, Daddy." Andy nodded in agreement.

He smiled at them. "I'm glad to know that."

Then he looked down, flipped through the rest of the journal, laid it down, and picked up another. He bent the old paper to create tension, then let the pages flick past his thumb one at a time until an entry grabbed his attention. He briefly formulated some thoughts about it and continued.

"Working on that exercise for Luke put a lot into crisp focus – awareness of all the seeking, all the hard heartedness, frustration, and disappointment… and most important, awareness of the lack of fulfillment and peace. I suddenly had clarity around it all. It was like the shadowy space of my subconscious was flooded with the light of awareness. And I suddenly felt all wrung-out on the inside… just gaunt."

"What does gaunt mean, Pappy?" Susie asked. Pappy looked over to Susie, leaned forward, and rested his forearms on his knees. He seemed to weigh his answer carefully, knowing that words were falling short, but that perhaps an image would help express what he was trying to relay. He shifted his gaze down to Leela, then sat back and looked softly at Susie.

"Do you remember the other day when we were driving to town, and you saw that dog walking real slow? You could see every one of his ribs because he was so hungry… and he was hanging his head low with his tongue out?"

With an emotional intelligence that belied her years, Susie nodded with an enthusiasm tempered with just the right amount of somberness. She said,

"Yes, I remember. He looked so *sad*."

"Well, even though I looked good on the outside, sort of like Leela or Frankie here…" The duo looked up when they heard their names, and Pappy joined Susie in a glance at the healthy dogs with their gleaming coats and happy eyes. Then he looked back to Susie and said, "…on the inside, I felt like that sad dog. Maybe worse."

The sense of Pappy's pain infused the brisk evening air like the oil spills in pristine ocean waters I had recently seen pictures of at the Earth Archives Exhibition. Susie let the mass of heavy energy disperse, and then softly spoke.

"That's really horrible Pappy. I can't even imagine it."

Pappy smiled at her tenderly. "Yeah… thanks sweetie…" He seemed at a loss for what more to say.

"So, all that's to say the sudden awareness I got from that exercise was an important catalyst for all of the transformation and change that came after. I'm forever grateful for Luke, and for his willingness to push me like that. He planted the tiny mustard seed of awareness in the most kind and indirect of ways." Pappy closed his eyes briefly and smiled. "Jesus… what a teacher."

"We're all on this journey home, and I'm confident we'll all realize The More at some point – whether on this side of the veil or the other. And I'm happy to be able to tell you that it's a lot of fun if you find it while still on this side." Pappy smiled wide, his joy and peace so evident. "Though I'm certain what's on the other side is incredible too!"

"You know that story in the Bible where Jesus says something like, 'Look folks… if you knock on the door, it *will* be opened for you!'?" Several heads nodded in recognition of the story. "Well, I had big faith that what was on the other side of that door was all I yearned for. And around the same time, I learned the imagery Jesus used didn't suggest a polite knocking. It was more like a desperate and relentless pounding… begging to be let in."

"Well, I'd been knocking all my life, but I realized I'd been doing it politely. And something about that imagery Jesus used resonated. So, I paused, reflected, and determined I was absolutely all in. It was find peace or die trying… and over the next few years I started pounding." Pappy smiled and then laughed hard. "If I'd known how much crazy was in store for me, I don't know that I would've." He winked.

"Jesus was right… in time, the door did open. And what I found on the other side exceeded my wildest hopes." He learned forward, rested his forearms on his thighs, and looked around at us with lively blue eyes.

"There is so much more to The More than anyone can possibly imagine."

Then he learned back, smiled, and pulled the colorful blanket over his shoulders. "Now, let's get into it."

CHAPTER SIX

TEN MINUTES

Pappy breathed out, then in deeply as he felt into the surfacing emotions, flipped deeper into the journal, and continued.

"So, that seeker experience kicked off a lot thoughtful consideration over the next many months about what I really valued and my commitment to those things. And I have to admit that even with as serious as I was about knocking on that door Jesus spoke of, there wasn't a whole lot of meaningful action right away. I didn't have a helpful guidebook for how to go about all that and I felt a little stuck since all I'd been doing wasn't really getting me anywhere. And I quickly found my old patterns of distracting and numbing weren't going to die easily either. Add to all that the fact that I was really busy helping clients navigate through the horrible financial crisis of 2008-2009. And, like I mentioned, home life was a bit more intense than either your Nana or I would have liked."

"Excuses, excuses. I know." Pappy chuckled. "I guess I'm just admitting that I went through all the fits and starts just like most anyone when they get serious about this stuff. I knew my commitment to finding The More was real, but I was a little lost about how to go about it. Luke was helpful, but he wasn't meant to be in my life much longer." Pappy paused briefly. "We'll get to that in a bit."

"So, when not distracted by the stuff of life, I continued with the familiar Christian motions when I had the time. And, like I said, even as sincere as I was, I admit those efforts were intermittent. I'm pretty sure that if anyone paid any attention to my life, they'd have thought everything was great. But if I'd ever played the 'fake it 'til you make it' game, it was during those years. I was faking being the content person I wanted people to see, but I knew very little about that expression was authentic."

"With all that was going on and all my inner turmoil, it came to a point where I really needed a break. Nana suggested I head down here to BV and spend time in the wilderness." Pappy smiled as he looked toward the glade of pines nearby, the jagged outlines of their highest reaches silhouetted like a mountain range against the starry sky.

"Your Nana knew me so well. She always knew it was in the wilderness where my soul would be able to calm down. I was chronically experiencing guilt and fear and the pain in my heart would keep me up at night, sometimes all night." His gaze drifted off again into the darkness.

"So, anyhow, it was in the forest where I could get some sense of the truth that my connection with God might not be as broken as I felt. Being in the forest just helped me pause, let all the thinking about the future and past go, and just be present to the moment. And in the stillness of those experiences, I could *sense* something restorative and beautiful, even if I didn't know how to process it mentally."

He smiled wide to acknowledge the standing joke. When any of us were with Pappy, it was common for him to suddenly light up with a smile and say, 'You know… sometimes you just have to pause and take it in.' And for his out-of-the-blue proclamation he would often receive a friendly eye-roll. This made me think of a story along these lines worth sharing to illustrate.

One perfect spring day when I was in high school, Pappy and I set out one morning to climb and then ski down Mt. Quandary outside of Breckenridge. We had enjoyed a steady climb of the final pitch under bluebird skies while I told him about a lot of stressful stuff going on in my life, and how I felt completely disconnected from any sense of peace. Pappy had listened well and hadn't said much except to ask occasional questions. After eating our lunch and enjoying what he would often call the 'symphony of silence' on the summit, we transitioned to ski down the east face. As we stood at the edge of the steep slope, he looked at me with great conviction and kindness and said, 'Don… the present moment *is* peace." Then he snugged his goggles over his eyes, tapped his pole against mine with a big grin, and dropped in. The short lesson went deep, and it helped me meaningfully over the several difficult years that followed. It is not an overstatement to say it saved and then healed me.

In my brief private reflections about that, I was surprised to realize all these years later Pappy had a history of pain like mine, and I know we were far from alone in our experience. It saddened me to think of all the people who still suffer from a sense of separation from what Pappy would often call 'All That Is', though that has changed meaningfully over the last many years, and that trend fortunately continues. My rumination ended with me thinking how prophetic the poet Lenon's words had been in *Imagine*.

Pappy continued, "So, I loaded up my bike and boats in our truck and hit the road. This trip was different though. I wasn't just headed out to play or blow off steam; the bikes and boats were just to help me clear my head out so I could be still and listen."

He thumbed past a few more pages before continuing, "You know that huge view of Mt. Princeton you see when you're driving into the valley from Denver?"

All nodded. I smiled as I thought back on my own reflections from earlier that week, and I was so enjoying getting some color for the sketch of my understanding about why Pappy considered the valley his spiritual birthplace.

"Well, of course you know I've always loved this valley and river. But there was a moment I'll never forget when God spoke clearly to me here. It was the first of several times, and it was those moments… those 'conversations'... that kicked off what your Nana and I called 'The Grand Experiment' – when we'd make a real-deal 'hippie' move with our lives."

"What's a hippie, Pappy?" Cecil asked.

Pappy should not have been surprised by the question, but he was. It was one of those moments when he suddenly felt very old. He smiled gently at Cecil and offered an explanation.

"Well, a hippie is a term that came out of a movement that happened a long time ago. It was a time when the four nation states of America were all united as a federation of many individual states called the United States. The US was at war against a much smaller country while it was also struggling with its own identity. And during that time, there were a bunch of young people who didn't believe in the war and other things about the US, like our economic and class systems, among other things. It's a story for another time, perhaps. I guess the point is that the hippies, or at least the original ones, put their actions behind their words and really lived out what they believed. They believed in community, love, getting back to an existence more in line with nature, and tolerance. Their call was 'Make love, not war!' And that's what they believed in and lived by, even while many thought they were pretty far 'out-there'."

Cecil seemed understandably confused. The life philosophy of the hippies had been the norm in his seven years of life experience.

Pappy decided not to elaborate, and continued. "So, the point is that hearing God on that drive to the valley kicked off a series of events that led your Nana and me to make a counter-cultural move that caused some folks to jokingly call us hippies. But it was the first time I was sure I'd heard God's voice, and that's what makes it worth mentioning since I'd hear it many more times over the next several months."

Cecil seemed satisfied and Pappy continued. "The whole way from Denver I was praying with so much sincerity. I didn't cry much back then, but I sure did on that drive. I was begging God with all I had in me to lead me to deep relationship with Him... pleading for peace and a settled soul."

I noticed how several of the kids were looking around at each other and the adults. One of the kids mouthed *Him?* to her parents, and so it seemed there was a little confusion about Pappy's consistent reference to God as 'Him'. It is true that when God was referenced, Pappy would often make it a point to honor both the masculine and feminine aspects – and that was only when he felt it was convenient to personify God at all. It seemed this evening he was comfortable defaulting to the language of the season he was telling us about, and the unspoken response from the parents was to let it go.

Pappy had picked up another journal and flipped a few pages into it.

"Like I've said, I figured I was missing something in the equation, and so on that whole drive I was asking in different ways for clarity about what more I could do… begging Him to tell me what I *needed* to do to enter The More. I sincerely offered my money, my career, a life of service work… *anything*! As we used to say it in the Christian tradition, it was all 'laid at the altar'."

"Well, as I turned that corner I mentioned, my heart was completely wrung-out. But as that big peak came into view, my thinking stopped and the most amazing feeling of calm washed over me. My mind felt nothing but spaciousness; there was no mental chatter at all. I was just awe-struck by the moment. The beauty of the valley unfolding in front of me, of Mt. Princeton and the other peaks, the cobalt blue of the Colorado sky offset by a few pillowy clouds. It felt… well… *holy*."

"I was so dumbstruck that I barely had the presence of mind to drive. There used to be a pull-out off the highway on that corner, and so I swung into it and put the truck in park. I rolled the windows down and turned the engine off. I remember a gentle breeze coming through the cab, and the air was that perfect blend of warm and cool on the skin. There weren't any other cars on the road and the silence that enveloped me was as still as my soul in that moment. It was just so beautiful. I can feel it right now as I talk about it."

Even his explanation of the moment felt holy.

"Then, I heard a voice."

Smiling, and with an obvious intention to keep the kids engaged, Pappy reached up with both hands, grabbed his earlobes, and wiggled them.

"But it wasn't with these old ears."

The children giggled with delight. When they sat in Pappy's lap, they would often take turns fiddling with his earlobes while he made funny faces at them.

The kids were soaking in the story, and Pappy paused for effect. Then he moved his hands from his ears and laid them on top of each other over his heart.

"It was in here. And it was so kind, *so* gentle." Pappy took in a slow breath, then let it out. "It very clearly called me by name and said, 'Will you just give me ten minutes each day?'"

Pappy let those words linger for a second or two, then continued, "And… that was it. But so much was said. Those words went deep in my soul and I somehow just knew it was God. And all God wanted was time with me… time of a different type than what I'd been giving up to that point. He didn't want me studying about him or *doing* things for him. It seemed He just wanted to *be* with me. I didn't know exactly what that would look like, but I knew it was right and I trusted more guidance would come."

Pappy paused to dry his eyes with the flannel on the cuff of his shirt. "'*Yes, God*' was all I said, and it was resolved with all the sincerity my heart could muster."

"Up to that point since the seeker exercise, my decision to address the void in my life was sincere and I'd acted on it as best I knew how. But in that request for just a little of my time each day… every day… I sensed God saying He'd fill that void if I'd just hang out with Him without any agenda. Way cool, huh?" Pappy beamed, but then his smile turned to a slight frown.

"I also knew that it was a gentle challenge, of sorts. If I couldn't consistently do the work of at least offering ten minutes every single day, then the reality was I just wasn't serious about the knocking." He shrugged.

The fire had died down noticeably, so there were expressions of gratitude when Andy got up, picked a few logs off the rack, carried them to the fire, and dropped them on the bed of glowing embers. Sparks exploded from the pit and performed a lively dance on the thermals as they rose toward the stars. We used the brief interruption to let our hearts catch up with all that had been said thus far, and within a few minutes the chill had been pushed back and Pappy continued.

"And that was it. I didn't 'hear' anything the rest of the weekend... and really didn't need to. That weekend, though, I made sure to spend at least ten minutes each day just sort of listening. I'd wake up and make my morning coffee in the silence of the forest, and just sit. It felt strange since I was so accustomed to studying the Bible and chirping at God with prayers in English, and stuff like that. I wouldn't call it meditation, though now I know it certainly was a form of it. I'd just pause and turn my attention to what God might want to lay on my heart. And it was so incredibly nourishing that I made time to do this a few times each day."

"I don't know how else to explain it except to say that God really met me with a simple, deep stillness that was unlike anything I'd felt before. Those short sessions were special, and that weekend I locked on that practice as being right for my next steps. It felt great to just relax and let go of the inclination to be doing something *outwardly.* It was that weekend that my *internal* journey really began in earnest, though everything that had happened before had certainly led me to that point."

"Well, it's an understatement to say I enjoyed the weekend and came home fully relaxed. Nana could tell something had happened, and we made time to talk all about it soon after I got home. She thought it was great and encouraged me to lean in more... and I sure did. Life didn't stop and it was as busy as ever, but I absolutely made sure to spend at least ten quiet minutes with God every single day. It has been said that if you take one step toward God, God will take ten thousand steps toward you... and I felt that happening during that time. I of course know now that had been happening all along, but I *really* felt it during that season."

"I had always used my seminary training and rigid theological framework when I approached the Bible. But that new style was much simpler. I'd still read the Bible occasionally, but I'd just let the verses and stories meet me where I was, without agenda. I stopped probing and twisting them around in my head, and just let them inform my heart... I let them be the Living Word. It was surprising how that shift in relationship to the Bible started making it so much more enjoyable. During those times, if I wasn't reading then I was simply contemplating life in the context of what I had read before or ruminating on an understanding I felt I was being led into. I never heard 'the voice' during those times like I had on that day on the drive, but I did feel a similar holy presence that became precious to me.

Pappy glanced down at his journal and thought for a moment. "It's important to mention that around that same time, your Nana and I were learning so much about so many things that were important to us, and we were realizing our lives just weren't in harmony with those things. Life just felt sort of synthetic. Everything was easy and wonderful on so many levels, but we were feeling compelled to explore another way of being that was different from our culture at the time."

"We yearned to be more in touch with the land and seasons, be less destructive to the Earth with our constant consumption of convenience, to live at a slower pace, to have less emphasis on the pursuit of things that required ever-more money. We were connecting with a desire to create more time in our lives so we could pour love into Andy and Betsey with intentional parenting, and to provide them with a childhood that we believed would be best for them. We didn't know what all that might look like or how to do it, but it's undeniable that we were feeling led toward something more as a couple, and also individually. What we believe was an actual call to follow God into the unknown in pursuit of that lifestyle would come in earnest very soon… and that was going to require *a lot* of faith. But God was being gentle with the process at that point by just planting a seed of interest that felt more like 'us' than 'Him'."

Pappy found another page in the journal and smiled. "As you know, Nana always had a very special relationship with God. While it looked a lot different around at that time, she was so sincere and was pursuing that relationship in her own way with her whole heart. We really trusted each other's sincerity about wanting to be faithful, and that trust was very important for the decisions soon to come."

"Ten minutes a day led to twenty and then an hour, and then more. I would wake up early before heading to the office to spend the time and would find more throughout the day and in the evenings too. Sure, I'd read other things than the Bible, and pray a lot too. But, more than anything, I felt like I was just hanging out with God in a way I never had before. I didn't necessarily feel deeply loved or completely at peace or intimately connected on a sustained basis, or anything like that. I just felt drawn into something that I couldn't get enough of. I guess I was just happy to be feeling like a relationship was starting… and it felt a lot different from religion as I had known it."

Pappy flipped a few more pages, and something stopped him that he felt compelled to share. "Even while I was enjoying that new sense of relationship, I believed God was something outside of me and far away. God was personified as a man somewhere way out there in what we'd call 'heaven'. So even with the new sense of relationship, He still felt distant – sort of like a far-away puppet master, or something."

Pappy paused. "Wow. One's understanding of God informs so much of how we live, doesn't it?" Pappy let the rhetorical question linger for a moment.

"Even so, I was feeling that new type of relationship really was the path I'd been seeking, and all I wanted to do was walk on it."

"The only two people I felt comfortable sharing the experiences with were Nana and Luke. And both were so supportive of both my new disciplines and the reality of my experiences. I remember that sometimes with Luke I'd admit to wondering to what end it was all for… how did all this 'wrap up?' Luke would encourage me to remember that months before I had defined myself as a 'seeker', not a 'knower'. And he said the answers would come as, and precisely when, they were meant to. He told me words have tremendous power, and that I was simply fulfilling what I'd stated about myself and that I should be satisfied with that for the time being."

Pappy turned pensive as he found another entry worth mentioning. "As I mentioned earlier, part of my work during that time was as president of a financial services company. The income was meaningful for us, but I knew we could get by without it since my personal practice was thriving apart from that more operational role. Nana and I decided that for me to find more hours to 'walk with God', I should step down from running that business and allocate those hours to this new path. That was a little spooky for us, but we knew deep down it was the right next step. Making that decision was the first really significant commitment to honor the 'all in' decision I'd made a few months before, and it was the first of many more to come."

"I resigned my duties and title, and I did use those hours well. I spent more time with Nana, Andy and Betsey… and a lot of time with God. I of course still went to work and took good care of my personal clients, and that business continued to grow. But I had freed up a lot of time, and so I was able to spend hours and hours a day just walking down the road with God."

"And yet, from that point forward it wasn't a delightful stroll along a manicured lane into a perfect sunset. Far from it, actually. I'd soon come to learn there are two miles of ditch for every mile of road."

CHAPTER SEVEN

THE FUTA CONNECTION

Pappy sat back for a minute and took a pull from his mug. Then he set it beside him and flipped through more yellowed pages. "Let's see…" Pappy said, lost in thought. "Where to go from here?"

"Time is a funny thing, and we experience it in such a linear fashion. Maybe we don't understand time as well as we think?" He looked up, the question directed at everyone, yet no one in particular. Even with as interesting as that conversation could have been, nobody seemed inclined to answer. It was clear this evening was to be about Pappy, and the family did not want to risk getting sidetracked with a dialogue.

But privately, I had started to wonder about that notion. The more Pappy spoke and connected with the story and emotions of that poignant season from so long ago, the more it seemed he was fully living it in real time. And to watch him, I wasn't sure he wanted to be there. He seemed to want to move away from the weight of the recollection, a weight that had cast a heavy vibe over our gathered family as we sat quietly in the half-light, sharing in his progress and his pain.

Pappy picked up the next journal, flipped through the entirety of it, then set it down and picked up another. *What was in all those other entries?*

"Aha! This is it!" Pappy declared with an enthusiasm that jolted us. "This is the next meaningful part of the story. And it's good timing too, since it's a fun bit, and this has gotten a little heavy. This is about the time I referenced a few minutes ago… the time when this whole story really takes off in earnest. You know how I was saying earlier that Nana and I were feeling led toward a different style of life? I mentioned that everything was great in our lives by most anyone's measure… but that we just weren't settled in our souls, and were feeling led to be the change we wanted to see? Well, this is the part when we went down to Chile and really connected with the vision for what that could look like. I'm *so* glad I have these journals… so many important little details about all this that I'd have forgotten otherwise."

"Ok. So, let me back up to where I left off about the ten minutes a day inspiration leading to *a lot* of time with God. That pattern went on for many months and continued to accelerate. I was learning a lot – more than I ever learned in seminary. But even as I absorbed more head knowledge, I continued to yearn for the feeling of love and connection with God which the Bible suggested was available. Nana and I used to talk about wanting to get 'diddley-dooed' by God, something like in the fairy games Betsey played as a kid when she'd pretend to turn one thing into another with a whimsical stroke of her wand." Pappy cut a fun look toward Betsey, who rolled her eyes and smiled.

"Now I'm a pretty smart guy, but I used to be really stuck up here." Pappy said as he pointed toward his head. "But even for me, I was at the point where head knowledge and theological frameworks just weren't satisfying." Pappy then softly pointed to his heart. "It's like I'd sit for hours and listen to God… and I really did love being in that space, but it felt more one way than any relationship I'd really want. I'd think I'd hear God say 'jump', and then feel my only appropriate response was 'how high?'. I willingly said it, but I just wanted to *feel* the love… not just believe it might touch me some day in the future. And I didn't know what to do with it since everyone in my life seemed satisfied with that being the way it was when it came to God. 'His ways are not our ways', and all that. But it just felt off for me… and it was breaking my heart." Pappy shook his head quickly and sighed.

"I mentioned this earlier, but it's important to understand… I was seeking something *outside* of me, and that was a huge part of the disconnect." He drew a breath, threw his arms out wide, and looked around with a soft gaze. Then he lifted his hands and framed a dense cluster of stars, looked up for a moment, then let them fall back into his lap.

"I just thought that's what you did. Just keep reaching farther, looking harder, asking God to lead you to Him, waiting for a touch…" The light of the fire revealed moisture in Pappy's eyes as he blinked hard and rubbed them with the edge of his blanket. "There was a lot of undoing that needed to happen in me before I could truly see."

"And yet, looking back, I guess the heartache I was feeling was just a part of what I needed. It was telling me something was wrong, but I couldn't figure out what it was. I was in the wrong headspace to do that. In fact, the issue was that I was in my head, period. *I* was placing too much in the way, carrying the burden of too many assumptions that were rooted in my ideas of who I was, how I practiced my religion, and what God was like. The great irony was that I was unwittingly doing myself a huge disservice by building a strong identity around being a man of great faith. And my faith required a tight theology that stuffed the mystery and expansiveness of God into a neat little box that didn't allow God much wiggle room to engage with me in the way *He* knew was best. He knew better than to give me what I wanted in the way I wanted it."

"But since I wasn't *feeling*…" Pappy shook his head. "No, it's not about feeling… that's the wrong word. It was a *knowing* I was after… a deep, intimate *knowing*. And I didn't have it, which I know sounds kind of funny to hear since I was 'spending so much time with God'… but I didn't. "And so, true to form, I just doubled down with my efforts. The pursuit of a sense of connection, a deep knowing of God's heart, was becoming all-consuming."

"So anyhow, back to the story of how Chile came about. Simultaneous to my spiritual pursuit, Nana and I were learning a lot about a different way of living that appealed to our souls. We had a hard time qualifying it precisely, but we knew it was different and our thoughts bounced around while we tried to understand what was making our hearts flutter."

Pappy lifted himself slightly off his chair and shifted his weight. Leela accommodated his new position by arching her spine over and around his feet, then she indulgently scratched the side of her head on the flagstone paver. As Leela settled, Frankie – ever energetically connected to Leela - pushed himself a little closer to the fire, let out a long sigh, and settled in deeper too.

"Ok, so as y'all know, rivers are sacred to me. And we've gotten awfully serious with all this spiritual talk, so this is a fun story about an adventure in South America. It's an important part of the bigger story, but definitely less heavy."

Several of the children who had started to look tired perked up. Pappy noticed their renewed interest and it seemed to please him. "That trip had two parts to it: the kayaking I did, and the hiking with Nana. They're both important. Which do y'all want to hear first?"

"*Kayaking*!" Cecil blurted, then looked around self-consciously while his parents smiled. If anyone in the family had inherited Pappy's passion for the river, it was Cecil. Pappy looked around to see if anyone objected too strongly, and it seemed hearing another river story was ok if it was an important part of his transformation.

Pappy delighted in Cecil's enthusiasm, and he looked at the boy while talking to all of us.

"Well, little man, it's a pretty good story… but it's actually not so much about the kayaking… so keep that in mind. It's about a connection I felt on that river down there, and how that connection primed me to hear some answers I'd been seeking."

"You know how I was saying earlier that I often felt something powerful when in the wilderness? Well, I'd never identified whatever that was as a connection with God, or that God would use the wilderness and the activities I enjoy as a way He'd communicate. My understanding of God just didn't allow for that... like I said, I had God in a neat little box. But that time down in South America on that big water was different. It was unlike anything I'd felt up to that point. It was like God said, '*Sit up and pay attention!*'"

"I don't know where I heard about it... likely from one of the river blogs I followed back then... but I believe to this day it was God's leading to learn the Futaleufu down in Patagonia was to be dammed for a regional hydro-electric project. And it literally hurt to find that out."

"The Futa was... and I'm happy to say, still is... a crown-jewel for big water boaters. But in those days, massive dams were being built to meet the surging demands for electricity in remote areas, and the Futa dam was slated for construction to begin within the year. Deep down, I felt a strong need to interact with that river before it was changed forever and while it still had its wild soul."

"Big water always drops me deep into the zone... and especially back then. My mind would go blank as I focused all my energy on holding my line through all the chaos. I always felt so in the moment... so..." Pappy paused again, as if to make sure he hadn't already overused the word. "Connected." He shrugged and continued. "I was always so in my head all the time back then, so if there was ever a time when I wanted... when I *needed*... to feel clear headed and connected, it was then. And I believed the opportunity to interact with the Futa was the ticket!"

"So, I started researching the viability of the trip. It was early fall that far south which meant the lower flows would offer technical, steep, and less friendly rapids than during peak season. But even at lower flows, the Futa was supposed to be pushy big water fun, and while the logistics of the trip were a stretch, they seemed doable. I of course needed to chat with Nana about it for the green light, and so I 'threw out a fleece' to let God weigh in on what I was sensing. I knew it was a really big request and figured that if she was ok with an impromptu trip like that then it was truly meant to be."

"You've got to understand that ask was no small thing. I was asking the mother of our two young children if I could go run some big, remote, consequential, unfamiliar water far away from any search and rescue teams or medical care. I figured if she said yes, it would be almost miraculous. And even if she did, all the circumstances and logistics would still have to come together. Let's just say it was a long shot. So, I asked her, and God bless that woman, she understood what I was asking and even knew the real why behind the request. When I first laid out the plan for her, it seemed to land a little funny. But she rolled it around for a few minutes, and then with all the sincerity in her awesome heart, she said, 'Absolutely! And I'm coming with you!'" Pappy radiated joy in the recounting.

"Well, everything just sort of came together from there. My mom was available and wanting time with her grandkids, so we flew her out to Colorado to stay with Andy and Betsey. My work calendar was surprisingly light during the weeks we'd be gone, and I was able to easily move the commitments I did have. I found a company willing to put together a private trip for us, and it turned out the head of the outfit was available to guide me. He was a former pro kayaker who knew every rock on the river… and to make it better, we'd be with three of his raft guides who were training to be safety kayakers. If there was a way to run that river with a high probability of a safe and successful outcome, that was going to be it!"

"Nana would ride with the cataraft that was going to be following us for support – and so suddenly it was all set! With a small crew and raft support, we were going to be able to explore all the whitewater of the Futa and stay in a remote camp at the confluence of the Futa and one of its tributaries named Rio Azul. It was perfect."

“The week came to set out for Argentina, then on across the border to Chile, then further south to the outfitter’s primary outpost in the tiny mountain town of Futaleufu.” Pappy’s countenance changed significantly. He looked over at Andy and Betsey and smiled gently at them, then looked back at the rest of us. “I wrote a letter to Andy and Betsey in case I didn’t return home.” Pappy paused for a moment to let that statement paint a clear picture of the nature of the trip and how important it was to him.

“I had the chops and didn’t really think the worst would happen, but it certainly was a possibility. So as Nana and I left the house, I gave the letters to my mother and asked her to give them to the kids if something went wrong and whenever the timing felt right to her. I’ll never forget the way she solemnly accepted those letters. But she’d always encouraged my adventurous spirit, and while the tone in her voice was sad, her lively blue eyes practically shouted, *I understand, son*.” Pappy got a bit choked up by the memory of his beloved mother.

“After all the fun and adventurous travel to get to the outpost, it was finally time to get on the river. A few other raft teams had joined our excursion, and this was great because it made for a fun group vibe. They were adventurers from all over the world who had arrived for the same reason… they wanted to be on the enchanted river before it was dammed. Soul boaters, man.” Pappy smiled and winked at Cecil, who was wide eyed and leaning forward as he hung on every word.

“Well, we got right into it on day one. After gearing up in town and then a serious off-road drive to the put-in, we enjoyed a mellow stretch in the most beautiful blue-green water you’ve ever seen…. and with some fantastic Class III and IV rapids for just the right amount of spice.”

“It was the first Class V… it’s actually a V+… where things got real. Its name is ‘Throne Room’, and when I saw it I knew I’d found what we’d traveled for. I remember every second of that run.” Pappy laughed a little as he added, “The rapid got its name because just to look at it caused even the best boaters to have an uncomfortable feeling in the bowels. For me, it was a Throne Room of another type: a seat for The One I was pursuing."

"So much of the stuff you've heard me say over the years about rivers and life are lessons I learned on that trip. It turned out God was going to introduce Himself to me in a way I wasn't at all prepared for, but which changed me forever." Pappy took a slow and deliberate sip from his mug.

"Anyhow, we had to scout the rapid to make sure I felt ready for it, and the raft teams wanted to see it too. To do so, we had to make a sketchy scramble up a cliffside to a small overview about a hundred feet above the river… and as soon as the raft teams saw the full scope and potential consequences of that rapid, they decided to walk around it."

"Well, it was gametime for me, and my bowels were indeed rumbling! Sean was the lead guide and the owner of the outfitter I mentioned. He knew the river well, and had also seen plenty of good boaters get it handed to them in that rapid. We were standing beside each other looking down at the river when I said, *Giddyup!*"

"Sean snapped his head, then turned to face me square. He clearly didn't appreciate what seemed like a cavalier attitude, and decided it was time to give me a reality check."

"He said something like, 'Look man, I know it doesn't look like too much from up here… but this rapid is the real deal. With the way this stretch channelizes, the flow is going to feel very different from what we've paddled so far. The line is ideally right, but it's hard to hold at these flows… and the push is going to be straight into the rock if you're offline. You simply *have* to make that move above the rock. It's day one for you, and you haven't gotten used to this type of water yet.'"

With a twinkle in his eye, Pappy continued. "He even made it clear the portage was easy and that there was no shame in walking. Then he stuck it to me, 'Are you *sure* you want to do this?' I had respectfully looked away from the river to face Sean as he talked. Eye to eye, I indicated I understood and then walked back toward the cliff and scampered down to another small outcropping trying to gain a better view. I hooked my left arm around a small tree, leaned out over the gorge, and took a long, careful look at the whole length of the rapid. I could tell it was rowdy, but it was calling."

"While scouting, my nerves were balanced by my confidence… and that intersection of skill and challenge was just the cocktail I needed. I climbed back up to the group and nodded at Sean. He nodded back, then immediately started working his way toward our kayaks far below. Then I looked at Nana and noticed her eyes were filled with the most intricate blend of emotion - so full understanding and concern. I smiled, walked over and kissed her, then pressed my forehead against hers briefly. Then I turned and followed Sean."

"The raft teams decided to watch from above, and Sean and I were to meet them downriver after they finished their portage. Since the lower part of the rapid where the rafts were going to put on was long, busy, and could easily cause a flush-drowning if someone fell in, Sean decided the safety-boaters should stay with the raft teams to fish out any swimmers. So, it was just the two of us without anyone setting safety… full commitment! It took us about fifteen minutes to work our way back down cliffside, and calming my mental chatter along the way wasn't easy. I remember my mind barking at me the whole hike down: *Are you insane? There is no shame in a walking! What about Andy and Betsey? Nana?* I almost bailed several times on that short hike."

Pappy fell silent. He set his mug on the ground, grabbed the arm rests of his chair, pulled himself forward and rested his forearms on his thighs, then seemed to connect with that moment from long ago. It was a typical fun Pappy adventure story, but it was obvious to us all how much that particular experience had meant to him."

"It's hard to explain the attraction to this kind of thing, and I've always disliked the adrenaline rush that comes with it… it correlates too closely with fear for me. Adrenaline… or that kind of a rush… wasn't why I was there… farthest thing from it. I'd always enjoyed the adventure and sense of connection with the wilderness while boating. But that time, I believed I was there to meet God somehow… and I was willing to risk my life for it. In some strange way, I just knew that run needed to happen."

"We finally got to our boats. Mine was borrowed from Sean, and so it was unfamiliar to me. I hadn't bothered to dial in the outfitting for the easier stuff we'd been running, so it took me a few minutes to get my knees and hips really locked in. Sean noticed me fiddling around and used it as another opportunity to give me an out. He was like, 'Hey, we can easily pop out and walk it from here. You've got to understand… once we ferry across, we're committed. We'll be pushed too far downstream to ferry back and there's no portage on the other side.'"

"I remember thinking walking was probably the smart call. It was ski season back in Colorado, and the boating season many months before had been mellow because of the low runoff. I hadn't boated anything big in a long time, and the scale of everything down there in Patagonia was completely unfamiliar to me. As I looked downstream, I couldn't even see the massive Throne Room rock over the bedlam. The monkey in my mind was slamming his cymbals hard!"

I smiled, privately remembering so many chats with Pappy about calming the 'monkey-mind' when I'd be terrified during the crux of some adventure we were on together. And how many times had I used that lesson with life's other challenges?

"I took a quick look at Sean while I locked myself into my boat and started working through my pre-run routine. He was slowly putting on his helmet over a deeply furrowed brow, and was likely struggling about whether he was being a responsible guide by letting me put on. I went ahead and dunked my helmet in the river to fill it up, then poured the water over my head."

A few smiles flashed from around the campfire. We all knew that act of reverence had to be performed before Pappy ever put on the river.

"Then I clipped it on – and cinched the strap a little tighter than usual!" Pappy looked over at Cecil and we followed his gaze. The child's pent-up energy seemed set to explode like laser beams out of his wide eyes.

"During our scout, Sean had explained we'd need to ferry to the other side, pick our way downstream through some large rocks on the river's edge, then position ourselves just upstream of the narrow tongue of smooth water that led into the rapid." Pappy chuckled. "That tongue was so small I hadn't been able to see it from the cliff… I just had to trust it would be there!"

"So, when we were ready to go, Sean looked at me, smiled wide and said, 'We call this the Hairy Ferry!' He balanced his paddle across his deck and shoved hard with both hands off the soft moss that covered the bank. Then he quickly grabbed his paddle, set his angle, buried some beautiful, strong strokes, and was swept downstream while he ferried to the other side. Even after seeing Sean make the ferry confidently, the pucker-factor was *so* high for me! I knew if I messed up, the river would pull me backward into the rapid off-line, into a series of nasty holes and waves, and straight into, and maybe under, the menacing Throne Room rock."

Pappy paused briefly before continuing. "You probably all know how it is in moments like this, no matter what activity puts you into this state… the thinking needs to shut off and you have to rely entirely on skill. So, I said a quick prayer, breathed out, tried to clear my thoughts, and shoved off the bank. And as soon as my boat hit the water, thoughts came rushing back in… that monkey started jumping up and down, screeching, and clanging his cymbals harder than ever!" Pappy laughed and briefly made cymbal clanging motions with his hands while wiggling his body dramatically. Then he settled back into his chair and continued. "Even though I was anticipating a hard shove from the current, I wasn't ready for that kind of power! Now back in my head and not trusting my skill like I should have, I immediately over-paddled on my strong side, blew my angle, and started moving quickly downstream. The river seemed to want to push me straight into the chaos… it felt like it was testing me."

"Then instinct took over. I snapped out of my fear-fog, braced hard to offset the downstream shove, and got my hips under me. I threw in a quick pry stroke on my right side to correct my angle, then paddled hard to the other side and ended up a little downstream of Sean. My heart was pounding as I looked at him with eyes the size of golf-balls and barely held onto a slippery rock while I bobbed in the small eddy and tried to catch my breath. I'd snapped out of my headspace long enough to make the ferry on skill and instinct, but the mental chatter had fired back up while Sean worked his way through the rock garden and elegantly slid his boat next to mine."

"'Hairy, huh?' he said as he slapped me on the helmet. 'Great work. Just follow my line in. You've got this!'"

"I was about to tell him I wasn't sure, but as a good guide should at that point, he paddled into the current about twenty feet, put in a power stroke on his left side, leaned downstream into a small tongue no wider than his hull… and was *gone*!" Pappy snapped his fingers to indicate how quickly the current had taken Sean.

"Well, I had all of about two seconds to decide what to do, and it seemed staying put was the worst option since I thought I needed to see his line through the rapid. I put in two hard strokes, punched through the eddy line, and ferried over to where I'd seen him commit. I saw the narrow tongue, set my angle for it, then felt more acceleration than I'd ever felt before in a kayak!"

"The tongue offered an obvious line to the top of the first wave, and I paddled up it, caught some air off the crest, and scanned quickly for Sean…"

"*I* want to do that!" Cecil called, unable to control himself, and to the amusement of all.

"It was a wild ride Cecil, that's for *sure*!" Pappy laughed, thoroughly enjoying his great, great, great grandson's enthusiasm. And Cecil was clearly pleased thinking Pappy was telling the story just for him.

"In that split second, I didn't see Sean, but I was able to get calibrated. The tongue disappeared completely on the backside of the wave, and any further view of the line through the rest of the rapid was obscured by the chaotic water. It was all happening so fast!"

"Well, at that point there wasn't any option but to flow on and figure it out as I went. Sensing I wouldn't have to make any quick moves left or right, I put in a stroke on either side and then felt the smooth water under my hull, so I knew I was right where I needed to be. I was lifted onto another wave and I remember seeing Throne Room rock about twenty feet to my left. Then my eyes caught the bottom of Sean's boat just to the right of the Throne Room floating perpendicular to the current and twitching awkwardly as he tried to hit his roll! I saw him go over the steep drop upside down and disappear, and then suddenly something clicked. My mind drifted away, everything slowed down, and I saw a line through the havoc that looked good, and…"

Pappy sat forward to the very edge of his seat, all these years later enjoying a hit of dopamine from the memory. "Then I felt it… *whoosh*!" Simultaneously, he opened his eyes wide and raised his hands a little above his head while his long fingers fluttered gently.

"*Connected*!" He smiled wide, his toothy grin on full display. He extended his arms out to either side elegantly. "No time. No space. Completely in the moment. And it felt like I was one with *everything*. I was in the flow *within* the flow!" Pappy's tone seemed almost self-deprecating. He seemed aware that the moment he was describing was ultimately his experience alone to understand the importance of, and that it was impossible to use words to describe. He looked around at all of us, shuffled back into his chair, and adjusted the colorful blanket around his shoulders.

"From there it was easy, and I flowed on for the most beautiful ride. I saw Sean just below the Throne Room where he had rolled up and was starting to work his way through the long run-out. Then I noticed a small eddy on the right, just barely upstream of the massive boulder… and it called to me. It was a micro eddy right middle of all that whitewater, and I needed to be there. It was wonderful… I was in that river but *not* in the river. The river was like a portal or something; I'd traveled somewhere else."

"I set my angle for that eddy and pulled in easily. I rested there completely at peace with all that chaos all around me, and I just took in the sacredness of it all. There was no more fear at all and I felt disconnected from my body, completely absorbed in the moment. The whole experience maybe lasted ten seconds, but it felt like minutes… it was like time had expanded somehow. It was 'the long second' some folks talk about. And there are lots of ways to experience it – bikes, mathematics, skis, dance, meditation. Whatever the way, it's sacred and profound… and it changes you."

"As I bobbed in the eddy with the crux of the rapid behind me, I looked downstream to check on Sean. He was behind a small rock looking upstream to keep eyes on me, and I gave him the *All Good?* signal. He patted the top of his helmet while hanging his head and shaking it as if say, *Yes… but that was humbling*. I threw him a peace sign to indicate I was *all good* too, and he headed on downstream to meet up with the rafts. I took a deep breath, closed my eyes, and settled deeper into the magical experience. I remember thinking I *was* the waves… the rocks… the fear… the confidence… the air… the cold… the danger… the peace. It was just so…" He paused, shook his head slowly, and smiled softly. Words had failed even Pappy.

"I don't know that I've ever shared that experience." Thank you. He pressed his palms together loosely over his heart and offered a slight bow.

"Anyway, no more fears or concerns from then on. There was one more move from the eddy, over the relatively easy waterfall cascading off the steep lower aspect of Throne Room rock, and then on downstream to meet Sean. I took in a deep breath, offered a prayer of gratitude, put in a stroke, and flowed on."

Cecil fell onto his back breathless. He seemed completely exhausted, as if he had paddled Throne Room with Pappy. We all loved it. What a delight to see how children immerse themselves so fully in whatever holds their interest.

"Well, that was a fun little story, and I share it because something significant happened to me in the Throne Room. It felt like I'd dropped into some sort of spiritual current and had been primed by God for inspiration. And it's a good thing I paid attention, because we were being carried quickly toward a new vision for our lives. Very soon, everything would change."

CHAPTER EIGHT

THE VISION

"After that first day on the water, we settled into a rhythm of boating during the day and then reconvening at the outpost sometime in the late afternoon. The small camp was *so* cool. It was completely off grid, and yet it had some really clever amenities we'd enjoy as a part of our river-life routine: a wood-burning sauna would knock the chill of the river off; a cold rinse in the outdoor showers would revitalize; a quick change in our cabins; then to the small dining hall for a communal supper where a husband and wife team prepared and served incredible banquet-style medals for everyone. It was an international group – folks from Israel, Australia, France… all over the world. There were about twenty of us, and we'd enjoy lively and long dinner conversations on a range of interesting topics. It was great to get the perspective of folks from other countries and cultures on important issues, and that kicked off awareness of a big part of what your Nana and I love so much about traveling."

"At the rough-lumber table there were these really cool homemade candles supported by little wooden holders made from sections of local trees with the most unique dark and light grain. We'd mark the passing hours together by the size of the wax puddles pooling over the holders… and by the number of empty wine bottles." Pappy winked to Andy and

Betsey about some story that was only theirs, and which we'd probably never know.

"Dinner sometimes turned into full-blown party, and we'd head out to the beach, build a huge bonfire next to the river, and talk and listen to music until early in the morning." Pappy pointed in front of him to the large river-rock firepit. "This firepit right here was inspired by those nights! It was an incredible trip… just fantastic."

"But what really made it special for both of us was the resonance we felt with a lifestyle we got to see firsthand while hiking in the countryside. Sean and I ended up getting injured in Inferno Canyon on the fourth day of boating, so we had to call it quits for the week." Cecil sat back up, ready for another intense story, but Pappy only winked in response to Cecil's unspoken request, and continued.

"My injury was just to my shoulder, so light hiking was still an option. The raft crews were also ready for a break, and so on day five, Sean put together a trip for all of us to hike up and visit the coolest homestead I've ever seen, even to this day! To get there, we had to ferry a couple of rafts across the Azul and over to the trailers, and then we drove for about thirty minutes on the rough road upstream and put back on the water. We enjoyed a mellow drift for about a mile, then one of the guides pointed out a small trailhead on the bank opposite the road and we oared over to where we could access it. After a short hike up the hillside, the pitch crested into an opening roughly the size of this part of our property where we're sitting now. Not too big and not too small… about five acres, or so."

"Well, Nana and I immediately connected powerfully to that little farm. And I was just on the other side of my mystical experience in the Throne Room, so I was taking everything in with a heightened level of amazement and joy. But, that place… wow. It landed!" Pappy pointed at his heart.

"A quaint wood and stone cabin with solar panels laid haphazardly on top was perched on a lush hillside. It had a dramatic mountain range as its backdrop, and gardens and outbuildings framed the property on either side. Mind… *blown*!" Pappy lifted his fingers to the top of his head and made an exploding motion.

"It was misting that day, and a light fog was rolling through the mountains… the moisture felt so vitalizing and nourishing. I remember a massive hollowed-out tree trunk next to the cabin served as a shower, and was supplied by a nearby spring with gravity providing the pressure. That same spring provided the cooling element for the refrigerator, which was just another hollowed out log propped up on a frame at about waist level and filled with water. The fences were all made of rock and stone sourced from the surrounding woods. The garden was a beautiful mess, with an incredible variety of food growing haphazardly in an assortment of raised beds. To my untrained eye, it seemed someone had just stood at the edge of the garden and cast a bunch of random seeds into the area. But it had worked! That garden apparently provided most of the food for our meals at camp… and we ate *a lot*! It was just so cool… a wonderful orderly mess of organic wholesomeness."

"Our thinking minds couldn't make any sense of the place, and yet it somehow just 'felt' right. After all of us poked around for a bit, we harvested our food for the rest of our stay and toted the wooden crates and cardboard boxes full of produce back down to the rafts for the short float back to camp. I remember noting that our normally boisterous crew sat in silence as we floated since the experience had hit each of us in a special way. And for your Nana and me, that experience would forever change our lives. I remember sitting next to her holding hands over a box of dirt-covered carrots and potatoes. We knew something special was happening, and the unveiling process was so much fun."

Betsey took the natural pause in the tale as an opportunity to suggest a break. She held up her empty cocktail glass and mouthed silently to Pappy, *Refresh drinks?* Pappy smiled and nodded while several adults followed Betsey's lead toward the house. Pappy quietly watched them go, evidently pleased that his audience seemed to be having a good time. A few of the younger kids were fast asleep, and their parents carried them to their beds while a few of the older ones scuttled to the nearest cabin for a bio-break. Pappy stood up and his face took on a pensive look as he twisted left and right several times, then bent over and flat-palmed the flagstone for a few seconds. Then he walked to the woodpile, grabbed a log in each hand, and tossed the logs in one at a time. He watched them catch flame and decided to add two more.

Nobody else got up, so those of us still at the fire made small talk for a few minutes. Most of the conversation revolved around really enjoying getting to know Pappy better, and consensus was that it had been an interesting story thus far. As Pappy said again that he appreciated our interest, one of the boys said, "Pappy, you're *crazy*!"

Pappy smiled, winked, and said, "You know what? I asked myself one time if I was… and we all said 'no'. So, I guess I'm ok!"

Andy smiled, shook his head, and cut playful eyes at Pappy, "You're living in a crazy world when the crazy feel sane!"

Pappy grinned broadly at Andy, shrugged, and then said to his accuser, "If you think what you've heard so far is crazy, then strap in!"

Folks had drifted back to the firepit, and once everyone was settled, Pappy continued.

"The next day, the raft crews left to enjoy a mellow day on the water. Sean and the kayak guides needed to make a run to town to take care of some business at the main outpost, and Nana and I stayed behind at camp to have some downtime together. After breakfast, we visited with Gary and Divine, the old hippie cooks who'd been taking such good care of us all week. We helped them peel some carrots for supper that night while we made small talk about the homestead we'd visited and how smitten we were by it."

"Divine said, 'Well kids, if you enjoyed that then you should go wander back behind the camp… there's a landscape full of beautiful little places like the one you saw yesterday. It's as if time hasn't touched this area.'"

"*That's changing!* Gary grumped, making a face that matched the angry skull on his *Patagonia sin represas!* t-shirt."

"Nana and I didn't take Gary's bait to transition the conversation, and we agreed a stroll through the area sounded perfect. Divine suggested we walk straight back from the kitchen to a gate at the back of the property leading to a large pasture. She told us to walk straight across it and we'd find a road somewhere on the other side that would offer easy walking."

"Then Gary finished peeling a carrot, plopped it into a massive copper pot, and said 'Just be sure to keep an eye out for Mr. Ed.' Well, Nana and I of course exchanged quizzical glances, and then looked back at the two of them. I remember Divine smiled just a little too big for comfort, as if she felt a need to offset a legitimate warning… and said something like,

"'Oh, don't worry about that. Gary is a grouch. Ed's just an ornery old horse who has a problem with people walking through 'his' pasture, and he's been known to get a little feisty sometimes.' With some ceremony, Gary wiped his peeling knife on the dirty rag slung over his shoulder and held out his arm to reveal a nasty scar. As he rotated his forearm slowly, we saw a jagged mess of scarred flesh at least four inches long that ran along the top *and* bottom."

"He looked up at us with a wry smile, and said, 'Yeah. Nothing to worry about.'

Well, your Nana and I were a bit spooked, but Divine tried to assure us again with an unenthusiastic, 'Don't listen to him… it'll be fine. Gary had something to do with that bite too.' She cut a sharp look at him, and said to us, 'Here, let me put together a lunch for you.'"

"Now, we knew Gary well enough to know the cantankerous exterior was really a front, and that he was probably just having some fun messing with a couple of wide-eyed city-slickers. So, we shrugged the warning off and told Divine we thought it would be a fun little adventure. Then we thanked her, glanced at Gary while he smirked back at us, and headed to our cabin to trade flip flops for shoes and stuff rain gear and water bottles into our packs. As we walked from our cabin back to the kitchen, Divine came out to give us an assortment of wax-paper bundles tied together with string. While we put them in our packs, she pointed us toward the gate."

"As we said thank you and started walking, she said 'Seriously, don't worry about ol' Ed… just make sure he isn't in view when you start crossing the pasture.'"

Pappy laughed. "Well, you can imagine that parting comment didn't do anything to ease our nerves. But it added to the adventure, and we were excited for an afternoon together of just wandering without agenda. We got to the entrance of the pasture, lifted the wire off the top of the gatepost, leaned it away from the fence, and stepped through." Pappy's eyes widened as he pushed the blanket off his shoulders to enjoy the warmth of the blaze. "I have to say, I was freaking out a little bit!" Then he leaned forward and locked his attention on the kids with a playful intensity. "I mean, I was envisioning this massive, black horse with fiery eyes and jagged teeth…" Pappy made his best effort at a scary face, but seemed to know he couldn't pull it off and smiled.

"Anyhow, from that fence line we could see the whole pasture and we didn't see any horses, so we started walking. And when we were about a third of the way across, we heard dogs barking. We looked at each other, laughed nervously, and scurried on at a little peppier pace than we'd started with! We made it across uneventfully and were glad to find the road was right where Divine had said it would be. We climbed over the old wooden top rail which was loosely set in stacked stone on either side, and which was still wet from the heavy rains the day before."

"We didn't really know where to go from there, but decided to walk what we assumed was generally upstream along the Futa toward where we thought we'd eventually meet the Azul tributary. The old dirt road had a strip of vibrant green grass running down the middle of it, and Nana set out on one track while I started walking on the other beside her. The road meandered away from the camp and river toward the mountains, taking us deep into a completely foreign landscape which we agreed somehow felt familiar and grounding to us. I'll never forget how the sun broke through the heavy clouds early into that walk, and how after only a few minutes we were overwhelmed with such a delightful petrichor."

"What's petrichor, Pappy?" Susie asked. Pappy looked at her, smiled, and said,

"It's the smell of the earth when the sun heats her up after a rain. It's one of the ways she says she's happy!"

Susie was always barefoot and seemed most content when outside. We could tell she had connected with the explanation and had entered deeper into the story. She smiled at Pappy, touched the patch of grass near where she was sitting, and let him continue.

"We saw a sign warning drivers to keep an eye out for children walking to school, and about a half-mile later noticed a small building high on a hill behind a couple of small farms and connected to the road by a thin trail. We assumed it must have been the local schoolhouse, and we commented on how amazing it was that people were still living such a simple lifestyle. A vision was being sketched for us, one with beautiful color to be filled in soon." Pappy grinned as a slight breeze wafted through the valley, making the flames and smoke dance.

"A couple of miles later, the road we were on intersected another where a tiny church stood humbly at the junction. The double-doors didn't have any hardware except the large iron hinges nailed to both them and the heavy timber doorframe. The doors didn't appear to be locked, so I shoved on one to test it. The only resistance was its weight on the rough cement floor, so I lifted it slightly and leaned into it to create an opening for us to squeeze through. The windowless space was bare except for about five rows of wooden pews and a small pulpit on the far side with a carved image of the crucified Christ hanging on the plaster wall behind it. I remember the paint on Jesus was faded and cracked, and the worn colors seemed to give the piece of art a timeless dimension. The paint of the eyes had been retouched, and it seemed Jesus' passion had been captured in them particularly well. The low ceiling was vaulted, and the quality of light streaming through the narrow windows cut into it made the space feel enchanted. Nana and I were struck by how peaceful the energy in that little sanctuary was, and we decided to take some time to be quiet and pray. It was in that tiny, remote, South American country church where we made what ended up being the final plea for clarity about what was welling up in our hearts."

"After twenty or thirty minutes, we shouldered our packs and squeezed through the opening into the fresh air. I pulled the heavy door shut and met Nana at the little iron gate separating the road from the church. She softly said, 'How perfect.' I nodded, acknowledging what was stirring in our souls. Then I took her hand and we kept walking."

"Divine was right. The area was interspersed with picture-perfect homesteads much like the one we'd seen the day before. We admired the differences between the houses and the layouts of the small farms, all of which were tucked into groves of trees a good way from the road. As we walked, the sounds of silence were broken only by the occasional dog barking, cow mooing, or maybe a goose calling in the distance. And within that silence was a profound message our hearts were slowly tuning into."

"The sun had come out in earnest, and the drying dirt allowed us to move along at a nice pace. After a short while, we came to a fork in the road where we realized we were hungry and decided to take our lunch. Divine had packed cheese and dried sausage, hearty slices of seeded bread, a small assortment of vegetables and fruit, and a few brownies. We ate slowly and talked about our time in Chile, how the travel and community had been so restorative for us, and about the kids."

"Most important, we recognized how the homesteads, landscape, and simple lifestyle were so in tune with what we'd been learning, thinking, and feeling during the many months before. Neither of us could put precise words on it all, but we knew our sense for what was in store was being crystallized that afternoon. We finished our lunches and continued to talk while we nibbled on the crumbs found in the creases of the wax paper."

Pappy paused briefly to indulge in the memories, then slowly earmarked a page and set the journal on the growing stack composition books. He picked up another from the unread pile, worked his way through its entirety, then flipped back to one of the first pages.

"I don't remember who said it first, but we started talking about our need for some family values that could help guide us as we made big life decisions, since we'd been feeling a bit thrown around by one idea after another. The challenge was that most anything was an option for us, and our enthusiasm about an idea could shift easily based on something as fleeting as a mood. We realized we needed to establish a set of immutable values that would serve as a North Star for our family. We talked about what was important to us individually and as a couple, and what we wanted to instill in Andy and Betsey. And we figured that if we could get some core values in place then we could start really focusing our attention on the lifestyle that would support those values."

"It was getting to be afternoon, and so we decided to press on and keep the conversation going while we walked. The fork to the right was clearly not the main road, so we took it. And as we walked along, it surprised us how quickly we landed on our four primary values… almost as if the thinking was inspired. They're the same values that guide our family today, and which you are all well-aware of: love; harmony; family; community."

"Then we started walking past a homestead that was unlike the others. I've got to describe it to you, because that little homestead clearly informed the vision for what had been a loose idea up to that point. The house was set back about one hundred feet from the road. The exterior walls were dark logs which we assumed were cut on the property since the trees around the quaint home looked similar. There were a few large windows, their frames painted in a dark rustic red and snugged up under a large overhung shake-roof. A plume of smoke was rising lazily from the stone chimney. The yard to one side of the cabin had a few tidy firewood stacks, and on the other side was a truck where a large dog rested under the open tailgate. Strewn about the property were an assortment of old animal-drawn farming implements, and a couple of sheep grazed contentedly while chickens and guinea fowl scratched at the earth and ate the bugs they uncovered. Either side of a large, messy garden was visible behind the house, and it looked a lot like the one we'd visited the day before."

"We were both stopped in our tracks by the setting, and then we heard the alarm system kick into gear! It was wild… and we ended up employing the same system on our little farm a couple of years later. The guineas started squawking, which made geese honk from somewhere behind the house. All that racket got the attention of the dog, which made us a little nervous… but he just lazily shifted his head toward us without even lifting it off the ground. I guess he was satisfied we weren't a threat, so he barked once and all immediately went quiet! Very cool."

Pappy shook his head slowly. "I was so smitten by the scene that I sat on a stump and just watched for a long time. It was magical… the interconnectedness and interplay of that little farm was so obvious and so beautiful. There was just this natural order and simplicity to things that felt so different from our lives in Colorado." Pappy seemed to drift off briefly to another place again.

"As Nana stood behind me and took the scene in, it was all settling deep in her soul too. She had the presence of mind to snap a picture of me sitting on that stump watching, and that image captured the moment when our prayers for clarity were answered. I finally stood and we walked along for quite a while in silence."

"Somewhere along the way, Nana said, 'We need to do something like that… just like that little farm. We need to connect to whatever that was, and help Andy and Betsey get connected to it too.'"

"I looked at her and said, 'Yes, we do.' I'm sure that when we voiced that commitment with such heart-felt energy, a door was thrown open for us in the Universe. I took her hand again, and we strode along taking turns painting a picture of a new life for us that looked a lot like that homestead, and which seemed to sync perfectly with our new value system."

Pappy laughed as he said, "Of course, we had no idea how to make something like that happen, and were completely overwhelmed at the thought of how many big and little details would have to come together for it to become reality. But the beautiful die was cast, and we figured we'd leave it up to God to get all that sorted."

"The small road had turned away from the mountains back toward the Futa, and after about a mile we heard caustic noises that sounded like heavy machinery. We continued walking, and eventually intersected with another dirt road that was obviously the main artery serving the region. We took a right and walked toward the Futa with the sounds of what must have been a rather large worksite growing louder. As we rounded a bend, we suddenly found ourselves in a scene that was so disturbing that right then and there our commitment to our new vision for a simpler life was cemented."

"There were several trucks along the side of the road, and about eight men were managing some long rusty cables about three inches thick that were being dragged up the road by a big dozer. The men didn't take much notice of us, except to motion for us to stay clear of the cables. About fifty feet ahead of us, the country dirt road transitioned to a brand-new bridge made of bright steel that looked so out of place in the ancient landscape. It turned out the cables were the remnants of the old walking bridge that had connected the idyllic little region we'd just explored to the other side of the Futa, and then on to the larger cities in the area. There were a few men near the cliff between the cables and the bridge and they were setting spiked metal poles into the ground to serve as a rough guide for the cables so they didn't drag against the new bridge. They all seemed friendly enough, and some even offered smiles and waves to say hi. They were taking turns managing the cables, and Nana walked over to a couple of the men who weren't busy. She was able to find out they were excited because that day the bridge had been completed, so trucks carrying heavy equipment and supplies could now get to the massive worksite of the new dam more directly."

"We walked out onto the bridge and looked downstream, the pristine river and countryside now framed by glaring steel. As I looked downriver, the final few feet of cable slid slowly over the edge of the cliff and were unceremoniously dragged through the mud a few more feet. The low rumble of the diesel engine stopped, and several men walked toward the cable with grinders. The refreshing silence was short lived, because in just a few minutes a generator fired up and the men started cutting the old cable into manageable sections."

"It was all just too much for me. I could feel the pain that was about to be inflicted on the whole ecosystem and landscape when that dam was finished, and I felt a deep personal conviction. That moment created an internal conflict that stayed with me until we got our act together globally and made the complete switch to truly clean renewables… the enjoyment and wonder of electricity juxtaposed against so many of the negative consequences of creating it. The contrast between that scene and what we'd experienced while wandering the countryside was just too much for me. I knew I had to do something, and I knew Nana felt the same… even if what we did seemed ultimately insignificant in the grand scheme of things. To employ Gandhi's phrase again, we had to 'be the change we wanted to see in the world'."

"As we walked off the bridge together, we noticed a small trail along the cliff that paralleled the river and we rightly assumed it led back to the camp. Fortunately, we'd walked a large loop… and that was a good thing because we were deep into the afternoon and getting back before dark was going to be tough if we'd had to go back the way we'd come."

Then Pappy lightly added, "Plus, the last thing I wanted was an introduction to Mr. Ed after dark… even if he was just a feisty little pony!"

CHAPTER NINE

THE PROPHET

Pappy closed the journal about Chile and dropped it onto the pile, then glanced at the dwindling stack of fresh journals on the other side of his chair. "Oh, y'all are going to enjoy this one!" Pappy laughed, "Wow… I haven't thought about this in *years*… " Seeming a little stunned, he stalled for a few seconds before reaching down to pick up the next composition book. Before he grabbed it, I caught a glimpse of the cover. I could barely make out 'Crazy Town' scrawled in large, faded letters above the numbers 2010.

"Well, as y'all can imagine, that trip to South America was transformative for us both, but we had no way of knowing *how much* change we'd be experiencing over the next several months as we careened toward fulfillment of the vision. I'll tell you this though, we were absolutely committed to following God's leading, whatever and wherever that meant. And it did get crazy. I think it was ultimately a beautiful kind of crazy… if that makes any sense. Y'all can form your own opinions though. God knows, this is the part where things really went into the deep end!"

"But before we get into it, it's important to note that there was a lot of excitement immediately after our walk through the countryside in Patagonia. We spent the last few days of the trip hiking and hanging out, and just talking all the time. Hours and hours." Pappy paused, clearly savoring the memory of that time with Nana. "Yep, it was down there that we got our family values sorted and started letting the inspiration for a different kind of life take root meaningfully. And those were no small things for this family."

"When we got home, it was immediately back into the busyness of parenting, working, socializing, and all that. It was fun to be back, but we were changed people, and with a clear idea for what we wanted to do. The lifestyle we were enjoying was wonderful by most anyone's measure, and certainly by the measurement of what was then 'The American Dream'. For *us*, though, it just didn't feel quite right."

"Seemingly upon request, and rather suddenly, we had been given clear insight into a life that appealed to us on a 'just gotta-do-it' level. A life that would allow us to live closer to the land in a way that supported it while it supported us, to be a part of the organic movement, to be a part of the solution rather than what we felt was the problem, to steward a healthy and interconnected ecosystem, to live in meaningful community with others. We knew it was time to *do* it, rather than just keep *talking* about it. We yearned for space in our day-to-day lives to be better partners, parents and people. And, beyond our own experience, we absolutely wanted to give a gift to Andy and Betsey too… the gift of what we believed would be a meaningful connection to a beautiful way of life that was increasingly lost in our culture."

"More than anything, though, we wanted to know we were living in alignment with what we always called 'God's will'. The Bible reading, prayer, and quiet times had been consistent for many months, and that sense of 'sit up and pay attention' in Chile hadn't waned at all. My desire to feel God's love on a personal and intimate level hadn't been satisfied, but I kept doing what I believed was my part."

"I had connected to something beyond myself while down there in Patagonia, but I still didn't have a context for all that as a spiritual experience. Back then, God was way beyond me, outside of me… on a throne up in the sky, or something like that. I didn't have any point of reference for Him being in the eddies of a river, or in the shadows of a forest, or in the sunshine. And much less in the very beating of my own heart! If I acknowledged 'spirituality' at all, it was confined to a specific religion which I had been taught was the only way to God. And really, so much of the conviction I had was ultimately just because I happened to be born in a place where people around me believed that way. So, let's just say I had a very rigid architecture and understanding for how someone could experience that which is beyond us." Pappy paused and stared into the embers for a few moments, lost in some other memory. Then he smiled and looked up.

"I actually used to get upset when people would say they were 'spiritual but not religious'… annoyed the hell out of me." Pappy shook his head in a sad sort of way, though it was unclear what he was thinking. It was hard for any of us to imagine our big and open-hearted patriarch being at all dogmatic.

Pappy seemed to briefly debate offering a quick side note, then decided to share what was on his mind. "It's sorta funny that I just framed my thought about those spirituality vs. religion comments that way. *Hell*… I mean, what an interesting and loaded topic *that* is! What you believe about it has such important ramifications, doesn't it?" Pappy let another rhetorical question sit, and then quickly continued, "A deep dive into the history and cultural understanding of the notion of hell sure was of great benefit to me around that time… but no time to go there now. Let's just say that's one monstrous rabbit hole!"

Pappy turned a few more pages of the journal, deciding where to lead us next, and smiled.

"At the same time that we were feeling enthusiasm about a simpler lifestyle, a tremendous opportunity had come up for me professionally with a firm that catered to the ultra-high net worth community, and the role I was being recruited for would have catapulted me into 'the big leagues' quickly. I entertained the recruiting and had easily made it through several rounds of interviews, including the big dinner out with Nana, the partners of the firm, and their spouses. During my final interview later that same week, which was really just a formality before starting the job, the managing director put a recording device in front of me, pressed record, and said, 'Will you please state what is most important to you? Then, also please speak to what your ideal life situation will look like in ten years?'"

Pappy chuckled. "I know y'all can't picture me in a suit and tie and polished shoes and all that. But there I was, all suited up at a huge conference table with the senior partners. This was a real *moment*... the defining kind... a sliding door type of moment. I'm sure they were wanting me to say something profoundly ambitious that would make them believe I'd be a top producer for their firm. And it felt to me like my ability to state with clarity what it was that I really wanted was an important final test for them. That was such a great exercise, and it was wise of the partners to do that. I believe we should all take the time occasionally to dig deep, be brutally honest with ourselves, and state clearly what it was we hold as our highest version of self."

"Well, I took a long minute to think, and they seemed to be appreciating I was taking it seriously and not just saying something to get the exercise behind us and move on. What came up from inside was no surprise to me, but I sure was nervous about saying it out loud in that setting! I knew the desire I felt was right though, and I felt I had no choice but to declare it. I initially thought the exercise was a test by the partners of that firm, but suddenly it felt like more of a test from another Source. With my heart beating so hard I thought my tie might be bouncing on my chest, I leaned forward to make sure my voice would be captured by that recorder, breathed in deep, then let it flow out:

'What I want is to know God. I want my life to feel completely intertwined with His, and to be at peace in that alone.'" Pappy's eyes opened wide and he laughed hard at the memory.

"I was just so tired of feeling the separation from what I *knew* was possible. That beautiful conference room had huge windows that framed a gorgeous view of Denver's front range. And when I said that, I was of course only using my 'inside voice'…" Pappy winked at Kell, who then shoved Susie playfully, all about some trouble they got into earlier. "…but I felt like I was out there on one of those peaks shouting with everything I had in me! I wanted to know Truth and all it had for me. For the first time, I was ready to declare that to the world, and to make it a statement of my very reason for being. At that point in my journey, I just wasn't willing to tell those partners something I knew they wanted to hear but which wasn't true in my soul. I was there, on record, in that huge boardroom, letting those folks know what I was *really* about." Pappy settled back into his chair with a smile on his face, adjusting his blanket around him. "Let's just say that I don't think it's what they wanted to hear."

A loud pop from the fire startled everyone. Like a canon salute, the noise aptly served to emphasize the importance of that moment in Pappy's life – his soul's declaration, and in the most improbable of circumstances.

"The senior partner who was going to be my mentor looked at me in a way that wasn't judgmental or angry, or anything like that. He just seemed completely perplexed and was struggling as mightily as a duck in a windstorm trying to come up with a response!" Pappy's Southern colloquialisms never failed to amuse.

"Well, nobody said a word, but you could just feel the energy in the room shift. There was no need to cast my vision for the next ten years, though that would have been a great exercise." Pappy laughed and pulled some hair that had fallen over his face behind his ears. "How crazy would *that* have been? What if I had told them I wanted a simpler life on a homestead because I felt God was leading me and my family that way?" Pappy laughed more and shook his head gently.

"It really was a great moment, though. Now that I think about it, I believe it was a statement the Universe heard loud and clear, because things started happening fast from there. I realized at that conference table that nothing else mattered to me, and I trusted that if I followed the prompts that came from my seeking then everything would work out better than I could ever imagine, and on every front. Even so, it was a little tough to realize I'd just said all that to what I thought at the time was one of the best professional opportunities I'd ever get! It's hard to follow those prompts when the stakes are high. Leaving all the high-end finance world offers to go live on a farm was a serious downshift, and it was tougher for me than I'm able to communicate right now. While I did want peace, there was a lot to walk away from that was great and which I truly did enjoy... and which made life really easy. But the ideas that had coalesced into the vision for a simpler life felt like a calling, and moving toward all that was just something I couldn't *not* do. But I still had no idea how to pull something like that off."

"Back at my job, things were getting a little less stressful, since the country was moving out of the financial crisis, largely because of massive intervention by the central bank. And because the recovery was being artificially supported, I started to form a strong opinion that it wouldn't succeed. That opinion then led to a growing concern that the crisis could return with a vengeance, and with a truly devastating result that threatened my family's wellbeing. My timing ended up being off, but I was a young husband and dad who of course felt responsible for protecting his family from what I saw as a potentially very hard and even dangerous paradigm. So, all that was added motivation for a homestead." Pappy smiled in a way that seemed like he was offering himself forgiveness for the fears he carried during that time.

"I thought a little farm in the woods that had some water and a garden could serve as a nice support for us should things turn bad. I even started forming a strong narrative around the idea that God was leading me – protecting us – with this drive for a simpler life... though in retrospect I might have run with that too far. I don't know though... maybe I was just a little ahead of things."

"Whatever the case, right or wrong, there was no doubt that I could find all sorts of support for my concerns. It didn't take but a little sniffing around, and one could find lots of smart people laying out a solid case for how things were going to come crashing down soon! You know how it is, a person can find support for almost anything they want to take a position on. So much of life is dictated by what you focus on… how you think about things."

Pappy paused for so long that we were wondering if he had lost his train of thought, but then he told us something that shocked us.

"I used to operate entirely from a paradigm of fear. It was a natural way of thinking for me, though admittedly not very evolved. My reptilian brain was always looking for things that could hurt me or Nana or the kids – that deeply embedded instinct to always be on the lookout for the sabertoothed tiger ran deep in me. My nervous system was constantly in a heightened sympathetic state… on the defensive, stressed. I felt so angry… and often for no good reason! It was an awful way of living, but I don't think I was actually aware of just how off-kilter I was. It was just my ego's default setting, and that way of being was lived out by so many in our culture at the time… often without realizing it. I was often even told by my dad to use fear as a motivator, since that mindset was what had helped him to be financially successful. But as a kid, I watched him operate in a constant state of stress and fear, and that's actually a major catalyst for what eventually became my life's work in exploring the nature of wealth and how people relate to it."

It was interesting for us to get some insight into the seminal thinking of what ultimately became Pappy's professional thesis. He continued. "I love that man though. He was my father, after all… and it was all he knew to offer when I'd go to him for advice, especially in the early days of my career when things were really stressful. Papa J was the best. He was always there for me, and was just offering what had worked for him when he was at the same stage in life. In his later years he even apologized for guiding me that way."

"Anyhow, point is that all my successes up to that point were definitely because I was running hard from my worst fears – fears of the embarrassment of failure, financial ruin, loss of vitality. Sadly, and even though I wasn't aware of it at the time, the reality was that even my relationship with God had a lot of fear in it." Pappy paused. It was obvious he was inclined to get into an issue that was very important to him. But he decided not to, and just said, "I'm sure I'll get into all that later."

He continued. "It took me so long to see that there are only two fundamental ways of being: fear or love. And I'll tell you what… I was operating *entirely* in the former back then. My neural pathways of fear were carved in my brain as deep as the Grand Canyon. So, the desire to live more simply just for the beauty of it was starting to be infested with thoughts of the farm lifestyle as a good 'fallback position' for our family should things crash. I wish I hadn't carried that fear into the experiences that were to come, but it was all just a part of my journey."

"So, I continued investing significant energy into time with God… and, also energy toward making sure Nana, Andy and Betsey would be provided for, no matter what might happen. And so, there I was building up all kinds of fear-based provisions – food and water storage, guns and ammo, gold - all the while diving deeper into the Bible and quiet times!" Pappy shook his head and smiled gently, as if again forgiving himself for decisions made in the past.

"With every bit of it, I believed I was being led by God! And I do still believe I was, in a way, and don't want to diminish that. But it was getting a little, well… messy. Even so, the momentum around it all kept building. Most of my fear-based posturing was happening on a personal level, even while Nana and I kept discussing homesteading and all the positive experiences we believed doing that could offer our family. So, the movement toward the homestead idea started to take on a kinda strange but exciting vibe."

"The beautiful side of it all really was great, and very much in line with all I've talked about so far. We were looking at land and small farms all around Colorado, and were doing things like attending gardening and composting classes to get ready. It was a lot of fun, and so I don't mean to paint it as if it all went completely nutso… again, all that fear-based thinking was more in my private ruminations. Nana never operated at all from fear, and she didn't much like the stockpiling she saw going on. But she deferred to me, trusting I might know things along economic lines which she didn't, and also because she trusted my pursuit of God."

"A few months went by, and we were solidly back into the rhythm of life after our experience in Patagonia, and a commitment rolled around for me to go on a trip for a board I was involved with. I can't remember if I was President or President-elect at the time, but the Financial Planning Association was having some event out of town for a few days, and I had to be there. During one of the afternoon sessions, I remember sitting in that huge meeting room and feeling like I just couldn't take it anymore. My mind was consumed with thoughts about knowing God, feeling His love, a simpler life, and protecting my family. So, since I couldn't pay any attention to the speakers, I went upstairs to pray."

"After sitting in my suite for a while praying and listening, a call came in from someone who I had decided not to speak with anymore. Sam and I had been introduced a few years before for networking purposes. He was a nice guy, was really successful, and his network was powerful. But something was just 'off' about our interactions, and so I had decided not to pursue a relationship, even though he kept calling me every few months."

"For some reason… probably because a part of me thought it might be divine intervention, since he called right after I had asked for guidance… I decided to take the call. If I had known then what I was getting into by taking that call, I'm not too sure I would have! Always clear in hindsight, isn't it?" Pappy laughed. "Here's where this part of the story starts to get particularly spicy!"

"After a few niceties, Sam cut to the chase, 'We have to meet, and soon! You've been laid on my heart by God, and I have something important I have to give you.' Well, I was a bit stuck, and immediately regretted taking the call. But I paused and considered the context and timing again, and thought better of blowing him off. So, we set a time for a breakfast soon after I was scheduled to get back to Denver. I chose the place solely because I had good experience with getting in and out of that restaurant fast!"

"When the morning for the breakfast appointment arrived, I got there on time and Sam was already waiting for me. I hadn't been seated for more than a minute before he pulled a book out of his satchel, and I noted how his behavior felt hurried and awkward. While he pulled the book out, he was saying, 'Read this. You need to read this. I read it and have met the Prophet. I'm making sure to get this book into the hands of anyone who God lays on my heart. Promise me you will read it!'"

"Well, I didn't owe Sam any favors, and y'all know I don't like being told I *have* to do anything. So, I just asked him why he thought I might have been laid on his heart. He didn't respond, and simply said, 'You just have to. I don't pretend to know why.' Then, just like that…" Pappy snapped his fingers for effect. "… he got up and turned quickly to go. When he did, he bumped into the waitress who was coming to fill our mugs. Coffee spilled on Sam but he didn't even seem to notice… he just said he had another meeting to get to. It was just so *bizarre*! He wasn't interested in catching up at all, or in networking, or anything like that. He was there missionally, and considering the season I was in, there was something powerful about that to me."

"As Sam scurried out of the restaurant, I gave the waitress a *Well, that was strange* look, and placed an order. Then I picked up the book, wiped off the splashed coffee with a napkin, and opened it to get a feel for it. It was written by some guy named John who was called – or who called himself – 'The Prophet.' The book was billed as his true story about being completely sold out to God and his faithful day-to-day walk in consistent response to what he said was direct leading from the Lord."

"Now, that got my attention for a lot of reasons. There weren't many people... if any, actually... who I knew who were completely 'sold out to God'... and so that was intriguing. Plus, I'd been reading plenty about other people's opinions on how to discern God's will, what people thought 'The Kingdom of God' was, how to feel God's love... and other topics like that. Most of those books were written by academics with an opinion based on their theological framework. So, that book was potentially a refreshing read! I decided to read the first few pages while I enjoyed my breakfast. Let's just say it hooked me hard and fast... and I decided I'd take one man's experience over a whole bunch of folks' opinions any day. And this guy had a lot of incredible experiences... *if* his accounts were to be believed. Before his hurried exit, Sam said he knew John personally and had talked with several eyewitnesses who had verified many of the stories. So... pretty compelling, right?" Pappy looked around to see if there were any obvious opinions one way or the other about his interest. There were no obvious smirks or raised eyebrows from around the firepit, so it seemed the unspoken consensus was the latter.

"I had blocked the day as my one personal day for the week, so I decided to go home and dive into John's book more. On the drive home, I was praying the whole way, asking God to lead me through the book, or to be protected from its messages. I remember the sincerity of that prayer so well. It's part of the reason why I still to this day believe that even with as crazy as things got, it was all exactly as it was meant to be."

"We had a dog named Blue at the time." Susie had been lying down on a blanket next to the fire. She suddenly sat bolt upright and said with some desperation,

"Isn't Blue the dog that got shot by your neighbor when you were living on your farm?"

Pappy smiled and explained that he wasn't ever a hundred percent sure... that they knew for a fact that Bear and Billy were shot, but they weren't sure about Blue.

"I want to hear that part of the story, Pappy. That's so *sad.* I just can't imagine that!" A couple of the other kids chimed in that they, too, wanted to hear.

Pappy smiled. "Ok, we'll get to that part soon… and if I have the time, then I'll tell a great story about all that. It was hard, but it actually all worked out beautifully with that neighbor."

Susie laid back down and shifted to get comfortable. Piccolo emerged from the darkness and walked over to Susie. He climbed up onto her chest, circled once, and laid down.

"Anyhow, I was just going to say that as I sat down to read, Blue lay down in the living room near me and the energy in the room felt really peaceful. The bit I had read in the restaurant had struck a chord, and the strangeness of the day had made me excited to settle deep into my old reading chair and dive in." That leather chair was quite an heirloom for our family. It was now an almost completely worn-out piece of furniture, but it still had a prominent position in Pappy's study and he still spent a lot of time in it. It was in that chair where Pappy said he 'had it out with God'. I don't think anyone could even begin to count the hours of prayer, study and meditation that have happened in that chair.

"Well, let's just say it swept me up! I read that book from cover to cover in one sitting! If everything in that book was true, then it was an incredible story about a man who seemed to know God the way I desperately wanted to… and I'd never met anyone who could claim that! After I finished, I put the book in my lap and just sat there taking in all I had experienced during the wild ride those pages offered. After a while, I picked the book back up and flipped through the last few pages of the epilogue and some credits and such. Then I noticed that John actually lived close by and had listed his website and email address."

"Y'all know me and how I roll right into things." Pappy smiled at Andy and Betsey who looked back at him with playfully raised eyebrows and smiles that said *yep.* "So, I picked up my BlackBerry and I…"

"What's a BlahBurie?" one of the kids asked.

Pappy laughed and said, "It's actually one of the very first devices we were able to use to communicate with one another without wires attached to walls. That was the name of the company that made them, and so that's what they were called." The kids, and even some of the adults, just couldn't wrap their minds around the idea of wires for anything, but nobody wanted to sidetrack Pappy by asking for further clarification.

He continued, "I picked up my BlackBerry and I emailed John. I typed something about how I had just finished the book, and how I appreciated him putting it all out there and that perhaps we could visit in person sometime since I was in Colorado too."

"I sat there for a few minutes longer, and then decided to get up to stretch my legs and grab something to eat. Just as I was about to stand, I saw the little red light on the top of the phone start to blink, indicating I had a message. I opened it and was surprised to see the message was John responding to my note! All it said was 'Thanks, brother. How about we visit now?'"

"Whoa! I was surprised! What was I supposed to do with *that*?" Pappy slapped his knee and laughed. "The current of that day was strong, and so I just sort of went with it. I thought, 'Why not?' and responded with something like, 'Sure! I'll come your way. Where to?' I didn't want him to come to our house, since I didn't know the guy personally yet. John offered his address, and I looked it up on my road atlas since the address wasn't familiar. Back then, the satellite mapping services weren't reliable, and so I didn't use them." Pappy smiled, noting the group had appreciated his pre-emptive explanation.

"I wrote down the directions on a piece of paper, hopped in the car, and headed over to his apartment. After a while, I was deep into a sketchy part of town that I had never been to. Some intimidating dudes were sitting on their porches drinking from bottles wrapped in paper bags and watching me real close as I drove by several times in my flashy Audi, since I couldn't find John's address right away. And with each pass, my mind was telling me about all the horrible things they were cooking up for me!" Pappy widened his eyes to add fun emphasis to the story. This was funny to us, given that the story was coming from a man who we only knew to never judge anyone by appearances, and who could get along with anyone.

"When I finally got to John's apartment complex, I drove around the building hoping to find a place to park where I could keep an eye on my car, since I'd just spent a lot of money on some new wheels, and I was sure someone was going to try to steal them. I finally just had to be ok with whatever was going happen, and so I parked a ways from John's building, locked the car, and walked toward John's unit."

"The apartment complex was pretty run down… lots of trash around, broken windows, cracked cement walkways with weeds growing through, siding falling off, and such. I walked up to his door, and just as I was about to knock, it swung wide open. A man with unkempt, brownish-blonde hair, glasses, and a chubby face filled the doorframe. I remember I had to take a step back because while he wasn't an intimidating person, he came on real strong… but in a good way. I just didn't know what to do with his energy. His smile was a bit snaggle-toothed, and his teeth were stained various shades of brown. He had a big paunch that pushed his huge t-shirt away from his waist, and he was wearing shorts and flip-flops. Even though he looked sort of sloppy and off-putting, his genuine enthusiasm about me being there was just so friendly and engaging. I liked him immediately."

"'Come on in, friend!' John said, while he reached out his hand for a shake. I took his hand, and when he had a hold of me, he pulled me into his tiny home. Maybe that should have spooked me a bit, but it didn't. It was a little surprising, but was super friendly and so it somehow didn't feel weird at all. So, instead of punching him and running away, I entered into the living area, which also served as his dining area. Behind that was a galley kitchen strewn with dirty dishes. The most well-worn Bible I'd ever seen was open on the table surrounded by three chairs that didn't match, and there was a concordance next to it that looked as worn as the Bible. Papers with handwritten notes were all over the table and floor." Pappy laughed a laugh that had an affectionate tone to it.

"He seemed completely content in the space. Most of the folks I knew then, and even I at the time, would have been apologizing for the small apartment, or maybe offering some excuses for how such conditions were only temporary. He didn't though. He just offered me some water. Nothing else. Just water. Tell ya what!" Pappy laughed, "I could have gone for a two-finger tumbler of something particularly strong at that point! But that wasn't gonna happen. He just waited for my response, and I accepted the water out of politeness… and to give me a moment to get my bearings."

"John grabbed a used cup from a nearby convenience store out of the cabinet and filled it from the tap, while he eagerly told me to have a seat anywhere. The closest chair to me was an old recliner that had grease stains all over the upholstery, and disintegrating foam swelling up against the few remaining threads of the armrests. And I remember thinking the rats would enjoy nesting in that armrest." Pappy laughed more. "I was still wearing my nice clothes from that morning, and so I was hesitant about taking a seat and adding to my losses for the day, since I was sure my wheels were being stolen as I sipped the brownish tap water from that grimy cup." Pappy paused for a moment before continuing, trying to determine where to go next with the story.

"I was about to sit at the dining table when he strode over from the sink, grabbed one of the chairs from the table, and walked with it the few feet over to where I was still standing. His movement forced me to sit down on that recliner, and so I awkwardly flopped into it while he placed his chair very close to me. It was all so uncomfortable and yet totally comfortable at the same time… really strange. He sat on the edge of his chair with his forearms on his knees and looked at me intensely for a few moments. He smiled wide, and I remember the authenticity and graciousness of that smile suggested he had an internal state which I'd longed for all my life, and that energy called to me. He kept smiling with those crazy eyes, intense but gentle. Then he shifted his weight into his backrest, leaned the chair up on two legs, and locked his fingers over his big belly." Pappy leaned back and tried to puff out his stomach and lock his fingers over it to mimic John's actions. The posture was ridiculous considering how lean Pappy was, and some of the kids giggled.

"That guy didn't sugar coat anything or dance around or bother with pleasantries. He would just get right to it whenever you talked with him – and that time was no exception."

"'So, what brings you here?'"

Pappy smiled, "I told him that I honestly wasn't too sure. I explained that I had read his book on Sam's recommendation, that it had resonated, and so I had sent him the note… and that suddenly there I was! I was frank with him, and admitted I was a little confused by it all. He suddenly brought all four chair legs back to the floor and sat for a long moment just looking at me. I'm not one to back away from a gaze, and so I stared back at him. It wasn't like we were playing chicken or anything like that. It's just that we both were locked on each other, and I swear it was as if that man was looking right through my eyes and deep into my soul. He finally spoke, and it was like the conference room all over again, but in a totally different context. He had this really steady voice that was soft without being gentle, and he asked, '*What do you want?*'"

"Well, I had a pretty tough persona in those days, and I didn't like feeling pushed. Maybe it was the way he had stared at me for a while, which was just socially awkward. Maybe it was too soon in the conversation for me. Maybe it was because we just met. I don't know, but I felt a little irritated. And at the same time, I felt like it was an opportunity to state again very clearly what I wanted more than anything. In the boardroom with the partners of that firm months before, I had said what I wanted relative to all the things the world could offer. If this guy was actually a man with some sort of direct pipeline to God, then I decided this was an opportunity to state my desires in no uncertain terms relative to all the spiritual world could offer. Even though I was a little irritated, I sensed it was an important moment which I needed to take seriously – like this time, it was directly between me and God. So, I told him very succinctly, 'I want to know God.' And I just let that hang out there."

As Pappy flipped through a few more pages of his journal, Frankie and Leela suddenly sat upright and focused their ears and noses out in the pitch darkness beyond the light of the fire. They bolted in unison, and after a couple of seconds we could hear them barking as they ran into the wilderness. "They sure do love to run deer." Pappy said as he chuckled. "But they wouldn't know what to do if they ever caught one." Pappy laughed, thumbed past a few pages in the journal, and landed on something that prompted his next comments.

"Well, John seemed to genuinely receive that, but he also seemed to be evaluating the sincerity of my answer… and then he said, '*what do you really want?*' As you can imagine, that pushed me a little harder. It's like that brought the intensity of the conversation up several notches, and it got *real*! I looked straight into his eyes for a long second or two, set my pitch to a serious tone, and very slowly said the same words, but with a lot more heart, '*I want to **know** God.*'"

"I was expecting him to lean back and reflect on my statement, or ask a clarifying question, or something like that. But, before I knew what was happening, he had laid his hand right on my forehead. I remember wanting to slap it away, punch him in the throat and scurry out of the apartment, but I couldn't! My world went upside down… my axis was just *way* off. I couldn't have slapped his hand away if I had tried, much less stand up and walk! I couldn't react at all. I was completely paralyzed! I felt so dizzy, and remember sinking my fingers into those worn out armrests so I wouldn't pitch over! John continued to hold his hand on my forehead while I fought to get my bearings. Then I suddenly felt a warmth flowing through me, and it had an electric sort of power to it. I was outside of time and even space again… sort of like in that eddy on the Futa, but different. It was so wild."

"He asked again, '*What do you want?*' His fingers got heavier on my head, or maybe he was squeezing me a bit, I don't know. But the feeling got heavier, and the meat of his hand pressed harder into my forehead. I felt a sick feeling in my gut, and it start working its way up through my heart. And then I just… and y'all know I don't cry much… well, I burst into tears. Then whatever loose semblance of any grounding I still had dissolved completely! *Poof!*" Pappy threw his arms out in front of him with his fingers wiggling as if to illustrate what he felt had happened emotionally. He slowly flipped past a few more pages. *What was written on all those pages he was passing by?* I wondered.

"Then I felt something different. It wasn't so much like the room was spinning anymore as I was full-body tumbling through space. I cried and tumbled and allowed the disorientation to take me wherever I was supposed to go. It is to this day one of the few big cries I've ever had, all with that prophet's fat hand on my forehead!" Pappy laughed at the memory, a laugh which seemed to honor it. "So much emotion poured out of me, and then my answer left my heart and came up through my throat and out of my mouth and I said, 'I want to *feel* God's love. I want *peace. I want more.*'" Pappy's eyes were welling up with tears. "Well, after I said that, everything just sort of settled quickly. John took his hand off my head and sat back in his chair."

Pappy let that part of the story sink in for a few seconds before continuing, "Y'all, it was wild… like *beautiful* wild. I felt completely cleaned out inside. I felt the love and the peace I had said I wanted… and it changed me. In that moment, I knew for sure that *more* – that intimate felt-sense of the peace and love of God - was possible and was available to me and everyone else. I didn't know it then, but I was being granted a taste of what I'd eventually have as a permanent state. It was amazing… and was all I had hoped it would be."

"So, I just sat there for maybe a minute, sort of dazed and bathing in that new feeling. Then John looked at me with a profound sort of kindness and said, '*You need to be baptized*'. I felt exhausted and elated at the same time, so I didn't resist the suggestion at all… even though the elders at my church would have been disappointed, since they didn't believe in adult baptism. I had noticed a dirty pool filled with algae when I was walking up to his apartment, and I was so in the moment I said something like, 'You have a pool over there!'"

"John laughed and said, 'Now isn't the time. You and your wife together… and definitely *not* in that cesspool!'"

"Now that blew me away. We hadn't talked about Nana at all. Even though I'm sure he saw my wedding band, he had no earthly way of knowing that she was going through a lot on her own spiritual journey… and was feeling very strongly that she needed to be baptized!"

"He said, 'Come to our gathering tomorrow night. It's at eight. I'll email you the address after you leave'. Now, I really can't put words on how I felt after all of that, but it was *good*. I told him we would be there."

"He hadn't moved his chair back from me yet, and so he was still sitting close… uncomfortably close. I didn't care though. I was just sort of pleasantly stunned and was fine staying seated for a few more minutes. But he wasn't finished. He just sat there, not really paying attention to me. It was like he was *listening* to something I couldn't hear. Then he suddenly focused his attention back to me. Y'all, his eyes had *changed*. They had this incredible burning intensity as he looked straight at me, and said something that absolutely would have been impossible unless he really was in touch with God. He said, '*You are a farmer. But first, the wilderness!*'"

"Well, I was straight-up *dumbstruck*, and y'all know that doesn't happen to me! I sat there like a bump on a log and just stared at him. Now, I don't know exactly what he meant, but he had just told me was I was going to be a farmer, or in fact that I already was, at heart! How in the world could he have come up with that? I mean, to look at me with my flashy car and clothes, wouldn't the idea of me as a farmer have seemed ridiculous – the farthest thing from his mind? That statement was just too much for me, considering how much energy Nana and I were putting into the idea of starting a homestead."

"That was it though. That was all he said. After that, he seemed to come back into himself and the intensity was gone. He just leaned back in his chair, laughed a big belly laugh, and said, '*A farmer! I have no idea what that means! We'll see you tomorrow night!*'"

"Then he abruptly got up, walked over to the door and opened it. The fresh air filled the little room and helped bring me back to my senses. It saddened me, but that moment of peace I'd experienced had left as quickly as it had arrived. I was back to my old self… though changed in some way I couldn't qualify. So, I stood up and walked toward the door and extended my hand to shake his. He looked at my hand then back at me, then leaned in and gave me a great big, full-bodied bear hug. I was used to 'bro-hugs' from guys, and this wasn't *at all* like that. This was intimate and beautiful… powerful. He squeezed me tightly, kissed me on the jaw and whispered in my ear, '*Be a leaf in the wind, brother. Just let go and float.*' Then he let me go and slapped me on the back in a super friendly way, wagged a finger toward my chest while looking at me directly, and said, '*Tomorrow night!*'"

"I walked on out to my car in a bit of a daze. Now, they weren't, but I don't think I'd have even noticed if my wheels had been missing! The whole interaction had only lasted a few minutes… I don't remember how many, maybe fifteen or twenty… but some *serious* ground was covered! I mean, what was I supposed to do with all *that?* The overall experience, and specifically what John said, wasn't something I could just ignore. I mean, I guess I could have… but, I'd have felt like I was turning away from the very counsel I'd asked God for. On the drive home I was *reeling*. But I also felt surprisingly light about it all. I remember I was grateful, excited, skeptical, and concerned all at the same time. I prayed the whole way home, asking God to please not let me be led astray, since I'd already decided I was going to see what that relationship held in store."

"When I got home, Nana was still out running errands with Andy and Betsey. So, I poured myself a stiff drink and sat back down in my chair and let all the energy of the day flow through me. Then I heard the garage door open, followed by the familiar sound of Nana's Land Rover pulling into the garage. I knew she was going to be surprised to see my car in the garage, and so she'd likely be asking how my day was soon after she came in. How could I possibly explain?"

"We had an open floorplan in that house, and the garage entered to the kitchen through a little entrance hall. From the kitchen you could look across the large granite slab of the center island, through the dining area, and into the living room where I was sitting by the fireplace in my chair. I didn't feel inclined to get up and hide to avoid the inevitable question from Nana. So, I only had a moment to think through what to say. That crazy day had just been what it had been, even if it was hard to make sense of. And so I just figured I'd tell her about it all, and exactly as it had happened."

"Well, sure enough, Nana opened the door and held it for Betsey to come toddling through. Andy was close behind her, and they ran around the kitchen island toward the stairs that led down to the playroom. They saw me and cried out in that way that melts a father's heart, *'Daddy!'* and came over and gave me a hug. After a few minutes of saying hi, they got off my lap and went off to the playroom with Blue right behind them, obviously appreciating their energy."

"As she set a load of groceries on the counter, Nana acknowledged me with her typical, *'Hey, babe'*. Then she looked over at me, 'You're home early. Everything ok? How was your day?'"

"I smiled at her, threw back the last of my drink, and set the glass on top of John's book. '*Gotta minute?*'"

CHAPTER TEN

THE WHIRLWIND

"Well, Nana didn't know what to make of the story about me and John, but she trusted my dedication to seeking God. She wondered if I thought John was an important part of that pursuit, and I said I didn't know but that I'd like to at least take steps to find out. So, she agreed to go to the gathering John suggested we attend. We managed to find childcare for Andy and Betsey last minute… which was no small thing… and we took that as a validation, of sorts.

As we drove to the address John had emailed me, Nana wanted to hear again why we were allocating an evening to something that felt so 'out there' to both of us. As you can probably imagine, I really didn't have any good answers for her except that for some reason it felt right to me to go. Nana was just the best…" Pappy paused again to let the emotion surge through him. "She was always up for an adventure, and we were so united in our pursuit of God during that season. She just said, 'Ok. Then you know I'm game.' We were just following the breadcrumbs, y'all! There was such a great energy to the new twist with John and his community that I *still* reflect back on that time with so much fondness… even though it was a big part of what contributed to a lot of pain for me and Nana."

"The neighborhood we eventually pulled into was similar to the one where John lived. It was raining that night, so we walked to the front door of the tiny house quickly and we saw that it was cracked open behind a heavy, wrought-iron safety door. The iron creaked loudly when we swung it open, so knocking wasn't necessary. From just inside the door, we heard a voice whisper enthusiastically,

'*Come on in!*'"

"I pushed, and the door met a spongy resistance. That room was so packed that people had filled the whole house and were pressed up against the door! As we entered, we saw people crammed onto sofas and spread all over the floor and against the walls. John was on the other side of the room, leaning against the soot-covered fireplace. He and I made eye contact as Nana and I entered, though he didn't make any special gestures to acknowledge us being there. Someone was offering a heartfelt prayer asking that Jesus' spirit would sweep through the gathering. People were swaying and hands were raised and there were lots of sincere and loud *Yes Jesuses!* Sam was seated in a large chair near John, and he made enthusiastic welcoming gestures to usher us in further. Smiles, nods and small waves were offered us from most of the folks who didn't have their eyes closed in prayer, and we had the sense we were immediately 'in'. There was no turning around."

"That was unlike any gathering I had ever been to, Christian or otherwise. That kind of welcoming spirit is far more commonplace these days, but it sure wasn't the norm back then… at least for us! John was the leader, but he didn't assert himself or take any position of authority over the group, except to encourage folks when someone would chime in about what they believed God was teaching them. He might occasionally offer his thoughts about a passage that had been referenced, or he would encourage someone to further unpack something they had shared... but, that was really it. It was like decentralized spirituality!"

Pappy laughed gently at his play on concepts with a subtle mix of enthusiasm and sadness. Long before the Defi|Climate War, promoting decentralized finance and protecting the earth's ecosystem had been strong values for our family, with Pappy as a primary advocate of both. His conviction was no small part of the reason why Dad and Greg were in Washington, D.C. for the peaceful protest that fateful day when the government lost its grip on crowd-control efforts, and Greg had died.

"I mean, I was well aware that in the Bible, Jesus tells folks not to call anyone 'teacher' – but there wasn't a model of that anywhere that I was aware of. In fact, in all the churches and Christian gatherings I had been to, there was always some sort of spiritual hierarchy in place. So, being with a group that seemed so healthy, but without any one person telling the people how to think, was just *so* cool!"

Pappy pointed to the kids and smiled. "Let this be a really good lesson for you young kids. That man controlled that room in the most beautiful way the whole evening. He never once demanded attention or respect… but he was constantly *commanding* it. And make no mistake, there is a big difference!" Pappy winked at the kids, knowing they were likely confused, but satisfied that a seed had been planted about good leadership within decentralized structures.

"When he did speak, he had this air about him that made me and Nana willing to listen, not only to what he had to say, but also to the folks who obviously had so much respect for him. And he never took credit for any insight or wisdom he offered. If someone tried to give him props, he'd just say something like, 'The Spirit is flowing!'"

"Everyone had a Bible in their lap. As a new verse or passage was brought up, all you'd hear were hands moving quickly across worn pages to get to the passage. It reminded me of the 'Sword Drills' we would have in my elementary school."

"What's a Sword Drill?" Kell couldn't help asking, eager for another story.

Pappy shifted courses elegantly, always eager to engage with a child's interest, and smiled at Kell. "Well, now, those were something else!" Pappy said, laughing. "This'll be a fun side note, and it's worth sharing because it'll give you a little insight into my very early years and how so much of my religious beliefs were because of my upbringing and community." Pappy looked at the kids, and decided to qualify briefly, "...an interesting and powerful sort of forced group think."

"I went to a pretty strict Christian elementary school when I was about your age, and there was a huge emphasis on knowing the Bible... and the first part of knowing your Bible was how to get around in it. For Sword Drills, we'd all gather – all the kids in the whole school – and we'd sit crisscross-applesauce on the gym floor with our Bibles in front of us. It was called a 'sword drill' because a lot of Christians called the Bible 'the sword of the Spirit' which is referencing a passage many of you probably are familiar with."

"Bibles had to be placed just so." Pappy deftly sat on the ground in the manner described to illustrate, then grabbed a journal and placed it ceremoniously on the flagstone in front of him. He slowly looked around at all the kids, who were very much engaged, and most certainly imagining being in that gymnasium with hundreds of other kids with their Bibles in front of them. Several adults caught each other's eyes in amusement as they noticed most of the kids had sat up and crossed their legs while Pappy wove the brief tale.

He delighted in the children as he created the tension around what would happen next. "Then, the principal of the school, who was this really stern-but-kind woman who always wore long black skirts and white frilly tops and high heels, would hold a microphone so that it would cover her mouth. Then she'd gaze out at all of us with great ceremony." Pappy grabbed one of his flip flops as a prop to illustrate. He held a long pause, masterfully playing with the children's vivid imaginations. "Then, she'd quickly call out a random verse, pause for a moment, then call it out again to make sure we got it. Then she'd let that reference linger for a few seconds... and then came the much awaited, 'Students... draw your swords!'"

"Suddenly the whole room would be filled with the sound of pages flipping... it sounded like a huge flock of birds taking off the water! The first person to find the verse would lift their Bible up over their head, like they were drawing a sword from its sheath. All this happened while the teachers walked up and down the rows. Once someone drew their sword – and it was usually several kids at once - the teachers would act as judges about who was first. Then the nearest teacher to that kid would check to make sure he or she had gotten it right."

"If it checked out, it was considered a win and that kid would get to stand up in front of everyone, take the mic, and read the verse out loud like a little champ!" Pappy quickly stood up with his chest puffed out and held the journal open in his hand and the flip flop in front of his face. Then he feigned reading to the crowd. As he sat back into his chair, he continued, "But, if that kid hadn't gotten it right… well, now that was a problem! It was considered dishonest and prideful, and that kid would have to take 'the walk of shame'. The teacher would stand in front of them frowning while the student gathered their Bible and backpack and had to walk out of the gym in front of everyone."

"It was crazy intense… but then, that whole school was, actually." Pappy pulled the blanket around his shoulders and said, "I remember one time I said a bad word and I had to stay after school and write some Bible verse about how the tongue is bad on the chalk board two hundred times! Anyhow, that's what Sword Drills were."

"What do you think of that, Kell?" Pappy probed with sincere interest. "Well, gosh, I don't know what to think about that, Pappy."

"Fair enough, Kell. Fair enough." Pappy smiled at him, and then at all the kids, very gently.

"Anyhow, in that gathering in that little house with John's group, I remember being so impressed with their familiarity with scripture. That impression quickly translated into a sense that they were the sort of committed Christians Nana and I had been wanting to find for a long time. It sounds judgmental, or harsh, or something, to say this now… but we felt we had found what we might have called 'true believers.'"

"We had been standing right inside the door for several minutes, taking it all in, when couple across the room toward the kitchen caught our attention and scooched over. They motioned for their teenage children to scuttle over with them to make room for us, so we smiled and decided to take them up on their offer. We awkwardly dodged legs and laps and made our way to the space, which was just barely big enough for us to squeeze into. We crossed our legs, opened our Bibles… and then, *whoooom!*" Pappy smiled and threw his hands out toward us from his heart. "We were completely swept up!"

"It was just *awesome*. Hours went by. The sense of community and love was nothing short of incredible. People just loved Jesus and the Church and were desperately hungry to learn more about God and to hear what the 'Living Word' might be teaching them." Pappy laughed, obviously enjoying remembering the moment.

"Well, before your Nana and I knew it, we were wearing borrowed bathing suits that hardly fit because they were so big. And we were getting baptized in a rundown hot tub on the back patio of that house! It was so special… so sacred… so sincere and raw and beautiful… so unifying for me and Nana. There we were, in a situation that our friends would have probably thought was straight-up *nuts*, and we were loving every minute of it! Actually, we knew it *was* nuts by our society's norms, but we didn't care. We were *all in*! John and I shared a glance when I was going under the water, and his gaze went somewhere deep in me. Something magical was happening, and I just knew my life was about to change. And to make it all even more fantastic, guess who was baptizing me?"

Pappy paused for effect and looked around. "*Sam*!"

Pappy leaned forward and waved his hands lazily in a whirling motion over his head "Well, from there it was just a whirlwind! We started hosting Bible studies at our house, usually with John. Folks from the neighborhood would come over, and… well, I just don't know how else to say this other than how I used to say it… the Spirit would *move*. It was just incredible… wild to be a part of. We never knew what would happen in those gatherings."

Pappy laughed and flipped through a few more pages. "Oh, you'll love this one! This is a great example of how bizarre things were getting… and, also an example of why I paid John some real attention."

Pappy shifted his focus my way. "Don, would you mind refilling me again? The ratio of honey to water that last time was perfect. And maybe throw in a bag of green tea?" Pappy extended the cup to me once again and I walked toward the kitchen as quickly as I could, not wanting to miss much. But I was a little stiff, and moved like it. Pappy noticed, and suggested we all take another break.

As I walked across the patio, I overheard Pappy say, "Let's get the wiggles out for a few minutes. And look, no offense taken at all if anyone is tired and doesn't want to listen to an old man prattle on anymore. Please feel free to duck out and go to bed." I noticed through the kitchen window that while everyone did take the opportunity to stand and move around a little, nobody left. A few shuffled their chairs a little closer to the fire. Pappy was still standing when I returned and handed him his cup.

"Thanks Don." He smiled at me, somehow acknowledging our long history together with that brief glance. I had refilled his cup so many times in the past, sometimes with coffee, sometimes water or tea, and more than a few times with his favorite reposado. I smiled back, hoping he saw I was trying to say 'my pleasure' – and could understand the depths to which I meant it.

Pappy sat back down and got himself comfortable while everyone else did the same.

Then he picked up the journal he had been working from and found the page where he had left off. "Ok, yeah, so I felt I should share this little story about that time, because it's an example of the kind of thing that would happen a lot in our Bible study gatherings, things that played a big part in our willingness to really listen to John."

"One time, a sweet young mom who was a new friend of ours came to one of our studies. After a while, she was crying and talking about how she felt so distant from God and wanted to know more about the Bible and God's will for her life, and so on. It was all heartfelt, and the group was clearly touched. When it seemed like she had said all she was going to, we were just allowing the silence to linger while she dabbed at her eyes with the sleeve of her shirt. She was too self-conscious to even look up."

"John was sitting on the hearth in front of the fire, and the woman was sitting on a sofa all the way across the room. Then, all of the sudden, he stood up and hurled his Bible at her! I mean, he full-on reared back and *chucked* it right at her! It almost walloped her right in the chest, but she dodged just in time! Well, she looked up at him with eyes still teary and as wide as golf balls! I mean, we *all* had surprised looks on our faces... it was so out of character for him! As soon as that Bible landed on the cushion beside her, John yelled while he pointed at the worn-out Bible, *'Then spend time with Him! Read it, woman!'*"

"Well, I didn't know what to think! I looked over at Nana, and she was as wide-eyed as me and everyone else. I thought about calling the whole thing off right there, asking him to leave, and then apologizing to our new friend... and to the whole group for that matter! But something kept me from doing so. Somehow, things moved quickly past that awkward moment... like the momentum of the meeting up to that point just swept us on past all the crazy."

"After the study was over and we were all mingling for a bit, I noticed the woman was over in the kitchen by herself sipping on some coffee. I walked over and apologized for what had happened, and acknowledged how ugly that must have felt. Well, I couldn't believe her reaction! She looked up at me and said, 'Oh, no, no... John *is* a prophet. What he did was exactly what I needed. God has been laying that same message on my heart for months. He absolutely is a *true* man of God!'"

Pappy laughed as he noticed the looks on our faces, which were uniform in their surprise. He continued, "And that's how it went for a few months... just wild experience after wild experience that made little sense, but which continued to build John up as someone with some sort of special connection to God. He never asked for anything from us, except that we spend time 'in the Word' and stay in fellowship."

"Nana and I got closer and closer with John over several months, and we started sharing our hearts with him about how we were feeling led. He continued to consistently encourage us to just 'be leaves in the wind' and 'listen to the Spirit'. He'd say that kind of thing all the time, and it would drive me nuts... I remember I'd get *so* agitated. I felt like he didn't understand how much weight I was feeling about our circumstances, or how hard it seemed to 'hear God'." Pappy's eyes rested for a moment on something he had written in his journal.

"That was really tough for me. I mean, *how*... right?" Pappy looked around to see if the pain he had felt about trying to discern God's will for him and his young family resonated with anyone. "How could I be *sure*... in the moment-to-moment of life, and with the stresses I was carrying about potentially uprooting... that I was 'hearing' God and not just myself? I felt a strong need to be *certain* if we were going to make the huge leap that we were considering. I mean, I'd do anything if I knew it was God telling me... but, I questioned that all the time. After all, there were so many stories of people who thought they'd 'heard the call of the Lord' and had done crazy things like bombed abortion clinics, killed other people, and wrong-headed stuff like that. I think I was a little scared I was losing it a bit." Pappy smiled, and it seemed he was holding his memory of the man he used to be gently.

"Anyhow, John and I would often go on long walks and would talk for hours. I was usually focused on that particular issue - knowing how to *hear* God, and how to maintain confidence in that hearing. I remember one time he had come to spend time with me near my office in a busy part of town on the outskirts of downtown Denver. We were walking along the Cherry Creek trail, and after about a mile, we passed a homeless woman who my heart went out to. I felt prompted to engage with her, but decided not to act on the impulse. John was nearest to her, and he stopped and bent down. Then he leaned in close to her and whispered something in her ear that I couldn't hear. Then she shed a tear and reached up, touched his face, and offered him a toothless smile. He pulled out his wallet, and I was able to see that all he had was a $5 bill – and he gave it to her."

Pappy looked over at the kids, who seemed understandably confused. "Back then before cryptos, we used paper for currency... for money… and that was a pretty good amount of it back then in that situation… especially for a guy who didn't have any income and only lived on what God provided him with."

"As we continued walking, I couldn't help but ask him about that interchange since it was a perfect example of what I was trying to understand. I said something like, 'We've passed at least ten homeless folks since we started walking. Why did you engage with her and not the others?'"

"I remember he smiled at me with a knowing smile that was becoming familiar, winked, and said, 'You felt it too, didn't you?'. I admitted to having felt something, but also said that I considered whatever it was as too vague to be anything I'd act on. He just smiled bigger, looked at me, and said, 'The Spirit is looking for boldness… for people of *great faith*! You've got to start learning to trust that whisper, and respond!'. Well, y'all, that went *real* deep. I wanted to be bold for Jesus more than anything. I committed right then to listen… and *obey*."

Pappy touched his ear with one hand and placed the fingertips of the other hand against his chest, almost as though he was using a stethoscope on himself. He looked pensive for a long moment. Then, slowly, a grin spread across his face and he nodded contentedly while he looked out over his family. Then he turned his attention back to his journal. Sometimes words were absent Pappy's best lessons.

"A few more months went by, and the momentum continued to build with all that stuff. What a season! We had found an incredible community that was passionate for Jesus, and we were learning so much about being in community others, and Jesus' teachings, and how all that related to our lives. Andy and Betsey would run around playing made-up games in whatever random room we'd find ourselves in while meeting in little gatherings all over the city." Pappy laughed. "And, let me tell you, they were *random* places – basements of banks and back rooms of old coffee shops and places like that. Interestingly, we never met in a church building."

"Nana and I had started to share with John and the group more and more of the vision for our lives that had started in earnest in Chile. Over those months, it had crystalized into a beautiful picture in our minds – a picture which we were starting to *feel* as our reality. John and that community were so supportive. Our new friends would lay hands on us, pray that we'd have ever greater clarity, and for circumstances to come together to make it all a physical reality. The energy, emotion… and visceral *feeling*… being put toward the vision was tremendous."

Pappy reached for another journal while holding the current one open in his lap. He scanned the new one and seemed satisfied that he was remembering something correctly. "During that time, and at John's suggestion, I had started a 'boldness' project of 'listening to the Spirit' and responding whenever prompted without any thought. This would mean sometimes striking up conversations with strangers, or turning left instead of right while driving somewhere… or just pausing what I was doing and praying when prompted… and all kinds of stuff like that. I have so many awesome stories from that experiment!"

"One of those moments is really worth sharing, because I think it illustrates the wild ride we were on and how I was learning to trust what I started calling 'the voice'." Pappy directed his attention to the children, who were still completely absorbed in the story. "You've got to remember – this voice I'm talking about is in here," he pointed to his heart, "not here." He pointed to his head. "You little ones need to learn to listen to that voice. If you can sense it has love for others in it, then you can trust it. If it doesn't, or if you can't tell, then be careful." He let that settle for a moment as he looked at each of them. The adults seemed to appreciate the quick lesson, and the kids seemed empowered by it.

"So, here's the story… and it's an important one, since it put me firmly on the path of trusting the voice. One night, at 3:00 a.m., I was woken up by it. Like, bolt upright sort of woken up! It was powerful… and loud. That time it seemed audible, even though it couldn't have been, since Nana remained sound asleep. Well, it said to me in no uncertain terms: *Go hug Vicki.* That woke me up quick and completely. I sat up, shook the cobwebs out, and thought I must have been just having a crazy dream. But then, fully awake, I heard it again: *Go hug Vicki!*"

"Well, I was completely at a loss… willing to do anything, but with no idea what the voice meant. I didn't even know a Vicki that I could think of. I rolled out of bed and stumbled to the living room to my chair. I figured that since I had no idea what any of that meant, I'd just pray and listen more. I noticed my BlackBerry was blinking at the charging station in the kitchen, and I felt prompted to check it. I had a firm commitment to never do that until my quiet times in the mornings were over and I was ready to begin my work for the day. But most every action I took those days was prayerfully considered. So, I double-checked the inclination with a quick prayer, and I felt the prompting to check again. So, I picked the cellphone up, opened my email, and saw a note from a prominent and beloved man in our community asking for prayer for my mentor, Luke, who I mentioned earlier."

"Apparently, Luke had been in Montana fishing at a friend's ranch and had suffered a terrible aneurysm while on the river."

"What's an aneurysm?" McLean asked. Pappy focused his attention on the little girl and said,

"Well, in this case what happened is that a tube carrying blood in Luke's brain broke. Blood went into places where it wasn't supposed to be, and that caused really bad problems… like the kinds of problems that kill."

McLean nodded solemnly.

"The email said Flight for Life had just flown him to a hospital in Denver, and he was in the Intensive Care Unit at the hospital fighting for his life… and then that I remembered Luke's wife's was name was Vicki! Well, y'all,

I just about dropped to my knees when I remembered that… and, I didn't have to sit down to pray about the next steps!"

"The hospital was on the way to my office, and I had a really busy work schedule that day. I knew I needed to Go hug Vicki, though I had no idea how to contact her or how I might make that happen. I had only met her once, years before, so it wasn't like we were close friends, or anything like that. Even so, I figured I'd start my day early, swing by the hospital on the way to work, and see what God had in store with the 'hug' idea. I showered and dressed quietly, trying to not wake Nana up. She stirred just as I was leaving the bedroom and asked where I was going. It was still super early… around half past three at that point… and I was in the flow of something personal and sacred. So, I just said I was going to the office early. I figured I could explain it all later… whatever 'it' was going to be."

Some bats had started flying overhead, swooping into and out of the heat rising from the fire, and Pappy was completely absorbed in the memory of that experience. The event was clearly a seminal moment for him, and the memory of Luke and the impact his beloved mentor had made in his life was a combination of thought and emotion that seemed to overwhelm him. We all waited respectfully in silence while he watched the bats for a few long moments more before continuing.

"I got to the front desk a little after four. It was quiet – eerily so – and this long, white hallway extended way back behind the desk and was lit up bright by the harsh light. Nobody was at the desk, so I walked around it, then down the hallway, and ended up at the door to the waiting room for the ICU. I had been assuming Vicki and the family would be in the waiting room, and that the hug would be a pretty straightforward thing. But when I went in nobody was there. I felt completely out of sorts, and a little bit like I was losing my marbles with the 'hearing from God' stuff. But I couldn't quit just because it didn't play out like I'd imagined it might."

"I sat for a while in the room, thinking maybe Vicki would come in. But she didn't. It all felt so weird, even with as early as it was. That was a busy hospital in the middle of Denver, and yet I hadn't seen staff, or any of Luke's family, or any other folks there for other patients in the ICU. Then I had an idea to go find the chapel, thinking maybe I'd get some clarity about next steps there. I hadn't seen it on the way in, so I decided to exit the waiting room using a door that was across the room from where I'd entered. As I walked into the new hallway, I looked down it to the right. About fifty feet from me were two glass doors that led to a parking lot. It was all so eerily quiet – something like you'd see in a mystery movie just before a jump-scare. Then I looked left, and had one! The heavy door at the end of the hallway clanked loud when the latch sprung on the push bar. The door swung open – and do you know who walked through that door with her head hanging down? It was her… *Vicki*!" Pappy laughed, smiled widely, slapped his knee, and let the energy of that moment pass through him.

"I can't say I was really surprised… too many things like that had happened over those last few months. I was getting woken up at three in the morning all the time back then, and with all sorts of little prompts I'd respond to with affirming outcomes. But there was a lot more commitment to this one… and it was more dramatic. I think that experience with Vicki was the experience that made me so willing to listen and obey when the *big* call came!" We all wondered what that might have been, but Pappy wasn't ready to address that yet.

"Well, I started walking toward her with an obvious purpose. I have to say, it's more like I was *being walked*… it all just sort of happened. She looked completely fragged out. But she sensed someone headed toward her, lifted her head, and seemed to try to make out who it was headed her way. I saw the recognition in her blood-shot eyes when I was about ten feet from her, and her face softened as she recognized me. She called out my name and said, '…what are *you* doing *here*?'"

"I didn't answer. I just quickened my pace to close the distance between us. I said, 'Oh Vicki… ' and gave her a big, soft bear hug. I whispered in her ear, 'God told me to come hug you, so here I am.'"

"Well, then she just came all undone. She pulled me closer, put her head on my shoulder, and let a few huge sobs come out. She was already pretty cried out, and so the crying didn't last that long. She said,"

"'I've been here all night back there with Luke. It's touch and go, and I'm so scared. I'm just now heading home to get some rest before the kids arrive.' I released the hug, looked her deep in the eyes and just smiled with as much compassion as I had in me. My tongue was completely tied. There was nothing that was supposed to be said by me, and I knew it."

"'Thank you,' she said. 'I mean it. Thank you. I've been all alone here all night by myself and in so much pain. This is exactly what I needed. You're an angel.' I still didn't feel led to say anything, and so I didn't. I just gently stepped aside, smiled and nodded, and let her walk on by me so she could head home and get some rest."

"She shuffled on toward the parking lot while I stood in the hallway. I was completely overwhelmed at the feeling of being used to bring such comfort to another human being. It was beautiful." Pappy paused and wiped a tear from his eye. "There was an electricity sparkling through me that I'll never forget. Vicki looked back and lifted her hand for a little wave as she leaned into the door to push it open. Then she walked out into the dawning light. As I watched her exit the hospital, I remember thinking the sun was coming up on a whole new paradigm for her… and about how fragile and volatile life can be. Luke died a couple of weeks later, and I still miss him. Vicki said until the day she passed on that the hug I gave her that morning was one of the best she'd ever gotten."

"Those were my days during those months: working; parenting; husbanding and friending; praying; studying; listening and obeying. And during that time, Nana's and my excitement about the farm idea was building more and more. And at the same time, I was also feeling increasing conviction about hard times to come, and so I was feeling some urgency about getting prepared for that. While it was hard to discern my voice from God's with certainty, I did feel I was being led powerfully to move boldly toward the life we were envisioning. Almost as important, Nana believed it too. We had a whole host of reasons that I won't get into here for why we had such conviction... but they were reasons that were just too outlandish to ignore." Pappy looked from Betsey to Andy, and they both smiled back in a silent, respectful acknowledgement.

"But at the same time, I was increasingly nervous about making a move like that! The stakes seemed very high. I mean, it was a huge risk to drop all we had built together in pursuit of a completely new and different way of life that was totally unfamiliar to us. Was that all just me looking for a new challenge to spice life up a bit... or was it *really* God inspiring all those ideas? I started having a strong sense that not only were we to build the homestead for our family... but also for our Christian brothers and sisters, so they could have a shelter from what I believed was a coming storm. I know it sounds nuts – it did to me too – but, more than anything else, I wanted to be faithful. I knew I had the kind of bold faith that John said God was looking for... but, still, acting on it at that level was challenging."

"Well, as you can imagine, I ramped up the prayer and Bible reading big time trying to discern next steps... I became completely focused on getting an answer. Then, after a couple of weeks, I decided to fast and pray for a month." Pappy flipped through a few pages.

"It was a frustrating month, for sure, since God seemed completely quiet during it. All those little experiences of hearing the voice completely dried up... and I was confused and humbled. I kept asking and listening though. I maintained my fast faithfully, had all-night prayer vigils, and set reminders on my calendar every thirty minutes to pause, pray and listen. On the thirtieth day of August 2010 – a day I'll never forget – I was woken up again at 3:00 a.m."

"I heard the voice the same way I had on the *Go hug Vicki* night. It clearly told me to read a certain passage in the Bible. It was a passage I was not at all familiar with, but I knew I'd heard the instruction loud and clear. It's a wild thing y'all, to go from fast asleep to being woken up by a powerful voice coming from somewhere inside you. It was cool in one sense, and sort of intimidating and disconcerting in another. I had no response in that moment except to be in complete awe. After the shock wore off, and because I trusted the experience more quickly that time, I got up and walked out to the living room to my chair. I sat down, rubbed the sleep out of my eyes, picked up the Bible and set it in my lap, then offered a quick, 'I'm here, Lord.'"

"Let's just say the passage couldn't have been a more perfect answer to my prayers. So, that morning my heart was overwhelmed with a conviction that was to carry me for the next several years during all the great and hard times to come. I had been given our answer, and we were to move… and *then* - no dilly-dallying. I was sure we were to start the process that very day! And I knew, deep down, that it was a meaningful call toward The More. For me, and for our family." Pappy smiled at all of us.

"Nana had been completely understanding and validating through everything up to that point: all the John stuff; my listening and responding to 'the voice' project; the concerns about the economy… all that, and so much more. She was the only one who knew the intensity of my seeking during those days… none of my friends knew about it… and even John and the folks in our little group didn't *really* know. She had admired my dedication, and when it came to getting an answer about starting a farm, she had trusted it would come when it was supposed to. But my sudden conviction and timeframe would not be an insignificant thing for us, and I knew it might be hard for her to swallow. The timing was not ideal for a bunch of reasons, and the idea had taken an interesting and serious twist with the conviction I felt to care for others, should the economy actually collapse and cause the kind of suffering I thought it might."

"Nana's support was critical, and I knew telling her it was time to start the process that very day would be pushing her hard. I mean, it pushed me too! So, I 'threw out a fleece' as a final validation, and out of respect for our partnership. I'd tell Nana what I'd heard that morning, and what the passage meant to me. If she was supportive of it, then I was 'in' a hundred percent. If she wasn't, then I simply had to keep listening, and would chalk that morning up to a wild experience and would look for another way to interpret the passage 'the voice' had told me to read."

"Like I've said, she was going through some amazing transformations of her own, and I really trusted her intuition. We were absolutely in it together and I had to have her approval for something like that. For her to have said 'ok' would take a bit of a miracle – or certainly, I believed, would have been inspired by God. Well, I laid it all out there, and she absorbed it without any questions. Then after a few minutes, and knowing full well what was on the line, she just said, 'Ok, here we go!'. And that was it! Just like that..." Pappy snapped his fingers. "It was suddenly settled. We were leaving everything we knew in a huge step of faith."

Pappy shook his head slowly. "What a partner. What young mother with such dependent kids would be willing to completely remove any sense of stability and comfort in that season of life?" That observation seemed to land hard with the moms around the firepit. I thought about me, Naomi and Jenny, and the new baby. Would we have that kind of faith? Would we be willing to step away from everything we know in response to an internal 'voice'?

Even hearing the story, I couldn't completely wrap my head and heart around what was shaping up. Pappy looked around at us all, his vibrant blue eyes glistening in the firelight.

"Pretty remarkable, huh?" Then he leaned back in his chair and stared up into the starlit heavens. "Well, Nana was a remarkable woman."

CHAPTER ELEVEN

HOME

Pappy continued to stare up at the stars for a long moment, then blinked hard and took a drink from his mug. He scratched his head, glanced at his journal, and continued.

"We didn't waste any time, and started looking for properties in the mountain west that same day. In short order, we almost pulled the trigger on a small farm right here in Buena Vista, but it ultimately didn't feel right. It was *hard*! It was one thing to commit to moving and starting a farm, but entirely another thing trying to discern where that would be and what it would look like. It was exciting though, taking bold actions in faithful response to internal promptings and convictions."

"After a while of searching, we started having conversations about the possibility of moving out of state. One of our primary values was family, and we only had a few members in Colorado. We loved them, but they were really busy with their lives and we rarely saw them. So, we started thinking we could look at the Southeast to be closer to my side of the family. That was a bigger deal though… even more risks. Primarily, I'd have to move a long way from my business - and back then, we weren't living in a remote working environment like we are now. But as we opened that door of possibility, there were immediately several back-to-back events that pushed us over the edge and into a breathtaking pace of significant change."

"As a part of my process for discerning whether I was actually following God's will or going crazy, I had been in close communication with my family, since we were super-tight and they knew my heart so well. My grandmother, Mema, was a key player in this part of the story. She was a woman who loved God and had lived in intimate relationship with Him ever since her son, and my namesake, had been struck and killed at age fourteen by lighting. One summer, a lightning bolt from a sudden, freak storm blew him off the bow of their ski boat right in front of her. Can you imagine? As she dove again and again trying to find his body in the dark water, God spoke to her. He said something like, *Peace, Hazel. He is with me now*. In the rare times when she'd tell the story, she'd tell us she was flooded with a peace in that moment – a peace that had persisted ever since."

"She was our matriarch, and I loved and respected her so much. So, naturally, I valued her opinion on all I'd been processing over the last many months, and so I ran it past her in a long conversation one afternoon. After listening gracefully, she not only validated my sense of calling but even offered us a cabin she owned on Lookout Mountain, Georgia to live in while we got things sorted. My dad had also generously said we could have a few acres on the backside of our family farm in a tiny town outside of Atlanta, Georgia. He said we could stay for as long as we wanted in the farmhouse while we built. That was a particularly attractive option, since the 'farmhouse' was a recently renovated antebellum mansion that had been in our family for generations."

"So, we suddenly had two intriguing options in a concentrated area of the Southeast, and the flow seemed to be pushing us gently that way. We shared all this with John, and he organized a gathering so our little community could pray over us. He was increasingly vocal in his support of me and Nana as faithful and bold believers, and also of our vision which had developed so much since its initial catalyst in Chile. With those two options, it seemed the only logical next step was to fly to the Southeast and check things out. But don't y'all find it's a little frustrating that the light is often only cast for us as far as the next step?" It was another rhetorical question.

"I wanted the light to flood the next steps we'd be taking for a long time… and the landscape around the path too, for that matter! But that wasn't going to happen, so I had to trust things would progressively become more clear as we just faithfully submitted to each step of the journey as it was revealed. And that meant hopping a flight and exploring those new options in the Southeast. So, things already weren't going as we'd anticipated… we hadn't really considered leaving Colorado. And, like I said, that made everything feel much more consequential. But it was what it was, and it was nothing if not a big adventure for us. We booked a flight and landed in Atlanta a few days later with Andy and Betsey in tow."

Pappy picked up another journal and scanned through the pages of it.

"Being in the South in the spring is one of the more special experiences someone can have. The landscape and air quality is magical, and the people back then were so friendly… and the lushness and flowers! It is gorgeous on so many levels. We landed in Atlanta where I grew up, made the rounds to see family and friends, and then headed up to Rome to get the lay of the land in the community that would be closest to us if we were to end up on dad's farm."

"There were a few funny things that happened right away. One time, we saw this run-down little church with a bunch of people gathered in front of it, and some sort of carnival going on… well, carnival is a stretch." Pappy chuckled and glanced at Andy and Betsey, who were old enough at the time to start remembering this part of the story. They both smiled back, appreciating as adults all that fed into the rich experience they had as young children.

"There was one of those bouncy houses and a water slide and food set out on tables… so, *something* was going on there. Always up for a good time, needing some intel, and figuring being Christians was a good enough connection point, we pulled into the parking lot, hopped out of our car and walked up and said 'hi'. Those folks were thrilled we'd stopped by... and were definitely confused... all at the same time. But they were gracious with their authentic Southern hospitality, and we ended up sitting in old, discolored plastic chairs eating fried Twinkies and chatting with a few folks while the heat radiated off the asphalt in a way that's just impossible to..."

"Fried *Twinkies*?" Cecil blurted out, unable to control his enthusiasm over the mysterious concoction that simultaneously elicited intense disgust and intrigue. "Really, Pappy? You ate a Twinkie that was *fried*?"

Pappy laughed. "Yeah, the South is its own place, little man. It's hard to explain the charm of it. And you'd be surprised how well fried Twinkies and vanilla ice cream go together!" You could almost see the gears in Cecil's head churning. He looked over at his mother with eyes full of curiosity, obviously imploring her to make the concept of such an indulgence a reality for him. There were a few giggles as she looked at Cecil, laughed, and said, "Absolutely not, honey!".

Pappy smiled and continued, addressing the broader group again.

"We weren't thrilled about it, but there's that old saying, 'When in Rome...', so we just went with it – Twinkies, fried chicken, and platters of things with all sorts of unnatural colors. The irony wasn't lost on me and Nana either. We were on a scouting trip looking for a place to start an organic farm, and some of our first food was about as far from anything organic as one can dream of!" Pappy laughed. "We were just having good fun with it though. It was all such a wild ride, on even the smallest levels. Well, those folks were so kind to us, and that kind of thing happened a few times during our stay. We were quickly falling in love with the realness of the multi-faceted 'Southern charm'. The heat and humidity were almost unbearable on that trip, but we didn't care. We were on an adventure and just felt so... *willing*... so *submitted*."

"Nana and I were all swept up in the process, and it was a real highlight of our marriage, since during that crazy time we felt so deeply united as partners. And, more importantly to us, we felt united around our faith and commitment to following God together. It was so energizing… and overwhelming… all at the same time."

"Well, after only a couple of days in that area, Nana and I both felt strongly that the opportunity at our family farm wasn't the right one. That was a bit of a heartbreaker, since the property was stunning and we'd have been able to live in a fancy house on hundreds of acres. But, for reasons we couldn't ever really nail down, we just couldn't come to a peace about it… and that was of course critical for us."

"So, then we drove to my mother's house about an hour away on Lookout Mountain, and we enjoyed a day visiting with all the family who lived there. My sister, Hailey, volunteered to watch Andy and Betsey the next day so Nana and I could really cover some ground in the area to look at our options. And the first order of business was of course to head over to Mema's cabin and scope that out."

"That next morning, a heavy swirling fog had settled on the mountain, and fast-moving rain clouds would sweep in and then out, keeping everything soaked and feeling water-logged. Mema's cabin was in a transitioning area that was still considered pretty rough by the folks who lived on the nicer frontside of the mountain. As we pulled into the general area, we occasionally spotted some attractive homes. But, along the winding side-streets, there were mostly just dilapidated trailers and houses, broken-down cars, and trash heaps… and scary looking stray dogs wandered around aimlessly in small packs. It was a really poor area." Pappy chuckled and said, "So, without even seeing her cabin yet, we weren't feeling too good about that option. It wasn't at all what we had in our minds… a cozy little cabin in snugged into beautiful woods. The whole area just felt sort of nasty."

"We finally got to Mema's property and drove a little way up the muddy driveway, but there were two huge fallen trees that blocked us from driving all the way to the cabin. We were between rain showers, so we parked, got out, and walked the remaining few hundred feet. Well, as we got closer, we saw it was in rough shape. The old cedar siding was covered with some sort of black growth. The woods were encroaching on the house, and it seemed it wouldn't be long before the forest reclaimed the whole property. Tree branches were growing through the dark screen of the front porch. The roof was missing shingles, and the guttering had pulled away from the house over the little stoop which offered the only obvious place to enter. It had a dark and creepy feel to it." Pappy's eyes grew wide, and he shuddered for effect. Kell giggled, but the other kids looked a little spooked. Pappy nodded and raised his eyebrows.

"Mema had told the current tenants that we'd be stopping by while they were at work, so the door that opened off the stoop and into the kitchen was left open for us. Before even entering, let's just say our enthusiasm about the prospect of living there wasn't high. But when we opened the door and walked in, we felt our decision was made. A couple of skinny cats scurried out, and the scent of their urine slapped so hard we had to pull our shirts up over our noses to try to filter the fumes."

Suzie wrinkled her nose at the thought.

Pappy went on. "The linoleum in that tiny kitchen was pulling away from the base of the fake-oak cabinets, and the countertops and sink were covered with dirty dishes and food scraps. Another cat – and probably one of the mangiest I've ever seen – was perched on a little shelf across the kitchen in front of some creepy figurine dolls. The linoleum of the kitchen transitioned to the carpet of a tiny living room, and when we stepped on that carpet it literally squished, and the cat-pee smell got even worse."

Pappy laughed. "Nana and I looked at each other, and at exactly the same time, said, *'Nope!'*. We didn't even walk around the rest of the house. We just walked right out, certain God surely wouldn't want us in conditions like that! We got to the car and drove around the winding roads in silence… stunned that our obvious and easy options weren't turning out to be so obvious or easy… and wondering what might be a next step."

"The family farm near Rome hadn't felt right, and thus far, Lookout Mountain hadn't either. I think we were both a little sad and confused, and so we just drove along without saying much. After a while, the clouds started to lift, letting the sunlight in sporadically, and we commented on what a huge difference some sunshine made. We decided to head back to Hailey's house, pick up Andy and Betsey, and get ready for supper with a bunch of family at Mumsie's."

"That evening during our family gathering, we had a chance to visit with Mema. After explaining our experience out at her property, she got pretty upset. She had no idea her cabin had fallen into such a state of disrepair, and she told us that she had rented it in good faith to a couple who worked in student ministry, and that she had trusted them so much she hadn't bothered to check on things. Mema was old and couldn't manage the property herself, so the deal had been that those renters would take good care of the place for her, and that in exchange she'd let them live there nearly rent-free. She was so disappointed to hear it was in the shape it was."

"Well, that upset me. She had bought that property years before to satisfy a dream she had of owning a little cabin in the woods. That impulse buy was a significant nod to the fond memories she had of her childhood in Gatlinburg, Tennessee, where she played for hours every day in the mountains of what became the Great Smoky Mountains National Park. Those folks living in her cabin were taking advantage of my Mema, and I knew that one way or another that just wasn't going to stand. That night, I spent a lot of time praying with Nana and asking God for guidance about it all. Our disappointed spirits had settled a bit, since we'd had a few hours between us and the experience in the rundown cabin. We recommitted our willingness to go anywhere, but were still confused and needed some clear direction. I remember going to bed that night feeling this weird mix of confusion and trust."

"The next day was Sunday, and for reasons I can't remember, we decided to go to a church we'd heard about on the back of Lookout Mountain where all the farms were. It was called Mountain Meadow, and it had been started by a wealthy, big-hearted church on the frontside of the mountain as an outreach to the community on the backside. Well, what Saturday had offered in gloominess, Sunday offered in beauty! I can't really explain how different things felt, but what had been depressing the day before was spectacular that next Sunday morning! The road that led out to the church ran along the brow of the mountain and offered a huge view of patchwork farmland that extended out across the rolling hills of Georgia and on into Alabama." Pappy beamed at the memory of that view.

"The green was so vibrant. Dogwoods and forsythia and all sorts of other flowers were in full bloom. We rolled the windows down to let in air, and it had a perfect temperature to it... and smelled sweet! Just *nothing* like the day before. After a while, we turned off the brow road and onto a street where we'd been told the church was. There were still rundown trailers and trash and all that, but somehow it just felt different. The area sure didn't seem like a place for a church, until we came around a bend. And then we were treated to one of the most delightful scenes you can imagine!"

Pappy looked over at Andy and Betsey. They obviously knew the property and had clear and fond memories of it. It was fascinating watching how the three of them looked at each other, so much being said with their eyes in only the briefest of glances.

"There was this huge building that looked like a barn, out by itself in a field. It was made of rough-cut lumber and had enormous windows trimmed neatly in green, and with a matching metal roof. Cars were parked all around it in a sort of haphazard way – I mean, just a classic country church gathering! The building had these massive sliding doors that were pulled open, and some long linen curtains danced in the draft that blew through the building. Children of all ages were running around the field together, in and out of the building, while their parents visited with coffees and pastries in hand. We didn't see anyone who looked like they lived on the 'backside' of the mountain, and we came to find out the church had become a popular place for folks from the 'frontside' to attend, even while efforts to reach out to the local community were in earnest. It would take us some time to figure out just how tight and closed-off the mountain community was, and that had made it hard for the church to fulfill its mission-oriented goals. But at that point, we just welcomed the huge shift in energy that the scene affected in us… and we were eager to *worship*!" Pappy smiled and threw his hands up.

"The time there was just what we needed. The community was open-hearted and loving, and the pastor was even someone I'd known from my university days! He still to this day stands out in my mind as one of the kindest and most humble people I've ever known. After the service, as folks were milling around, a young man who turned out to be an elder of the church invited us over to his house for lunch, and we gladly accepted."

"We drove back to mom's house to change and to make a quick turn before heading back to the address the man had given us. I didn't know the area, and so the address didn't ring any bells for me. Mom was delighted that the momentum seemed to have shifted for us, and that there was a renewed possibility we might end up living near her after all. Ever the Southerner, she insisted we did not show up empty handed. So while we changed, she somehow whipped together a beautiful platter of food which she gave to Nana as we walked out the door."

"The family we were visiting were named the Jestroms, and all we knew was that they had kids about Andy's and Betsey's ages. So, we headed back out the brow road and were surprised to turn down a street that seemed to be very near Mema's cabin! The area was still rundown, but instead of the 'ugh' feeling we'd had the day before, we noticed and even commented on how it all felt so 'real' to us. It turned out the driveway to the Jestrom's property was within easy walking distance of Mema's cabin. We pulled off the street onto their driveway feeling like something was shaping up, and I remember exchanging glances with Nana." Pappy got a little choked up again and paused to regain composure.

"Their driveway dove steeply off the road, then transitioned to a small bridge over a creek which was running heavily from the recent rains. Then it took us through some dense rhododendrons and pitched back up and to a four-way fork. That property was affectionately known as 'the compound'…

a place we'd heard about at church earlier. Apparently, several years before, four families had bought twenty acres and had divided the parcel equally. They built their homes together so they could live in close community, since they were good friends and had started their families around the same time."

"We checked the directions, took the fork to the right, and slowly rolled under a magnificent canopy of oak branches and green leaves, then into an opening that seemed to be the yard for the Jestrom's home. When we entered that opening, Nana gasped, and I stopped the car. Y'all, we were just in awe of the scene in front of us. The kids even chimed in with slow *wows*!"

Andy and Betsey grinned at each other as Pappy painted the scene.

"The most perfect white house was in front of us. It had black trim and a red door, and an abundance of Southern charm. There were two porches, one upper and one lower, both extending across the front of the home. On the lower porch, there were several men visiting while holding Mason jars filled with sweet tea, and the women were sitting around a table on the porch. One of them was pregnant, and she was gently rocking in a chair while holding her large tummy and laughing at something one of the other women had just said. The elder who'd invited us over noticed we'd stopped the car, and he waived for us to drive on down the gentle slope and park next to the house. I mean, it could not have been more quintessentially Southern and idyllic!"

"I was immediately smitten with all that… and even more so because none of the adults seemed bothered at all by one of the kids arching way out over the lawn… and I mean *way* off the deck. He was barely holding onto an old tire hanging from a rope tied to a huge oak limb at least thirty feet above. He couldn't have been more than four years old, and he was holding the tire with one hand while he waved with the other to his parents, who just sort of nonchalantly smiled and waved back. Then the kid kicked spasmodically to turn the tire so he could face the children he was about to come back down on like a little wrecking ball. It was *awesome*!"

Pappy put his thumbs in his ears and flickered his fingers around and said, "Some of the girls on the ground put their thumbs to their ears like this and mocked the kid on the swing, like they were daring him to try to hit them. He accepted the challenge and came down fast and hard, trying to kick them all. They laughed and dodged just in time, and made more faces to taunt the kid on the swing he arched and came back down for another pass."

"I remember all four of us just sat there trying to make sense of the scene. It was just so foreign to us and our suburban, safety-wired brains. Somehow though, I knew each of us was registering it all as perfect. I remember turning to Nana and saying, 'Are you kidding me?' She smiled, reached over, touched my forearm, and simply said, 'God is good.'"

"We had a delightful visit that afternoon. We learned about the broader intentional community they were trying to develop in the area where Nana and I had driven aimlessly the day before. They made us feel so welcome. They were all committed to intentional parenting and community… values that were obviously very important to me and Nana. In particular, the lonely and seemingly solo aspect of mothering she'd experienced in Colorado was such a challenge for Nana, and the idea of sharing the load with other moms was understandably really attractive to her. And while we visited, Andy and Betsey were immersed for hours in one game after another with the kids."

"Apparently, the church we'd gone to that morning was serving as a rallying point for that community of folks who'd moved from the frontside of the mountain to the backside, and which was now spread across the backside. Nana and I were sure we'd been led there, and that it was all an answer to prayer… and we eventually said as much to the group. They knew what we were looking to do, at least with the homesteading… I didn't share about my sense of calling to help others in the event of an economic collapse. They understood, and were really helpful by giving us some great leads on some land in the area that we'd only have known about by getting the kind of insider scoop they were offering."

"The next day, everything just sort of fell into place. We called a realtor who was the local land expert, and who was also a friend of one of the guys in the church. Mondays were typically his day off, but he said he was willing to take us around, since we were scheduled to fly out Tuesday morning. By the end of that day, we'd made a solid cash offer on an incredible twenty-five-acre tract of raw land in a gated community close to the church building!" Pappy laughed again, "We didn't know how it would all come together from there, but the realtor said it was highly likely our offer would be accepted. So, we just figured next steps for us would be revealed when they were meant to be... we were really learning to go with the flow during that season. We told Andy and Betsey that we'd likely be moving there, and because of their great experience with their cousins at my mom's house, at the church Sunday, and then at the Jestroms', they were thrilled. On that trip back to Colorado, we were all on a real *high*... I mean, what a *ride*!"

CHAPTER TWELVE

THE WILDERNESS

Pappy seemed to be delighting in the opportunity to weave his tale freely. He had shared a lot up to that point, which had painted a rich background for the season of transformation he would soon be explaining. Frankie and Leela sauntered back into the gathering, energized by their evening adventure, and walked over to Pappy. He smiled, reached down to give each of them a quick scratch behind the ears, and affectionately said,

"Good pups."

Satisfied, they took their positions at his feet, and settled in. Then Pappy leaned back into his chair, re-wrapped the blanket around his shoulders, and continued.

"Things moved quickly after that trip… quicker than we might have liked, actually. We got word the day after we returned to Colorado that our offer on the land had been accepted, so we just stayed in the flow and started telling folks about our plans to move. We had various cohorts of friends, and depending on who we were talking to, we shared different details of our decision. Some would understand certain aspects better than others, so we were a little careful with how we relayed things… though in my case, and in retrospect, I didn't do it as well as I'd have liked."

"Since John's community had been supporting us closest in our pursuit of God's will, we recounted the experience in the Southeast to them... and they were so encouraging. It felt like there was a real urgency to it all for us. After the initial disappointments about our family farm and Mema's cabin, everything had come together so easily. And we interpreted that as God wanting us to stick with the fast pace that had been laid on my heart."

"Well, making a move like that within an accelerated timeframe wasn't easy! There were a lot of logistics that had to fall into place: the sale of our home... which, by the way, we were horribly upside-down on financially after the 2008-2009 crisis; getting financial affairs in order; stepping down from work and board commitments; figuring out what to do with school for Andy and Betsey; trying to offer some sort of rational explanation to friends and work relationships; and on and on."

"I'll never forget telling my business partner about all the events that had led up to me finally feeling convinced that God was calling me and our family to build a homestead. He was a good friend and was the first person outside of John's community I told the whole story to." Pappy chuckled at the memory of what must have been an incredibly awkward conversation.

"When I was done, he just looked at me for a long moment and said, 'I don't know what to say. I don't *think* you're crazy.'" Pappy laughed and added, "His tone said loud and clear that he wasn't too sure of that!"

"And I couldn't blame him. I knew it made little sense, if any, by the standards of society's norms back then. I mean, who up and leaves the type of life we had in Colorado to head off to the woods on the back of some random mountain, just because they felt God was leading them? Plenty of folks give up their lives to go into dedicated missions work within established ministries... and folks generally think well of that kind of move. But that wasn't the case for us. It's not a stretch to say it was just blind faith, but no less dedicated to God."

"Well, my business partner's reaction pretty much summed up the thinking of most of our friends outside of John's community. Folks loved us, but they thought we had lost our marbles. They just couldn't comprehend the decision, except to offer a few comments here and there about it being 'cute' to start a little farm. And even though they were supportive, many of our new friends in John's community clearly considered the whole thing to be pretty far 'out there'. But at least they encouraged us in our boldness and admitted that they admired anyone so willing to follow God that faithfully. It had a lonely feeling to it, for sure. Nana and I were unmoored and heading out into some unchartered waters."

"Ultimately, though, the overwhelming logistics started miraculously coming together so well that it made us feel we were absolutely doing the right thing. Our faith was definitely tested by the stresses of the move, but as we stood fast and trusted, the hurdles just crumbled one by one… and usually at the last minute! We sort of got used to that… and there are so many cool stories of the things that happened during that season of our family's trust-fall." Pappy laughed, flipped through the journal some more, presumably past all the stories he was choosing not to share. Then he paused and looked over at Betsey. It seemed he knew she would remember a particular memory he was about to share.

"This little gem sums up so much of the experience for me… the reality that I was laying it all down to follow God. Now, I've always been something of a car guy, and I think the whole experience was most 'real' for me when we drove as a family to the Toyota dealership and traded our two nice vehicles for a Prius… a car that back then represented a real commitment to environmental sustainability because it relied mostly on electricity to run." Pappy paused at the memory. "Yeah… that was a really big deal for me!" Betsey clearly did remember the event, and something precious had been shared between the two of them during it. Betsey just smiled and winked at Pappy, and he winked back.

"As we drove off the dealership lot, with all of us crammed into that little hybrid, I remember feeling like that was the point of no return… and it was! Everything just kept moving really fast from there, and it was an incredible season for our family."

Pappy frowned slightly. "Now, I'm not saying everything went as smoothly as we'd have liked it to. And a pretty good illustration of what I mean is that it turned out the only option for housing that made any sense was for us to take Mema up on her offer for us to live in her cabin while we built on the land we had bought!" Pappy shook his head slightly at the memory. "God works in funny ways. But we were just in the flow, and we weren't going to let the type of roof over our heads deter us from the bigger vision and sense of calling!"

"Finally, it was time to roll away from Colorado. The moving truck wouldn't be at the cabin for about a week, so we hit the road and enjoyed a big road trip to the Southeast. We finally arrived on Lookout Mountain in the evening, around sunset." Pappy smiled wide. "And when we pulled up to the cabin, we were absolutely blown away by the transformation. My mom, sister, and Mema, as well as some folks in that church community I told you about earlier, had made some big efforts to make us feel welcome. The fallen trees had been cleared, and all that had looked so dreary and even dangerous on the outside had been fixed. They had the nasty inside professionally cleaned, and had even installed flower boxes on the windows and had filled them to overflowing with beautiful arrangements!"

"So, the thing we were most concerned about... introducing the kids to that little cabin and telling them it was our new home for a while... ended up being a non-issue! The kids were thrilled, and as soon as the car parked, they jumped out and ran into the house. After a few minutes, they came back out and started running around their new yard, which was considerably bigger than what they were used to in Colorado. It was a full-blown forest full of possible adventures for them! Nana and I sat on the stoop off the kitchen that evening and watched Andy and Betsey explore the edge of the woods together, then delight in the wonder of seeing fireflies for the first time. I'll never forget that night, just taking it all in and holding it all in my heart with profound gratitude." Pappy slapped his knee and his voice elevated in his enthusiasm. "We had made the move! I mean, we had actually *done* it! We followed our hearts and stayed in the flow... and it had happened! It was a huge adventure that was so fun and rewarding, and yet absolutely terrifying, all at the same time. But ultimately, it felt so right."

"A few days later, the moving truck rumbled down the driveway at about nine in the morning. As the movers were bringing in the larger furniture, three or four cars pulled up and about ten men hopped out. Well, we didn't know about it, but the Jestroms had coordinated a group from the church to help us move our stuff in and get settled… and some of the women came by later with casseroles. It was just normal for them, but all that meant so much to us since one of our values was community. We had some wonderful friendships back in Colorado, and there was absolutely a sense of community there. But, while we certainly appreciated what we had, we yearned for community of a different sort too… a sort that we couldn't really articulate, but wanted to experience. We hadn't really thought much of the fact that our friends back in Colorado hadn't offered to help us move. That was just the way things were back there… everyone was busy with their lives. But the way that Lookout Mountain community immediately and sacrificially came around us brought what had been only a sense for something more into crystal clear, practical reality. What a way to kick off what we had started calling 'The Grand Experiment!'"

"It took us a few days to settle in, and then it was time for me to start getting after it with the construction. Some things had been laid on my heart to build, though they made no sense financially, or even practically." Pappy chuckled. "I can only make sense of it all now as another test, of sorts… though I don't pretend to understand the psychology – or psychosis – behind all that." Pappy laughed a little harder as be continued. "And those crazy things were all about making sure the property was a place where a lot of people could be provided for in the event things really did get bad. There was a big problem though… we couldn't find any builders who weren't booked out for at least a year, or more! Well, that was disheartening since I didn't know how to hang a faceplate on a light switch, and neither your Nana nor I knew if carrots grew off trees or out of the ground! We couldn't do it ourselves, and so we felt really stuck."

"There we were again, not knowing how it was going to get sorted, and left with only our faith that it would be. Sometimes that waiting was really challenging for us though. And those initial months there turned into an extended season when we wondered if we had 'heard incorrectly'. Or, when we were really vulnerable and honest, we'd even wonder if we had made a big mistake. We were at a real standstill, and simply didn't know what to do at that point."

Around the firepit, I knew what was going through the family's collective minds. There we were on one of the loveliest properties one could imagine, knowing that every bit of it quite literally had Pappy's and Nana's hands on it. They were able to do most anything when it came to construction and permaculture design. And their aptitude for aesthetics and gardening were actually sought after by folks building retreat centers and small farms! To imagine them not knowing how to manage the scaling out of a project was almost unfathomable.

I took a moment to look around. The soft light pouring through the windows of the perfect little cabins dimly illuminated the property. It was all just so lovely: the idyllic ranch home and outbuildings; the still waters of the cold-water eddy-bath reflecting the stars in the night sky; the meandering Zen-garden walking paths seemingly set in motion by the firelight, and then disappearing into the darkness like rays from a muted star. Pappy and Nana had designed it all, and had built most of it themselves.

As if he knew what we were thinking, he said, "I really didn't know the first thing about construction, and that's no exaggeration! I was *completely* out of my element. All I knew was that many folks had said that whenever building did begin, we'd need to have the building envelope established and have a driveway in. Apparently, that was a lot of work and was going to be expensive, considering how far back the main structures were to be from the road. So, I decided that I just needed to trust that it'd all come together, have faith, and focus on the next step… just follow the light into the next step. I had a strong back, a sense that I could probably figure out a chainsaw, and twenty-five acres of thick hardwood forest that needed to be worked into an opening for a house, a barn, and a pasture. As if that wasn't enough to keep me busy, I also had to cut a driveway big enough to allow heavy equipment onto the jobsite." Pappy shook his head. "If I'd have known how much work was in store for me over the next few years, I don't know if I'd have started!"

He chuckled, "We didn't even know enough to understand that excavating and clearing was an entirely different skillset from building. We just thought builders did all that as a part of their process… didn't even know the difference between a contractor and a builder, for that matter. And nobody had told us to start looking for excavating companies. I guess they all wrongly assumed we knew *something*." Pappy laughed more as he reflected on the scope of what ended up being a massive project. "I was also wanting to save money where I could, since I was pretty sure the project was going to stretch us financially. I figured I'd at least start taking trees down, so that part would be done and out of the way for whenever we could find a builder."

Pappy took a sip from his cup as he flipped through a few more pages. Suddenly he laughed hard and spewed some of his drink. As he set the cup back on his armrest and wiped off the journal and his chest with his sleeve, he said,

"Y'all are going to get a kick out of this. I needed to get some tools so I could get to work. So, I drove our family three-quarter ton recreation-rig-turned-work-truck into town to the local hardware store feeling *bonafide*! I was wearing some brand new Carhartt pants and Chippewa work boots that didn't have a scuff on 'em. I was even wearing an older Eton dress shirt that I figured I could allow to get dirty… and I'm pretty sure I probably was wearing it tucked in! I'm certain I looked every bit like the noob I was, but I didn't feel that way walking across the parking lot. No sir! I was striding with a finance-turned-mountain man swagger."

"When I swung open the doors of that store, it was probably the equivalent of the greenhorn who decides to have a drink at a legit saloon full of rough cowboys. You know the scene. It's the one where he throws open the creaky swinging doors to reveal himself wearing a white rhinestone rodeo outfit complete with ten-gallon hat, tassels, sparkly boots. Then suddenly the piano quits playing, and everyone turns to stare." Pappy chuckled, looked down, and shook his head. "I sauntered on into the store and wandered aimlessly up and down the aisles among all these tough looking mountain men who knew exactly what they were doing. I was quickly starting to feel out of place, and that was a whole new experience for me. I was game, though… and had a good attitude about it. I knew I'd get it figured out in time, and so I swallowed my pride and tried to find the section of the store where they kept the saws."

"After a while, a guy about half my age walked up with the kind of enthusiasm that suggested he'd drawn the short straw, and asked if he could help. I did have enough awareness to notice he was obviously amused at the site of me. I took it all in stride… but I *sure* wasn't accustomed to feeling that way! I explained to the young man that I'd be clearing about seven acres of land, which would mostly involve cutting down large oak trees and clearing stumps. When he heard I'd be doing it by myself with no experience, he just said, 'That'll take a minute or two.'"

I suddenly noticed many smiles and raised eyebrows around the fire. Now we knew where Pappy had picked up the euphemism he often employed, and I could tell the family took some pleasure in the knowing.

Pappy picked up on the acknowledgement and smiled, then continued. "I enjoyed how understated that mountain culture was… and how they'd stay out of your business unless you invited them in. Well, I was quick to admit to the clerk that I knew nothing, and I even made some self-deprecating comment about how he probably already knew that. That seemed to soften him a bit, and put him in a position which he seemed to appreciate… and so he ended up being super helpful. That was a great lesson for me. I don't think he'd have been as helpful if I'd acted like I knew what I was doing. It could have even been interpreted as insulting – that a newbie like me might possibly think he could just jump into an experience like that and employ a skillset most learn over many years."

"Anyhow, he showed me the different types of saws, bars and chains, their intended uses, how they worked, and all that. Then he volunteered some general safety and cutting tips... really helpful and important stuff, like how to read the grains and wind-loads stored in the trunks that would make the trees fall very differently from one another. You could ultimately only learn most of that stuff from experience, but a lot of what he shared I'm sure ended up saving my life more than once... or at least kept me from getting seriously injured. Interestingly, he never suggested any safety equipment like chaps, eye or ear protection, or even a helmet! It just wasn't how they rolled... they might occasionally carry some cotton swabs to tuck into their ears if they were going to be sawing all day, but that was about it for safety gear. I think I lost thirty percent of my hearing just from all the sawing I did those first few months!" Pappy put his fingers in his ears and screwed up his eyes, then sighed. Now we knew, too, that our need to speak up when talking with him from any distance wasn't entirely age related.

Pappy laughed. "As I listened to that clerk talk, I was pretty sure he was actually telling me not to head out into the woods by myself with those saws. But that just wasn't an option for me. I was there because I felt a deep calling from God to be there, and to get that project done. With the way I thought about things back then, that meant I needed to be *doing* something at all times! It's hard to imagine now, but it never crossed my mind to just sit still and wait for things to come together. It's just how I was wired back then."

"So, I ended up buying three saws for different types of felling and limbing, a few other pieces of related equipment, and a weed-eater so I could clear the undergrowth around the trees for access to the cutting zone. I left the store feeling happy and ready to get to work, and I threw all the gear in the back of our truck and drove straight to the property. I wanted to get after it that same day... and I loved every bit of it, at first. There was something so raw... so powerful and real about firing up a chainsaw and working land. It was hard and dangerous, but it was satisfying in ways work never had been for me. I worked hard all-day dropping trees and cutting them into manageable sections, then I'd use a cant hook to roll the larger sections together. Then I'd huck all the limbs onto the top and set the massive pile on fire. At the end of all that effort on that first day, I'd taken down three trees and had piled two of them for burning." Pappy laughed at himself, "I was too exhausted to finish piling the third."

"As the sun set that evening, I walked along the route for the driveway I'd flagged a few days before and counted the number of large trees that needed to come down. I didn't even count the pine or saplings, since I was realizing those were relatively easy to take down compared to the large oaks. It turned out the driveway alone would require cutting about eighty trees. Then I counted about twice that for the building envelope. I remember walking back to the truck that evening thinking I could get it all done in about eight months, maybe less." He shook his head.

"Well, was I ever the optimist when it came to what I thought I could get done! Still have that fault, actually." Pappy winked. "I drove back to what we were still calling 'Mema's cabin' and had a meal with Nana and the kids that I'll never forget. I felt like such a manly man!" Pappy laughed as he beat his chest with his fists, making all the kids laugh. "And I went to bed that night and slept deeper than I'd ever slept."

"When I woke the next morning, I was so sore I could hardly move, and I ached in areas where I didn't even know I had muscles. I knew I had to keep putting one step in front of the other though, and so I rolled out of bed and pushed through the pain to pull my clothes back on. I'll tell you what, too… after only one day, I didn't look quite as much like a noob in those clothes… they were filthy! It's worth mentioning that as I pulled my pants back on, I noticed a couple of ticks lodged deeply on the inside of my left leg. Now, I grew up in the Southeast, so I didn't think much about it. I just picked them off and flushed 'em down the toilet. And those were the first two of literally hundreds I'd pick off over the next few months. They're now the scariest things in the woods to me… and have been ever since that season. We'll get to that bit in a minute."

"Well, I got my hinges going and waddled out to the kitchen for a cup of coffee and a quick bite with the family. I acted like I was feeling a lot better than I was, kissed Nana and the kids, slowly climbed into the truck, and started the fifteen-minute drive back to the property. When I got there, I was surprised to see the two burn piles were still going and were kicking off so much heat I could feel them from ten feet away! Just feel the heat kicking off that fire there from those little logs…" Pappy pointed lazily to the fire in front of him. "…and now imagine logs at least four or five times that size, and piled about ten times bigger than in this pit here! Those piles were so hot they'd take your eyebrows and arm hair off if you were within three or four feet of 'em! But the heat from those fires felt good in the chilly early mornings… especially as the fall turned to winter."

"Anyhow, I got to work that day and finished cutting, piling and burning the third tree I'd started working on the day before. Well, that little project took over an hour, but it helped get the soreness all worked out… and so then then I really got to it! Clearing cutting zones, felling trees, limbing, cutting up the trunks, piling it all up to burn. Rinse and repeat day after day after day… for months!" Pappy held up both arms in a body building pose. Then he made eye contact with the kids and playfully kissed each bicep, making the children laugh again. "I got in the best shape of my life out there in those woods!"

"The first couple of weeks… even month, or so… I was having a really good time. But after a short while, the fun wore off. I was in the woods by myself all day, every day. I can't count the number of times I almost dropped a tree on myself or the truck, or had the saw's bar kick back on me nearly lopping off a leg or foot… and sometimes even my face! The work was quickly turning from fun to scary as I realized how dangerous it was, and suddenly the whole project had become a real test. To mitigate risk a bit, I'd watch a lot of YouTube videos about how to clear land safely, and I learned a whole lot over those initial months. So, over time, I got more and more efficient, and settled into a rhythm of working hard for thirty minutes and then taking ten minutes off. As the rhythm of the work became familiar, my mind would wander while my body worked."

"Of course, during all that time I hadn't let go of my seeking, and I had been recently impressed with a book titled *Practicing the Presence of God* written by a lay monk named Brother Lawrence. In a manner similar to what he explained in the book, I tried to make every movement a prayer of dedication, every action a 'knock on the door' Jesus tells us to knock on. Mostly, I just kept asking God for direction about next steps. And I didn't hear *anything*. At *all*! I didn't even have any sense of comfort that I was doing the right thing. I never got angry at God or anything like that… I was just sort of hurt. There I was, having left it all behind, trying to be faithful to what I believed was God's call, scratching away at clearing some remote land on the back of a mountain in Georgia… and I felt all alone. I had no sense of God's presence, and I remember thinking, *'What kind of friend treats their buddies like this'*? But I shoved that line of thinking down, and chose to continue with the understanding that God just didn't operate within that kind of friendly relationship… and so I'd just continue on as a faithful servant." That was another surprise to the family. Pappy often talked about his friendship with Jesus, so we were confused about this. It made what was to come all the more interesting for those of us who knew Pappy well.

"To stay sane, I held onto the conviction about what I believed I'd heard that night months before… and I'd also often spend time thinking back over all the amazing things that had happened since. I've found that when things feel tough, it's a good practice to pull back and keep the bigger picture in mind. It sure helped then."

"I was feeling so lonely during those long days and didn't have any intimate felt-sense for God's love for me, even while I still believed it was possible. Making it worse, other than faith, I still wasn't showing much of any authentic 'fruit of the Spirit'… and that was getting harder and harder for me to accept. In fact, I was still wrestling with a lot of habits which I judged myself harshly for… habits which I believed wouldn't be in my life if my religious and spiritual-life was 'right'. But I just didn't know what more to do. So, I just pressed on."

"Five or six months doesn't sound like much time. But when you're in the woods by yourself working like that every day, with no clear direction on next steps and no end in sight, time moves *real* slow. I asked everyone I could think of if they knew a few folks who could help me, but it seemed like everyone who could have helped was busy on other projects and wouldn't be available for a long time. So, I figured that was just my lot, and kept plugging away."

Pappy let out a long sigh. "I don't know that I've ever felt so alone as I did during that season. All my friends were back in Denver… and I rarely had time to make any new ones. Even though the community there was definitely open armed, they were all really busy with their own lives. So, opportunities to visit outside of Sunday mornings and occasional evening Bible studies were more the exception than the rule. Nana was busy managing Andy and Betsey back at the cabin, and she was enjoying a precious season with them while they homeschooled. When I was at home in the evenings, we didn't have much time together since I'd fall asleep from exhaustion shortly after putting the kids to bed. I was a grinder though, and so each day I just kept doing all I could see to do, trusting that in time there would be a next thing."

"I remember one day when the loneliness, uncertainty, and sense of distance from God had me feeling really down and distracted… and distracted while doing that kind of work is dangerous. As I was plugging along, I hucked a heavy limb toward a hot burn pile just like I had done hundreds of times before. When I released the limb, I tripped and pitched forward toward the fire. I landed with my arms outstretched, and barely caught myself just before my face smashed into a huge section of red-hot oak at the base of the fire. I felt my eyebrows singe straight down to my forehead, and I'm pretty sure my hair would have singed down too if I hadn't been wearing a cap. Fortunately, my hands found something to push against, and I shoved away from the fire hard. That pitched me to the left of the pile, and I rolled away from it fast. After a rotation or two, my ribs slammed into a stump on my right side, and that stopped my rolling. The sharp pain from that hit was so bad that I couldn't breathe for a moment. After I finally did catch a breath, I gently felt around where I hit the stump and it didn't seem like anything was broken. Then I noticed my hands felt hot, and I looked down and saw that my gloves had partially melted onto my palms. I sat up fast and ripped the gloves off, but then the pain in my ribs made me lie back down. As I lay there, I broke down and allowed myself to start crying."

"I mean, what was I doing? I was physically exhausted, and even after all the clearing experience up to that point, I was still out of my element and knew it. We were burning through our savings far faster than anticipated, and I couldn't figure out where the money going… and that was maddening for a financial planner! After the move to Mema's cabin months before, it seemed the momentum had stopped, and little seemed to be coming together smoothly. I had led my sweet family during a really important time in our lives to a tiny cabin in the middle of nowhere. My remaining work relationships, which I relied on for a trickle of income, were tenuous, at best. And to make it all worse, our family wasn't spending much time together… which, as you know, was one of the main considerations for the project in the first place! I was just feeling so, so beaten down."

Pappy paused for a few minutes, clearly feeling into that sadness and frustration. Then another breeze came from down valley and chilled us all, but livened up the fire. A few of the sleeping children unconsciously burrowed deeper into blankets their parents had piled on them. Pappy eventually pressed on.

"That was all so tough for me. I know there are lots of ways to look at it now… but at that time, it felt so hard and raw. I just couldn't understand why God didn't show up and at least offer some comfort… but always fell back on the default, *His ways are not our ways* line of thinking that was so prevalent in my religious paradigm when things didn't make sense. It's impossible to put words to the level of fatigue in my body… but moreso, in my soul. I *ached*. Somehow, though, my sense of calling continued to drive me on, day after day. And some days were certainly better than others. I was only sure of one thing… that I just needed to keep pressing on in faith. But the fun and excitement and sense of adventure had *definitely* worn off. Now, I obviously didn't know it, but things were about to take a positive turn. I think there's an old saying about how that works… something like it's darkest just before the dawn, or something like that. Well, that was definitely the case then – what was figuratively and literally a wilderness season."

"After explaining to some folks at church one Sunday how slowly the work was going, I was introduced to a man named Ryan. He was one of the members of the church who'd lived on the back of the mountain his whole life, was well thought of, and was apparently a good builder. For reasons which I never fully understood, we'd never crossed paths at church, and nobody had ever suggested I meet him until that morning. So, after chatting for a bit, I figured I'd take a flyer and asked Ryan if he'd be willing to come out to the property to help me drop and stack a few trees I was intimidated by. Well, he was a man of few words, but he did say 'sure', and it turned out he wasn't busy the next day and we agreed to meet early in the morning."

"When I pulled up to the edge of the woods at the start of my roughed-in driveway, Ryan was already offloading a tractor with a big contraption on the back and some forks on the front. I didn't really understand how the tools would be used, but, by then, and after a few experiences with some of the locals, I'd learned to keep my mouth shut and just watch."

Pappy laughed at the memory of the story he had decided to share. "Since I was pushing deeper and deeper into the woods with my clearing work, I'd bought a four-wheeler and landscape trailer to tote my gear to the jobsite. So, I pulled up, parked next to Ryan, and offloaded all my gear next to his tractor. Until that moment, I'd been so proud of my little work rig… all my manly tools and gear. Well, Ryan fired up that tractor and I realized right away that I'd been playing pee-wee the whole time I'd been scratching around in those woods. The rumble of the diesel engine disrupted the silence of that cold mountain morning, and suddenly it felt like some *real* work was about to get done." Pappy smiled, interrupting himself, and said, "I appreciate all the electric vehicles these days, but I admit I still miss the sound of a diesel engine."

Betsey chimed in, "Oh I know it! I still can remember the smell… that used to be one of my *favorites*!"

Pappy winked at Betsey. He laughed again, this time a little harder, and said, "Oh this story gets better! Knowing deep down that I'd be more in the way than helpful, but not wanting to admit that to myself or Ryan, I instead opened my mouth too quickly and actually asked him if he wanted me to walk ahead of him with the weed eater and cut a path so he could get his tractor through the woods!" Pappy shook his head at the memory. "Well, Ryan just looked at me for a *long* moment, trying to figure out just how ignorant I was. And the longer he stared, the smaller I felt. After a while, he just said, '*nope*'."

"Then he put his tractor into gear and moved it slowly to the edge of the rough opening I had created. From the tractor cockpit, he dropped the big thing down off the back, turned around and looked at me, and told me to stand back. Then he put the implement into gear. It lurched to life with a lot of mechanical whirrings, which I quickly recognized as heavy metal blades spinning from under its deck. It was only then that I finally realized the thing was basically a massive mower that could take down small trees. He started rolling into the woods, easily pushing the forest out of the way while the mower cut a wide swath. I hung my head, walked over to the truck, and laid my little weed eater in the bed. Then I picked up my saw and walked behind Ryan along the path he was cutting." Pappy was having fun with the self-deprecating humor. "I had to tuck my tail so many times during that project… and let's just say that feeling 'less-than' got to be real familiar!"

"Now, Ryan was a skilled operator, and as he worked his way down the driveway, he'd use the forks to easily lift large loads of logs and slash I hadn't been able to manage, and dump them onto the burn piles. What I later learned was called a 'Bush-Hog' was doing the clearing work in minutes… work that would have taken me hours to do. Well, we *got after* it that day!" Pappy slapped his knee as the energy of the memory coursed through him.

"I was Ryan's little monkey on the ground, sawing trees into sizes he could manipulate easily with his forks. I'd cut, he'd pile, then I'd set the pile on fire and move along to the next section of land to be cleared… and the Bush-Hog behind him was constantly cutting, making the work zone look like a proper clearing. It seemed to me that in our first half a day together with his equipment, we'd accomplished what would have taken me a full week to do without it."

"That day during lunch break after he easily took down the two massive oak trees I was unwilling to drop myself, Ryan asked what I was up to with the property. So, I shared the lovely vision Nana and I had for a homestead – the simpler life we envisioned, and a little of the 'God calling' aspect of the backstory. A slight, but obvious, shift in Ryan's countenance seemed to indicate he sincerely appreciated that we saw beauty and value in the life he and his simple community cherished."

"While sitting with him in the stillness of those woods, I felt prompted to venture some of the concerns I had about hard times to come, and some of the rationale behind those concerns like a central bank that seemed out of control with its money printing, increased polarization of the classes and social unrest, the devastation of the environment which was creating a host of serious challenges, among other things. The strongest part of the prompting, though, was to specifically share my sense that the farm would be a place where folks could be taken care of during what might be a challenging season."

"Well, I'm embarrassed to admit that I stuffed that prompting down. I just didn't have the guts. I sensed some sort of rapport developing with Ryan, and I didn't want to blow the start of a potential friendship with a mountain local. As you can probably imagine, when I shared that stuff, I was usually met with some vibes I didn't like... that message was understandably off-putting for most." Pappy paused, and then chuckled. "I'm pretty sure a lot of people thought I had lost it... and who wants to be friends with a crazy man? Worst was, I couldn't blame them. I knew it sounded far out there, and maybe I should've kept my mouth shut more than I did. But I loved my friends. And when I shared my concerns, it was truly out of concern for them."

"Anyhow, in that moment with Ryan, I was conflicted about sharing more, and I stuffed the prompting down. So, we just sat there beside each other on stumps, and enjoyed the silence of the woods while we ate our lunches. After a few minutes, and completely unaware of the internal debate that had raged in me about sharing more with him, he turned to look at me. Our eyes met, and he held my gaze for an intentional, long moment, and said, "Any other reasons?"

"Well, that question punched me in the gut, and I knew I needed to go there. So, I resolved myself, yet again, to accepting whatever judgements or loss of budding friendship that might happen after I shared the crazy stuff. I smiled and said, 'Well, yeah... there's more to it.' And I went on to explain."

Ryan listened well, and he held space for me to speak my fill without interruption. After I stopped, he let all I had said linger in the cool mountain air between us. Then he started speaking freely. He basically explained that he held the same convictions, and for reasons similar to mine – thoughtful consideration of world events, and a sense of an internal call that he believed was from God. Well, I was shocked! I wasn't used to that kind of response.

But I sure was relieved… and was, of course, thrilled! It was immediately clear to both of us that a real friendship was forming."

"He went on to talk a bit about his story of 'coming to Jesus', and it was fascinating. Some of his testimony illustrated just how far I was from the big city and my professional network back in Denver. He illustrated the scope of his transformation by sharing he used to host Ku Klux Klan rallies on his farm! But that because of Jesus, he now loved serving the black communities in the inner-city. Ryan had such a powerful testimony, and was a man of great faith…"

"What's a Klu Lux Kan?" Susie asked.

Pappy was jolted out of his narrative abruptly by the question. But he paused, thought for a few long seconds, and answered. "Well, Susie, it's tough to explain. The KKK was a large group of men in the South who were full of hate for anyone who didn't have white skin. They had strong beliefs about white people being a superior race, and they often used the Bible to defend those beliefs. They did terrible, awful, things to black people… even killed a lot of them. It's hard to believe, but when we moved to Lookout Mountain, their influence was still around… and that was really uncomfortable for us." Pappy stopped to see if the rather brief explanation would satisfy. The looks on the faces of the children indicated they couldn't wrap their minds or hearts around that level of hate, and Pappy didn't offer anything further. He decided to just press on with the story, likely assuming the kids could talk with their parents about all that if they had questions.

"Well, anyhow, Ryan and I really did end up hitting it off, and that first day with him was indeed the start to a fantastic friendship rooted in a profound dedication to Jesus. He was a giant of a man, physically and spiritually. He was only about six foot two, but his presence was enormous. I'll never forget his hands. They were tough and leathery, and seemed to be the size of a catcher's mitt. And his strength was simply incredible, even though to look at him you'd never guess it. So often, I'd not be able to lift something, and he'd come over and hoist it easily. He was a walking encyclopedia about mountain living too… a world of knowledge that was new to me, and which I just couldn't get enough of. His understanding of life was as ancient as the Appalachian Mountains and the culture that had crafted that understanding over many generations. He always carried a Bible with him too, and he took every opportunity to talk of God's grace."

"That first afternoon together, he shared a lot of great ideas for our project. He could tell from my occasional responses that I knew very, *very*, little about how to accomplish what we were wanting to on that mountain. And as we talked, he seemed to be developing a real compassion for me and my family, as well as a unity of spirit and mission with us. That night, we worked hard late into the evening under his tractor's flood lights. As we were finally putting our tools away back at the trucks, he said he wanted to help. He offered that he'd be available in a few of months if I still was looking for a builder. Well, I was of course greatly encouraged by this and took it as a sign that suddenly things were turning around. We shook on it… and suddenly I had a builder who had an absolute conviction about, and commitment to, our vision! I took this as an almost miraculous answer to prayer, and was super excited about it all! I drove home on a real high, and Nana and the kids were already asleep when I got back. So I stayed up for some time in my chair offerings thanks for the day and the turn of events."

"The next morning, I woke up excited. The previous day had illustrated the power of hydraulics for me, and I'd easily justified the expense while working with Ryan the day before. I decided I needed a new toy!" Pappy laughed. "While it definitely wasn't in the budget, with Nana's blessing I took the day off and headed down to the local tractor dealership, and I was there when they opened. I wasn't looking like such a noob by then, and the sales guy treated me as a peer, so long as I didn't act like I knew more than I did. Within a few hours, we'd decided a 28 horsepower Kubota was the perfect tool for my needs. Then I loaded up on all the other stuff that went along with it, like a trailer and various implements, repair parts, grease guns, and all that kind of stuff. I was *fired up*! I'd just taken a huge leap past buying a few saws and a weed eater! I'll never forget hauling my new tractor home. It felt so *legit*, and I had a newfound enthusiasm for the clearing work!"

"When I got home, Andy and Betsey came running out of the cabin, 'ooohed' and 'aaahhhhed' much to my satisfaction, and danced around the trailer asking me to unload the beautiful orange machine. So, I climbed into the cockpit and fired it up. When I did, they both had such fun, childlike versions of the same stunned response I'd had the day before when Ryan fired his up. When the machine roared to life, they both fell quiet and just stood there slack-jawed and flat-footed. I smiled at them so they wouldn't be afraid, and rolled the rumbling machine slowly off the trailer. Then I put it in park, lowered the large bucket to the ground, and motioned for them to climb in. To their great delight, they scurried over and settled in, and I raised them up and down and drove them around the property. Nana had come out onto the front porch to see what the commotion was all about. It was such a classic scene, and I'll never forget it. She was wearing a flannel shirt and a Carhartt vest she'd come to love. And her jeans were tucked into her muck boots. She was holding a mug of coffee with one hand, and had the other tucked into the pocket of her vest for warmth. She smiled at me with a wonderful look in her eyes, and I smiled back. It was one of many moments like that which we'd share during that season. Those moments were so special… times when we'd both feel such full hearts as our vision came together. Yeah, that was a memorable morning."

Andy chimed in. "Wow, Dad! I remember you used to let me drive that thing around when I was only, what, five?"

"Yeah!" Pappy laughed "…and you were driving a D6 dozer shortly after that!"

Andy shook his head, dumbstruck that he and Betsey somehow hadn't been killed or seriously maimed during that season. Some of the boys looked at Andy with envy.

"We spent the rest of that day together as a family, just knocking around the cabin and playing in the woods. Then we enjoyed a great family supper… and wrapped the evening up with time around the fireplace just talking and wrestling, and that kind of thing. It was magical… a real hint of what was to come."

"Before sun-up the next morning, I worked for about an hour with a headlamp on in freezing temperatures, trying to figure out how to get that tractor secured back to the trailer. It wasn't as easy as the salesguy had made it look the day before, and so I was humbled yet again. I was having the hardest time trying to figure out the lever-load binders that would tension the chains so the tractor would be held firmly in place on the trailer. Andy had been wakened by the chains rattling against metal, and had walked out onto the driveway in his PJs and was watching. Finally feeling sure I had it all sorted, and not wanting to look incompetent in front of my son, I walked over and gave him a high five and a hug and tousled his hair. Then I walked to the truck, hopped in, fired it up, and started to pull out of the driveway. I hadn't moved ten feet, when I felt the rear end of the truck lurch up violently, then noticed a flash of orange in my rearview mirror. I looked back just in time to see the tractor flop off the back of the trailer and start rolling slowly down the driveway toward the house where Andy was standing! Well, not only had I not latched the huge machine onto the trailer well, I'd also left it in *neutral*!"

"I was *freaked out*, man! I slammed the truck into park, jumped out, and managed to hop up into the cab of the tractor while it rolled along toward a wide-eyed Andy. I was so unfamiliar with the cockpit that I couldn't find the brake, and so I just steered it so it would roll uphill, away from Andy and the house. Well, Andy was delighted by all this, and put up quite a little fight when Nana came out to take him inside. He so wanted to come with me, and it saddened me that I had to head back out to the property and away from the family after such a great day together the day before."

"As Nana scuttled Andy toward the house, she looked at me with a concerned expression that said so much. I was heading out to the woods by myself to do dangerous work with chainsaws, and now with the addition of a powerful tractor I didn't know how to operate. Her look said everything, and she was right about every aspect of her concern. I was completely out of my depth, but my sense of mission kept me stubbornly pressing on. Then there's also the powerful pull of boys with their toys!" Pappy winked at the kids. "I looked away from Nana, fired up the tractor, drove it back onto the trailer, and got it chained up. And that time, I did it right with a little help from YouTube. Good or bad, that's how I learned almost everything during that season. Trial and error, and lots of near misses."

"That's for sure!" Andy said as he glanced at Betsey, who looked back at him with a smile and nod. Andy chuckled, shook his head again, looked back at Pappy, and said, "It was an incredible part of our lives, Dad. I'm glad you and Mom decided to make it all happen. What a childhood."

Pappy smiled back at Andy, and then at Betsey for a moment, and continued, "I had a lot of fun learning how to use the tractor, and made what felt like real progress with the clearing over the next few weeks. But, as an inexperienced operator, the dangers of work with heavy equipment made the risks of a chainsaw seem insignificant. I'm certain I was supernaturally protected during that time, just as much as Andy and Betsey were."

"Well, the novelty and fun of the work with the tractor eventually wore off too, and the work became familiar and routine again. Time started to really drag on again, and the stuff with God wasn't any better. I was encouraged that Ryan would be available soon, and that certainly added some motivation. But his availability still seemed a long way out. The sense of loneliness really started getting bad, and it messed with my headspace. When I think back on it, I believe I was being tested to determine my resolve and commitment. As a father, I always said things one time and then expected the kids to obey." Pappy cut another soft glance at Andy and Betsey. "And during that season of my life, I believed God must handle his kids the same way. So, just continued pressing on as I'd been doing for many months by that point."

“Then one day, soon after a brief lunch, I saw three men and a woman picking their way through the debris-strewn worksite. They looked as uncomfortable in those woods as I'd been months before... and that means they looked downright silly. I turned off the tractor and watched them from the cockpit as they awkwardly moved toward me, tripping over undergrowth and limbs. It was strange. I sensed something was wrong, and I asked God what it could possibly be about. They were clearly intent on speaking with me, and so I rested the hydraulics, hopped to the ground, and waited for them to approach. The stillness of the forest enveloped me, and it had a foreboding sense to it.”

“Well, it turned out those folks represented the homeowner's association for the development. After the obligatory pleasantries, they dropped a bomb on me. The association had apparently decided the nature of the project we had planned would not be allowed! They yammered on for a while about the reasons for the decision, but I just heard ‘wablah, waahl wabblalah...’” Pappy made a funny face while his hands gestured like sock puppets saying nonsense words, and this made the few kids who were still awake laugh again.

“I couldn't believe it! Before buying that land, I'd spoken with the then-president of the association and had made our intentions for the land *very* clear. He'd said it wouldn't be any issue, since our lot was so large and was removed from the rest of the development. Now, it's true that some of what we wanted to do had always been disallowed in the covenants, and I knew that going into the purchase... things like a well, open pasture and livestock, solar, and other stuff like that. So, I'd really pressed him on that stuff before closing on the property, and we'd even signed a written agreement of understanding which the president said the HOA had all agreed they'd honor.”

“But the woman in their little group was the new president of the association, and she said that I needed to file a complete and detailed plan for the entire project so they could be certain that everything in our plan was in line with all the covenants. She said the agreement I'd signed with the past president had been reviewed by their attorney and wouldn't hold up in court, if we got to that point. Well, I just felt this crazy mix of anger and broken heartedness. I looked at the past president who was standing right beside her, but he wasn't willing to look me in the eye."

"The woman handed me a legal-sized envelope, and then got a verbal confirmation from the past president that he had witnessed the delivery. She explained the envelope had a letter in it from the association's attorney, and went on to explain that I was in violation of the covenants for working on the property without an approved plan in place. She looked pleased when she said I was to do no further work until all that was squared away."

"I took a moment to gain my composure, and said something like, "So y'all have been watching me all these months come back here and work and invest in this property… and are just now bringing this to my attention? *Really?* You think this is an appropriate way to handle things?" And I made sure to glance again at the ex-president as I said that. The current president responded by saying I was to be in touch with their attorney if I intended to push back against any of it. Then they turned to walk away. I'd had enough experience with HOAs back in Colorado to know what had just happened meant they were serious. So, I watched them walk away and stood there just sort of dumbstruck."

"When they were finally out of sight, I walked over to the nearest burn-pile and tossed the envelope onto it. I never did open it. I backed away from the fire and sat down on a stump, feeling completely numb. My hopes and dreams for that property – and all that faithful hard work over many lonely months - turned to ash quicker than those pages did." Pappy grew quiet and stared into the firepit. A smoldering log interrupted the silence by breaking apart and dropping into the embers below.

"I was so bummed out and embarrassed. *I* didn't even have the energy to load up the tractor and gear, and finally just started wandering through the woods back to the truck. I didn't even have the heart to walk along the driveway I'd successfully cut, the same drive which just that morning I was so proud of and was a symbol of all the progress I'd made. I couldn't believe I was in that situation, and started to throw myself a real pity-party. But I finally pulled myself together and drove back to the cabin where I'd have to face Nana and the kids in my shame. As I drove, I kept repeating over and over, *'My ways are not your ways'* and *'Not my will, but Yours, be done.'"*

CHAPTER THIRTEEN

A GOOD SEASON

Pappy rapped his fingers on the wooden armrest of his chair, and let the emotions from that memory flow through him. "So, I rolled up to the cabin completely dejected. I mean, that visit from the homeowner's association was a real kick to the teeth and I was embarrassed, so when I walked into the house, I kept it all to myself. Nana was surprised I was home mid-afternoon, but I told her I was tired and had decided to knock off for the day. I just didn't feel like explaining what had happened right away since we'd developed some high hopes for that property. I felt like I had let her and the family down completely, and on so many levels. Even with my earnest attempts to chalk it all up to God's will and surrender to it, I was beating myself up pretty badly for a while there."

"At supper that evening, Nana could tell something wasn't right, and she eventually asked what was bothering me. I admitted I was frustrated by something significant, but I requested that we talk about it all later that night. So, after Andy and Betsey were asleep, we took some time to visit on the porch. As we rocked slowly in our chairs, I explained what had happened and what I believed were our very limited options moving forward. Your Nana was amazing, as you know... but her true colors really shined in that moment. She was completely certain it was all part of God's plan for us. She was sure I'd learned, or was learning, whatever I was supposed to… both with all that time in the woods by myself, and also with the recent twist. She had such great faith."

"She gave me the space I needed to wallow for a long while, and just sat beside me as we rocked gently with the dogs resting contentedly at our feet, and listened to the soft sounds of the southeastern woods. Finally, she said, 'Well, I *see* you and I know this is confusing and hard. But I should share some thinking I've been doing… bottom line is that I've grown *really* fond of this place. The kids and I love it here, it's really starting to feel like home to us, and this location makes a lot more sense with the way our lives are coming together here with proximity to your family, our friends, and church.' Then she laid the crux of her recent thinking on me, 'Mema gets what we're up to… maybe she'd be willing to sell this place to us. I know that would be a dramatic shift, but considering the circumstances and our options… what do you think of that idea?'"

"Well, it's an understatement to say it took me a few minutes to wrap my head around that idea, and for all the reasons you can imagine. I'd spent months working hard toward, and investing heavily in, the goal of getting my family *out* of that place! And in all that time and effort, I didn't have any insight into Nana's growing affinity for that little cabin. We just hadn't been spending enough time together. How about that, though… how about your *Nana*? What a partner! There she was, the mother of two beautiful kids, living in a run-down cabin in the woods, twenty minutes from the closest grocery store and even further from all the other conveniences we had enjoyed in our comfortable suburban life back in Colorado… and she was *enjoying* it?" Pappy let the question linger, not expecting an answer. I could see that several of the mothers who already held Nana in high regard were now even more impressed with her.

"Well, I was still *reeling*, and I had a hard time recalibrating quickly to such a significant change in plans. I remember being aware that I wanted to hold onto the frustration I was feeling, and I of course knew that wasn't helping me at all. It was weird. I felt like I *wanted* to be grumpy about it. I think I wanted all my hard work to be seen, or something… to be recognized for all I'd endured back there in those woods. I certainly didn't feel I was getting any recognition from God, and I can see now that my ego just wanted to be recognized by someone."

Pappy shook his head and chuckled. "The ego is such a wily rascal. I knew better, but I just didn't want to 'be a leaf' that night. I wanted to be appreciated, and to stick with the *plan*… and I was wanting Nana to join me in a little pity party! But that was unnecessary, and wasn't going to happen. It was helpful, too, that by that point I'd learned enough to know that having expectations and intentions were two very different things. Expectations were too often the killers of my joy, and this was an opportunity to let some big ones go. It was of course still humbling and frustrating, but it seemed to be where the flow was taking us. And the reality was that her idea was a good one for a lot of reasons. So, I thanked Nana for being Nana, rocked forward and leaned over to give her a kiss, stood up, and walked off the porch into the front yard while she walked inside."

"The dogs had followed me across the yard to the edge of the thick woods, so I knelt to pet them for a moment. And then, literally, right then and there, as I was petting the dogs and working hard to guide my confused emotions toward a posture of complete surrender to what was… *wham*! Download! I saw it all! I stood and started walking and seeing a complete plan for the property unfold down to the smallest detail. It was a wild experience, and while it was happening, I was very aware that I was being *guided*! I saw every aspect of the homestead we were to build… the driveway, barns, pastures, fencing, the remodeled cabin, the pond, the workshop… *all of it*! The whole thing only took about an hour… it was just incredible. What a shift! And, more amazing than the vision for the physical property was how my emotions had shifted. I was suddenly authentically excited and ready to act on all I'd seen!"

"Even looking back on it now, it seems like the turn was super-fast... and it *was*... but it felt right. There was also the fact that I'd be on the property with the family all day, every day... and that was so much more in line with the more beautiful aspects of the vision we had. I had no idea how to pull all the building stuff off... but Ryan would, and he was going to be available soon. I was so excited that I could hardly stand the energy in my body. As I walked up the stairs of the front porch to go inside, I paused and offered a sincere *Thank You* to God for the clarity. Then I walked in through the front door."

"Nana was already in bed, and I flopped down beside her, completely exhausted. What an emotional ride that day had been! I was still in my work clothes and smelled like diesel fuel and sawdust. Before I could tell her what had just happened, she told me to go take a shower. I did, and my mind spun while I watched the dirty water at my feet circle and then flow down the drain. Then I dried off and went back to bed, and I told her how much I loved her, and about what had happened with the ideas. She encouraged me not to get too far ahead of myself, and that we'd just take next steps the next day and talk to Mema. I knew she was right, but I also just knew building on Mema's property was going to be the next step… and that knowing was *electric*!" Pappy slapped his leg at the memory, then shuffled restlessly in his seat.

"I couldn't sleep that night. My mind was shifting from excitement to fear and back again, over and over. One of my biggest concerns was how to pull it all off financially. We'd already spent a lot, and we needed to do everything in cash since no lenders would take on a building project like ours. Starting over definitely wasn't in the budget, and I was feeling overwhelmed by all that. But I had to trust, and just take next steps. I woke early and made breakfast for the family, which the kids loved… and I did too. Then, after we'd eaten, I called Mema and ran the whole idea by her."

Pappy grinned, "I swear, that woman was a *saint*! She was a hundred percent on board and was even enthusiastic about the prospect of seeing her little cabin evolve into its potential… absolutely incredible. She told me what she'd sell it for right there on the spot. It was expensive, but very fair. So, it was a deal! Even though finances were obviously a huge part of the project, and I had a lot of fear around money at the time, it all felt too much like a 'God thing' to let my faith falter at that point."

"There had been constant ups and downs over the many months, and there was definitely a lot of uncertainty at that point, in particular! But, with that exchange with Mema, it felt like I was back in the flow." Pappy laughed again, clearly enjoying the energy of that memory. Then he raised his eyebrows. "I didn't know how fast the current was about to start moving though!"

"I've never been one to waste much time. So that very morning, Nana indulged me as I walked her around the property casting the vision for what I'd foreseen for the property the night before… and less than twenty four hours since I was working hard on a fully committed basis to our other property! She just looked out over the dense woods, and then toward the little run-down cabin, with a befuddled look on her face. Then, she turned and looked right at me and said, 'Well, I trust you! Have fun with it all! I'm going to get back to the kids. We have a busy day with school.'"

"That was it! Just like that, the whole project had changed. The flow had taken a very different course than anticipated, so I just kept my hips loose, put in a paddle stroke, and stayed with it!"

I smiled to myself. While Pappy apparently had a harder time staying in the flow as a younger man, we only knew him as someone who seemed to model his life on the elegant dance of boating down a river. He lived within the pattern of intention, movement, response, and flow… ever tracing the harmony of life's river-song.

Pappy looked up from studying his journal. "I didn't want to do too much around the property until we'd closed on it, and that took some time to set up. So, I used that brief pause to rest and hang out as much as I could with Nana and the kids, and to do little things around the property to get ready for the big push. During that week or two, I thought a lot about what the approach to the construction should be. Nana and I decided the first clearing effort should be directed to the large garden area. We were eager to start working with the land, and to turn what we'd learned about permaculture into a reality."

"So, the closing finally rolled around, and the property was ours. That same day I started working on clearing the area where the garden plots would be. It was hard work, but the whole time I delighted in being on the same land as Nana and the kids. Over those months, we'd do a lot of work together as a family, and it was always just a blast. I think I still have pictures somewhere of that early stage in the project. It was so cool to be setting fence posts and tilling soil and building garden beds together. We felt like a unit, and things seemed as if they'd suddenly gelled for us. We were actually living the vision!"

"And it got even better! One day, I saw a call coming in from a college buddy of mine named Mark. Mark lived in the area, and he was calling to let me know that a good friend of his, and an old fraternity brother of mine, was looking for land on Lookout Mountain, and Mark was wondering if I knew of any other larger lots for sale in the development where our lot was. I told him I was actually going to be selling mine, and explained the reasons why. Well, within a few days, I was meeting those two old friends at the lot I'd spent so many months clearing. Because of all the scratching around I'd done, my buddy was able to more clearly see his own ideas for the property, rather than just a bunch of thick woods. He immediately fell in love, and offered me three times what I'd paid for it! We shook on it, and that was that! Another quick closing, and then I'd suddenly been compensated well financially for all that effort. And that infusion came right when we needed it to keep things moving along on our new property."

Pappy picked up another journal, flipped through it and smiled. "Then things got *really* fun! I'd finished clearing the land for the garden, so that project was meaningfully under way. We also bought some chicks and some temporary coops that we planned to use until the larger coop was built. Then, coming back from a daddy-daughter 'date day', Betsey and I found two tiny, abandoned puppies huddled together in the middle of the street, shivering. We decided to take them home and ended up keeping them, since there were no animal pounds serving that area. So, all of the sudden, we had chickens, seedlings under grow lights that needed tending, four dogs, and Andy's and Betsey's robust terrarium. There was a lot of life all around us… and we were *loving* it. The kids and Nana were enjoying homeschooling. And when she wasn't teaching, Nana spent all her time figuring out all that would go into the massive gardening project. We did all kinds of things that were so foreign to us, but which we had a lot of fun figuring out."

Pappy laughed at a journal entry. "Here's another funny quick story! You kids'll like this. Nana had learned that a successful garden depends on good soil. Well, that seemed obvious enough, but we learned then that good soil is no simple thing! She learned nutritious soil was dependent on good compost, and that worms are critical for composting. So, we ordered a whole bunch of worms from an online store named Uncle Jim's worm farm. This worm community would allow us to get our compost going in earnest, and also to start brewing 'worm tea' to feed our seedlings."

The children were obviously curious about the worm tea, but they resisted interrupting.

"Well, late one afternoon, we got a call from Joe over at the post office. He let us know our worms had arrived, and that we needed to head over and pick them up right away, or they wouldn't fare well overnight. So, we loaded up in the Prius and drove the ten minutes to meet him. The instructions that came with the worms said we should put them in a big bin for a night or two with some food scraps so they could stabilize and settle in. Then we could incorporate them into our compost pile and 'tea' brewing system. We took the instructions seriously, and planned to follow them to the letter when we got home."

"On the drive, Nana explained the idea of permaculture to the kids, and how we wanted to create an ecological full circle with the garden." Pappy smiled. "And that was how we ended up naming the project: Full Circle farmstead. It wasn't a big farm, but it certainly wasn't a tiny homestead. It was a Farmstead… and we were all about full circles, on so many levels. So, it stuck. We eventually had a logo and website created, and had a blast over the years selling at the local farmer's market under that brand. And, in time, we developed a great reputation too! You've seen the same banner we used at the farmer's market – it's hanging out in the coop now as a fun reminder to me and Nana of those special days."

"Now, you kids are going to love this." Pappy grinned at the cohort of children who were still awake and obviously enthralled by the story, determined to make it to the end. Their tired eyes glistened with anticipation in the firelight as Pappy continued, "We got a big plastic bin, re-read the directions about how to prep it, put the worms in, and poked a lot of holes in the top. Then we set it on the floor in the living room, said a quick prayer over the worms, and went to bed. The next morning, Nana woke up earlier than me, and headed to the kitchen for some coffee. I heard something like 'ewww... Oh no! They're... *they're everywhere*!' The kids woke up, and after a few seconds I heard them laughing and shrieking. They came running back to our room shouting, 'Daddy, Daddy... wake *up*... the worms have moved in!'"

"Well, I didn't' quite know what that meant, but based on what I'd heard from Nana, I had a feeling we'd goofed somehow with the overnight worm storage. I got up and shuffled to the living room while I rubbed the sleep out of my eyes. Nana, Andy and Betsey were all standing with looks on their faces like, *What do we do?* I scanned the room, noting the brown sofa and hardwood floors seemed to be wiggling, and I couldn't make sense of the bizarre scene for a moment. Then it all clicked as my focus crystallized and my brain connected to the context, and I saw there really were worms *everywhere!*" Pappy wiggled his fingers. "I don't know what made them want to leave the bin, or how they waddled out from under the lid, but a few thousand of them sure were motivated!" Pappy laughed. "We spent the next couple of hours picking wiggly worms out of every nook, cranny, and seat cushion in that room."

As Pappy had anticipated, the kids were enthralled, and Andy and Betsey were immediately held in even higher esteem.

"Anyhow, it was one funny story like that after another for months. We learned lesson after lesson after lesson that way. It was really all just managed chaos, and we were enjoying every minute of it."

"Ryan was going to be available in just a couple more weeks, so the actual construction was soon to begin. I'd done a lot of clearing while waiting for him, but I was at the point where I needed more help to get things moving along meaningfully. Well, I'd been flip-flopping between fear and trust for months about the money, since I knew the project was going to cost a lot more than we had. But it was really hard to figure out exactly *how* much, since I didn't have any experience with financing that kind of thing. It was a love and faith project if you've ever seen one, and so I definitely approached it all with more of a 'ready – fire – aim' approach than I should have! I was aware of that, and money was obviously a very real consideration, so Ryan and I took an afternoon to work up a budget. With the funds we had, we could get it going and make some good progress. But, after working through the numbers, it looked like I was going to need about $250,000 more than we had. Now, back then, that was a lot of cash, and I didn't know where it was going to come from. I was admittedly spooked!"

"So, I of course prayed, and then just tried to leave it all in God's hands. And I also did what I could do. I suited up and went around town, talking with more bankers and trying to sell them on why it was a good idea for them to lend the money. But they still weren't interested… at all. Even trying to trust, I was getting stressed and was really questioning my stewardship. I had sensed many months before that perhaps I should have paused and waited on God before buying the twenty-five acres that ended up not working out. And so, I tried to apply that lesson in this case. I eventually quit trying to line up funds, and decided to trust that somehow it'd all work out – though I just didn't see a way. I of course didn't want to commit to Ryan and start something, only to not be able to finish. But how could we have been brought along that far, only to ultimately fail?" Pappy put his hands to his temples, then slid them down his face and sighed at the memory. "It was trust-step after trust-step. And I wish I had enjoyed those steps more, but I have to admit that with every step forward I carried a lot of fear. You'd think I'd have learned by then that I could trust, but I hadn't… not fully. And I think that all goes back to wondering if I could really trust a God who I believed only accepted me conditionally. But I won't get into that yet."

"Ryan called one day and told me I should focus my attention on getting a driveway put in. He explained some heavy equipment was going to have to get on the property early on, and that the current access wouldn't work. I'd already flagged where the drive was to go, and had cleared some of the smaller trees, but I had no idea how to build a driveway! Ryan knew it, and offered some helpful advice. He knew I'd gotten pretty good with a saw and tractor, and he said the clearing should be easy for me. But he said the stumps of the larger trees were going to be the real problem. They had to come out, the holes filled in and the drive graded before the gravel could be laid. I'm sure he saved me a lot of trouble by telling me to not even try to remove the stumps with the tractor. He said he'd come over soon and we'd think through the best approach… but that what I needed was some heavy equipment – dozers, excavators, and that kind of thing. He knew I didn't know how to operate tools like that, so renting was out of the question. And he said all the excavating crews he knew were busy. So, that was disheartening. And, not knowing what else to do but keep plugging along, I just got back to work clearing, tried to suppress my fear, and trust it would all work out."

Pappy laughed and flipped through more of the journal. "And it sure did work out… and beautifully! I have another story about how this came together – and it could be a whole book in and of itself. But I'll just give you the highlights, since it ties into the need for heavy equipment… another crazy story that could only have been God at work. I know I've said a few times already that I was religious back then, but… I mean, I was *dogmatic*. As I saw it, there was only one true path to God – the path I'd fortunately been born into and been taught about all my life. And, frankly, I just thought anyone who didn't hold the same understandings was wrong and was even at risk of eternal damnation. I could still love anyone who didn't believe as I did, and could respectfully disagree, but at the end of the day they were wrong." Pappy paused, and in the brief silence the surprise among the family about this unfamiliar version of Pappy from long ago could be felt.

"During a class to become members at that delightful church I told you about earlier, I ended up getting a bit sideways with the pastors over a couple of theological points. The issues turned into a pretty big deal, and the whole thing really saddened me and Nana because it was becoming clear that we were going to have to make a change in our church community. One evening, after the debate between me and the pastors got pretty heated, one of them suggested we check out another church that might be a better fit for us. He wasn't at all mean about it, but it had just gotten to the point where it was clear that we needed to move on. The name of the church he suggested was called Peace Community Church."

"I don't know exactly what it was that made him suggest Peace, but we went that very Sunday." Pappy laughed at a memory. "And when we walked in, let's just say that it was immediately clear to us, and to that very close-knit community, that we 'weren't from around those parts.'" Pappy laughed more at the memory of it, but then a look of real sincerity came back over his face. "When we walked in, we stuck out like sore thumbs. But the folks there were so open and friendly and loving toward us. Just incredible… they made us feel welcome immediately."

"Now, you've got to understand, Peace was unlike any church we'd ever attended. It was made up of people who'd lived on the back of the mountain for many generations, and we could immediately feel the deep sense of community they shared… a community which we were decidedly not a part of yet. Great folks… wonderful, actually… but they were a part of a culture we hadn't spent any time with, and we just didn't know how to relate to them. We felt we were really out of our element."

"Well, none of that silly socio-economic stuff ultimately mattered, and we were in for a real treat with that group of believers. We didn't have much in common with those folks, except, as Nana and I used to like to say, 'our humanity, and Jesus'… and that was *more* than enough! After a while of greetings and friendly chats, we settled into a worship service that was unlike anything we'd ever experienced – including that first Bible study with John's group. *Hours* went by like *minutes*! We'd sing for a bit, then the pastor would teach for a bit, then folks would start chiming in with stories of the miraculous things that had happened to them during the week. And then it'd be more singing, teaching and testimonies... it all just sort of flowed, and we were completely swept up in it."

"One woman was completely out of money, but she had to get to work. Her car had run out of gas on Tuesday, but she had prayed, and had somehow managed to drive to and from work the rest of the week on an empty tank – and her gauge wasn't broken! Another man praised God for his five-year-old daughter's miraculous healing from club feet – and the daughter then stood up and raised her hands over her head pointing both fingers at the sky in acknowledgement of where she believed her healing had come from. Another woman shared a story of a miraculous 'all clear' from cancer... a situation the church had been praying about for a few weeks."

"I mean, it was just amazing! We'd occasionally hear about that kind of faith community, but it's hard to believe something like that exists until you actually see it – or, better yet, experience it. Simple and complete faith was the norm for those folks... in a very real sense it was all they had. There just weren't other resources like we were accustomed to in the more affluent churches we'd attended. They had to live by faith in something beyond themselves to simply to get by. And it was like the more faith they had, the more miracles happened! So, as you can imagine, the worship was powerful, and the teaching was *real*."

"After the service, the pastor and his wife introduced themselves to us. His name was Chris and hers was Courtney, and we immediately liked them. Courtney had the ability to make you feel like a best friend within minutes of meeting her, and Chris was a kind man of few words, but when he spoke, it counted." Pappy laughed and smiled at the fond memory of this obviously beloved couple. "Chris's voice was just great. It was like this beautiful blend of Willie Nelson and Elvis. I won't even try to mimic it... completely unique!" Andy and Betsey were both smiling at the clear memories Pappy was flooding light onto.

"Courtney asked what had brought us to their little church, and we explained that we were living just up the road, and that the pastor over at Mountain Meadow had suggested we check it out. They were good friends with him, and said how highly they thought of the folks at Mountain Meadow. But then Courtney looked at me with an intense gaze and said, 'But why are you *here*?' I could tell she meant something like, 'What is an educated and well-heeled family like yours doing on the back of the mountain… and specifically, in our church?' She didn't mean to make us uncomfortable at all. She was just surprised and sincerely interested, since it wasn't the norm."

"Well, a kind but serious question deserved a respectful and serious answer. I felt compelled to lay it all out there, but had the mixed emotions similar to what I had with Ryan that day in the woods. Why risk losing new friends right away? But the experience with Ryan had encouraged me to remember to be faithful to 'the voice' – those subtle internal promptings. And I guess the afterglow of the experience that morning and all the 'Praise the Lords' and 'Yes Jesuses' had a hold of me. So, I offered a brief overview of our desires to live more intentionally and simply, and to pour more into the kids. They received all that fine, like most anyone would. But then they both waited with expectant looks for me to keep talking, as if they knew there was more. So, I expanded a bit, and offered some of what the farm vision entailed for us. And then I just collapsed into the moment and let it all hang out." Pappy laughed. "I did the churchy version of a 'mic drop', and shared how I also felt a strong call from the Lord to build a property that could be a refuge for folks in what I believed were some tough times to come."

Pappy laughed harder. "Well, your Nana looked at me like I'd completely lost it! She had this smile on her face that looked polite enough to Chris and Courtney, but I knew what she was thinking… *Are you kidding? You're going there? Now? Do you really want to have any community*?"

"Chris stepped forward to close the short distance between us, reached out his hand to shake mine, laid a strong left hand on my shoulder, and looked me square in the eyes. He didn't seem upset, and I took that as a good sign, so I accepted his offer and was met with the type of strong-but-friendly grip that I was getting used to when meeting mountain-folks. Then he pulled me toward him in a way that felt friendly but intense. He continued to hold his gaze, and it felt like he was scanning my soul. Then he said, 'Welcome, brother!' Right after that, Courtney reached her arms up to the heavens, looked up, muttered a *Praise Jesus*, then extended them out to hug Nana and pull her in for a hug. She exclaimed, 'Oh my *Lord*! Y'all *have* to come have lunch with us! This is just too amazing! Praise the Lord!'"

"We accepted the invitation, and quickly wrangled Andy and Betsey who were running all over the church with some new friends. Then we and a lot of other folks drove down the mountain to an all-you-can-eat buffet in a large shopping center. We all pulled into the parking lot at about the same time, and I noted how most of the folks were climbing out of their work trucks. I chuckled to myself about how we must have looked to them while we piled out of our Prius, but nobody seemed to care… and I didn't hear any snide remarks about the hybrid vehicle like I was getting accustomed to from the locals. We all went inside and enjoyed a great meal… well, the food was awful, but the company was wonderful!"

"We made small talk for a while, and they asked a lot of questions about the scope of the work for our project, how we were handling school, and the like. So, we shared about it all as best we could, and threw in a few funny stories about all we were learning the hard way. I even shared how I didn't really know how it would all come together, since we were facing some real challenges with the construction. Chris prodded for some specifics, and I referenced stuff like the immediate issue with the need for heavy equipment, manpower, and even loosely referenced the costs. We admitted we didn't have it all figured out, that so much of it was a faith journey for us."

"Throughout the meal, we of course asked questions of them too, and had learned a lot about them, the area, and community. And toward the end of our lunch together, we learned a little about Chris' and Courtney's more recent history. It turned out that Chris had owned a successful excavating company for about forty years, but had set it aside to commit to the church full time a few years before. Courtney was his faithful partner in the ministry, and they were a beloved team in service to their community. It was beautiful to hear about all they'd left behind to follow the leading of their hearts. They really were kindred spirits, and Nana and I delighted in getting to know them."

"Well, that lunch went deep into the afternoon, right up to when evening services were set to start. So, we all piled back in our vehicles and headed up the mountain to the church building, where we continued enjoying fellowship. When we pulled up, I couldn't help but see the building in a new light… and a light I appreciated. We'd learned during lunch that the slightly dressed up metal building had been Chris' garage for all his heavy equipment before he had shut down his company."

"We stayed for the evening service, and enjoyed every minute of it too. The room was full of mostly the same folks, and the worship and prayer and preaching were just as full of energy and enthusiasm as that morning had been. We finally left at nine… and we were some of the first to leave! We'd spent all day completely swept up in the most wonderful and authentic experience of community. And Andy and Betsey had loved it all too. Nana and I went to bed that night speechless… just sort of absorbing the beauty of the day."

"So, I was in a real jam when it came to getting the driveway done, and I admitted my frustration to Ryan. We'd agreed to meet the Monday afternoon after what ended up being our surprise experience with Peace Community the Sunday before. The goal was to come up with a gameplan that might not necessitate a driveway right away."

"Well, that Monday rolled around, and I was still on a bit of a high from the day before at Peace Community. I was in this state of pure trust… and I'm sure that had a lot to do with the amount of faith I'd witnessed all day the day before. So, that morning I was doing a lot of sawing when I heard what sounded like a powerful engine working hard to make it up our street. That didn't quite register, since large trucks were rarely back in that area where we lived. I was working to rough-in the driveway, and there was about fifty yards of woods between me and the street where the noise was coming from. I heard the engine power down to idle, then men's voices, then chains rattling and clanking, and I naturally felt inclined to figure out what the commotion was about. I set my saw on a stump, and walked through the woods toward the noise. When I got to the street, I saw a huge, parked truck towing a lowboy trailer loaded with an excavator and a skid-steer. The man who was fiddling with the equipment looked familiar, but I couldn't place him. I started walking toward the rig, when suddenly Chris came walking around the back of the trailer. I was so confused… I just wasn't too quick to put two and two together that morning!" Pappy laughed.

"Chris saw me, and walked toward me with a wide smile on his face. He looked at me and said, 'You'll be needing some tools for this job. These are some good ones I kept after shutting my company down… should be perfect for what you're doing out here. They run good, and you can have them for as long as you need. All I ask if that you keep 'em greased and pay for the fuel. The dozer is on the way, and should be here soon. Where do you want 'em?'"

"Well, you can imagine how I felt… but I just didn't know what to say. I was completely speechless! Chris had just offered me a huge gift, and we both knew it. We looked right square into each other's eyes, and I gave him a sincere, quick nod." Pappy lifted his left hand, pointed two fingers at his eyes and generated a playfully intense look. Then he pointed with those same two fingers toward the children and swept across the whole crew, making eye contact with each of them. "Everything that needed to be said was in that look, but I still said, 'Thank you, Chris. In front of the house will be great.'"

"He nodded and turned to Tony, who I then remembered as one of the friendly greeters from Peace Community who'd been the first to meet us when we had walked in the day before, but I didn't recognize him in his work clothes. Chris told Tony the machines needed to be taken up to the house, so Tony and the other guy finished the offloading the lowboy just as another truck with a large bulldozer rolled up with a couple of other men. I invited Chris to the house, and we walked along where the driveway was going to be. I told him I had no idea how to run the machines, and that I was a concerned about screwing up such a gift. He just laughed, and in that twangy voice of his, he said encouragingly that if I could run a tractor then I could figure out those tools. Well, I didn't say anything, but I wasn't too sure about that!"

"Nana came out to greet us, and the three of us visited on the porch while the men drove the machines toward the cabin and parked them, their powerful engines still rumbling, and creating a vibration through the whole house. Andy and Betsey came out, wide-eyed at the impressive display of power next to the little cabin. Andy was fascinated with 'diggers' at that age – and now there were three different types parked in his front yard!" Andy and Pappy exchanged a fun glance.

"I was so in the *flow* with all that was happening suddenly... I just knew a good season was upon us! I sensed something special was shaping up, and that we were about to get *real* busy. Nana could feel it too. We knew what kind of progress a tractor allowed for, but these machines were going to take things to a whole new level. Chris could feel our appreciation, and he simply said, 'Hydraulics are one of God's greatest gifts to man. Y'all are doing good work here... important work... work Courtney and I believe is God's work. We're just glad we can help y'all out a little.'"

Pappy cast another glance at Andy, and chuckled. "Andy was sitting with us on the porch, and it was obvious he was about to come out of his skin with excitement over the possibility of getting near the diggers. Chris had kids and grandkids of his own, and he understood full-well the fascination boys and men share about heavy equipment. 'You want to hop up in that dozer, Andy?' Chris asked. Andy's eyes widened, and his flabbergasted expression said it all. 'Well, why don't you and your Pappy hop up into the cab of that D6 over there… just see how it fits you.' Andy didn't have to be asked twice. He offered a quick *Thank you pastor!'* and ran down the steps to the side of the huge machine that towered over him. Tony had powered down all the engines before the men said their quick hellos and goodbyes and walked back to the trucks to wait for Chris. The top track of that dozer was high above Andy's head, so he waited for me to walk over and help him up. But I was so green, I didn't even know how to get up into the cab, much less how to operate the thing!"

"Chris knew, and kindly walked over to the side of the dozer with me and pointed the way up into the cab. Andy and I climbed up, while Chris followed and stood on the track beside us. Then he leaned in and gave me some basic instructions by pointing at the various controls and what they were for. I asked him if he was *sure* he was comfortable leaving the machines with me… I wanted to be really clear with him that I had zero experience as an operator. I was concerned that he only knew men who'd grown up working equipment like that, and so he might be taking some basic levels of knowledge for granted. He understood though, and said, 'You can't break the machine. Just go slow and play around with the levers and pedals and what-not. You'll figure it out. You just make sure you don't break yourself, or these precious children of yours! I ran over one of my favorite dogs a few years back. So, accidents can happen to the best of us. Again, just take it nice and easy and you'll be fine. I've got to meet some folks over at the church. The key to each machine is in the ignition. Here's my phone number. Just call if you get into any trouble.' He tore a piece of paper from an address book he kept in his front shirt pocket, wrote his phone number on it, and handed it to me. And with that, we shook hands again and he walked off toward the street."

"Well, Andy was eager to fire it up and feel the rumble, and his patience had about run out. I watched Chris walk away for a moment." Pappy paused and then interrupted himself with something he just had to say. "What an incredible gesture. That man was an angel in my family's life. And I call him my pastor to this day."

The he continued. "I looked at Nana. And she was looking at me in a way that acknowledged the magnitude of the gift and her appreciation of it… but that also expressed a whole lot of concern!" Pappy laughed some more and continued, "I knew she was right. But I didn't know what else to do except smile and shrug my shoulders. She nodded with a reluctant *go-ahead*, and I shifted my attention back to Andy and the array of knobs, pedals, and levers. And while I tried to get my bearings, he fiddled around with the controls pretending he was operating it."

I finally choked down the lump in my throat and decided to twist the key in the ignition. Having learned my lesson about not engaging the brake that morning months before when I'd almost sent the tractor right over Andy and into the house, I pressed down on it… or at least what I thought I'd remembered Chris saying was the right pedal. Then I turned the key, and the dozer roared to life. I noticed Betsey jump a little, and Andy and I just sat there together in the cab, overwhelmed by the raw power that we were theoretically in control of. But neither of us were willing to touch a control while the engine was on for fear of plowing down the house!"

Pappy laughed hard at the memory of another story. "In fact, the first time I tried to get any meaningful work done with that dozer, I knocked myself out cold!" Pappy laughed more, reached up and rubbed his head. "I hadn't thought about the physics of a heavy-duty track machine like that. Dozers have a heavy blade on the front, and I just didn't consider the physics of the small ledges we had all over our property at that point. So, I rolled over one not thinking anything of it, and once that blade was out over the fulcrum far enough, suddenly the twenty-five-ton machine bucked me up into the steel ceiling of the cab. I woke up some minutes later in a crumpled heap on the floorboard with the dozer still throttled and pushing down a huge oak tree!" That story gets even better… but no time for that now." The kids, and it seemed the adults too, seemed a bit disappointed. Only a person with too many stories passes up an opportunity to tell a good one.

"So anyhow, Ryan came over that afternoon and saw the machines. He smiled and said, 'Well, the stumps aren't an issue anymore. God is good!' I smiled back, and we walked around the tools together. While he looked them over closely with his trained eye, I told him I didn't know how to operate them. But I'm pretty sure he already knew that. He was gracious about my ignorance, and gave me another quick run-down of the various controls in each machine. Then he hopped up into the excavator, drove it slowly it over to the roughed-in driveway, and pulled the massive tool up to a huge oak stump. He waved from the cab for me and Andy to come over and watch. Just then, Betsey came out on the porch with a fantastic multi-colored outfit, complete with pink cape and cowboy boots, hands on hips and elbows out, wanting to join in on the fun." Pappy winked at Betsey. When she tried to wink back, a few nostalgic tears were released.

"Yep! Little Doctor Sissy-Pants was hardcore… always game for anything!" She said.

"Yeah…" Pappy laughed, shook his head, and smiled gently back at Betsey. "That character cracked your mother and me up!" The family laughed together at the image of Betsey as a little girl, so full of spunk. Betsey was an old woman now, and the vital and vibrant image of her as a little girl was a lesson for us all in and of itself.

"So, Nana walked back inside, and the three of us walked over to Ryan. He showed me how to pick away at the roots of the stumps with the teeth on the bucket so their hold on the earth would break and you could easily lift the stumps and set them aside. Then he put the tractor's forks on the skid-steer and built a few big burn piles… then got back into the excavator and piled the few stumps he had quickly cleared on top. Next, he hopped up into the dozer and pushed a bunch of dirt, pointing out how important it was to keep the blade from bouncing, or I'd end up with a wavy driveway. So, I just had to repeat the process he'd shown me over and over, and then we'd be ready for gravel and Ryan would be able to start the building."

"Ryan scratched around a little more while the kids wandered back to the house, and he offered a lot of little pointers to help me out. He was an artist with that equipment, and I just sat there on a stump watching him in awe, knowing, once again, that I was completely out of my element. He hopped out of the dozer and walked over and said,

'The stumps and the piling are easy. You'll get that bit quickly, no problem. But the dozer is a different animal. You'll figure it all out though. Just keep an eye out for your kids and dogs!' He must have known about Chris' recent experience with his dog. 'I've got to get back over to my job site and finish cleaning up. I'll call my gravel guy to get that set up for you… his name is Tony, and you'll like him.' Ryan snickered playfully as he added, 'And he'll like you too, considering how much money you're about to spend with him! How long do you think you'll need?' Well, I had no idea, but I said a week. Ryan nodded, and that was that. So, I had a week to figure out how to work those machines, get the long driveway path completely cleared, and the dirt pushed and graded."

"That wasn't the hardest part, though. The money issue was still weighing heavily on me like a cold, wet blanket. Ryan's bills were about to start rolling in heavy on a weekly basis, and I just didn't have what it was going to take to finish the job… far less, actually. Ryan of course knew about it, since we'd worked on that budget together, but when I reminded him, he just said, 'It'll all get sorted. You just keep putting one foot in front of the other. God's got it. You have to have faith, man!'"

Pappy shrugged. "Well, that was good counsel… and so I refocused on the tasks at hand and trusted that as I continued to step into the unknown, God would take care of the details like money. I got pretty good with that heavy equipment in short-order, and I was able to get a beautiful, meandering driveway ready for the gravel on time. With no communication between me and Tony, he showed up in a massive dump truck first thing in the morning, and on the day that marked a week since I'd last seen Ryan. That's just how that entrenched mountain culture worked. You agreed to something with a handshake, and it happened."

"Tony hopped down out of his cab, shook my hand, and asked me to show him the whole driveway. We walked the length of it, then back to his truck. He didn't say much, but when he did it was usually hilarious, and it turned out I did like Tony a lot and we became friends over the years to come. After we got back to his dump truck, he just said, 'Got it.' I could tell he was doing some figuring based on his many years of experience, which had started as a young boy when he'd helped his dad do the same kind of work. I didn't want to interrupt his thinking, so I just watched and didn't ask any questions."

"So many of those folks I met in the trades were geniuses – the complex math they'd do as naturally as I breathe was staggering. But I never met one of them who thought of themselves that way. As Tony thought about all the variables of laying the gravel, he walked to the swing gate on the back of his truck, counted the links on a heavy chain hanging from it, and set a certain link on a hook on the side of the bed. Then he climbed up into the cab and backed the truck up so that his run would start right at the beginning of the driveway. He throttled the engine, started raising the dump bed, put the truck into gear and let off the clutch. Just as he started rolling, he raised the dump bed to the final angle he'd determined he needed so the perfect amount of gravel would fall out of the measured gate-opening. And he went on to lay that first layer of gravel across the whole drive perfectly. I mean, think about that! He'd just synthesized a whole bunch of data points in his head… like distance, speed, gate-width, flow rate, gravel size, lift angle… and he'd done it all perfectly! Amazing. Over the course of the day, Tony made a few more runs like that, and suddenly our driveway was in. And I was *really* proud of it!"

"Nana came out with the kids to admire the work. She gave me a knowing kiss, recognizing how important it was, and how hard I'd worked on it. We spent a few minutes together, and then they walked back to the house to press on with schooling. Shortly after they had gone back to the cabin, and while I walked around on the gravel feeling a deep sense of satisfaction, I felt my phone vibrating indicating a call coming in. I pulled it out of my pocket and looked at the screen. It was my mother." Pappy's eyes flicked up to the stars for a moment before he continued.

"I answered, and she didn't carry on with any of her typical Southern small talk. She just got right to it. 'Honey, I have something very important to share with you, and I need to tell you in person. Will you please come over and meet me… and can you come right now?' Well, part of the reason we'd moved there was for family, and she only lived about ten minutes away. She didn't typically ask things like that of me, and so I said 'sure' and drove straight over. During the drive, I was concerned she might have a serious health issue, or that there was some other bad thing going on, my fear-based way of thinking in full effect."

"But just before getting to the house, I was stopped by 'the voice', and I had to pull over. I sat there for a few seconds and then said, *Yes, Lord?*. It was the first time I'd experienced that in a long while, and I'd really missed it."

"I had *yearned* to hear it again, and I was trembling. *You have been faithful, and are about to receive what you need* was all it whispered to me. Well, all I could do was respond with a really intelligent, *Huh?*. I was completely at a loss, but then I suddenly had a deep knowing that whatever it was that mom wanted to tell me about wasn't something to be afraid of. Nothing more was offered, and I let the sacredness of that moment pass."

"When I entered the house, I heard her call out, 'I'm in here'. I entered the kitchen, and she was sitting at the table. She looked at me and said, 'Take a seat, honey.' I did, and then waited for her to speak. I was feeling completely swept up in the moment… like I was just sort of watching it all happen."

"She said, 'Son, I hope you interpret this as a real affirmation… and that you can see you are part of a plan that is so much bigger than you.'

Mom had always been my biggest advocate for the Grand Experiment, and not just because it would bring me and the family closer to her, but because she really believed in what we were doing, and on all fronts. 'I am going to give you a large amount of money. This money is coming *through* my account, but the person giving you this gift wants to remain anonymous. So, please don't press me at all about details.' She paused again, and her silence made everything feel really sacred… even miraculous. She pulled out her checkbook, and…"

"What's a chec….' Before Cecil could finish his question, one of the other kids had kicked him and whispered harshly,

"It's an old-fashioned way for trading money… we learned about it in history… now, *shhhh!'*

Pappy smiled. "That's right, we used to trade money with paper, and a check was one of the main ways back then." He continued, "Well, she finished writing, and tore that check from of the book. Then she slid it across the table to me."

"I stared at it without picking it up, and had to read it twice. I looked up at Mumsie, who was looking at me with tears in her eyes. She knew what those funds meant to me and for the project, even though she had no idea about the stress I was carrying around finances. And she certainly didn't know the specific sum Ryan and I had determined I'd need to finish the work. I looked back down at the check again and smiled. That sort of thing had become somewhat common, but it never got old… but that moment was on another level." Pappy paused and cleared his throat. "That check was for $250,000!"

"Well, from that point it was *on*!" Pappy slapped his knee, and his enthusiasm was infectious. "Ryan's crew showed up a few days later and got to work, and Chris had spread the word about our project among his community of skilled tradespeople. Suddenly, I had heavy equipment on site and plenty of manpower, so we started tackling multiple projects simultaneously. We cranked *all* day, *every* day, for over a year! We had one crew building what we called The Barn, which would end up being a gorgeous, finished space for community gatherings like yoga, Bible studies, movie nights, and things like that… and it was also the place where a lot of people could be housed in the event that a hard season did befall us. The downstairs of The Barn was finished too. That's where the kids' homeschool room was, and also an office for me. So much was going on: pastures were being cleared; a large pond was put in, a well; a root cellar; outhouses; fruit tree orchards; a solar power system; livestock barns; gardens and chicken coops… and so much more. It was a huge project. And, on top of that, we were completely remodeling and adding onto Mema's little cabin!"

"I wasn't as green by then, and during that project I worked side by side with all the laborers and tradespeople. In fact, I *out*worked every one of them. Well, every one of them except a sixty-year-old Mormon man named Lavoit who I just couldn't seem to tire out… and who became a dear friend. I showed up for work before anyone else, and I worked long into the evening after they left. I learned so much every single day, and it was a blast. I admit I carried my same old push-hard intensity during that time, which wasn't particularly attractive to Nana, since I was always in go-mode. But I was enjoying having a project in full swing, and a sense of purpose – and I just charged the whole time. Nana was continuing to enjoy the season with the kids and garden, and we were delighting in each other during that time. And as much as she was celebrating all my accomplishment with the construction, I was celebrating her success with the kids and the gardens."

"I was free to think things up and then create them the very next day. I spent most of my time with two master carpenters who also knew how to plumb and do electric work, so working with them gave me an education I'd always wanted. They also became good friends, and we developed a real respect for one another. When I wasn't with them, I was working on one of the other projects we had going on. The only time during the week other than Sunday's that I'd take off was on Fridays while Nana worked as a physical therapist in the local school district. Fridays were 'arts and crafts' day with the kids, and that was technically a part of their homeschooling.

During the whole construction process, I was able to be around the family a lot, but those Fridays were special."

Betsey couldn't resist chiming in. "Oh, Daddy, that was so much fun! Most of our friends were in school cutting up posterboard into animal shapes and adding glitter and paint, while we were building duck houses and garden trestles and all kinds of stuff with you!"

"Yep!" Pappy said as he laughed, swept up in the energy of this part of the story. "You were running a framing nail-gun at age five! Do you remember when you first asked to try it? I warned you it had a heavy kick... but you were determined! You leaned into it with all the weight in your little body, and it knocked you right on your butt as soon as you pulled the trigger. But you got right back up and repeated that process again and again until you got the hang of it!"

The kids all got a kick out of this and laughed. Betsey looked at them while she playfully stuck her tongue out.

Then Pappy felt compelled to add, "You got pretty good with it quickly, though!"

He smiled. "So special. It's also a miracle the two of you didn't get seriously hurt those days!"

Pappy flipped through one of the few remaining journals. "It was such hard work, but it was a blast. We got so much done in such a short period of time. And I've gotta add this. It's a funny scene that stands out because of all it represented. It's when we finally ate our first meal sourced only from our land."

"Now to digress a bit and set the stage with a funny-but-serious story, Dad had a small herd of bulls and cows that needed to be tended to, so we had to harvest most of the bulls. And before you judge that as cruel, let me tell you something... a herd with twenty bulls and only three cows is *no bueno*! Those were some pent-up, angry bulls... *dangerous*!" Pappy winked at me, and cut playful glances at some of the other guys. While the women rolled their eyes at Pappy's low-brow humor, it was clear that they could, in fact, imagine a situation like that being bad.

"So, I learned a little about how to rodeo and work the herd into a pen, and then the bulls onto a trailer. Now *that* was some crazy work! Those bulls were so angry that they'd charge us, and try to mash us hard up against the pen rails. One of the guys I was working with allowed a bull to get his head under his butt while he was running away. That bull cranked his massive neck, flicked his head, and sent that poor guy soaring up over the pen. He landed down hard on the top rail, and right on his ribs, then flopped down to the other side out of reach of the still-angry bull… and that was it for him for the day!"

"We finally got the ones we wanted on the trailer, and I worked with a local butcher to process some beef for our freezer, and some to sell. There was a sort of sacred solemness to that process. We definitely wanted to get a better understanding of our food supply, but harvesting bulls and chickens was hard. And the contrast between that and harvesting from a garden ended up having a profound impact on me. That experience changed my relationship with food forever…"

Pappy paused, and we all knew him well enough to know he was tempted to launch into a monologue on regenerative agriculture. But he stopped short, smiled, and continued. "Anyhow, point is, between the meat and the salad, that meal represented *a lot* of work! And that night, we were having burgers and a huge salad from the garden… and some new little chicks we'd just picked up were walking around on the table while we sat down to eat. The salad was beautiful, with peppers, tomatoes, snap peas, and green beans on it… and here's the part you kids will think is funny. After the sincerest blessing over a meal I'd ever offered, Nana lifted the first bite of her salad to her mouth. Then, just as it almost reached her lips, a bright green inchworm stood up and wiggled around!" Pappy laughed and wiggled his pinky finger in front of his face. "A cute shriek came from Nana while she pulled the fork away from her face. It was so funny! The little critter kept standing on the leaf of lettuce that was on her fork. It was wiggling around and calling out, 'Nooo, giant woman… please don't eat me!'" Pappy pitched his voice and wiggled his arms and body to mimic the worm. "Now, that's a real-deal organic salad for you!" Pappy laughed.

"Did she eat the worm?" the kids called out, almost in unison.

"Nope. In fact, Andy and Betsey insisted on taking the little guy back out to the garden so it could continue on as a part of the whole system. And Nana and I shared a real moment over that. What Andy and Betsey did with that inchworm blessed us – a lifestyle that was so foreign to us was already becoming a part of who they were."

"Well, in short order, we had Full Circle Farmstead up and running, and with a full offering for the local market that was being met with rave reviews. The raw land had been converted to the loveliest little farmstead you've ever seen, and we settled into the rhythm of our version of what we'd been so inspired by down in Chile." Pappy added, "It turns out it wasn't a 'simple life' at all… but it was beautiful, and rich in its elegance."

"Andy and Betsey played out in the woods for hours every day between school sessions, and I'd become a half-decent jack of all trades while Nana delighted in the opportunities for solitude and contemplation which the garden offered her. We were so in touch with each other, the land, the seasons, the livestock, the plants. The folks at Peace Community had become dear friends, and we were still very close to everyone over at the compound. Nana and I often commented on how amazed we were that the family values we had put so much energy toward had crystallized so perfectly. So much love. So much harmony. So much family. So much community."

"It was a really good season." Pappy paused, and seemed to draw the wonderful emotions he associated with that time into his heart.

Then he slowly added, "I'm so glad we had that time, because the seeming perfection of it all was about to shift."

CHAPTER FOURTEEN

STORY TIME

We were so grateful for all Pappy had shared. But he had pushed his limits with cutting too many of his stories short, and we wanted a zinger. Before he could flow into what was obviously going to be the more intense part of his transformation, Jenny spoke up.

"Pappy, this is really special for us all to hear, and I know you're just getting to the main part. But you're killing us by shortening, and even skipping, so many stories! Take the time to give us a funny one!" Jenny was one of the older teenagers, and all the kids looked up to her. Emboldened by Jenny's request, and anticipating Pappy would concede, a few of the children started rousing those asleep so they could hear a fun story. A few just couldn't wake, though several did. And suddenly there was a whole gaggle pressing Pappy with high pitched *Yeses* and *Pappy, you have tos*!

Pappy delighted in this interruption. He leaned forward, rested his elbows on his knees and looked at the children with a playful intensity.

"Well, I do have a good story or two. And it does seem it'd be fun to play around for a few minutes. Do you want a funny one, a sad one, or a mix of both?" Pappy's exaggerated facial expressions mimicked the themes he was offering, and the kids were swept up in the idea of choosing from a smorgasbord.

"Oh, what fun! What are some options?" Jenny asked.

"Well, let's see..." Pappy leaned back in his chair to think, as Piccolo worked his way around Leela and made a pass by his leg to let him know he was there. Leela's head lifted, and she gave Piccolo a lick just before the cat hopped lithely into Pappy's lap. He laid his head into Pappy's chest and rotated it so his neck was exposed. Pappy seemed to know exactly what to do, and started scratching the old cat until we could hear its loud purring. Pappy looked down and smiled at Piccolo for a moment while he quietly worked through his library of preferred tales, then he looked up at us.

"Ok, so there's the story about our neighbor shooting three of our dogs that I referenced earlier. That's a sad-funny combo, but it ended beautifully and has a great lesson in it."

"Then there's the crazy story about when our neighbor literally blew up a house on our street just because he didn't like the guy who lived there. Let's see, then there's the time your Nana had to hook up heavy chains to the truck and pull our tractor out of a big fire before it exploded... with me on it! Or the time we herded bulls and had to lasso them from four-wheelers... and how they ended up getting revenge on us in a big way!"

Pappy was in a flow rattling off options for the kids, whose excited faces looked as if they were in a candy store with overwhelming choices, and most of the adults had similar expressions. The topics seemed so far-fetched that our collective thinking would have been more along the lines of wondering if he was serious, had we not known him well enough to know they were probably all true.

Pappy had stalled briefly, but then kept going as if he were just getting warmed up. How many more could be possibly have? That man lived big, and in a sense, had experienced many lives during the 120 years we were celebrating with him that evening.

Pappy glanced over at Andy and smiled. "Then there was the time when Andy accidentally set our chicken coops on fire, and we had to fight a huge blaze for hours as a family late at night. And another one when I mashed my toe really bad in an accident on the tractor... and to relieve the pressure, I had to drill through my toenail out in the shop. I hit the nerve while Andy and Betsey watched, and they nearly passed out when blood splattered everywhere." Pappy winked at Betsey, who shook her head in return – the memory still obviously an unpleasant one for her.

"Let's see, so many... Andy lost his first tooth while he and Betsey were skinny-dipping in a mud-puddle... then there was the time I accidentally shot one of our goats in front of Nana and her mother. I got in all kinds of trouble for that. Oh, and that reminds me of a good one... the story of the mini unicorn."

"Yes!" McLean suddenly squealed breathlessly. "We want to hear the story of the mini unicorn!" There was voiced agreement among all of us, and it was decided.

Pappy smiled. "Well, that's a really good one... one of my favorites." He winked at McLean.

Pappy leaned forward and rested his forearms on his thighs. He was holding his mug between his knees by the fingertips of his left hand, swirling it in small circles. Then he lifted it to his mouth, took a sip, and began.

"So, we had pretty much just started the project, and were still as green as green could be. We didn't know *anything*, but we were jumping right into *everything*! My dad lived in Atlanta, and he called one evening during supper to say that he'd just attended a party at a farm up in Rome. Apparently, the folks hosting the party were raising money for some charity through an auction, and two Nigerian Dwarf goats were in the mix. Papa J had entered a bid on them just to help the charity, and with us in the back of his mind in case he won... and he did! Of course, he didn't want anything to do with the goats, and so he was calling to ask me if we'd want them. They were apparently still at that farm and were ready to be picked up. Or they could be left there, and his donation would just go to charity and the farmers would keep the goats."

"We were all gathered around the table when he called. So, I held the phone away from my ear, put it on speaker, and explained the option to the family. Nana, ever up for tending to animals, and loving the adventurous prospect of an entirely new type, immediately said *yes!*. Andy and Betsey quickly followed by squealing their excitement too… and then, Betsey, cute as could be, and after saying *yes!*, asked what Nigerian Dwarf goats were." Pappy winked at Betsey. "Papa J explained that they were tiny adult goats… about the size of Buddy. Now, Buddy was our beloved little hound who was about thirty pounds, about yay big." Pappy held his hands up to approximate the size, about three feet apart and two feet high.

"Well, the thought of two tiny pet goats sent Andy and Betsey into a high-spirited tizzy. Dad heard us, and that settled it… and I remember him laughing at that. He had worked so hard as a young man to get *off* the farm, and he just couldn't wrap his head around what we were doing out there, or why, after all we'd built in Colorado. He never did wag a finger at me though, and to his credit, he was having fun with it all. Even though they were divorced at the time, he and Mumsie both were so supportive of our family during that wild season, every step of the way. So were Nana's folks, for that matter. This family here…" Pappy swept his arms to embrace us all "…this family… we all stand on the shoulders of the giants who went before us." Pappy nodded solemnly, then chuckled.

"Well, looking back, I'm not sure if Papa J was giving us a gift, or if he knew how much trouble goats could be, and was messing with us. Whatever the case, the day came for us to go pick them up at that farm in Rome. We'd watched a few YouTube videos about goats, and had read enough to know we'd need a pen of some sort. So, I spent a few days building the coolest area for them behind the house. It was pretty big, with boulders to climb on, wood ramps so they could stay up high, and all kinds of neat features."

"Fun side story… it turns out I'd used weld-wire rather than woven-wire for the fencing. And that ended up being a big mistake because it had allowed one of the goats, who we ended up naming Diablo, to rip his way out of the pen when Nana's folks came for their first visit. Diablo sauntered toward them, and as he got closer, he saw his reflection in the shiny red paint of their brand-new car. And he snapped! He bounced up and down a few times, then rammed his reflection and dented the door badly. Then he hopped up on the hood and pranced around like the little devil he was!" Pappy laughed and the kids thought that was hilarious.

"Anyhow, let's just say that Nigerian Dwarf goats are *lively!* We loaded up as best we could on some basic goat knowledge, and then naively drove down to Rome with a large crate to tote them back in. We met the farmer, and she gave us a good run-down on what to expect, and how to tend to them. We went over to the holding-pen where she kept the kids, and y'all, they were so *cute*! All these little baby goats were sort of bouncing around, running into walls and each other… you know, 'kidding around'. They were full-on *spring loaded* and curious about *everything*! I should have seen what was coming, but we were all smitten. So, the farmer helped us load up the two that were ours, and we thanked her and drove back to the cabin."

"Now, you've got to understand something else before I go any further. Your Betsey here, she was a real lover of this sort of thing. She was also only about three or four when we started the farm. So, she wasn't the best at tending to live things, even if she did love them lots. At that point, she'd lost a fish, a turtle, her pet chicken named Chick-Chicken, and a cat. And she adored each one of those animals, so every loss was really hard on her, and Nana and I were getting seriously concerned about her developing some sort of attachment disorder."

"Well, now all of the sudden we had two goats to tend to. One was a billy and one was a nanny, and Andy and Betsey were both eager to claim one for their own." Pappy was now getting swept into his own story. "The billy was black and grey with two huge horns and some of the biggest ba…" Pappy caught himself and paused, as Betsey rolled her eyes. Then he pressed on with a wry smile. "He was an all-male billy goat. And we could tell by the way he was ramming the cage the whole ride home that he was a feisty one. The nanny was white, and had these two deformed horns which at certain angles looked sort of like a single horn was growing right out of the middle of her forehead. The billy was named Oreo, but like I mentioned a moment ago, we changed his name to Diablo a week or two later, and for good reason. The nanny was named Star. Diablo had a blue collar and Star had a pink collar… and that's important to remember for the end of the story."

"Betsey had fallen in love with Star at first sight, and had immediately claimed her as her own. Andy was always a laid-back kid, and was happy to take Diablo. As we pulled up to the cabin, we were all excited to introduce them to their new home, and we felt like real-deal farmers with livestock in the bed of our big truck!" Pappy laughed at himself with the big laugh we all loved.

"So, when we got back to the farm, we were eager to get them into their new pen and watch them start their new life with us. Nana and I got out of the truck while Andy and Betsey tumbled out behind us, and we all walked around to the back together. I dropped the tailgate and hopped up into the bed while Nana positioned herself behind the tailgate. Diablo was making it hard for me to get the gate of their pen open, since he kept trying to ram my hands when I'd reach to unlock it. But I eventually managed, and held him back with one arm while I got a hold of Star with the other. Star was pretty content and let me pick her up without any resistance. So, I lifted her out of the crate, shut the door, and locked it. Well, that sent Diablo into a *rage*… I mean, he just went nuts! He was jumping up into the top of the crate so hard he was literally lifting it off the bed of the truck!"

"I scooched across the rough bed-liner while cradling Star and handed her to Nana. Then I turned my attention to Diablo. And as I turned to face the angry little fireball, I caught a flurry of activity out of the corner of my right eye. I looked over toward Nana and saw Star kicking hard, trying to get out of her arms. She was suddenly angry as a hornet about something, and a goat can *kick*! Between the uni-horns and the kicking, Nana really had no choice but to try to set her down. As she started to lower the little nutso temper tantrum, Star kicked hard out of Nana's arms and landed on the bed of the truck. Then she bounced up and down a couple of times on the tailgate before leaping off, and then bounce-walked her way over to some grass at the edge of what was going to be the pasture. She stopped suddenly, and then turned to face us. While she looked at us, she took a bite of grass and stared, chewing slowly." Pappy leaned farther forward, puffed out his cheeks and made a chewing motion with wild, crazy eyes.

Then he sat back into his chair and pulled the blanket around his shoulders. "Now, there are three things you should know before going any further. First, the lay of the land is important. I'd cleared most of the trees for the pasture, but there were a lot of stumps yet to dig out. Those stumps were hidden by a lot of thistle… stuff that grows in long strands with really sharp prickers, and it was so strong that it'd trip you up if you didn't watch your step. Nasty stuff. So, the area where Star was heading was not a place you wanted to be running wildly. And our property wasn't fenced yet. It was surrounded by a rough road that had been cut after my neighbor, Danny, had set his land on fire a few years before, and it had gotten out of control. The forest service had pushed a dozer through the woods to create a fire break, and our property was visible from many points on that route. Well, Danny and his large family were delighted with the 'free' road the forest service had installed. It wound all through the woods and they could ride around on their four-wheelers shooting deer at random."

"And three of our dogs!" Betsey chimed in.

"Yes, that was tough." Pappy said, but moved on.

"So, that brings up my neighbors… and this is the second thing you need to know. The land we'd bought from Mema was apparently land that our neighbors somehow still believed was *theirs*. It's a long story about how Mema ended up purchasing it, but let's just say that they didn't take too kindly to new folks in the area, and they certainly didn't have much respect for contract law. Well, we were just getting to know each other, so I was trying to be a good neighbor, and was kind and respectful whenever we'd interact."

"In the early days of the project, Danny would routinely ride right onto our property on his four-wheeler just to flex a little. He always had a cooler of cheap beer fastened to the handlebars, and a big revolver on his hip, which he said was 'for snakes'. And, just to add a little extra color on the picture I'm trying to paint for you… do you remember a few minutes ago when I referenced a neighbor blowing up another neighbor's house? Well, that was Danny. Even so, my property was right next to his, and I wanted to get along, so I tried to make a good impression whenever we'd run into each other."

"That brings up the third thing you need to know… what I was wearing. Now, there was a dress code where we lived, and you'd better be abiding by it if you wanted to ever even have a shot at getting along with the locals. Loosely, that code was work boots, jeans, a t-shirt, and a trucker cap. And I'll tell you what, your boots had *better* be well-worn." Pappy chuckled again at the memory of his first day at the hardware store. "That was it… and you didn't see much in the way of variation on that theme. Also worth mentioning is that men back there tended to do all the building and wrenching… they dealt with the larger equipment and livestock almost exclusively. The reality in that culture was that anything small was for the women or kids." It was easy to sense the women around the firepit bristle at that, especially considering how much women and their strength was celebrated in our family.

"Well, I'd taken the day off from working the farm so we could drive to get the goats. And for some reason, I'd put on what I used to wear in Colorado… flip flops, khaki shorts, an old blue and white Hawaiian shirt that I used to wear on ski and river days, a visor, and sunglasses." Pappy smiled as he added, "Let's just say I definitely wasn't in uniform."

"So, that's the context and what you need to know. So now, back to the story. Star had worked her way deeper onto our property, and in the direction of Danny's farm. While I tracked along with Star, keeping my distance and trying to act nonchalant, Nana looked at me with a bit of a panicked look that said it all: *I don't know how Betsey will hold up if she suffers another loss!'"*

"I agreed, and decided to take more action, and with the kind of determination only a father protecting his little girl's heart can have." Pappy glanced over at Betsey, who was smiling ear to ear.

"The best immediate idea I had was to grab some of the goat feed from the truck and sort of crouch-waddle toward Star, holding out the feed and trying to sweet-talk her into coming to me like I would with a puppy." Pappy set Piccolo aside, got out of his chair, and replicated the ridiculous motions, which made us all laugh.

He continued as he reclaimed his chair. "Well, Star didn't come, and I could tell she was not at all interested in me coming any closer to her either. Even so, I waddled a little further toward her with an intention of grabbing her real quick by that pink collar. I managed to get within about ten feet, but she knew exactly what I was doing. She slowly finished chewing a mouthful of grass, looked me right in the eye, and then sprung straight up in the air! She landed, and did that weird goat-bouncy-trot-thing, and was quickly another twenty yards away from me. She was getting deeper into the manky thistle area, and I *really* didn't want to be dealing with that in flip flops and shorts! So, then I stood up and tried walking around real slow, just acting sort of easy-going, like I didn't have a care in the world and wasn't at all interested in her. I'm sure it all looked absolutely absurd, but a man'll do anything for his daughter." Pappy winked at Betsey again.

"I think in her mind, she was playing with me. But I was all business. She let me get to within a few feet of her, and just as I was thinking I had a shot at being my little girl's hero, Star quit chewing and gave me that same look. I knew she was about to bounce away again, so I sprung first. No luck. I was of course no match for a goat *designed* to evade predators... all of which are much faster than me." Pappy laughed at himself again.

"Anyone who grew up on a farm would have known that... so, there I was, acting like a real noob again. I even remember thinking it was embarrassing enough in front of Nana and the kids... and I was grateful that nobody else was watching." Pappy winked. "Or so I thought."

"Then, suddenly, Star seemed like she was bored and done playing with me, and she started covering a lot of ground quickly... bound-loping toward the fire-road where my property met Danny's. Well, let's just say I was *triggered*, and I was going to get that little goat if it killed me. I took off running after her, naively confident that my stride could outmatch her bouncing. As I sprinted, I felt like one of those cartoon characters whose feet circle their ears when they run in high gear – like the RoadRunner, or something. I could hear Andy yelling, *Get 'er Daddy, get 'er!'* My legs were getting ripped to shreds by the thistle, and it seemed I was tripping on every stump along the way. I mean, I'm sure I looked completely possessed... arms and legs flailing, charging through prickers, all cut up and tripping while chasing a tiny white goat with a pink collar that was easily eluding me."

"Star loped along, right off our property, across the fire-cut, and onto Danny's farm. Now, I didn't ever dare cross that property line, since I was pretty sure I'd have been shot... literally. But, in that moment, I just didn't care! I didn't break speed at all, and I was in full stride in my flip-flopped-Colorado-hippie-dippie outfit when I started crossing that road. Then, suddenly, I was stopped-still by something I sensed to my right."

"In that same moment, the daddy-care possession left me, my senses returned, and I remembered it was Saturday. Now on Saturdays, Danny and his dad, Mark, liked to ride around on their road shooting stuff. With humiliated horror, I realized it was them I had sensed, and I instantly knew the entire scene had been fantastic entertainment for them."

Pappy shook his head with the memory while he let everyone absorb the scene. "Now, in all my efforts to get along with the mountain neighbors around our property, there were two relationships most important to me. And they'd just witnessed something for which I'm sure they had no framework for understanding. It would have been all the same to them had they seen me skip across our pasture wearing nothing but a glitter bikini."

"Well, I just stood there flat-footed for a long second before turning to face the shame. I realized there was nothing I could say that would offset the narrative they'd already formed. Like I said earlier, mountain-men communicated mostly with their eyes. So, I decided to not say a word, and just take whatever abuse they were going to delight in dishing out. I rotated toward them, and steeled myself. Sure enough, there was Mark behind the wheel of their huge side-by-side. Danny was sitting beside him, literally riding shotgun. He had the butt of his twelve-gauge propped on the top of one muddy boot, with the other extended out over the hood. They were both casually reclined as if they were watching TV on their couch in their living room. They were of course in uniform, and I noticed both Danny's jeans and his filthy-white t-shirt had a fair amount of blood splattered on them, likely from something they'd just shot. Their faces were expressionless, except their eyes, which were clearly viewing me as an idgit!"

"In that lingering glance, *so* much was said! They knew they were in the power position, and were absolutely loving it. Since I was standing on their road, I knew I risked a fight if I didn't look away first, so I did. After all, small things back there turned into fights… and sometimes those fights turned into multi-generational feuds! I mean, these were the men who'd shot and killed three of my dogs, blown up my neighbor's house because they didn't like him, and Mark had apparently even shot his neighbor in the leg over something trivial right before we'd moved in. I looked down at my flip-flopped feet and thistle-shredded legs. Having looked away first, the power-play bit was over. So, with my last ounce of pride, I looked back up at them to take whatever thumping was about to be doled out."

"Mark took a long swig from his can of cheap beer, then spat his heavy wad of chewing tobacco over onto my property. He looked at me and said,

'Bet'chur huntin' a goat ain'tcha?'

Danny was looking at me with a stare I couldn't quite qualify the meaning of, but for which I had a pretty good sense. He held his gaze for a long moment, challenging me to respond. Well, I was at a loss, and he knew it. With a wry smile, he slowly turned to his dad and said,

'Goat chathynk? Heyll, I don*thinc*so. 't'seems arnew nayberhere is inta chasin' migit unicorns!'"

"Well, Mark thought that was just hilarious, and about choked on the new wad of chewing tobacco he'd loaded, while some spittle escaped the corner of his mouth and dripped onto his shirt. While he wiped his chin, Danny recovered from his own guffawing. As their mocking laughter tapered, they must have decided their afternoon's entertainment had ended, so Mark fired up the side-by-side and put it into gear. I stepped aside, pretty sure they'd run me over if I didn't. Mark emptied his beer can, chucked it over onto my property, and mashed the accelerator. As the machine lurched into motion, Danny lifted the butt of the shotgun off his boot and swept the business end of it past me, then laid it across his lap. They rolled on past, laughing and punch-shoving each other like a couple of ten-year-old boys." Pappy paused and laughed with everyone else at the story, which just seemed beyond belief.

"Well, I was used to feeling a little out of my element... but not like that! That experience of being mocked directly to my face was a first for me. And it was a great lesson, too. Those men didn't know me, and I didn't know them either. From that moment on, no matter how much I didn't understand the actions, thoughts, or convictions of another person, I'd always try to *see* them, and be kind, you know? It's probably good to add that over time I became pretty good friends with both Danny and Mark. Wild, huh?" Pappy smiled.

McLean spoke up for all the kids, "What about *Star*?"

Pappy's eyes lit up as he was reminded of how the whole story wrapped up. "Well, it's actually a fun and happy ending! I stood on the road for a minute more looking for Star, but couldn't see her anywhere. And you can imagine, I wasn't too interested in walking onto Danny's property, knowing he and his dad were close by with their guns, and would have probably had a good time making me dance. So, I made the walk of shame back to the family, and explained that Star had gotten away. I was relieved to find out that nobody had seen me interacting with Danny and Mark. I don't know if my pride could have taken another blow that day. It was tough. We were all sad, and the whole thing made us feel like farmer-failures. But fortunately, Betsey seemed to take it ok rather than fall apart. Nana and I explained that Star would likely be very happy out in the woods living on her own, though we both believed it was more likely she would be a meal that night for one of the many hungry wild dogs that roamed the area."

"Then we all turned our attention to Diablo." Pappy chuckled. "He obviously had a sense something bad had happened, and was standing in his cage calmly, looking as nervous as a cat in a room full of rocking chairs! Calm didn't last long though. Just as soon as we got him into his pen, he started shredding the fencing with his horns. So, my afternoon quickly shifted to trying to keep him from getting out, and then farm-life just sort of went on that day. After trying to deal with Diablo for a few months, and having nothing but lots of trouble, we gave him to a local farmer who said he could handle him."

"Several years later, Mumsie sent me an article from the local paper... and yes, this was during the time when folks still got a lot of their news that way." Pappy looked at the kids, who were fond of always calling him old-fashioned. "The article was about two tiny goats that were living in the wild on Lookout Mountain! Sure enough, one was a white nanny, and one was black billy. They'd apparently been thriving on the rocky ledges of the north face where they could avoid predators! Someone had snapped a photo of them, and that photo was in the article."

"I showed it to Nana and the kids, and we were slack-jawed! The picture was black and white, but we could see the white goat was wearing a collar, and the picture even highlighted what we knew was Star's deformed unihorn! And Diablo, the little Houdini he was, must have somehow escaped from the farmer and reunited with Star!"

Andy and Betsey reacted to the memory with warm smiles.

"I remember that!" Said Betsey. "That made me feel so good to see that picture!"

Pappy could tell that story had been a fun ride for the family, and he smiled with satisfaction. "How was that one?" Pappy asked, as he looked at Jenny. She smiled back, and before she could answer, McLean practically shouted,

"I want a mini unicorn!"

Pappy laughed and said he'd see what he could do about that.

CHAPTER FIFTEEN

CRACKING OPEN

Pappy took another long sip from his cup, then paused for a few moments. "I haven't told that one in ages… funny stuff. There were so many memories made, so many lessons learned. I could prattle for days and still not do the season justice. Even with all its challenges – which we're about to get into – I never had any regrets. It was such a rich time… and in so many ways, it shaped the fate of this family."

"Now, I know all this was kicked off by an interest in how I went from an angry guy who killed things he loved just because he was a little upset, to… well, whatever I am now. It has been fun for me to take this trip down the lane of memories, and I'm glad we put some color on the sketch, because now you have a lot more than just the general context for what comes next… the meat of the story. All the things that happened along the way were important parts."

"And that's the way it is with pretty much everyone else's journey too. I mean, the businessperson who seems to be an overnight success was usually about twenty years in the making. The wise woman gleaned her insights over many years, and after living through high highs and low lows." Pappy paused. "Everything counts. But now it's time to get to get to McLean's question directly… to talk about the stage of acute change in my life."

Pappy drew in a deep breath and slowly let it back out while he looked around at us, the pain of the memories he was about to share from long ago evident in his eyes.

"While so much great stuff was going on all around me, I still felt malnourished, like that stray dog, in the way that mattered most to me. During that whole season, the unfortunate reality was that I was being swept along in an undercurrent of fear. I think I was ultimately afraid 'The More' might not be available... that with all my effort to connect with God in a way I desperately wanted to believe was possible, that perhaps I was just chasing a false hope. I carried a profound sadness and frustration, even anger. Even when circumstances were so good, I just couldn't shake off those emotions. And to make it all worse, I beat myself up for it... I *believed* I could have more peace, and so I wondered where I was failing God, myself, and those I loved."

"Folks who've heard this story over the years have told me I was blind to all the ways that God was so obviously showing profound love for me. And that's not really true. I wasn't blind to all the beauty and grace. Not at all. But that's sort of the point. I knew The More ultimately didn't have anything to do with circumstances, good or bad. I mean, that's a timeless truth that I'd always been well-aware of... that putting hope in circumstances, whether present or future, is a sucker's game. I was yearning for something that I knew transcended, and at the same time undergirded, any circumstances. I certainly wasn't blind to all the 'God winks', as Nana used to call the good things in our lives. But I just couldn't connect with the Wellspring flowing through it all... a sense of oneness with the All-In-All that I knew was possible. Instead, the monsters of fear and anxiety seemed to be tightening their cold, bony talons around my heart. For me, the good was pretty much drained of its color without a sense of intimacy with the Source of all the good."

"I was doing everything I knew to do in an effort to be faithful to God and, cultivate that relationship. Because, like I've said, I thought the 'abundant life' – meaning a beautiful spirit, peace, and contentment, and all that – would come as a function of that path. But it just hadn't, and by that point I had no reason to think anything would change. With all I'd experienced, the reality was that I was the same anxious, sad, mad… hard… man. I was starting to realize that the religious approach I'd put my hope in as a path to intimacy with God was failing me, and that was unnerving."

Pappy picked up the second-to-last of the journals and flipped a couple of pages into it. He seemed frustrated with his inability to put his experience into words accurately. "It was a lonely experience, and it's lonely in the retelling of it too. I think you have to experience this kind of suffering to understand it. That's the way it is with any type of pain, I guess. It's one of the great joys of my life to know none of you have had to endure this particular type, even while I know there has been plenty of sufferings of many types amongst us over the years." Pappy paused and looked at our large family. His gaze seemed to acknowledge each of us, and all of us, at the same time. "But even with your individual challenges, it has brought me a lot of comfort to know you've been able to see through the veil more than I was able to in my much younger years."

"Worship through music had always been special to me. And an acoustic version of a song was released around that time called *Oceans*, by a band named Hillsong United. I remember when I heard it for the first time, I thought, '*This* is a dangerous song!'. It was this beautiful prayer in which the singer was pleading with God to take her where faith would be tested to the utmost, where 'feet will fail'… and to then find Him in the *mystery*. Now, that was a hard-core concept for me, since I had a pretty well-defined understanding of what God was and how He'd show up. So, the idea of letting go of any expectations and qualifiers threatened the very way I understood and tried to relate to God, and I believed it was dangerous to potentially open myself to evil influences. It felt really risky."

"I related to God through a well-developed system of theology, and so I had Him in a neat little box that I could wrap my head around. And, I came to realize over the years that even with the best of intentions, that box was keeping me from experiencing God the way God can be most fully experienced – expansively, without borders! Frankly, I don't know why I wanted to worship a God who I could understand. It seems sort of arrogant looking back on it. But my heart was right. I'd been taught, and had accepted, that the approach I was using was the *right* way – that theological looseness was *dangerous*! So, for me to be willing to accept God through, and even as, mystery, and then to be willing to go wherever that sense of Him might take me, was a *real* stretch."

"The reality of that proposition meant I'd have to be willing to lay down the very bedrock of my existence – Christianity, as I understood it at the time! I know now that was a big part of the issue… religion had become my idol, and was keeping me from experiencing God. But I obviously didn't know that then. I was doing all the 'right things', and yet my soul was at a point where I had to admit that approach had failed me. That was hard and unsettling, but it felt kind of exciting too."

"I felt a strong call in that song! I listened to it over and over, and the more I did, the more my heart resonated with it. Once I had the words memorized, I'd sing along with all the earnestness I could muster… and so I prayed that prayer *so* many times. As I prayed, I could feel my heart pushing against its comfortable, albeit rigid, boundaries. But I was a seeker, and I wasn't going to turn away from the quest for soul satisfaction, no matter the cost!"

Pappy's face became serious and pensive. "I was of course still studying the Bible and praying a lot. And what I kept coming back to was this concept of 'knowing God'. It was something I just couldn't relate to, since the version of Christianity I had been taught only gave this a lot of lip service, but didn't really hold up the kind of knowing I was reading about as being of paramount importance… knowing God was to be accomplished through right thinking and various disciplines, and that approach might satisfy the head, but risks leaving the heart unsettled."

"As best I could tell from reading interpretations of Jesus' teachings in the Aramaic language he spoke, 'knowing' God meant something intimate and all-consuming… like this sense of intimacy so profound that one feels they're in union with God. And that idea felt like heresy to me. But, I was haunted enough by my lack of that experience that I had to open myself to the possibility that there was more, that maybe I'd had it wrong. I knew I was like one of the 'whitewashed tombs' Jesus spoke about. I worked hard at being good, doing good, and looking good. But inside, I felt dead. And I sensed Jesus whispering in my ear to push in deeper, to venture where my faith would be tested, to keep seeking. At the same time, I wondered if that whisper was a demon leading me astray." Pappy shook his head slowly.

"So, I doubled down on time in scripture, praying and studying, all in a completely committed effort to 'know God'… but this time with the added dimension of trying to surrender to the mystery." Pappy laughed gently, and added, "It's funny… trying to surrender to mystery while you're studying. The two approaches aren't mutually exclusive, but they're close!"

"Anyhow, around that time, I also started a little project. I searched for examples of folks who were expressing what I believed was possible for someone who knew God the way I was starting to believe the Bible spoke about… Christians who sensed a profound intimacy with God, who had authentic love and peace welling up in their very being which poured out of them effortlessly." Pappy paused and smiled.

"The person who came closest was your Nana. During that time on the farm, she was the most content and peaceful person I knew because of her spirit of surrender and trust. She was smart, and had an informed spirituality that was generally grounded in evangelical Christianity, though she didn't take the religious aspect of it, or any particular system of theology, as seriously as I did. But just before moving to the farm, she'd gone through a tough season as a young mom with two particularly needy toddlers. I'd always known her to be a content, happy-go-lucky person by nature, but she'd developed quite a bit of anxiety during that time and was feeling really weighed down by the burdens of that season. But after a Bible study with some women called 'No Other Gods', she just completely let it all go. I know now that she took the crucial leap of surrendering to the mystery of it all and chose to trust that which was beyond her... which she certainly understood as the Christian God. And right after she did, she settled into a deep place of peace, freedom and trust which stayed with her forever after that. I think there were some important lessons I could've learned from her example, if I'd had the eyes to see. But I guess I wasn't ready for them yet." Pappy held space for a few moments for our collective, beautiful memories of Nana to linger.

"While she was no small exception, and while I'm now quite certain there were others who were very content in their evangelical Christianity, God just wasn't bringing them to my awareness at that time. Now, please don't get me wrong. There were a lot of nice people who loved God and who were kind, gracious, and generous. And you've even heard stories tonight of some beautiful interactions with some special people who took their faith very seriously. But, as I'd have a chance to get to know them, I'd find they were typically suffering meaningfully in various ways. And the root of that suffering always seemed to be their theology which insisted they understand themselves as sinners who disappointed God. There was a common insistence on sticking with the idea of original sin, being a disappointment to God, and living in a fallen world. And that insistence was crucial for them, because elevating those ideas made Jesus' sacrifice on the cross seem bigger. The humility in that posture had a patina of beauty, but a tragic undertone. Even John had related to God that way."

"And the reality was that I'd subscribed to those same ideas all my life, too. But as I opened myself to new ways of thinking and reading the Bible, it seemed Jesus was calling us all to something very different... something fragrant! This is what I was referencing earlier. He called it 'life in the Kingdom', and that's about all he ever preached about... rarely about his death or coming to die for us for our sins, or stuff like that. He spent a lot of his time talking about a peace and joy that would transcend understanding, if we'd just choose to let ourselves see it. In fact, he even told his disciples to go out and preach the good news of the kingdom of God, then report back to him. I mean, he was still alive, and in the Good News they were go preach, there was no mention of his death on the cross or a sacrifice for our sins. Now I don't want to diminish his death, and all it might have meant. But, eventually, there was no doubt in my mind that he was most interested in a way of living rather than beliefs about his dying."

"And since a very specific understanding about my sinfulness and his death had been such a foundational part of my theology, I started allowing doubt about *everything* in. It was just a little at first, since I was too afraid to let it all go yet. But, since I was realizing my earnest seeking over many years had led me no closer to what I knew was possible, I was increasingly comfortable with the paradigm of mystery. My understanding of God as something separate from and outside of me remained, but my convictions about how to relate to that 'Other' were loosening meaningfully."

"At that point, my studies and prayers had drifted outside the box I'd always stayed in. And I realized that in our modern translations of the Bible, we often use the word 'repent', which most folk are taught to interpret as meaning 'say you're sorry and change your ways'. But that's not particularly faithful to the meaning of the original language. A better translation is arguably to 'change one's mind', or to 'choose to see differently'. And so, then I started thinking that perhaps Christianity wasn't really so much about saying sorry and then believing a certain story about Jesus. It seemed increasingly clear to me that he was talking about seeing differently, and then allowing a profound transformation to take place in one's experience with life."

"And there was something else happening while I looked for examples of folks who seemed to have a connection with The More, but in my religious self-righteousness I didn't see it as a good thing at the time. A lot of the examples of folks who *did* seem authentically content, joyful, and at peace were people from outside any Christian community. In particular, they were often a part of the yoga community. And, add to that my experience with one of the carpenters I worked with every day for hours. I mentioned him earlier. Lavoit was one of the most selfless, loving, kind, joyful, and at peace people I've met to this day. And he was very committed to a religious tradition that most Christians I knew back then would call a heresy."

"There is a whole lot more to all of this that I don't want to get into here. I'll just say that during that time I think my prayer was being answered, and I actually was falling into Mystery. I was starting to open to the idea that perhaps I'd misunderstood everything for all those years, and that was a really hard thing to allow myself to realize. Something fundamental was shifting, though, and I was more open to following God in a different way than ever before."

"I increasingly allowed myself to deal with challenging questions about my theology with intellectual and heartfelt curiosity, rather than with a defensive posture. And that was hard, since it was like the sands of my faith were being pulled out to the vastness of the ocean with each wave of thought that challenged what I held as true. Over time, I couldn't avoid the fact that there were just so many different seemingly legitimate takes on religion and theology – and all from folks who *sincerely* loved God. And that was just within Christianity!"

"What really baked my noodle was reading things like the Tao Te Ching, Bhagavad Gita, and even Jesus' teachings on the Lord's prayer in his native tongue of Aramaic! And I quickly realized there is so much beauty to find in *all* the religious traditions. The old rigid answers I'd always subscribed to just weren't holding up for me anymore." Pappy shook his head, then let out a long sigh. He smiled at the children, most of whom had fallen asleep while burrowed under warm blankets near the fire.

"Maybe I should get a little more granular. During that time, there were lots of hard punches landing on one of my *core* beliefs, in particular. I'd always held firmly to the absolute truth of the Bible as the inerrant Word of God, and that it was to be interpreted literally. But I eventually found myself appreciating the Bible more as metaphor and allegory than as something to be interpreted word for word. I did believe it was infallible – that the truths I could glean from the ancient, sacred text would never fail me. But I was letting go of my old, rigid approach to it. And that made it more alive to me, and I *so* enjoyed the new understandings that flowed from that approach! I continued following my heart, and my old paradigm started crumbling at an accelerating pace… and faster than I was comfortable with!"

"I kept leaning in, prayerfully following promptings, trusting I'd have clarity in time. But I was increasingly unmoored, and was losing a sense of self that was important to me. That was spooky. But it was like the more I was willing to open myself to new ideas, legitimate and challenging considerations kept presenting themselves to my awareness. Other specific examples are thoughts about the lost years of Jesus' life, the Nag Hammadi library and Gnostic Gospels, Paul's Gospel vs. Jesus' Gospel, and all sorts of things like that which started me down a path that my Christian friends consistently warned me about whenever I'd try to bring up the topics for discussion. Importantly, Nana was very concerned I was being led astray from the faith we both held so dear. And I understood her concerns, but I felt I was being pulled along… led… and I didn't want to stop."

"And one of the main considerations that pushed me to keep following the breadcrumbs were the stories of the earliest followers of Jesus. I mean, wow! What an alive… *something*! It sure wasn't religion that guided them, since Christianity didn't even exist at that point. As I understood it, those folks just followed something called 'The Way'. And their experience was so different from what I'd ever experienced, or even heard about, in our culture. They seemed to be a huge crew who intimately knew God, and clearly had the peace I yearned for. The experiences of theirs that I read about were nothing short of incredible! They endured all kinds of hardships *willingly*… and for something they'd *experienced*! They lived with a profound sense of community, and were so committed to a loving way of being that they just didn't care about possessions, or their own lives, or anything earthly!"

Pappy shrugged, then paused. Andy took the opportunity of that moment to grab a couple more logs and throw them on the fire. The chill of the early morning mountain air was setting in, so several of us scooched closer to the pit while Andy stoked the fire with a large iron poker. Pappy smiled appreciatively at his son, and continued.

"Around that same time, I read John Foxe's *Book of Martyrs*. It offered so many stories of men, women, and children who willingly died for their relationship with God... and often in horrible ways. They were dying because they claimed something akin to knowing God intimately... a message the religious and political powers of the time felt compelled to shut down."

Pappy looked around at us. "What did those people have that allowed them to be so at peace with the kinds of horrible deaths they died? All I knew was that it was different from what I had. And their mysterious experiences spurred me on, since they strongly suggested that what I yearned for was possible."

The next morning, after he was gone, we understood a little better why Pappy had pressed the points. All the man had ever seemed to care about since any of us had known him was to help people come into an awareness of who and what they are 'in Christ', as he would say. And he obviously believed some high-level introduction to some of the considerations he had wrestled with as a younger man might serve us.

"*That* was the kind of faith and experience of God I wanted... that I *needed*. It was the kind of experience that I wasn't going to settle for less than." Pappy smiled. "And I believed with all my heart that kind of knowing was still possible in modern times. Those brothers and sisters from long ago presented an example of what I'd been yearning for all my life."

"My tradition within Christianity spoke a lot about 'knowing God', but then people shied away from ever claiming that kind of knowing for themselves! And that never made any sense to me. A well-respected Presbyterian pastor in our community even *warned me away* from the kind of knowing I told him I was seeking! He actually said it was *heresy* – that it was rooted in a heretical tradition called Gnosticism. And he pointed out that one could find plenty of examples of modern Christian martyrs who held to the core doctrines of the evangelical church and had died for their beliefs. Now, he didn't say all that in a mean way. And, sure, even during that time when my deconstruction was beginning, and like most Christians I knew, I'd never have 'denied the faith' either – meaning I'd not have denied my understanding of Christianity. But, when I was honest with myself, that commitment was rooted more in a fear of going to hell, or a stubborn unwillingness to let go of religious head-knowledge, than because I felt intimately connected to God. So, the next step logically for me was to consider whether my theology and religion was actually *preventing* me from accessing the kind of relationship with God that the early Christians enjoyed. I felt like that was a fair consideration. But it scared me. So, further into the rabbit hole of mystery I went."

Pappy flipped a few pages further and continued. "I got to a point where I needed to pursue connection with no distractions. That meant I'd need to get away from all the busyness on the farm, and I said as much to Nana. Even while so many of the new things I was wrestling with were intriguing, at the time I was more hurt and scared since I knew my bedrock was cratering. Jesus said you can't put new wine in old wineskins because they'd burst. And I know now that's what was happening. My old ways of being and understanding just couldn't have handled what I was yearning for, so I couldn't receive at that point. But it was excruciating to let go and 'be a leaf', since those old wineskins were a big part of who I believed I was. And I still had a niggling concern that moving further down that path that seemed to lead away from all I'd always held dear was unfaithful. It didn't help that Nana and others who loved and cared for me continued to warn me with increasing earnestness. I was moving toward serious depression."

"Your Nana loved me immensely, and I *always* felt that. And, selfishly, I wanted her with me in my pursuit and suffering. I wanted to have *anyone* in it with me, for that matter. But that just wasn't my lot. As for Nana, she was fulfilled spiritually, and just didn't see my questioning as necessary. My other friends who I'd try to talk with would just warn me that I was going down a dangerous path that they didn't want to entertain at all. And, in fairness, when I'd start bringing this stuff up and try to wrestle it out with others, I wasn't a lot of fun to be around. I didn't want to disrupt other folks' faith, and I did understand and appreciate their avoidance of the stuff I'd bring up, since it was out of their commitment to God that they did so. What made that season so much harder for me and Nana was that because of the contrast of our spiritual seasons, we just weren't riffing with each other like we always had... and that hurt both of us on a deep level."

"But, out of her great love for me..." Pappy paused and smiled. "... and maybe because she needed a break from me... she suggested I take a road trip out to Colorado and spend some time alone in the wilderness. Well, she didn't have to suggest it twice! I wrapped up some loose ends at the farm, loaded up the truck, and within a few days I was deep in the Colorado backcountry. I ended up right here in this valley... just camping, fasting, reading, journaling, and praying."

"Well, the only thing I experienced during all those hours on the road and in the backcountry was silence. I felt absolutely *no* connection with God. I spent about four or five days back there, and finally decided God just wasn't going to offer me anything. So, I decided to break camp and head home where there was a lot of work that needed to be done. As I was rolling out of Buena Vista, I reached out to a few old friends in Denver to see if they wanted to visit for a bit. One buddy, Ellis, said he could grab some lunch with me. Two other buddies, Dean and Scott, told me to swing by Dean's house after lunch, and that Scott would head over and we'd visit for a bit there."

"After catching up over lunch for a while with Ellis, he asked what I was doing out in Colorado. We were good enough friends that I explained a little of the context. I told him that things were going well back at the farm in so many ways, but that I was really struggling spiritually. He cared, and knew how important that was for me. Ellis wasn't a Christian, and certainly wasn't religious. He actually wasn't even all that spiritual. So, I'd have considered him an unlikely person to help me as much as he was about to."

"He suggested I read a book called *The Power of Now* by a guy named Eckhart Tolle. I'd heard of the author, and I knew he was associated with what I used to consider a dangerous movement called 'The New Age'. Ellis said he had the audiobook and that I could take it with me for the trip back. Well, I didn't want to be rude, so I accepted the offer. But honestly, I had zero intention of actually listening to it, since I'd been indoctrinated with the belief that a faithful Christian would avoid teachings like that."

"But what was a little interesting to me was that I'd watched Ellis transform from a really aggressive and disliked-but-successful businessman to a softer person who was increasingly at peace and loved by those around him. What was happening in him was completely outside any work of God that I understood as possible, and that was really confusing and attractive all at the same time. If he thought the teachings of Tolle would help, then that testimony carried some weight for me. So, we went over to his house after lunch, and he gave me the set of CDs to listen to. That was it for my time with Ellis... but what an impact his suggestion would ultimately have!"

"Then I headed over to see Dean and Scott, and it was great catching up with them. They'd been good friends to me, even with all the abrupt changes I'd made when I left for the farm. And during our visit, they also brought something to my awareness that I hadn't heard of. I'd shared briefly about where I was spiritually and emotionally, and though they didn't struggle with any of that stuff the way I did, they did care. And they strongly suggested I look into working with my mindset. Basically, they encouraged me to start looking into some non-religious neuro-training modalities that would help me shift my process onto a more positive track."

"Now, they didn't suggest that doing so would be a silver bullet for my pain, but they could easily discern that I was operating mostly from a place of anxiety, fear, and lack of contentment with 'what was', and they wanted to help. So, I listened, and felt their concern for me. But I ultimately filed their suggestions away, and didn't give them too much thought, since what they were offering wasn't overtly Christian. It still amazes me to know that even while my religious foundation was crumbling, I was still trying to hold onto it!"

"Anyhow, the importance of that suggestion wasn't to be realized for a while longer, but they'd planted a significant seed. So, after a while we said our 'see you laters', and I hit the road. I had really missed those guys, and so I really enjoyed that visit. And, I didn't realize it then, but the reality was that even though I hadn't met God alone in the wilderness, He'd just met me on that trip through my old community of friends!"

"For five or six hours in the car heading east, I was barking at God. I was angry and frustrated that He seemed so distant, and I was saying as much in no uncertain terms. At one point, I even lifted both hands off the steering wheel and raised two fists to the sky. Then I let go of a nasty series of expletives… and flicked Him off. I actually gave God the double-bird!" Pappy laughed. "The way I was behaving made me wonder if a lightning bolt might strike me dead right then and there. On that drive, somewhere in Kansas, I acknowledged that what I claimed with my religious beliefs seemed unable to affect any real change in my life. I realized everything I'd built my life on seemed created more by man than inspired by God. And it felt freeing to finally and fully admit that to myself."

"But those admissions were just the opener for the real doozies soon to follow. As I drove along, I continued to reflect on my whole worldview and each of its constituent parts. Then I suddenly realized something that rocked me hard… something core. The way I saw it, I'd endured tremendous soul-suffering because of the way I'd received and internalized the Christian message. I almost mentioned this a while ago, but held off on addressing it then." Pappy paused, seemingly unsure about how candid to be.

"This bit is sensitive, and I'm reluctant to share it even now. But it's such an important part of my story that I have to if I'm going to keep this honest and transparent."

"My theology certainly declared that God loved me… no doubt about that. But there was a critical component to the bigger picture of what I believed that I just hadn't ever considered before. And that was that I'd always understood God's *acceptance* of me was *conditional*." Pappy's eyes welled up with tears. "And that hurt to realize. But there it was… and I had to wrestle with it."

"You see, the way I used to believe insisted that folks profess belief in specific understandings about sin, Jesus, and his death in order to be accepted by God. The good news was that if you did, then you were 'in the fold' and would have eternal life with Him in heaven. But, if you didn't… well, then you'd be separated from God for eternity… and not in a great place. I hadn't ever framed that message as anything but a choice everyone must make – a choice offered to everyone out of God's great love for all people… a loving offer which folks could receive or reject. But, when I reframed it, I couldn't help but seeing it *so* differently."

Another breeze flowed through the valley, this one stronger than the others. The flames in the firepit danced in the wind while we zipped up coats and pulled blankets around ourselves a little tighter.

"You see, I think even more than I wanted to feel God's love, I wanted to know I was *unconditionally accepted*. And I think all people share that as a fundamental yearning! So, suddenly thinking of God's acceptance of me as conditional was devastating, even if it was considered a choice. But what kind of a choice is it when the threat of something as serious as hell is presented as the consequence of not choosing as God insists you must in order to be accepted? I suddenly realized how much of my pain and suffering was rooted in that whole idea. If God, who I believed was love, had such a conditional conviction about His acceptance of me, how much less could I trust the absolute acceptance of the humans in my life – even Nana's? I realized that so many of the walls I'd built in so many areas of my life were because I didn't have a core belief that I was acceptable unless I did the right things." Pappy was clearly upset, and he shifted in his seat as if to allow the negative energy to run through him.

"What I'd held as a core belief all my life has a fancy name: the penal substitutionary atonement theory. It's still a theory that many folks believe in as absolute truth. I'd even studied it in seminary, and had learned how to defend it as a crucial element of the faith. But amazingly, it wasn't until many years later that I came to learn it was only that – a *theory*. A guy named Anselm of Canterbury came up with it in the early 1000s to try to make sense of Jesus' death in the context of his culture coupled with the words in the Bible. Well, the church adopted the theory more and more over the years for a host of reasons, though apparently certain factions embraced it more than others. And the tradition I grew up in certainly held that theory as one of its core dogmas, and if you didn't believe in it then they'd likely have said you weren't a Christian. So, all the realization I was suddenly coming into was very threatening to my sense of self since I still claimed to be a Christian and I thought that atonement theory was foundational."

"And I'll add this, since I'm on a little roll. It wasn't *just* my sudden understanding of God's acceptance as conditional that rocked me. There was more to it! The way I'd always believed, God couldn't just let the person who didn't believe the specific narrative about Jesus die, and let that be that! No. God's righteous justice called for that person - His own child, as the Bible calls all people - to be ruthlessly tortured for all eternity."

"Well, all of the sudden I was really concerned, since I knew I'd been led past the point of no return, and the floodgates felt like they'd been thrown open. I had to admit to myself that I didn't *want* to follow a God whose acceptance was conditional… much less one who had such a wrathful temperament toward those who didn't make the 'right' choice."

"But I also still believed the consequences of putting all those beliefs down were *huge*! I was torn between two paradigms, and suddenly a real terror started to set in… a fear that made any concerns I had about circumstances seem trivial. It was one thing for me to start realizing some of this stuff for myself, but what would it mean for our marriage when so much of that precious relationship was built on our shared faith? Then there was the consideration of how any rejection of my religion or theology might negatively impact our family and sense of community. Even more, what of the state of my eternal soul? And Nana's and the kids? The stress was becoming unbearable on multiple fronts, and I so wanted to shove that line of thinking away and stay cozied up in my familiar old beliefs."

"But something seismic had shifted. The nut had cracked, and I knew I wasn't going to be able to take comfort in those old ways of thinking anymore. But at the same time, I wasn't willing to let it all go just yet. I was terrified. And the stakes seemed too high to take that kind of trust fall."

"As I drove along, I wasn't angry anymore. I was just exhausted, completely overwhelmed by the new considerations that had flooded into my awareness during that time in the truck. After a while, I felt a nudge toward the set of CDs Ellis had given me, which were lying on the floorboard where I'd tossed them. I initially tried to shove the inspiration to listen away, but I just couldn't shake the prompting. On the one hand, I believed that opening myself to any alternative teachers like Tolle was risky. But, on the other, I'd just accepted that what I'd always subscribed to wasn't cutting it for me anymore."

"Like I referenced a minute ago, I'd flirted with exploring some ideas about Christianity that were a little outside the box, and had even read some texts of other traditions. But I'd never allowed myself to be taught by any teacher outside of Christianity. I mean, sure, I'd read plenty of other teachers' writings, and was loosely familiar with what was out there. But when I'd read that stuff, it had always been as an apologist with a Biblical worldview looking to poke holes in the author's positions. The prospect of giving Tolle's book an honest listen felt like a pivotal move to me, a decision not to be taken lightly. Even so, I loaded the audio and started listening with an open mind." Pappy laughed at his memory of his first few hours of listening.

"Honestly, I had no idea what he was talking about! It was all so foreign to me, and sounded so 'woo-woo'." Pappy swirled his arms around above his head with a loose motion, and to our amusement. "Even though I didn't understand a lot of what he was saying, I did get the gist… and I thought it was really good. His fundamental thesis was that the present moment is the peace of God. I could riff with that, and could even see how the Bible supported the notion."

"But I also realized that accepting that idea and the framework Tolle built around it would require a significant reframe of how I related to God and all of my *doing* for 'Him'. So, I was threatened and intrigued at the same time. And I kept listening. Tolle went on to say that all that exists is the present moment, and he emphasized that people don't feel at peace because they don't realize that and abide there. Instead, folks are lost in thought about the future and the past, neither of which even exist, *except as thought*! The future is only thought of what might be, and the past is only thought in the form of memory."

"Well, that's pretty simple stuff, but it blew my mind, and I gave some good thought to that idea, in particular, while driving along. Were my thoughts about who God was, and how our relationship should look, keeping me from *really* seeing? Was *I* the one putting conditions on *God*? Was all of my activity sort of 'unconscious' - meaning life was happening while I was lost in thought about what should be, or fears of what might be… and not really trusting God in the moment to moment?"

"I listened to that book straight through *twice* on the rest of that trip! It was like a new path had been set for me… a path on which, in fact, my 'feet would fail'. I'd just have to keep trusting where mystery was leading me. I finally got home and pulled into the drive late one evening, feeling completely refreshed and with the realization the trip had been a success, even if not at all what I'd anticipated."

"I believed that moving forward, I had to meaningfully shift my way of seeking and try a new way of relating with God. And I was excited about that! It turned out I had a long way to go before finding the peace and love I was pursuing."

"That was a weird place to be. My core religious convictions were damaged badly, but I held onto some of them... mostly out of fear, I guess. So, as I fumbled along from that point, I tried hard to just surrender and take the fall... be the leaf. But it was harder to do than it might seem it should have been." Pappy smiled, then quietly hummed the start of a tune.

"I remember playing that *Oceans* song one time when I was feeling in the flow, completely trusting whatever God might have in store for me. I begged Him to overwhelm me, to go ahead and break through whatever shells I had up that I wasn't aware of, no matter the pain. I actually wrote a lot about it here." Pappy flipped through a few pages. "I remember this season so well! And that day, in particular, that song-prayer was *so* meaningful to me... and I sang those lyrics with all my heart, yet again. The reality was that it was the prayer I'd prayed all my life, with *all* my seeking. But for the first time, I was ready... *really* ready... to be taken *anywhere*, so long it was where God wanted to take me. It was a whole new level of surrender, and I claimed the lyrics of that song with a new level of commitment."

Pappy released, then slowly unfolded an old, faded piece of paper that had been clipped to the page he had been reading from. He smiled. "Here are the lyrics. After that day, I carried this piece of paper around with me, ruminating on them intentionally and constantly, until I had them as an ongoing prayer in my heart. Do you want to hear them?" There were smiles and nods around the fire. The energy of the evening had shifted considerably, and this felt like the *real* stuff. Of course we wanted to hear.

Pappy laid out the page carefully in his lap, and began to read. His eyes grew moist and soft tears fell on the paper, smearing the faded ink. It didn't matter. He closed his eyes and continued from memory:

You call me out upon the waters

The great unknown

Where feet may fail

And there I find You in the mystery

In oceans deep
My faith will stand
And I will call upon Your name
And keep my eyes above the waves
When oceans rise
My soul will rest in Your embrace
For I am Yours
You are mine
Your grace abounds in deepest waters
Your sovereign hand
Will be my guide
Where feet may fail and fear surrounds me
You've never failed
And You won't start now
So I will call upon Your name
And keep my eyes above the waves
When oceans rise
My soul will rest in Your embrace
For I am Yours
And You are mine.
Spirit lead me where my trust is without borders
Let me walk upon the waters
Wherever You would call me
Take me deeper than my feet could ever wander
And my faith will be made stronger
In the presence of my savior

I will call upon Your name

Keep my eyes above the waves

My soul will rest in Your embrace

I am Yours

And You are mine

CHAPTER SIXTEEN

DECONSTRUCTION

Pappy paused for a while after reading the lyrics, his posture communicating serenity and pain. The sound of the rushing river rose to meet the silence, and swept us all into a moment of contemplative reflection. He held space for a few seconds more, then opened his eyes and looked around.

"You're kind for allowing me to take this trip. It has been special for me. Reflecting on all this makes me profoundly grateful for the life I've enjoyed, and the freedom I've lived it with since this season from so long ago."

Pappy smiled gently, but it quickly faded. "I wish I could tell you it was all great from this point, but I still had some hard miles to walk. I knew I was serious about my willingness to go to any lengths to find The More, and as you just heard, that prayer opens anyone who offers it to all kinds of possibilities. But the prospect of what might be ahead scared me a bit too, since I was starting to sense, at least in very general terms, what might need to happen." Pappy flipped almost all the way through the journal, and then back to the first few pages.

"Somehow, I intuitively knew I was inviting more deconstruction… and not just about my theology. I sensed I needed to be stripped down… to have things taken away that I wasn't aware were issues, but which must have been prohibiting The More in my life. I had mud on the eyes of my heart, and it turns out that mud was made up of all the things I identified with as 'me'. I just couldn't see who I *truly* was."

"And, interestingly, that was the hard bit… allowing God to show me, to receive that grace. I thought I'd been willing all along, but I really hadn't been. What I ultimately came into an awareness of wouldn't have been in line with what I'd been taught, and chosen to believe, all my life. So, I'd unintentionally been demanding God show up the way I expected Him to. Let's just say that I was finally exhausted by my efforts, and was ready to surrender expectations. But, like I said, I sensed there were more miles to walk, and with that prayer I was telling God I'd walk them, no matter how hard they were. I threw myself wide open to a new paradigm, and it was scary and exhilarating at the same time." Pappy leaned back in his chair.

"I never would have thought the religious framework that undergirded my faith was a big part of my problem. If I'd been told that earlier on, I wouldn't have been ready for it. I'm sure I'd have run away from a message like that – and would have run entirely because of loyalty to God. But it ultimately turned out I had religion and relationship in wrong order. And for my journey, that was a real problem… things had to be reset. It's sort of funny too, because I'd always heard catchy phrases about that all the time in church, 'Jesus wants relationship, not religion!' But it was my religion defined what that relationship should look like, and so I never enjoyed it the way it was meant to be enjoyed.

Pappy paused for a moment to collect his thoughts before continuing. "Religion, in its highest form, is *beautiful*… and I mean *all* religions. If someone is on the path of light and love, then who am I to judge how they got on it, or how they're experiencing it? Well, that's not how I felt back then… but that's what I ended up developing a real conviction about. When religion is being used to usher someone into a relationship with that which is beyond them… call that The One, or Source, or Ground of Being, or God, or whatever… then it's serving its ultimate purpose."

"But back then, I wasn't appreciating religion in its highest form like that, even though I thought I was. I didn't experience God the way my version of Christianity told me I should. So, I naturally assumed I was messing up somehow… and I carried so much sadness for so many years because of that. But there was a lot that needed to be stripped away before I'd be forced to deal with the bedrock of my faith. So, God started working on all the things that had to give before we'd get to that point. And during that challenging extended season, I dutifully tried to keep the framework of my religion standing, even while the sands under the structure were shifting seismically."

Pappy found an entry in his journal. "The letting go happened incrementally, over time. I started asking God to show me how *He* wanted to be related to. And rather than telling me in any sort of dramatic fashion, He just started laying questions gently in my heart. Why did I believe He needed me chirping at Him in *English* in my prayer life? Was there another way? And did He really need me doing *anything* for Him?"

"Did my relationship with Him *really* have to look the way I'd been taught it should?"

"I started thinking that maybe I should stop talking *at* God, and just listen. Maybe it really was as simple as Tolle suggested. Maybe just being present to whatever was, was all there was. Well, that certainly sounds simple enough, but it sure wasn't easy! You'll remember that I'd practiced awareness of being in God's presence while working on the farm… Brother Lawrence's approach in *Practicing the Presence of God.* But that was my only experience with contemplative practice, and I was sensing I was being led to something entirely different. I understood Lawrence's approach as thinking that everything I did was an act of worship to God – *doing* for Him. Tolle, and others who taught stuff similar to him, were encouraging a commitment to *being* present to whatever was, without emphasis on doing."

Pappy read an entry, and then chuckled as he decided to run down a rabbit trail. "When I look back on it, my absolute commitment to my religion kept me from hearing what God was whispering all along. Ironic, isn't it?" Pappy flipped back and forth a few times in the journal, careful not to tear the old paper. "Here's an example…"

"At a yoga retreat with Nana, years before in Telluride, I'd been introduced to the idea of meditation. And we'd both resisted the whole notion, since back then it was generally associated with Eastern traditions like Buddhism. Meditation wasn't in the mainstream then like it is now. In addition, this was back when we were a part of John's group, and so meditation just wasn't something I was open to. I'm confident it would've been frowned upon, and I didn't think I needed it, since I was doing everything I'd been taught a good Christian should. And not opening myself to potentially evil influences was certainly a part of that!"

"But, one time, after a flow class at that retreat in Telluride, the teacher suddenly started leading us into a meditation. Well, I freaked out a bit, even though she was just doing a good job leading a traditional class with a series of poses to get the wiggles out before the seated meditation. But it surprised me, and I felt like I was cheating on Jesus! I didn't want to seem rude and get up and leave the intimate setting, but I sure didn't want to open a door for Satan either!" This was fascinating to all of us, considering what a proponent and practitioner of meditation we'd always known him and Nana to be.

"I looked at Nana, and I could tell she was feeling the same way. I reached over and grabbed her hand and squeezed it three times like we always used to do: *I – Love – You*. We exchanged a glance, acknowledging we were on the same page, and decided to just go with it. We were both feeling God would protect us from anything evil."

"Well, it ended up being a *fascinating* experience for us both! I thoroughly enjoyed it and learned quite a bit about myself! We both did. We spent hours that evening talking about all we'd experienced, and all we believed God had taught us. That was it, though. Even though it had been a really cool experience, I just wasn't ready to do it again out of a sense of faithfulness, and some fear. And looking back on that, I think that's amazing, considering how close it brought me to a sense for the kind of relationship I was yearning for with God. It shows how committed I was to what I thought God wanted and expected of me."

"But that happened years before we were even considering moving to the farm. The point is that I was done with my old approaches and felt I had to try something different… even things that I'd been nervous to try before, and had even shunned. I remembered that experience with meditation, and decided I'd look into it. I thought I'd revisit the 'ten minutes a day' idea, but this time I'd just wait patiently and receive, rather than remain in a state of constant pursuit."

"But the problem with the idea of meditation was that I really didn't know how to do it! I'd only had that one experience, and the teacher had guided us. Other than that, it was a completely unfamiliar and foreign way to try to relate to God. I had no idea there was such a long tradition of meditation in Christianity, and I wasn't about to go looking to learn from a teacher outside of it!"

"In researching Tolle a bit to make sure he wasn't having an evil influence on me, I found out that he'd had an enlightenment experience many years before. Apparently, after his experience, he'd struggled to find words for how to describe it. But then he found the writings of a Christian mystic named Meister Eckhart. And because those teachings had resonated so much with Tolle, he'd changed his name to Eckhart. So, then I began reading some of Meister Eckhart's work. I felt safe enough doing that, since he was Christian, even if a controversial figure. But I was getting over the whole problem of letting my life and experience with God be dictated by what others told me was 'right' or 'wrong' and how to go about it." Pappy paused, allowing powerful emotions to flow through him, presumably stemming from latent frustrations related to group think about who was 'in' and who was 'out'.

"Soon after starting to read his work, a quote struck me: *The eyes through which I see God are the eyes through which God sees me.* Well, that didn't sound like any Christianity I knew! And after reading that, I could understand why the church had gone toe-to-toe with him! I mean, he was effectively claiming to be the same as God, and that wasn't going to fly with me either. So, my guard went up against Tolle too. And that's really too bad… his instruction would have helped me a lot during that season. But, again, I believed I was just being faithful and loyal to God, and I wasn't ready for that line of thinking… yet. I was grateful, though, for the seminal teaching he'd offered in *The Power of Now*, which was to commit to awareness of the present moment. I had at least taken that to heart, and was being changed by the practice of it!"

"Somewhere along the way, I came across a book called *Christian Meditation: Experiencing the Presence of God*, by a guy named Jim Finley. Well, you can imagine how intriguing that title was to me, so I'd kept his book on my reading list. I don't think it ever drifted to the top of the list because, frankly, I hadn't expected much. I'd read plenty of books about experiencing God over the years, but they always ultimately guided me to a sort of intellectual theological framework, and I'd assumed Finley's book would be similar. But when I finally got around to reading it, I realized it was *so* different! And it turned out the timing was perfect… typical of God, isn't it?" Pappy let another rhetorical question float among us. "The type of experience Finley addressed was about just *being with* God – no study or looking for Bible verses to tell me what to think, or how to relate to God… or anything to do, except sit and visit."

"So, I read the book and was fascinated by it, and I decided to start a meditation practice of my own. I felt comfortable about that, since Finley unpacked how rich the history of Christian meditation was. And I believe that single decision to commit to meditation was perhaps the most significant step in my whole journey! The general idea was to be still and open your heart and mind to God's whispers. But it was *really* hard work, and especially since it was hard to specifically discern any immediate and direct benefit from it."

"So, after a few months of feeling like meditation 'wasn't working', I read Finley's book again before quitting. And his words meant more to me on the second pass, because I had some experience with the practice. There was something I read that time that I'd missed on the first pass. He said something along the lines of *meditation is like traveling on airplanes.* You can go up ten thousand times and see the same thing… nothing particularly special… just clouds and sky… feel the turbulence, and all that typical stuff. He reminded me to keep in mind that with my consistent practice, I was still taking the flight, and that doing so was a good thing in and of itself. But he went on to say that if one flies enough, then inevitably they will see the most spectacular sunset… something so beautiful that they just can't make sense of the experience."

"Basically, he was telling me to be patient and kind with myself… and to avoid expectations. Well, that helped me a lot. I needed to just keep trusting the discipline of practice was paying off, whether I could sense it or not. Long story short, over the next many months of sticking with it, I was indeed blessed with some spectacular sunsets. Lots of boring 'flights' too… the majority, actually. But over time, I got so much out of the practice that I can honestly say meditating was the single most important factor in my ultimate transformation!"

"Some of the meditations led to a profound sense of vastness and mystery that was just so… beautiful… so peaceful, and deep. Whatever it was that I was meeting had a sense of holiness to it, and it felt like I was being introduced to something that wanted *me* to be a part of *it.* It's so hard to explain… maybe impossible. But most of what happened during that long season was just a series of little whispers to my soul, and many of those whispers were challenging questions about things I believed. So, trusting the process, I'd look into whatever might have come into my awareness during a practice, and I'd usually end up with an expanded paradigm and worldview. I was being led deeper, and the reality was that the way I'd always related to God was being obliterated."

"I do feel I should say that even though I knew I needed to keep pressing in with meditation, I was also still sort of spooked by the prospect of it. I mean, more than a few of the questions that would come up were of the type I'd always been warned might come from Satan himself... and I was well aware that the 'path to hell is paved with good intentions'. So, every time before I meditated, I'd pray with all my heart that God would not let me be led astray. I explained again and again that I'd follow Him wherever, but I needed to have confidence I wasn't being messed with. Then, I couldn't do anything but trust that if there was ever a prayer He'd honor, it'd be that one!"

Pappy glanced at his journal and seemed to wince a little at what he saw. "I was having an increasingly difficult time enjoying many of the things Nana and I had always enjoyed together – things like studying the Bible, worship, and even Christian community. And that disconnect was so hard for both of us. Again, I'm not going to get into any of that without her around... that's a longstanding promise we had with each other – that we'd not discuss much about our marriage without the other present. But I will say that after a while, she let me know she was concerned for me and the path I seemed to be on. I absolutely understood, and I so appreciated her love and concern for me. But the reality was that I just couldn't turn away from what I believed was the call of my heart... God leading me. I of course wasn't being intentionally callous... farthest thing from it. It's just that I was 'in' at all costs when it came to seeking God and His peace... *The More*. And I carried a lot of heartache over the budding realization that continuing on that path likely meant some sort of very real disconnect with Nana... and potentially Andy and Betsey, too. I couldn't imagine losing our connection, but it *was* happening, and we didn't know what to do about it."

"During that time, John came out for a visit to see what we'd been up to since leaving Colorado. His community was still thriving and had been praying for us all along. He came out to visit because he wanted to report back to them with an eye-witness account. I'd missed John, and it was great having him there. When he first arrived, we caught up for a few hours and we showed him around. He had a chance to see the vision that he and his community were such a significant part of only a few years before… and now with that vision almost completely fulfilled!"

"After a while, a few other friends had come over to meet John and visit, and we eventually found ourselves sitting around the fireplace eating brownies and drinking coffee. John took a moment to speak to our little gathering, and he couldn't have said nicer things. He went on and on about our faithfulness, what good stewards we were, how God was clearly behind the project… and stuff like that. I hadn't shared with him that the path I was on that was leading me away from the kind of orientation to God he was applauding us for."

"Then all of the sudden, his energy shifted. He looked me right in the eyes for a long second, and it got the attention of everyone. It was bizarre. The room sort of went wonky on me again like that day in his apartment, and his voice suddenly had a very different tone. He said with a strong voice, *'Never forget… you are nothing but an unprofitable servant.'"*

"Well, that was about the worst thing I could've heard at that point, considering my struggles to connect with God. Or maybe it was the best thing… depends on perspective, I guess. In retrospect, one could certainly argue it was a reasonable admonishment, or that I might have even misunderstood what he meant. He was quoting Jesus after all. But what I heard was a strong reference to the master | slave relationship, laced with the notion of conditional acceptance that I was really struggling with. That was an important moment, because bright light flooded the dark contrast between the way I'd been relating to God vs. what I knew in my soul was possible… what I was starting to get hints of with my new practices. And after that comment, I wanted to run even harder toward the new. I only saw John once after that time he visited us on the farm, many years later… and it didn't go too well. Let's just say he didn't have much appreciation for the religious changes that'd happened on my journey."

Pappy sighed. "Anyhow, there were lots of things like that over those months, things that wouldn't have been a big deal if my heart had been in a different posture… or if they hadn't happened in such rapid succession. But all together, they were making it really hard for me to hold onto my faith."

"For example, Chris and Courtney were excited to host a traveling minister who they said had a gift of healing. He had come to the mountain for a special service, and the event had been promoted meaningfully. Almost the whole community showed up for healing… lots of folks from all over the mountain. After a while, the minister asked for anyone who specifically needed healing for their heart to come forward. Well, I felt like he was talking right to me, since my heart was hurting more than it ever had at that point. The pain over the prospect of putting down everything you believe in, and have always stood for, is just excruciating. When it comes to religious conviction, no matter how much leaving the old for the new makes sense, it's still really difficult. I'd always believed in free will, but I didn't feel too free to make a choice that felt right for me, since the threat of eternal damnation and torture was hanging over my head."

"So, I marched right up there in front of everyone. I wanted to get a 'touch' from God, and if that minister could deliver it, then I wasn't about to allow that opportunity to pass me by! I walked up the stairs of the stage, then right up to him… and he leaned in close. He asked me what I'd come up for. I had tears rolling down my face when I shared a little about the pain I felt from my sense of separation from God."

Pappy stood up and raised his arms out to mimic the minister. "*'Well, child of God, get ready to feel the release from bondage, in Jesus' name!'* Then smacked his hand against my forehead. Well, I didn't feel anything except his slap… which was *hard*! A few moments went by, and nothing happened. I was saddened, and then sadness turned to agitation. I'd seen plenty of evangelists and healers on TV who did that sort of thing… and after being touched by the holy man, folks would fall and flop around. I'm not saying those aren't legitimate experiences, but it wasn't the case for me that night. I didn't feel or experience *anything*, and I wasn't about to pretend like I did. I just stood there and looked at him with tears still in my eyes while he looked back at me quizzically. As he realized that it seemed nothing was happening with the first person who'd come up on stage, and seemingly to avoid embarrassment, he just turned away from me and addressed the next person who'd come up. I walked off the stage, wounded deeply… not embarrassed at all… just sort of hurt and sad. With a lot of little things like that, I was really starting to throw the hands of my soul up in defeat."

Pappy sat back down and flipped back and forth through the pages. "Wow. These entries hurt to read. I can still feel the pain from that season. I had so many questions…" Pappy scratched his head. "I'd held onto some remnants of my old ways of relating to God. I mean, even habits that aren't helpful still somehow have a strange comforting effect… and those old habits also helped the family dynamics around that time… but, no more. I had lost all interest in Bible studies, singing, going to church on Sunday mornings, participating in Christian community, or anything like that."

"But that didn't mean I'd quit seeking! I started meditating three times every day for twenty minutes each session… and, as y'all know, that's a lot of meditation for a beginner!" Indeed, most in the family had joined Pappy and Nana for meditations over the years. And for those of us who didn't have a consistent practice, it was a really hard exercise.

"I fasted routinely, and I'd even hold all-night prayer vigils begging God to ease the pain I carried… to meet me, let me know I was whole. I'd only use the Bible to let the 'living Word' speak to me, meaning I'd read a passage or two and let the words roll around in my awareness, but without any agenda or theological framework to cram them into."

"Since I'd lost interest in going to church, the whole family decided to take a break from it for a while too… and that's a significant thing for anyone who claims Christianity and is serious about their faith! And, in fairness, we decided to quit going for other reasons too. We were realizing we needed a day of rest each week. The farm life was beautiful and rich, but it was also *a lot* of hard work. Then there was also the fact that after that healing minister's visit, Peace Community had started to fall apart for a host of reasons. That's a really sad story, and there's no reason to get into here. The point is that we just sort of quit on church."

"Interestingly, on those rest days on the farm, I started to vaguely sense God all around on that property. Frankly, I sensed something more beautiful than I ever did in a church, except on very rare occasions. On those days, I wasn't focused on all that needed to get done, and it seemed the property sort of gave back to me... the land and animals *ministered* to me. We'd never taken the Bible's suggestion for a day of rest each week seriously, and it was truly amazing how restorative it was to just pause completely! I don't really know how to explain it... sort of like a day-long meditation retreat, or something. I'd feel such a peaceful resonance with the land and plants and animals. And Nana and I did a lot of yoga on those Sundays too – often after we finished up our huge and leisurely family breakfast."

Pappy winked at Andy and Betsey, to which Betsey smiled and said, "Uh huh... like for *hours*!" Pappy smiled at the memory of those afternoons practicing yoga with Nana.

"Yoga was a practice we both enjoyed, and I think we spent so much time doing it together during that season because it offered our relationship a real connection point. Yoga is fundamentally a practice of union, after all. And the practice allowed me to experience some closeness with both Nana and God, though I don't think I'd have articulated it that way back then. Again, I had no understanding of those Eastern philosophies back then. So, I was just enjoying the time with Nana, and wasn't seeing those afternoons in the yoga studio for what they *really* were. I was just feeling closeness with something... and it felt *right*. You can probably see the theme of those rest days... certainly better than I could back then. Peace was *always* all around me. I just didn't know how to let it in... or better, enter into it. But I was getting a taste... getting closer... and that was enough to keep me pressing."

"Well, even though I felt some sort of soul evolution happening, I still hurt. I was just starting the slog through what was going to be a very dark valley for me. Looking back on it now, I can see that so much of my suffering was rooted in my resistance to what was, judging it as not ok. I just wasn't far enough along my journey to see how much suffering that was creating in my life."

"As I was realizing my religion and faith needed some sort of re-tooling, I also realized another important thing needed to change. I was fed up with the way my thoughts were torturing me. Meditation had helped me be more aware of my thoughts, and I was surprised to realize that they generally weren't friendly. Ever since my visit with Dean and Scott on my way back from Colorado, I was really interested in working with my mindset… and it seemed the time to do that was upon me. So, I spent some serious time trying to observe and understand my 'thought life'."

"I practiced a radical idea at the time… being an *observer* of my thoughts, rather than identifying with them. And over time, I became increasingly aware of the crucial fact that my thoughts aren't me. As the observer, I could watch the thoughts come at me, then choose which ones I wanted to engage with. But there were *lots* of 'em… it seemed my mind never stopped, and evaluating each thought was exhausting. Most of them were toxic and nasty, still rooted in fear… and I beat myself up over that observation because I believed that meant I didn't have enough faith. So, *then* I'd have a whole host of negative thoughts about all of that to deal with! Thought after thought after thought… spiraling ever downward about all kinds of things… it seemed endless! But, you're not beaten until you decide not to get back up. And I kept getting up… over and over and over again."

"Once I saw the pattern of negative thinking, I knew I could change it… and that was so empowering! So, I put a 'closed for revegetation' sign on the old, well-worn fear trail in my brain, and started clearing a new one. I was absolutely dead-set on never going down the old fear trail again… I just wouldn't let myself."

Suddenly, the sound of distressed chickens cut through the quiet of the late evening, and our attention was distracted. Frankie and Leela quickly stood up and sprinted toward the coop while barking aggressively. After only about a minute, both dogs emerged out of the darkness, sauntering toward us with a happy energy. Pappy greeted the duo, and they settled at his feet while he satisfied their desire to be acknowledged for a job well done.

"A dog's life... so simple, isn't it?" Pappy mused while he scratched Leela behind the ears. "Reading all of this, and telling this story, makes me sad for how many years I made things so much harder on myself than they needed to be. The reality is that life's pretty simple for us too, if we let it be. Dogs are great teachers." Pappy gave each of the mutts a couple of loving pats on their backs, then settled back into his chair.

I took a moment to watch the dogs, then looked around at the faces of my family. I felt love for each of them, and was grateful we were all together, sharing the experience of listening to Pappy. Then I focused my attention on the river beyond the crackle of the fire, and was barely able to make out the hooting of a great horned owl in some far-off tree. The moon had waned, so the brilliance of the stars in the night sky was awe inspiring. I looked back at Pappy, and he was smiling, seeming to delight in the moment as much as I was. Then he shifted in his chair and pulled at the thread of thought he had been using to weave the picture of his mental transformation.

"Trying to figure out what kind of new path to make forced me to get real clear about what it should look like, and where it should head. I knew I hated the fear trail, so I just figured I'd create whatever was its opposite. And that's love. And that was it! I realized it was that simple: fear or love... and it was my choice which trail to let my thoughts run on. I decided I was going to filter all thoughts through that simple rubric, and make every effort to make sure my thoughts were on the path of love." Pappy smiled, opened his arms wide, and held up the V-sign with his right hand like the old-modern hippie he was.

"Now, as cool as that clarity was for me, it challenged so much on a practical level. I had to answer the big question about whether I *really* believed God was for me. I mean, fundamentally, that's the ultimate question for all of us."

"I decided that whenever I questioned events or circumstances, I'd choose to trust God was for me, and that everything was part of a plan working in my best interests… in *everyone's* best interests… even while I was less and less sure who the God was that I was trusting in. That was a little strange, because there were lots of Bible verses and teachings about God's faithfulness… how He works all things together for good. But, for whatever reasons I'd never allowed that principle to *really* become a fundamental part of my worldview."

"Well, all that work on my mindset gradually made me even more certain the relationship with God I yearned for was possible, even while I was moving away from my strong religious convictions. You see, as I worked on creating the love path, life just felt better… I felt more connected to, well, *something* beyond me. And a big breakthrough came when I started realizing that maybe the reason I felt so connected was because love is what I was at my core… and that idea… that love was my home frequency… was a game changer."

"I had… and I *wanted*… to start letting in the idea that perhaps I wasn't sinful to my core after all! And letting that particular idea in was a huge blow to my faith, because the concept of original sin was a critical part of the system of theology I subscribed to… and that system was a crucial aspect of how I'd always related to God! I began wondering if I'd either misunderstood all the Christians in my life who spoke about, lived by, and taught the doctrine, or if there was some other disconnect with how I related to it. Regardless, it was time to let it go… and that was terrifying, and yet also refreshing and exhilarating!"

"After a while, I started to think my understanding of that doctrine was so sad… even tragic. Suddenly, my long-held belief of my inherent sinfulness made no sense to me. If fear and sinfulness were my natural states, then wouldn't the path of fear and wrongdoing simply feel better? If I really was sinful to my core, then wouldn't I delight in thinking bad thoughts and doing bad things? Well, I didn't enjoy fear-based thinking or actions that stemmed from it, and I certainly didn't enjoy doing things that were hurtful… in fact, quite the opposite. And did I *really* want to know a God whose acceptance of me was conditional?"

"It got pretty simple from there… the love and self-acceptance snowball started rolling and gaining some serious mass. When I wasn't feeling the vibes that I increasingly believed were my home frequency – love, joy peace, etcetera… then I'd employ various practices to reconnect. It was so simple and important, but not easy in those early years. Even with the new freedom I was feeling, it remained a hard and scary thing for me to start letting go of my religion."

"Our world is so much better now than it used to be. Fewer and fewer people subscribe to the theological and religious understandings that I used to. But my dream is still for us *all* to be aware of our connectedness to each other and to Source constantly. Can you imagine if that was our reality… the great vibes all around that we'd experience?" Pappy suddenly stood up and spun in a circle, as if lost in the music at a live concert. Indeed, this was his jam. Ever since any of us had known him, helping others feel and experience their connection to The One, as he often called God, was all he had ever seemed to care about. We all laughed a bit at his weird little jig. But they were laughs of affection and admiration. Frankie and Leela didn't even budge. They were always by his side and were so used to this sort of behavior that they didn't think much of it.

"So, anyhow, I guess the point is that I was consistently engaging with life very differently from how I had when my old religious constructs were strong. I was using meditation, yoga, non-judgmental awareness of the present moment, observation of my thoughts, among other modalities that weren't in line with my old religious approach. And it was a good thing I had those new practices, because I was going to need them in the challenging season to come."

"The constant deconstruction of my religious paradigm continued to be excruciating for me, no doubt about that. But I tried to handle the challenges with more softness than I had in the past… more like a river that doesn't try to move the rock but flows around it. I definitely got tripped up a lot, but that's part of what made it fun. I had to start somewhere, and the newness of it all was refreshing for me. So, when I tripped, I'd just get back up and keep at it." Pappy grinned. "I still trip and lose my sense of connection, as you know." Some in the family smiled back at Pappy. Indeed, he still made what many would call mistakes. But he was humble about it when they happened, and was quick to apologize if his actions had caused any pain. He seemed to welcome the opportunities to keep evolving into what he believed was his highest version of himself.

"Over those many months, I was led to a lot of authors who were new to me. They introduced me to all kinds of wonderful thoughts… thoughts that were like a tall glass of cool water after a grueling hike in a scorching desert. And I watched interviews with fascinating spiritual leaders from many different religious traditions. It was like I was getting to know myself through all those great teachers, and was meeting a cohort of long-lost friends."

"And I was at the point where I just didn't care anymore that most of those people were generally considered 'wrong' and even dangerous by my Christian community. That's saying something considering *I* was the guy who wasn't willing to celebrate Easter or Christmas with the family for a few years because I thought the pagan influence on those holidays was dishonoring to God." Pappy shook his head gently and smiled. It seemed he was observing, then forgiving, his past self for behaviors that were rooted in the best of intentions, but which were signs of a person who he just didn't relate to anymore.

"I was on a *ride*! Those teachers were offering ideas and frameworks for living that were helping me feel love and softness rising up from inside me naturally... I wasn't forcing it at all. They were feelings I'd always tried to fabricate, but which now were feeling *authentic*! It was groovy... but also a little confusing, since I knew I was growing into a better place using modalities and philosophies that I'd been warned about all my life. But I just kept following the breadcrumbs... following the fragrance of peace."

"After a while, I'd put a few new and very effective tools in my toolbox for handling life's challenges, and I guess God decided it was time to meaningfully test my renewed commitment to 'finding Him'... to entering The More. I didn't know it at the time, but the old me had to go... completely. It had been a long pursuit and process, but I guess it was time to turn up the dial. Be careful what you wish for, as they say. It was time to finish making the new wineskin, and that was going to require a walk through a dark valley."

"I identified as a husband and father, friend, successful businessman, provider, seeker, mountain athlete, farmer, and most important, Christian... even if I wasn't exactly sure about my dogma anymore. It's true that I'd been brought to a place where I could understand in my head that all those identities weren't really me... that they were just thoughts about a 'self' that I'd created. But I didn't own that on a core level yet. I was still holding onto my old self. And in holding on, I was exposed to constant triggers that had the power to break me away from my connection with my growing beliefs about my true self. The irony in that was that as a Christian, I held to the belief that I'd put the 'old man' away and was 'being made new'. But, I don't think I'd really understood what that meant. I'd bifurcated my false self into 'good' and 'bad' or 'new' and 'old'... but both were still my false self, my ego! I had to see that I wasn't any of the 'selfs' that I related to. Like I said, I didn't know what was coming or what I needed... but it turns out it was time for the spiritual equivalent of a drowning."

"Now, look, I know that some of these things would be seen as easy by others. I know I was mercifully spared the loss of a child or spouse or all the other horrible things that most anyone would say are the worst things imaginable. But, what I'm about to tell you about was *my* journey… it was what needed to happen for *me* to break through to the other side and enjoy all the freedom there. Some folks never have to suffer to get to the other side, but many *do* have to go through a hard season… the 'dark night of the soul'. They have to allow their ideas of themselves to be stripped away so they can really get to know their *true* selves. I honor everyone's journey, no matter what that looks like… and mine was about to get tough."

"So, one of the big issues was having to face the disconnect between my identity as a successful provider and the reality of my financial situation at the time. Let's just say we were in a fragile position. *Really* fragile. In faith, and in an effort to show God I was serious about laying it all down for Him so maybe He'd grant me access to The More, I'd spent every nickel we had to build the farm. When given the option to call it quits and hold onto some cash for a fallback position, I didn't hesitate to keep spending on the project. I believed I was called to make it as good a place as it possibly could be. So, in service to God and in what I believed was selfless sacrificc for others, we'd spent all the money we had. We'd managed to pull it all off with no debt, but we were out of cash. I'd maintained a small wealth management practice, and the income from that was just barely enough to get by… actually, not quite enough. I'd grossly underestimated the carrying costs of a property like that. So, let's just say that we were in a real jam."

"As I mentioned earlier, fears around money had always been huge in my life. So, finding or family in such a fragile position left me believing I was a failure. I felt I'd failed as provider, and was pretty far removed from any of my earlier successes as a businessman. Those were two of my most significant identities, and I was *very* attached to them… I used to carry so much anxiety around money and provision. So, keeping my head right while under such financial stress, and while losing those core identities, was just horrendous for me. As we spent the last of our cash, I was actually living one of my greatest fears… and I didn't see a way out."

"But, while the reality of our financial situation and my inability to provide was painful, I was still *determined* not to go down that old fear path. And, as you can imagine, there were suddenly so many opportunities presented daily to walk it. When I'd hung the 'closed for revegetation' sign on that trail, I'd meant it. Whenever I could feel that connection to my beliefs about my true self and God being for me was broken… which was often, during that time… I'd use my new tools to pause, turn, and walk down the love path. It was sort of a blend of open Christian spirituality and positive thinking humanism."

"I wasn't praying and asking for things anymore. I was just trusting in the flow… and holding on to the conviction that I needed to just stay in that home frequency and the rest would work out. It's hard to put into words how much work that was. Laying down a new neural pathway might have been the hardest thing I've ever done. It took so much attention to my thoughts… so much awareness and dedication. But you know what? It *worked*! I got more comfort from just submitting to what was, and trusting it, than I ever did by praying in my old ways." Pappy smiled warmly.

"I remember when things were really grim and I didn't have the cash to pay our tax bill one year. Rather than throwing a fear-based pity party, I decided to write myself a note. I was reading this iconic book by a guy named Napoleon Hill about mindset, and its fundamental thesis is that we are the authors of our lives. That was still a new concept to me back then, but even so, following his suggestion, I wrote down a statement that within five years' time, I would have the intimate relationship with God that I yearned for… that was still my main desire, after all, even with the messy finances. And I also wrote that I'd earn what was then a ridiculous sum of money in a specific year soon to come. Well, writing that note felt like a real Hail Mary. When it came to the finances, absolutely nothing was set up circumstantially to allow for anything to change. In fact, I was staring at circumstances that pretty much seemed to declare the opposite would happen. And I'd been pursuing The More sincerely for many years without meaningful result. But I was going to maintain my belief that God was for me, guiding me… and that somehow it would all not only work out, but be fantastic."

"Then, as if losing my connection with my religion, my money, and sense of who I was wasn't enough, I had a new issue to deal with… an issue I wouldn't wish on anyone… chronic debilitating illness. Over the course of many months, I'd started struggling mightily physically. I was too busy and focused on other things to allow myself to be distracted by this, until I just couldn't ignore the symptoms anymore: absolute exhaustion; joint pain; and excruciating headaches. I was constantly fatigued, and the pain in my joints would get to be almost unbearable. For months, I'd just figured I was hitting that period in life where things just slow down a bit physically. And I was working long hours doing manual labor, so of course I was tired. Then there was the fact that both of my parents had developed some intense arthritis when they were in their early forties, and my mother had always suffered occasionally from headaches. So, for a long time, I decided to chalk it all up to getting older… and true to form, I just pushed through it all."

"But one morning, I went out to the coop to collect eggs. I stood for a long time in that coop holding a large empty egg basket, and as hard as I tried, I just couldn't remember why I was there… and that *really* freaked me out. I'd been slipping gears cognitively for a while. The kids even started calling me 'Dory' after the forgetful fish in *Finding Nemo*. But I always just blamed it on being tired and barely having bandwidth to hold all the many moving parts of the construction project in my brain." That was still a classic movie after all the years since it had come out, and the kids knew Dory's character well. The few who were still awake grew very solemn when Pappy framed his cognitive decline that way.

"So, I walked back to the house carrying the empty basket and told Nana that something was wrong… that I couldn't remember why I'd gone out to the coop! She was always a very patient woman who would let things run their course for a long time without intervention. But she said she'd been noticing me slipping here and there over the last few months, and my forgetfulness combined with all the other symptoms escalated her concerns meaningfully. We agreed that I should get checked out."

"Well, *long* story short, it turns out I had a nasty thing called Lyme disease. Once we found the right medical counsel – which was no easy thing – the docs decided it was likely caused by all those tick bites I'd gotten while clearing the land years before. They'd infected me with Lyme and other co-infections, and the various infections had ultimately overwhelmed my immune system. The toxins were making my body go haywire, and I was spiraling downward fast. Well, that diagnosis was scary news for the whole family... and, with all the other things I was wrestling with, it felt *real* heavy for me."

"Thanks, God!" Pappy chuckled. "I mean, on top of everything else that seemed to be piling up, now I had to deal with a serious illness that could put me in a wheelchair for life, or worse? I mean, what else could go wrong? At that point, for me, only the loss of relationship with your Nana... or maybe Andy or Betsey getting really sick... could have made things any worse! But my health and vitality were intimately linked to other ego identities of mine. So, I guess God decided they had to go too. Everything I rooted my sense of identity in was crumbling around me rapidly."

Pappy scratched his head, then pushed away some of the hair that had fallen across his eyes. "My doctor was concerned the bugs and their toxins had crossed the blood-brain barrier and that we needed to go down the antibiotic route immediately. I didn't want to do that, considering how devastating I knew it would be to my gut... a hard option for an organic farmer! But I was a dad of young kids, and I needed to fight those bugs hard... and antibiotics were the heavy artillery."

"So, it was around that time when the tests of my new and rather fragile spiritual and mindset paradigms got really serious. It was one thing to train my brain to create an optimistic love pathway and choose to believe God was for me when dealing with the softer day-to-day challenges which might be spread out over many weeks. But it's entirely another to keep a commitment to that path while getting piled on with one thing after another! And, while carrying the burdens of all I've talked about, I almost buckled under the added weight of the threat of being an invalid husband and father."

"But, I just braced myself, adjusted to the increasing weight, and doubled down. Maybe it was tripled down at that point." Pappy laughed again. "As those crushing pressures mounted, I decided I wouldn't even flirt with any thoughts that weren't trusting, optimistic, and full of hope that all of the challenging circumstances were leading me to The More. The way I saw it, I just didn't have an option, and I guess I needed that exercise." Pappy smiled and looked at the kids. "The butterfly just flops to the ground if it doesn't push against the cocoon for a while." He winked. "I *needed* the hard work of getting that new pathway of love, hope, and trust cut in really well. I wouldn't wish it on anyone, but those circumstances offered the perfect opportunity for me to do the hard work… and it was cut that new pathway or die trying."

"Now, when it comes to the antibiotic treatment for Lyme, let's just say the cure was *far* worse than the disease. It was an awful process. I'd take a cocktail of antibiotics designed to rip open a bunch of the toxin-laden bugs in my bloodstream. Then, the toxins that would normally be trickling into my body slowly would be spilled all at once. I still have trouble taking pills today because of the association I still have with all the pills I took back then and their brutal effects on my system. I knew swallowing those antibiotics would cause me to be overwhelmed with the most intense pain I've ever experienced soon after I swallowed them, because the process caused all the symptoms to manifest at a really intense level, and all at once!"

"I'd be shut down for days. I think the headaches were the worst part of the whole illness, and the agony of them was exacerbated by the fact that I couldn't move around in bed to distract myself, because the joint pain was so bad. I was in and out of a bedridden state for a couple of years as I worked through those antibiotic cycles. I'd take the cocktail, endure the pain, start to feel better, and then it was time for another cocktail. Rinse and repeat. There's a lot more to that whole journey that I won't get into. But let's just say it was some real physical suffering."

"And, when I wasn't bedridden, I was trying to figure out how to make things work financially... an increasingly grim challenge, since the expensive Lyme treatments were all out-of-pocket expenses. I continued to choose to have absolute faith and confidence in the fact that all the challenges were part of an important process for me. But things were a *real* mess, and it was all I could to try to keep it together in front of Nana, Andy, and Betsey so they wouldn't be scared. Adding to all that, I was going through the crux stages of my intense spiritual crisis by that point, as I had effectively lost any sense of identity, since all the things I'd put my sense of self in had effectively collapsed. Like I said earlier, we all have different ego constructs that have to be dismantled to find who we really are, and mine were being stripped away painfully all at once. I wasn't feeling like a good husband or father or friend. My finances were a wreck, and I'd lost my health."

"And worse than anything for me, my faith in my religious system was pretty much gone, though I hadn't admitted that to anyone yet. I still believed that if I let go of all that entirely, and said as much publicly, then as the Bible says, it was going to be eternal torment for me. So, with all that was happening, I just couldn't go there yet... even while the religion I was holding onto offered no help for me during those trials. I'd soon discover that I had to let it *all* go. So, God mercifully allowed the hits to keep coming."

"During that time... and it's amazing to me when I think about this... but it's written right here..." Pappy pointed at his journal, "...my tenacity as a seeker hadn't waned. I was hurting so deeply, but my prayer was..." Pappy got choked up as he seemed to be feeling the earnestness of the prayer he offered so many years ago: *God, I don't understand what's going on. But Your will... whatever 'You' are... be done in all of this. If You don't plan to heal me from this suffering, please heal me through it.* I continued singing that Hillsong prayer too. Even then, when my feet were actually failing, I was willing… I *wanted*… to be led into what I was sure was available… as mysterious as it was to me at the time. I had faith, and I just kept pounding on the door… beaten, bruised, bloody, and barely able to stand – but, still knocking."

"It's certainly an understatement to say it was tough going. I was being forced at a relatively young age to answer the ultimate question: *Who am I?* I didn't have an answer for that… or, even any framework for the question, for that matter. I saw the carnage from my sense of identity collapsing all around me, but I didn't have any idea what was happening, or to what end. I just saw and felt pain. And my hope was in something I had no living examples for, but was still the vision of my heart. I believed that way of being Jesus spoke of, and those early Christians lived, was available to me. However, I was finally starting to accept that, for me, my religion was the one thing standing in the way of accessing The More."

"On the days when I was feeling ok physically, and to save a few dollars, I'd join the few who were still on the farm project's skeleton to get some work done around the property. They were good men who I counted as friends, and who were aware of our circumstances. Some days they'd even work for free, since they knew I was out of money. And that was humbling for me, but they were great friends who believed in the project and wanted to see it through – Chris, Ryan, Lavoit, and even the Jestroms."

"The Lyme treatments continued, and were incredibly expensive. Lenders still weren't willing to help, and I think now that maybe God was blocking that safety line. But I was really close to the real understanding of what it means to be 'broke'. The weight of all those burdens had me on my hands and knees. I just felt *so* dejected. So, all the hard charging intensity I was known for had been completely replaced by a profound sadness and sense of defeat."

"I was at the end of my rope, just barely hanging on, not knowing how to claw my way out of the hole we were in… even if I'd had the energy to try. My thoughts started drifting more and more consistently to a large life insurance policy that I was still paying on. So, I had some very real internal dialogue about removing myself from the equation so Nana and the kids could be immediately helped, at least on several important levels… and I was dead serious about that as an option. That's the type of fear-based thinking that would pop up all the time, and which I'd have to constantly swat away… awful fears about finances, the fate of my eternal soul as I lost my religion, my future physically, and even my concerns about my most precious relationships. I was deeply concerned about where things were headed for my family with an invalid husband and father who couldn't provide for them, and who'd already led them to a horrible financial situation. I was in such a bad place mentally that suicide seemed like a reasonable and loving option for how to take care of them, at least practically. I was also selfishly just tired of the struggle." Pappy stared into the fire for a long moment, and the sound of the ever-flowing river filled the silence again.

"McLean, you asked earlier if I'd really shot and killed one of my favorite pets." McLean brought her tired eyes up to meet Pappy's, and I noted her face had a very different expression than hours before when she had asked. "Here's that part."

"I was on a call for work, and it was really important… *a lot* was riding on that conversation. As I talked, I was looking out over the pasture watching the chickens free-range contentedly. My eyes scanned the flock, and then I saw our best mouser, Piccolo, hunting the chickens!" Pappy paused, smiled, and reached down to stroke the cat in his lap. "Yes, Piccolo. Ever since that time, every new cat we've brought into the family has been named Piccolo because of all this. Well, I felt distracted and stuck, since I was on a call and didn't think I could do anything about it. But then I saw him lunge at a chicken with an obvious intention to kill it. It barely escaped, and the flock was of course suddenly stressed and agitated… and then something just snapped in me."

Pappy took another breath as he shook his head. "I asked the person I was talking to hold for a moment, put the phone on mute, and set it on a shelf near me. Then I grabbed a scoped .22 rifle I kept in the closet. Piccolo had paused his pursuit and was sitting near a fence post watching the chickens intently. I drew down on him, and his body filled the optic. Likely sensing my energy, he looked toward me, and I looked right into his eyes through that magnified lens. He didn't move… just stared right at me. I thought to myself, *Am I really about to do this?"* And then, without much hesitation, and feeling completely numb inside, I pulled the trigger."

"It was awful. Piccolo was just doing what a good hunting cat does… and his capability along those lines was something we all admired him for! But I had no grace or compassion in my heart… nothing like that. Or, more accurately, I just wasn't present enough to pause and connect with it." Pappy smiled gently at McLean as she wiped away a few tears. Piccolo must have sensed the Pappy's energy as he recounted the story. He stood, stretched, and then settled back down into Pappy's lap, perfectly content. It seemed to be a gesture of grace on behalf of his namesake that wasn't lost on any of us.

"When the bullet hit him, he leapt about six feet in the air, landed on his side, then bounced around in pain. I went back to the phone, thanked the person I was talking with for their patience, and asked them to please give me another minute. Then I walked out to the pasture, put the barrel up to Piccolo's head, and finished him. I didn't care. It could have been one of the dogs, or maybe even a person at that point, for all I know. I wasn't healthy on *so* many levels… and that moment really showed it. I was dead inside."

Pappy had tears rolling down his face as he told the story, and we all stared at him in shock. A breeze blew and stoked the fire again, but the flames didn't bring any warmth.

"I hate to admit it, but so much about my old way of being is represented in that story. I think it was that day I finally just went all limp inside." McLean and Pappy shared another brief moment, and the sadness in their glances was something we could all understand.

"Well, months went by with me in that deadened state. Relationships were strained, the money situation had drifted into the realm of heavy debt on credit cards, and my health was awful. And things hadn't gotten any better spiritually either. I was just barely hanging onto any semblance of faith, and all my questions about the nature of God were overriding any attachment to a religious system."

"Around that time, I stumbled on a work by a man named John of the Cross. He wrote a book called *The Ascent of Mt. Carmel*, which is basically a book about what was then considered the typical spiritual journey. There was a part in it called *The Dark Night of the Soul*, and it really resonated with me. My soul just felt all blacked out. But there was a glimmer of light in that book. St. John had gone through his own soul-suffering, but things had turned around for him. His story offered a shred of hope, and I grabbed a hold of it."

Pappy flipped toward the end of that journal and smiled an exhausted smile. "Yeah, this part was the final nail in my coffin. This is where I died my first death." He paused before continuing. "You see, my mother was really concerned about me during that time. It was April of 2015, and Easter was rolling around, so she invited us all to attend a Maundy Thursday service at their church. Mumsie had always been such a support for me, and I could tell she was desperately wanting me to re-engage with church life. I didn't want to hurt her, so I agreed we'd all be there… even though that church, and all the dogma I believed it represented, was a significant trigger for me at the time."

"When Thursday evening rolled around, I sat in the service listening intently to all that was said by the pastor. He basically laid out the full and familiar 'Gospel Message'… or 'Good News'… that I'd heard so often over the years: all people are sinners unworthy of communion with a holy God;

God loved us all so much that he sent his son, Jesus, to die as an atoning sacrifice to God for our sins, and as the only way of salvation; only those who believe this, and in Jesus as the son of God – and also as God – could have eternal communion with God."

"Well, I just couldn't take it anymore. Right there in that sanctuary... right in the middle of Holy Week... I finally admitted to myself with firm conviction that I just didn't believe that message any longer." Pappy paused, obviously still impacted by the importance of that statement. "I should clarify that. I didn't believe those words in the way I'd always understood them... which, in my limited understanding at the time, was the *only* way to understand them. And that understanding *was* Christianity to me... my way of knowing God!"

"And since I saw God as something outside of me, I silently told God as much and in no uncertain terms. Immediately after doing so, I was in a bit of shock. I sat there wondering if I'd really just said that! Had I really just denied my faith? Had I just shut the door to what I had put all my hope in for so many years, and believed would lead me to all the fullness and peace that I believed was possible?"

"I sat silent and stunned through the rest of the service. When it was time to leave, I didn't have much to say to anyone, and so we just headed home. I wasn't about to tell Nana or the kids. It was all in my heart, between me and God at that point. I mean, I didn't know *how* to tell anyone and not cause all kinds of suffering in the hearts of folks who loved me. Because the way I understood things, I'd just resolved that I would rather spend eternity in hell being tortured than to believe in – or have any relationship with - a God who would employ such a system."

Pappy paused and let out an unfamiliar, soft sigh. It had a great sadness to its tone and sounded strange. "It's kind of interesting now... I could say every one of those words of the gospel message now and mean them from the bottom of my heart. They just mean something different to me now than they did then. Maybe I was all alone in understanding things the way I did. But I don't think so. And you know this is just my story... the last thing I want to do is trip up any of you if you think that evangelical Christian gospel is beautiful. I respect all paths." Pappy paused for emphasis, then continued.

"After that, something felt free inside me... free within the general numbness. Again, it's hard to explain. It was like a subtle light was flickering in my soul behind so much darkness. But it was hard to see, and even harder to focus on, considering how completely exhausted I was over everything that had transpired over the many months before that moment. If I had any energy, it went to pushing away thoughts about the implications of what that denial might mean for me, Nana, or the kids. I decided to privately just let the energy of it all settle in my soul, and then flow on through in its own time. And I did have one shred of hope offsetting the prospect of my eternal damnation. I hadn't denied my religion out loud... which, as I understood it, would be the point of no return."

"So, I wrestled with all that for a while without sharing the struggle with anyone. And rather than backing away from what I'd told God in the sanctuary that day, I developed deeper conviction about it. I could look back on my journey and know without a shred of doubt that I had only wanted God to lead me. I was willing to go anywhere, no matter the cost. And while I'd never have guessed that path would lead to me putting down the one thing I'd put my hope in, I was confident that I had been *led* there. And I just *had* to trust that! It was brutal though. I was so confused and scared, more than ever before. So, there I was... broken on all fronts. It was *not* a fun season." Pappy smiled and winked at us, indicating a good ending to all that suffering would soon be shared.

"Around that time, I was still going out to Colorado occasionally for work. And a couple of weeks after that Easter season, I was out here and mom called while I was driving to the office from a lunch appointment. We hadn't spoken since that church service, so we caught up a bit, just talking about nothing in particular. Then she revealed the real reason for calling. She knew me well, had sensed something was way off, and was specifically even more worried about me spiritually than she had been before. She brought up the Maundy Thursday service as a way to probe. Now, the *last* person I would *ever* want to hurt was my mother."

"But she asked me straight up, *Son, are you a believer anymore?* Well, I was stuck. I knew what she meant. She wanted to know whether I believed the way we both understood to be the only way to believe… the only true way to avoid hell and have relationship with God. The moment of truth was upon me, and I was stuck between lying or breaking my mother's heart."

"I asked her to hang on for a moment, and I pulled into a parking lot. She waited patiently, knowing it was a heavy question which we both believed had eternal consequences. And I'm not sure she wanted an honest answer. I stared out at Pike's Peak for a few long seconds trying to collect my thoughts. This was 'it' for me. I decided in that moment that to deny my experience would be to close the door on whatever it was that God had been, and was, doing in my life. Suddenly, Luke was there with me… I was in the boardroom again being asked what I wanted… in John's tiny living room on that worn out chair… on that stage with the healing minister… privately, in my chair having an all-night prayer vigil, *begging* for truth. It was like some crazy convergence of my heart's ultimate desire was being distilled down to that moment. I was at a supernatural confluence of the rivers of life, and the line through the intimidating rapids downstream wasn't clear. I knew it was entirely my choice, before God, whether I wanted to keep floating down the river of change I'd been on." Pappy paused and smiled. "Well, y'all know me and my love for big water." He winked.

"I cleared my throat. I told her that no, I did not believe the way I'd been taught to believe anymore. I denied the Christian gospel as I'd always understood it. And then I waited. I could hear her crying softly, and that broke my heart. Her crying was one of the hardest things I've ever heard. She didn't say much that I remember, except that she would be praying for me. After we hung up, I was just numb. My final, and most foundational, identity had just crumbled. I was dead inside."

"I sat in that parking lot without any feelings or thoughts, except being troubled a little by the 'belief' that I was now going to hell. And I didn't really even care about that at that point. I don't know how I could say I didn't believe in Christianity anymore, and yet still hold onto the belief about the consequences of hell for what I'd just said. I was all twisted up. Maybe it shows how deep the fear pathway had been laid over so many formative years. I don't really know. But that's where I was with it all. I had been desperately clinging to the very end of my rope. And in that conversation with mom, I'd let go and started a freefall." Pappy fell silent for a few moments.

"It's important to say that I never lost faith in something beyond me… call that God, or whatever name you want to use. But I'd lost any faith in my way of defining and relating to God… and that had undergirded *everything* I was about. I was completely unmoored."

"I went to bed that night in a sort of stunned stillness. By that point, I really didn't know how to pray… and much less who or what to pray to. I felt like I didn't know anything anymore. I had turned off my phone for the day, since I assumed Mumsie would have talked with Nana, and that out of love and concern for me, Nana might call to discuss whether I'd really 'denied the faith'. I was getting on a flight back to the farm early the next morning, and I needed the remaining time in that day to think about how to handle the unavoidable conversation with Nana that would soon be upon me."

"It was one thing for me to be willing to suffer the eternal consequences of what I'd chosen. But going back and telling the family would cause so much pain and confusion, and I was *so* sad about that. Even worse, I was concerned that if the way I'd previously understood things was actually right, then there was a very real risk I could lead my family onto the path of eternal damnation too… and, that was just *unthinkable* for me. I fought hard to come back to center… to hold onto my belief that God was for me, and that those were just fear-based thoughts that had no place in my new paradigm." Pappy's eyes welled up with tears. "The waves of fearful thoughts kept rolling in and crashing on me relentlessly. I was getting exhausting standing up after each thought, holding onto hope, and then getting slammed again. That night, my existence was seeming so pointless, even potentially harmful for those I loved."

"I called out that night harder than I ever had before. I *wept*... and I remember being surprised that there was any emotion left in me. I begged God to take my life rather than allow me to go back and hurt or mislead my family. I meant it, too. I know that sounds dramatic, but I absolutely meant precisely that... and with every fiber of my being. I begged God to kill me right then and there if I was wrong and could potentially lead others down the wrong path."

"I don't remember what time I drifted off to sleep, but it was late. I remember just lying there in that dark room for hours, alternating between complete numbness, confusion, and desperate sadness. And all that concern and emotion was laced with conviction that what I'd done *wasn't* wrong... that following the breadcrumbs to that desperate point was faithfulness, not foolishness. Then, after a while, I finally just let it all go. I mean, I dropped *everything*... and let it *all* go. I quit on my self-doubt, my self-judgement, my judgement of what *was*. I gave up judging all the pain. I gave up on thinking I knew anything about myself, or the way things work. I even gave up on hoping in The More."

"Then I drifted off to sleep... completely dead to every aspect of the self I knew... and, finally, at peace."

CHAPTER SEVENTEEN

ONE CONSCIOUS BREATH

Pappy closed the journal and set it on his lap. He sat quietly for a few moments and stared at the fire. The silence was deafening. Our beloved Pappy, who we had always known as a loving, deeply spiritual, wildly successful, happy-go-lucky patriarch had just been candid and vulnerable with us in a way that was rare for anyone. We all appreciated it, seemed to collectively realize that we related to his story in our own unique ways, and reflected on as much while we allowed the sacred moment to linger.

The last of the large logs on the fire broke apart and merged with the great mound of glowing embers. Pappy breathed deep, and said,

"That was a tough season." He chuckled softly at the understatement. "It's sort of ironic that so much of that pain was right-smack-dab in the middle of so much great stuff. Life, huh?" Pappy smiled. "But, for me, I still believe all that needed to happen for my outer purpose on this planet to be meaningfully set in motion. I had asked God for the full ride, after all. And every bit of my path has served an important purpose. The One *was* with me all along, as you'll hear in a moment." Pappy paused as he reflected and slowly shook his head. "I've been so humbled over the years at how many people have been positively impacted by that story… or at least bits and pieces of it. And what's to come too… which I believe is the best part, and explains what I've been all about ever since!"

The statement prompted the children who were still awake to rouse those who were asleep. Shoulders were shaken gently while light, whispering voices shared with waking ears what Pappy had just said. Tousled heads emerged from under heavy blankets, and sleepy eyes focused on Pappy, determined to hear whatever the 'best' part was to be. It was beautiful to watch the children want to listen.

He looked around the circle again at each of us. "This family… all of you… are one of my life's greatest treasures. Thank you for being here, for making these reunions such a priority!" He smiled, then bent down to pick up his last journal. Piccolo shifted, and patiently allowed Pappy to settle deeper into his chair before regaining his comfortable repose. Pappy skimmed the pages of the final worn composition book in the stack.

"So, we're a river family, and you've all had your fair share of swims when you flop out of rafts or need to exit a kayak… so you'll understand this. For that matter, anyone whose been held under water longer than they'd like will get it. You know when you've been under for too long, and your lungs are burning… and it's feeling really scary, and you start to panic a little?" There were acknowledging nods around the fire.

"Then, just as you're about to break through to get a breath, something prevents it… the raft floats over your head, or a rapid pulls you back under… or whatever. Then the whole situation goes from scary to terrifying? And your lungs are burning so bad, and your mind is racing so fast, that you're pretty sure you're dying? But then suddenly, you somehow do break the surface of the water! Can you picture the type of breath you'd breathe? Can you feel that when you think about it? It *literally* is the breath of life… and while you're taking it in, you are just overwhelmed with gratitude." With desperate eyes, Pappy quickly shifted forward in his chair and filled his lungs with a massive amount of air. Then his face softened as he settled back and let the breath out slowly.

"I mean, can you really imagine being sure you're dying, then suddenly breathing in so hard, and with so much gratitude, that it feels *completely* restorative... sort of like a new lease on life? Well, that's what happened to me that very same night."

"After falling asleep having surrendered completely, wanting to die so the pain would stop, I suddenly sat upright and inhaled the most incredible breath I've *ever* inhaled! It was just... amazing. I mean, I've had lots of cool experiences like that over the years. But this was the first, and it was powerful... and special. With that breath, I was aware of my connection to God. Not only did I know all was well, but I knew I *wasn't* stuck... that there *was* more! Suddenly, I'd been transported from believing... to *knowing*." Pappy smiled wide.

"With that breath *everything* changed. I suddenly felt so alive and peaceful that it took me a few moments to believe I hadn't died. It was just so... *beautiful*. And I was aware, and a little amused, that I couldn't identify the way I felt. Any memory of an experience like that just wasn't available to pull from for a reference point. But, at the same time, it felt so natural... I felt like I was at home... like I was *alive*!"

"I didn't know it at the time, but I believe now that I'd breathed what the Bible calls the pneuma. Loosely translated, pneuma means 'breath of life', or 'spirit'. I don't pretend to understand the mystery of all of that. But I do recognize that waking up that morning with that breath was a tremendous grace. I still don't know how to put what happened clearly into words. I don't know if it was my moment of salvation or enlightenment or a powerful satori or what... but I'll tell you this as a matter of *fact: everything* was different."

"I looked over at the clock on the bedside table and it read 3:00 a.m. Well, that was delightful for me, since I had such a history with that hour.

I just sat there for a while, stunned and staring at that clock with a goofy smile on my face. And time had a weird feeling to it, too. If I hadn't been watching the digital display, I wouldn't have known if a minute or an hour passed. As I turned my head back to center, I noticed it had this weird feeling to it, like it was on ball bearings or something… incredibly smooth and fluid. And that was absolutely wonderful for me because, remember, I had Lyme disease and nothing in my body worked smoothly or fluidly… most any movement like that registered high on the pain scale."

"And my vision had some sort of wild trail effect to it, too. I remember that as I turned my head, the red of the digital clock display sort of pulled out of the clock as a block of color, then transitioned into a muted red streak that disappeared gradually across my field of vision… sort of like a comet trail. After that, my eyes tried to focus on the blank wall in front of me through the pitch darkness." Pappy shook his head at the memory. "It was just the strangest thing. It was still completely dark in the room, and yet there was a twinkle… like an electric sparkle all around me… and *through* me! I don't know if I was seeing it with my physical eyes or with some sort of new spiritual vision, or something like that. But there was this new dimension to what I could see… and I *felt* it too." Pappy's smile had not diminished at all while he enthusiastically relayed the experience, and it grew wider as he continued.

"I had no headache, or joint pain… physically I felt *well*! It wasn't just my neck that felt ok. I didn't have any of the Lyme symptoms that I usually woke up with! And, that crackling energy stayed all around me, and was coursing through me. It was subtle, but I identified with it somehow *as* me. It was all just *so* bizarre."

"Then I turned on the bedside lamp and the room came into view. There were very few decorations, and the paint was a basic beige. But somehow the *beauty* of it all just absolutely overwhelmed me. It wasn't the mundane objects themselves that overwhelmed; it was the energy around them. Or maybe *through* them? I don't know. But it was all very unfamiliar and super positive. And while the inanimate objects didn't necessarily feel alive to me, they had a sort of energetic magic to them. Talk about good vibes!" Pappy laughed.

"I was starting to wonder if I could handle all that energy and newness! I fell back onto the pillow and stared at the ceiling, still smiling. Some time had gone by, and I still had no way to calibrate to the experience. I remembered how I'd fallen to sleep, but it felt like lifetimes ago. And I was completely detached from all that fear, anxiety and sadness. I felt vital physically… something I hadn't felt in years. I'm not exaggerating when I say I'm sure I could have gotten up and run a marathon. It felt *so* good to feel good!"

"I started laughing with delight, because I knew in that moment I'd been healed from the Lyme! I've never taken a day of good health for granted ever since. And it wasn't just physical healing I'd received. I noticed the incessant mental chatter just wasn't there anymore! My mind was at rest… completely at peace."

"So, I just allowed myself to lie there and feel all that… just *experience* it. I was simply aware. Everything just was at it was… and I wasn't demanding more of it! I felt so completely content, so full of love for life… so much harmony in my consciousness. And I knew with every fiber of my being that life knew, loved, and fully accepted me just as I was… and that I was an integral part of it!"

"The intense experience wasn't fading after several minutes, but I was getting comfortable enough with it to know I hadn't died. Then – and I don't know how to explain this either – the experience itself was somehow communicating with me… completely apart from any thoughts about it that I might have been forming. It let me know it wanted to linger a bit and, well… play. It was like it had a personality." Pappy chuckled. "I know that makes no sense. I'm trying. Again, so sorry… words fail."

"But that suggestion did bring my thinking mind into the mix, and I was aware of fearing that thought might jeopardize the experience. But, somehow I knew my individualized thought was ok both with and within 'the experience' itself. It was like my mind was invited to play too, and that 'the experience' even preferred a harmonious coexistence with my mind rather than treating it as a challenge, or enemy. So, since money was one of my biggest fears and sources of anxiety at that time, I figured I'd test the newfound sense of peace in a meaningful way. As beautiful as the experience was, I decided it was time to see if it was fleeting or was going to stick with me. And what better way to challenge the peace of the experience than with one of my most acute fears?"

"I thought about our challenging financial situation, and all the stressors associated with it. The awful circumstances had been haunting me horribly… and making me feel like a complete failure. But when I thought about all that, it was all still there… but there was a space around it. Years later, I heard Tolle explain this type of peaceful clarity precisely that way… and the explanation fits so perfectly! It was like I was back in that eddy on the Futa with the chaos all around me, but I was resting contentedly within it. The money stuff was important, of course. But suddenly, it wasn't *ultimately* important… and that made it ok. I just knew it was *all good*." The euphemism was one of Pappy's favorites, and now we understood why.

"I kept resting there, feeling so profoundly grateful for the peace, the healing, and the sense of profound love… love that was pouring into me, and through me… and yet, I *was* the love, too. Then I thought about the pursuit of so many years… the suffering and ego deconstruction I'd gone through in my desperate effort to connect with The More." Pappy paused and shook his head. "Well, the memories of hurt, dissatisfaction, and longing were all still there, of course, since my journey had been what it had been. But I realized the memories were just thoughts. And it was as if suddenly my story about those thoughts was gone. There was a recognition of my journey thus far, and all its steps… but no judgements or emotions about any of it, except gratitude. I felt held, cradled. And I loved The One cradling me with every bit of my being. And I knew It loved me. I was experiencing what I'd craved all my life… the love and complete acceptance of God. The More." Pappy paused and shook his head, clearly frustrated with the struggle to communicate the experience.

"And I felt a part of what was cradling me… a part of the experience, and all it was communicating. There was suddenly no separation between me, and… well, *everything*! I *was* love… and it felt like some beautiful alchemy of the purest versions of peace, joy, gratitude, compassion, and kindness you can possibly imagine. Then, suddenly, it dawned on me… " Pappy paused, furrowed his brow, and fought to maintain composure.

"The seeking… it was *over*. The door had opened, and I'd stumbled over the threshold into the room…. and The One was holding me. Well, when I realized that, I just lost it. I mean I came *completely* unglued… and the cry I had then was so incredibly cathartic and cleansing for me. I'd fallen asleep weeping from sadness and despair. And a few hours later, I was weeping with a profound sense of love and oneness with all of life! What I'd come into an awareness of was so far beyond anything I'd hoped for in my wildest imaginings. I'm sure I couldn't have taken any more love into my being, or I'd have burst. And in that moment, I knew I'd *always* been that love… that experience… that beauty. I knew it was my home state and always had been, and that for whatever reason I'd just been blind to that reality."

Pappy scanned a few more pages of his journal, obviously wanting to recount the experience faithfully. "Then I was aware of my essence as this dazzling light with so much power and beauty… the majesty of it was so raw. And all I wanted was to shine all that it was… all that *I* was… without any inhibition! And I had a great conviction about it, too! There was just too much beauty to allow it to be hidden. And why would I want to?"

Pappy paused to make sure he was heard very clearly on the next point. "And at the same time I experienced that awareness, I knew nothing of the experience was about *me*. In fact, there *was no me*, as we like to think of ourselves. I know this is sounding 'out there'. But it's like the beauty I recognized as me was the beauty of *all*… and *all* were the beauty of *me*. Ever since, I've yearned for people to see their own majesty, and to bring their own unique and inspired offerings into the world."

Pappy looked around to take in his surroundings, then spread his arms wide and wiggled his fingers. "In that moment of awareness, I could see the beauty of every single thing… the sacredness of it *all*. And I knew that same energy I felt so at one with was flowing through *all* things! I had an acute and keen sense that all is One… and that perspective hasn't left me since that moment. I realized Source is ever-manifesting in all sorts of diverse forms as the universe flowers and God reveals Itself to Itself… all the while knowing what It is, but wanting to experience the joy of the flowering." Pappy settled back into his chair and watched the embers dance as the fire offered the last of its warmth.

"Anyhow, using Biblical language, since Jesus is my guru…" Pappy winked at Jenny. "What I connected with was an overpowering sense of my position as a 'child of God'… of being 'connected to the vine'. I understood Meister Eckhart's statement that had completely perplexed me before: *the eyes through which I see God are the eyes through which God sees me.* While it took a few years to understand this, I came to realize I'd been granted what the mystics called union… oneness. With that experience, my religious and theological frameworks had been obliterated… and I wasn't sad about that at all. I felt free. That experience is something I'm certain I'd have been willing to die for if I'd been faced with the choice of denying the experience or being fed to lions, burned at the stake, or hung on a cross. I'd never deny it or its impact on me. Finally, I could understand those early Christians."

"*Many* have experienced this throughout history! I'm *nothing* special when it comes to this kind of thing. This is available to *everyone.* In fact, I believe what I came into an awareness of for myself *is everyone's home state of being.* It is our God frequency… the energetic resonance of all humankind. And we're all already there, we just need to see it… to simply be with it. And there are as many paths to awareness as there are people on the planet. Jesus was a man who realized and lived this state of awareness perfectly. Source used him as a vessel to flow through completely unfettered. And he made it very clear that anything he could do we *all* can do. It's like God was modeling through that one man named Jesus what was possible for us all – and was, in no uncertain terms, *calling us to it!* I mean, that seems pretty clear in the Bible, assuming Jesus' admonishments can be taken at face value. Jesus is the perfect incarnation story, and the world should be so grateful for his example so we can follow it. But I believe we're *all* the incarnation story! *That's* the good news as I see it! Our identity really is only ultimately found in The Universal Christ!"

Pappy leaned forward and stretched his back, then he sat back into his chair. "Now I know I'm getting a little excited… but I can't help myself. This is the *sauce*, y'all! If I'm going to leave a legacy, I want it to be that I was passionate about this good news and told others. And now you know the reason for my life's work! So, thank you for indulging an old man. As best I can tell, Jesus' whole message could be summed up as 'see differently and enter the kingdom!' For that matter, it's fundamentally the same message that seems to weave its way through *all* the wisdom traditions. And, as I see it, that's what it's *all* about. Jesus' teaching made so much more sense after my experience that night."

"There *is* a peace that passes understanding – that transcends circumstances, then somehow loops back to undergird them. And it is absolutely every single person's *birthright.* 'The More' we all seek in all our individual ways… *is within us!* And that awareness, and all the peace and hope that comes with it, can be found right where you are, no matter the circumstances. I spent so many years seeking something outside of me, only to find the wellspring had been within me all along." Pappy shook his head with a smile.

"Last thing I'll say on this is that the experience was keenly humbling. Relationship with God is relationship with The Eternal. And I realized that if I was moving deeper into relationship with The Eternal, then any pride I might have now, in the present, is just silly! In a very real sense, I felt like I was just beginning… and have ever since, too! There's no way for anyone to have any pride about the experience! And lots of people have a relationship like this, but theirs might or might not look like mine!"

"I certainly feel ok saying, or hearing anyone else saying, I 'see' or am 'in the light' or 'conscious'… 'enlightened' or 'saved' or whatever. But I don't know that there is a *final* stage in this process of moving into God – or one way to do it! I mean, maybe there is, but I'm not there in my understanding of it all. It does seem Jesus clearly called us to that level of awareness… 'Kingdom' awareness."

"You're all familiar with Einstein. He said it well… something like, 'There are only two ways engage with life: as if nothing is a miracle, or everything is!' And the miracle of it all is the ultimate mystery! By settling into the mystery and letting go of all my expectations for how God should show up… the conditions *I* had put on *Him*… then suddenly, God was *everywhere!* The Bible has a great phrase for this… *In Him we live and move and have our being.* And yet, even after this awareness, life is still life… just with a twist." Pappy smiled.

Then Pappy's focus shifted past us toward the river while another wide, toothy grin spread across his face. A few of us turned to see what he was looking at. Five or six bobbing bright lights were moving toward us quickly in what seemed to be the flow of the river. "Midnight run." Pappy said as he kept his eyes on the boaters while they emerged from the inky black of the early morning. "Good times. I knew they were getting on the water tonight. Those guys know every rock on this river – every rapid, hole, hazard. But running it at night… well, that's really something. It's the same experience as during the day, only different." Pappy chuckled. "Soul boaters."

Pappy smiled and looked intently at us. I sensed we were all a little confused by the 'same but different' comment about running rivers at night, though it did seem to illustrate what he was trying to communicate. We watched the pod of kayakers come into full view, their lights illuminating waving hands and big smiles. As they passed by, they called out something unintelligible.

Pappy laughed and waved back, then cupped his hands around his mouth and shouted, "Flow on, fellas!" He watched the boaters slip back into the dark, the beams of their headlamps quickly disappearing around the bend of the river downstream. Then his face turned solemn, and his mind was clearly elsewhere for a long moment. We would only understand where it had drifted the next morning. "Big water this week," he said.

Then his attention focused back on us. "That's what it's all about. Enjoying the human experience like those boaters out there… like us, right here. And at the same time, enjoying the experience of our divinity. I love the imagery of the cross. The vertical meets horizontal… spiritual meets earthly. That's it! It's all about living at that intersection of our humanity and divinity, and just enjoying the flow! That's what happened when I woke up that morning, figuratively and literally… and life has been a type of high-water midnight run for me ever since." He smiled. "The same, but different."

Pappy looked around with the twinkling life in his blue eyes that we all loved about him, and which we hadn't seen much since Nana had passed. His passion for the message, and for his family, and for all people, was so obvious. We so enjoyed gaining insight into Pappy's 'Why' that evening.

"So anyhow, after a while of lying there in bed absorbing the experience, soft light started streaming in through the window as the sun rose. Hours must have gone by in what seemed like an instant! Time was *jacked.* I had an early flight back home, so it was time to get myself ready and head to the airport."

"It was then that the experience got wild in a whole different kind of way. The physical experience was so intoxicating… it was like I was high on my own supply!" Pappy laughed with a big belly laugh.

"Just feeling the carpet underfoot was *awesome*! Then I got in the shower and was overwhelmed with the sensation of the water on my skin.

And on and on it went… every little experience was a sensory overload! As I started moving into my day, I was in this state of profound gratitude… flooded with appreciation for so many of the little things I typically took for granted. Everything really was a miracle!"

"What was even more fun was the way I saw people. And that morning, I was around *a lot* of people. Everyone was so beautiful! It's so true that when you see the beauty in yourself, you are free to see it in others. And I couldn't help but engage with folks! I didn't understand what was happening, and didn't really care to understand it… I was just going for the ride! The beauty I saw in others was my own beauty, and vice versa. And it's like the energy of that awareness was just flowing *through* me… and folks were drawn to me as much as I was drawn to them! And when I say 'me', I don't mean this bag of bones… this meat suit." Pappy swept his hands up along his body. "I mean *the energy that I am* was flowing *through* my physical form and connecting with the energy of others."

"I ended up having three or four delightful conversations with complete strangers, all of which went deep quickly. And, interestingly, each of those folks were really struggling with something in their private, personal lives. All I wanted for them was for their struggles to be absorbed and obliterated by an awareness of who and what they are. Well, I knew I couldn't force that kind of awakening to happen, but I could allow the good vibes to flow through me. And that felt like enough then, and always has since. Just be, and watch the magic unfold. It's a funny thing how even the smallest amount of light we allow to flow through us is often enough to push back a whole lot of darkness."

Pappy continued. "So anyhow, that whole day, the subtle, crackling energy persisted… all around and through me. I could see, or rather feel, the energy reaching out from my chest and trying to connect with itself in others. I could feel other people's energy hidden behind the layers of their senses of self… just like it had been for me. And it was like the energy flowing through me was reaching to pull itself out through what was holding it back. And I was just sort of watching it happen!"

"As the energy coming through me would reach out to folks, I'd often then find myself chatting with them. I could feel it was the raw humanness of our interaction that would soften their blockages... just taking the time to slow down and *see* people, to really listen. It's so simple. There's so much power in just holding space for people... just being with them in their experiences, whatever they are. It was all so new to me, and I was loving every single minute of it. With a few folks, their energy burst through their shells quickly and we were riffing with each other on a deep plane almost right away. With one woman, there was this wild, immediate connection. We didn't even say anything. We just sort of walked by each other and I could feel our energies connected like old friends... then they separated, at least to the extent any of us are ever separated. And her eyes said she could feel it too! So, we just enjoyed this lingering and engaged smile with each other while we passed. That was *really* cool. With others, I could tell they felt the energy coming from me, but their barriers were just too significant, and the sense of connection was inhibited. And all of it... every experience... was ok with me. I just felt compelled to simply be... and to let others be... and to let the energy do its dance."

Pappy suddenly seemed a bit talked out, but also refreshed by the memory of that morning. A lot of my attraction to Pappy suddenly made sense. I could feel his love for me and others. I could tell he completely respected my autonomy, individuality, and life experience. I had always felt something wanting to come out of me and connect with him, and I wouldn't have put those words on it over the years. But the way he framed the experience resonated deeply.

Pappy held up his hand and extended his index finger. "It was *one breath*. One. Conscious. Breath. Everything changed with the grace of one breath taken with awareness of who I am, and what I am a part of. And everything that has flowed since has been just that, too... just one conscious breath at a time and life has unfolded beautifully."

"Everything has been different since that morning, and the same." Pappy smiled. "It's *all* good." He paused. "Now, you hear me say that a lot... and 'it's all good' could be misunderstood as naïve, or even insensitive. I'm not saying everything has been the way I'd have chosen it, or that I'm living life perfectly… whatever that might mean. And I certainly don't mean every life circumstance could, or should, be labeled universally as 'good'. God knows, there is some tough stuff that happens. But like I've said, I absolutely believe in the perfection of the process and have complete trust in the flow… that The One is for me." Pappy smiled wide and breathed deeply. Then he took a sip from his cup, placed it on his armrest, and pulled the blanket around him.

"So, that's it. Betsey, thank you… so very much… for asking me to share all that. And, McLean, thank you for asking the question. I hope you can understand that in a very real sense, it was another man who shot the original Piccolo. My Christian friends would call him the 'old man'." Pappy smiled at the children who had fallen back to sleep, then at the family who had been so kind to him with their attention. Thank you *all* for listening. It has been one of the greatest privileges of my long life to have a chance to share all this with you." As he let his gaze linger on his gathered family, we could feel his love for us.

Nobody said anything for a few minutes. We all just sat still and absorbed all that had been shared. Then Betsey's daughter, Lauren, spoke up.

"Pappy, thank you for sharing all of that! It was such a gift to us. I'm pretty sure I speak for everyone when I say I can absolutely sense in you the energy you're talking about. It's part of what we love about you. And I understand what you mean, I think… that it's not yours, but is yours… and that it's something we all share and are unified by, whether we are aware of it, or not."

Pappy smiled at her. "Thank you, Lauren. Yes. We're all connected more than most realize." Pappy said with a wink.

Then Lauren spoke what was on most of our minds. "Well, I, for one, would sure like to know how things turned out. I mean, what a profound and sudden transition in your spirit! But the circumstances in your life were still really hard for you all. How did your new awareness affect how you engaged with all that tough stuff? I mean, that's sort of the ultimate test, isn't it?"

"I don't want to push if you're worn out, or be interpreted as dismissive of the experience itself and all you shared. But would you be willing to tell us a bit more? I mean, we understand what led to the turn, but how did you and Nana come through it – and out of it? And did this new way of being have a significant influence on all that?" There were nods all around the dwindling fire, and a voiced consensus that at least a little better closure would be appreciated.

"Well, thanks for asking, and I guess that is important to address. I agree… it's one thing to have some airy-fairy experience in a vacuum. But the real test of something like that is how it plays in tough circumstances. And you're right… I was at my breaking point before waking up that morning. So, yeah, if y'all want to hear it, I can give a pretty quick rundown of how things played out from there."

There were more nods around the fire, so Pappy reopened the last journal, flicked through it quickly, then set it aside again.

"I don't really need a journal to prompt my memories about this. I remember the season well. I remember it because things got worse… *a lot* worse. My physical healing seemed miraculous, and it took some time to settle into a belief that it was long-term healing. But it was real, and that was a huge gift. But all the other issues were still very much in play. And the only two things I could imagine making things any worse were about to happen. I was about to enter the refining fire. It's more hard stuff… but it turned out great."

"I'll lob this out there before saying too much, since it'll help calibrate you to my state of being with all the challenges to come. After a year, or so, without any language for the experience, I finally found some language from the Buddhist tradition that really seemed to sum it up. It's along the lines of the 'same but different' stuff I've been saying. There's a story of a teacher who is asked by his student what enlightenment is like. The teacher says that it's just like life as before, only you feel you're walking about two inches off the ground. That really made sense to me when I read it, and it's a great way to articulate my experience. Life keeps going. It's just that I felt I was in the world, but not of it... that the things of the world had grown strangely dim." Pappy smiled playfully.

"Another saying is, 'before enlightenment, chop wood and carry water; after enlightenment, chop wood and carry water'. I used to talk about 'connecting' to God on the river or wilderness, or whatever. And I don't know how to explain the difference between those ways of connecting and this new way. But the connection after that morning absolutely has had a different quality to it. It's a quality of an intimate love relationship full of peace. And it allowed me to sort of float through what I'll refer to again as the refining fire, even while I had to deal with the challenges on a practical level. It's like the confidence you might have when knowing someone has your back. I had this profound sense of resilience knowing I could deal with *anything* that came my way, because I was enjoying a profound, deep knowing of love and security that had me convinced everything was working together for good, no matter how hard it might be."

"And that's a good thing, because I was about to be forced to decide if I was going to fight to hold onto my newfound joy, or lapse into my old patterns and take the familiar path of fear and anxiety. A *real* season of testing was in store."

CHAPTER EIGHTEEN

RECONSTRUCTION

Andy suddenly got up with playful exaggeration, grabbed two smaller logs from the wood pile, and tossed one on the fire. Thousands of small sparks exploded into the calm night sky. "I should've known to put more on a while ago." He said, without looking at Pappy but with a wry smile. His lighthearted mocking of Pappy's longwindedness garnered laughs from the group. Andy was a quiet man, but often quite funny. And he was known to have a gift for bringing levity to the hardest of situations. Even after Greg had died in the D|C War, Andy had maintained an authentic elegance, grace, and even humor. Pappy got the joke.

"Haha, funny guy. This won't take *that* long… but another log or two can't hurt!" Pappy winked at Andy.

And that was true. The early morning hours were infused with a chill, and we appreciated the additional heat. Andy winked back at Pappy and tossed the second log. More sparks exploded from the pit, then drifted lazily into the sky. As I watched their joyful dance toward the stars on luminous display, it was as if they sought to re-establish their connection.

"Love you, Dad." Andy said as he took his seat.

The oak caught flame while Pappy scanned the last half of the final journal. We sat gazing at the fire, enjoying the mesmerizing effect the waves of heat were having on the bed of embers, as dark black transitioned to light blue, then orange, and back to black.

Pappy finally spoke up, "Ok, so my return travel pattern from those trips to Colorado was to fly into Atlanta, then drive the two hours north to our farm. And during all that travel after such an incredible morning, I enjoyed a sort of lifted feeling that is impossible to articulate."

"I finally got home a little after ten. Andy and Betsey were asleep, and Nana had waited up for me, but was about to go to bed too. She was always pretty worn out when I'd come home from those trips… which was completely understandable, considering all the irons she had in the fire while I was gone. So, that night we just said our hellos, then goodnights."

"It was hard, though. I was still energized and wanted to share all that had happened with her. I wanted to try to articulate the experience with my soulmate, and it seemed like doing so would help solidify it! But she needed to rest, and I knew the conversation required time and space since it was going to be hard to communicate it in words. I have a hard enough time doing it now, more than eighty years later… so you can imagine how much I fumbled back then! Right after the experience, and for years down the line, I simply had no language for it, except from some ideas outside our Christian tradition… and I knew that was likely to present a challenge. I was acutely aware the experience transcended any religious box, and I wanted to soar in the freedom of that. But I knew I needed to keep it as grounded as possible in the religious tradition we'd built our marriage and family on. And while I know now that Jesus' teachings offer some ideal language and metaphors for my experience, I didn't have that understanding back then… and I sure could've used it! I stayed up most of that night ruminating on the best approach, and ultimately fell asleep with no clarity."

"Even though I knew weaving Christian language through our conversation would make Nana feel more comfortable, I was pretty sure I wasn't going to be able to keep it confined there. I had a sense for the risks, and those risks concerned me, since the potential fallout was significant. Considering what I figured she'd heard from mom about our conversation, I didn't know how she was going to receive *any* attempt to relay my experience, since the denial of my religion alone was so important. The way she and I understood things back then, someone who did what I'd done was 'outside the fold' and was even considered 'dangerous to the faithful'. And in fairness, if someone had explained such an experience to me less than a year before, I'd have judged it all as absolutely wrong, that the person was deceived, and that the deception was 'of Satan'. So, I was in a bit of a pickle, and I knew it." Pappy sighed.

"As I drifted off to sleep, I realized my mind was *really* involved with thoughts about how the conversation with Nana should go, and I found myself really twisted up. And that was an important lesson, though I didn't know it then. Again, I didn't have any guidebooks for this. I know now that I should've just trusted I could be present, not think much, and allow Source to flow the right words through me. But I hadn't learned that yet."

"I woke early the next morning, and was surprised I felt pretty much the same as I'd felt the day before, with the sense of love and the crackling energy, and all that. It was still *way* cool and totally new, so I just tried to settle in and enjoy it. But that morning, I had more than just a beige wall to stare at! We had a big bay window that looked out over a green, sloping pasture, which then extended down to a lovely, peaceful pond. I remember the water was reflecting the blue of the sky, and the pasture grasses were tall, with a lot of wildflowers throughout. It was simply idyllic… we'd built something really special together."

"And when I looked out that window and took it all in, I was in awe of the beauty… almost dropped me to my knees in reverence. I think anyone would appreciate the view, but I was completely overwhelmed. I could hardly handle the raw majesty of it all. And I was *feeling* it, too… not just seeing it, but literally *feeling* it!"

"Suddenly, I was aware I needed to be in the air outside. So, I walked from our bedroom, through the French doors and out onto the screened porch. I closed my eyes, felt the air, and drank deeply from the sounds of life that only a farm in the South in the spring can offer. Even with my eyes closed, the beauty of birdsong and wind in the trees was still almost too much to take in! Then, playing with the experience, I remember deciding to open my eyes to re-engage the visual dimension."

"What happened was so cool! It was separate from the more general experience that had stayed with me since that breath. This was specific to the physical experience… when whatever is beyond this dimension is revealed in this realm. I used to think mystical experiences were only legit if you saw all kinds of bizarre things through your 'third eye'… auras, new geometrical shapes, cool new colors and energy patterns… stuff like that. Something like what you see in that wild artwork from folks who try to draw what they've experienced during a mystical experience. But what struck me that morning was the realization that without the overlay of my mind's understandings of life experiences, then what I was seeing, feeling and experiencing was the most amazing 'trip' one could have!"

"How much more diverse could you want something to be than the life that is unfolding in front of us all the time? I realized right then that familiarity destroys wonder and awe. It's like I could somehow 'see' more, since my mind's unnecessary activity had been reduced so greatly. I won't try to explain it further… I'm already sidetracked, anyhow." Pappy shot a quick, acknowledging smile at Andy and Betsey.

"Nana and I always liked to catch up over coffee in the mornings after my trips back from Colorado, and that morning was no exception. She'd calibrated toward a lighter morning of work so we could visit, and so had I. And it's a good thing we had the time blocked, because we needed every bit of it... and a whole lot more, actually. Let's just say that even with as much as we loved and respected one another, and as hard as we tried to have conscious conversation, it didn't go well. I tried to explain how full of love, joy and peace I felt, but I ultimately botched it. I couldn't keep it confined to Christian terms, and made the mistake of trying to bring in concepts from other traditions I'd read about to try to explain the experience. But all that understandably led to a lot of pain, tears, and hard questions." Pappy shook his head sadly.

"That morning, we only just began working through the issues that came up, and there were so many more that arose over the next few weeks and months. Working through everything took many years. Even as important as it is, I don't want to talk much about this, since Nana isn't here. But I will say it was one of the hardest parts of my journey, and Nana would probably say the same about hers. It was traumatic for her, and it never did get easy for her to think back on that long season. I'll offer a few comments so you get some insight into what we were dealing with, but not saying much to unpack it feels best. There are a lot of great lessons to be learned from our experience during those years, but her voice would need to be represented, and I wouldn't do it justice. And we don't have time for it anyhow... it could be a whole story in and of itself!"

"I will say that while I certainly never wished it, I understood the hurt I was causing with my attempts to share the experience with her. It seems I just dug myself into a deeper and deeper hole, causing increasing confusion and suffering as I tried to reframe and reword the explanation. And it broke my heart. I know now that trying to put adequate and accurate words on an experience like that is futile. And she, of course, had a really hard time trying to wrap her head and heart around what I was attempting to communicate. One of the main things she heard and held onto was that I'd denied Christianity." Pappy shook his head and frowned. "And it's of course true that in my ignorance I'd told her that. I just didn't know any better. It's hard to imagine I didn't understand the scope and diversity of the religion I'd dedicated my life to up to that point, but I didn't. I had no idea the evangelical tradition within Christianity only represented a rather small fraction of the broader community. And she didn't know that either. So, you can likely imagine how hard that must have been for her… especially as we thought about Andy and Betsey, and how to parent them. And what would our community look like moving forward… not to mention our own marriage? It was devastating."

"I'd of course tried to communicate as sensitively as possible, but the reality was that I'd made her head spin and her heart sad. Her confusion and concerns were legitimate, and the issues were significant. She suddenly had to wrestle with so many new and challenging questions… questions that no devoted Christian spouse would ever want to deal with. How could the God, and the spiritual path that was so healing and peace-giving for her, be rejected by her soulmate… the same man who'd discipled her for so many years? How was it possible that her seminary-trained husband had denied Christianity… and that after doing so, he felt better? She wondered if I'd been deceived, or that perhaps my experiences were delusions from the neuroinflammation caused by the Lyme disease. She was concerned that I may be in major trouble, yet also saw that I seemed peaceful, even happy. Pappy paused, and smiled softly. "And, ultimately, she wondered what love should look like in that situation."

"Pappy paused for a long moment, staring into nothing that we could see. Then turned to look at young McLean.

"But God was merciful during that season." Pappy smiled at the little girl as she sat staring up at him with tear filled eyes. "After a long time of great sadness, a little light finally came into our experience… and McLean, you'll appreciate this." She sat upright, obviously pleased that her simple inquiry hours ago had been the catalyst for such a story. He winked at her.

"It was during that time when I started retreating to the woods more… simply being in and with the environment, just appreciating the stillness. I'd often walk across the pasture, past the pond, and up to a rock formation deep in the woods. I'd pray there, practice yoga, meditate, or just sit and let myself be amazed by the intricate beauty of nature for hours. Well, Nana understandably didn't know what to think of me and the whole situation. She didn't like a lot of what I'd voiced, but she also couldn't make sense of the changes in me she was observing. She wasn't willing to label them as good, because she didn't trust the source of the changes. But she also wasn't willing to judge them as bad, since the changes were along the lines of more peace, joy, and love. It was so confusing for her… a really tough spot, since what she was observing challenged so much."

"So, anyhow, there was apparently a moment that convinced her to open herself to the notion that something good might be happening. I had nothing to do with it directly… it was a God thing, I guess. One morning, I was walking across the pasture on my way into the woods, and I didn't know it, but she was watching me from that big window in our bedroom. The way she explains it, the dogs were with me… something that'd come to be a constant since returning home after my experience in Colorado. But what was interesting to her was that the *cats* were with me too. We were apparently all walking along across the pasture together, just as happy as can be." Pappy laughed and slapped his knee. "It was the fact that the animals… the cats, in particular… were wanting to be with me, responding to something attractive and safe in me, that gave your Nana some hope. And that sudden and refreshing hope that maybe all was not lost… that perhaps God was, in fact, at work… kept her holding on and hanging in!"

"Getting through those challenges took a lot of love, commitment, mutual respect, trust, and trying to find humor where we could. We knew deep down that we were eternally connected in ways we didn't pretend to understand… and we took comfort and trusted in that connection. We learned over time that a marriage is the two committed individuals, and a third entity… that one plus one equals *three*." Pappy paused, debating whether to run down yet another rabbit trail. He decided not to, and continued.

"And there was the sense of loss of my community during that time, too. I knew what had happened to me was available to all, regardless of religion. But my experience and newfound way of being was, as far as I could tell, something foreign to my community at the time. I'd learned some valuable lessons about how to frame the experience so as not to offend Christians, but it seemed they just couldn't accept the reality of my experience. They didn't outright call me a liar… but they didn't know what to think of it all either."

"So I ended up having a hard time staying in that community for a host of reasons. Some of those reasons were related to frustrations I had about the pain and disconnect from God I'd experienced for so long, since I believed much of that suffering was rooted in my old beliefs… beliefs which most in that community held as absolutes. And based on several candid conversations with folks, I discovered I was considered someone to be on guard around, since I threatened norms. It felt like I was suddenly swimming the opposite direction of everyone I knew."

"At one point when I was still trying and failing to explain my experience, I told some friends that I felt 'one with God'. I knew it was a strong statement, but that was the only way I knew to say it at the time, and I remember hoping it might be celebrated. But, after that, I was considered more a 'wolf in sheep's clothing' and a 'demon masquerading as an angel of light' than a brother. One person I really cared about deeply even called me the Antichrist! All that might sound really mean, but it wasn't. I knew they were saying those things out of love for me… trying to bring me back. And it was fair enough, but it didn't feel great. I truly appreciated their concern for me and my eternal wellbeing. I mean, what kind of friends would they have been if they believed I was damned to hell and didn't then try to bring me back into the faith? I just confused them, and so I suddenly felt very much on the outside of something I used to cherish."

"So, a very important connection point had been severed with Nana, and also all my friends. A loss of community led to a very lonely, long season. I'd lost so much over the last few months, and was aware of that. But, somehow, and sort of like the exercise of bringing my financial situation to mind that first night after my breath, the peace had persisted. And so had the general sense of joy and love… which was great for me, but wasn't entirely a good thing, since it irritated folks to see me so content within so much loss. I think it made people believe I was aloof and detached… which is ironic, since that wasn't the case at all! I'd never felt more grounded in life! It's just that I'd lost judgement about my losses, and had completely surrendered to what was and was trusting in the flow. Then, after a long season with all that going on, another thing happened which was a major turning point."

"I'd traveled out to Colorado again for business, and I met up with an old, wise friend. I'd asked him to lunch because he was such a kind man, and I thought he might have some wisdom to share about what I was going through. He listened well to my explanation of my breath experience many months before, and what life had been like since. He responded with such tender kindness, then he shared something that changed my life forever… and likely our family's whole trajectory."

"I knew he was Greek Orthodox, though I didn't know the depth of his theological training within that tradition. He leaned across the table with an expression of joy, grabbed both of my hands with a gentle firmness, and slowly said with great conviction, 'You are experiencing the blessed state of theosis. And that, my young friend, is something to be profoundly grateful for.' I looked at him quizzically with tears welling up in my eyes while he continued. 'Your experience is decidedly Christian, though I wouldn't say exclusively so. Theosis is a core doctrine in Eastern Christian theology. You've had an acute experience, and it's important to know that it's also a process… there is much mystery here. Protestants in the West might call it salvation and sanctification.'"

"Well, I sat there slack-jawed for a long moment… I was absolutely floored! I'd never heard anything about the doctrine, and it dates back to the earliest Christians! I wonder to this day how I'd never heard of it, with all my study and formal seminary training. And I know that if any of you look into theosis, you'll find plenty of people who disagree with the doctrine... *plenty*. But, there are Christians who disagree about *a lot* of stuff! The fact that there was an enormous cohort of Christians who would've celebrated and understood my experience was more meaningful to me than I can possibly articulate. The reality was that by that point, I didn't really care too much about a religious box for my new paradigm. But being able to claim Christianity sure was important for our family, and for the community we cherished."

"So, that conversation was a profoundly wonderful gift for me. Feeling comfortable claiming Christianity solved a huge problem for me and Nana, and especially when it came to raising the kids. And I believe my reconstruction began in earnest around that time. As you know, I consider myself a spiritual mutt. But Christianity is my home tradition, and it's the primary language I use to this day. I definitely riff with the Buddha and Krishna... and the writings of Lao Tzu, and many others who I believe God spoke through. But at the end of the day, Christianity is home. It was also made life easier, since it was also the home tradition of our culture back then. Americans celebrated Christmas and Easter, and presidents even swore oaths on Bibles. We even used to have 'In God We Trust' written on our money!"

Then the teenage Jenny spoke up from across the firepit.

"Hey Pappy, sorry to interrupt... but, I have to jump in. I hear you, and appreciate all you're saying, but I'm really curious... what does theosis mean?" She was very involved in her church's youth ministry and service work, and was by all accounts a beautiful young woman inside and out. She had always taken her faith very seriously, and this was all clearly new to her.

Pappy took a moment to gather his thoughts, then offered, "Theosis generally refers to one's coming into a profound and experiential understanding that one is the manifested energy of God... while absolutely acknowledging one is not claiming to be God's *essence*. So, effectively, theosis seeks to explain the empowering and humbling experience of union with God. Does that make any sense?"

"I guess so." Jenny said. "But I do have *a lot* of questions about all that!"

"Well, Jenny, it would be a true privilege and pleasure to chat with you for a little while… maybe even tonight for a few minutes while it's all fresh, if you're inclined. But, sweetheart, please know that God has you *right* where you're meant to be for *your* journey. I don't want something I say in relaying *my* story to interrupt the beautiful life you're living, or the sense of connection with God you so clearly enjoy. We're all on this journey together, and one person's steps might be the same as others we're traveling with… or might not. We all just need to trust what's in our hearts and stay in the flow of love."

Jenny nodded, but it was clear all Pappy was sharing was a lot for her to absorb. Pappy smiled at her, then bumped his heart with his fist and gently cast two fingers her way. This was a holdover expression from when Andy and Betsey were growing up. It was just a fun, quick way for them to say 'love-to-you', and it was a gesture the family had adopted and employed over the years. Jenny did the same, and they smiled at each other.

Pappy continued, "Theosis did a good job of articulating how I felt after that breath, and how I've felt ever since. I'll be forever grateful to that old friend for his wisdom… he was a real angel in my life. He lapsed deeply into dementia not long after that, and we lost touch." Pappy held space for the memory, and was likely also reflecting of what a tragic disease Alzheimer's used to be in the West.

"For quite a while before meeting with my friend in Colorado, I'd been in a sort of no-man's land with my spirituality. And that was challenging, but good. It was fruitful for me to be wandering in that wilderness, because I was consistently forced to settle into the simplicity of what I'd come into an awareness of… and just rest there. I had to practice just being content with what was, and hang onto my deep knowing that God was always with me, in me… and for me. And I found that was always enough, even with all the challenges."

"So, after learning about theosis, God then finally led me to some teachers who pointed out the rich tradition of a mystical orientation to God that wove its way through *all* religious traditions... and those folks became tremendous new influences on me. They became my community in a very real sense, albeit only through the pages of books and on screens. But they pushed me to go deeper, to let go of any resistance, and to settle more and more into The More. And being bolstered in my new paradigm during that time was enormously helpful, because the challenges to come were about to turn up the heat on my refining fire meaningfully."

"During that time, as Nana and I were struggling mightily to rebuild our relationship with each other and our community, we suddenly had yet *another* series of significant challenges to deal with. Considering the challenges we were already struggling with, I'm surprised the brutal season that descended upon us didn't break us. It's one thing for a parent to be ill, but entirely another for your nine-year-old child to suffer." Pappy glanced at Andy, who smiled back. "Over the course of a few months... and I'll spare you the gory details... Andy's health started crashing for reasons we didn't understand. He started feeling weaker and weaker, then explained he couldn't think, had horrible nausea, and couldn't sleep. His symptoms quickly worsened, and then he started having a hard time breathing... and that of course took things from concerning to scary. It was so hard seeing your child's health unraveling like that, and feeling so helpless. Nana, though... she got *on* it! As y'all know, she was one of those people who was the full package... she was simply brilliant. She'd turned Harvard down for her undergraduate studies, and had chosen to take the science track at Duke University. Yep... the brains of the family!" Pappy smiled at all of us.

"So, when it came to medical stuff, that was her domain. Long, long story short, it turned out Andy had inherited specific genetics from me and

Nana… and so had Betsey, for that matter. When certain genes got turned on, we couldn't detox from biotoxins… especially molds. And all that's also probably what made my experience with Lyme disease especially rough."

"Our understanding at the time was that the situation was very serious. We've learned a lot since then about epigenetics, and we've even been able to turn off the genetic expression that caused this problem for us. But at the time, as we were learning about it, it was all new and really scary. We had a long medical road ahead of us learning how to manage all that… and the first few miles of that journey were awful. Chronic illness is no joke, and I didn't want anyone in the family enduring what I recently had… or worse."

"According to the docs who understood it, Andy's labs suggested he was dangerously close to lapsing into auto-immune disease. Interestingly, my labs and Nana's suggested we were on the precipice of something devastating too. And Betsey's indicated she wasn't far behind. So, all that obviously represented a huge new problem to deal with… and there were no obvious solutions."

"So then, in addition to serious new health concerns, going into deep credit card debt to pay the bills that had piled up, lack of community, a fragile business, and my relationship with Nana being, well, *strained*… there was yet *another* blow to come. Nana and I decided after *a lot* of research, prayer, and consultation with medical professionals that the wisest decision for us was to move away from the Southeast." Pappy hung his head and shook it at the memories.

"In the early stages of getting the whole mess sorted, and after we finally found the right medical counsel, our doc had said we should consider moving to a more arid climate. Well, that was a shock, and we just weren't ready to hear something that significant at that point. But after a few weeks, we developed a more informed sense for what we were dealing with, and we realized that she was right… and that we needed to move quickly. Andy's lungs appeared to be fibrosing – stiffening – and his consistent anxiety was turning into panic attacks. And the stress of everything going on during that season brought on some scary symptoms for Nana too."

"The doc believed Andy's lung condition might be reversible if we could get him into a clean environment and help him detox. For every ten buildings in the South, it was quite likely nine of them would be moldy, if not ten. So, if we were to stay, we'd have had to live in a bubble. And, as hard as it was to consider leaving behind all we'd built, living always on our guard against something that threatened our vitality so significantly wasn't an appealing option."

"We figured that back in Colorado, maybe three or four buildings would have interior molds, and that was a significant enough delta for us to decide to make the move. Buildings just weren't built as well back then as they are now, and folks didn't know about mold toxicity, or the realities of sick-building syndrome… or anything like that. We know now those things were responsible for so many of the mystery illnesses people used to struggle with, and our experience with all that was a major catalyst for THRIVE | CO."

"So, we decided we had to leave the farm." Pappy put his head in his hands, rubbed his forehead for a few seconds, then looked back up.

"Whoa… that was *so* tough. All that had led up to the Grand Experiment, all we had just built, all the beauty it expressed, and all the investment of heart, time, money, and faith… it's just impossible to relay the heartache about moving we that suddenly carried. It was like one of those awful scenes in a movie when a hero is getting beaten up really bad by a bunch of thugs for a long time… then he tries to stand up, and someone hits him again with a devastating blow and knocks him down again. That season really did feel like that. Just *brutal*!"

"But, when your child's health is on the line – and your whole family's too, for that matter – you just go with what you think is best, even if you don't have *all* the data you might want to make such a big decision."

Making that move was a real leap of faith with the science of the day, and so much of the pressure of that decision fell on Nana."

"Now, a move might sound easy enough to do. But please try to appreciate the lay of the land, and how challenging that was going to be. First, we had no money, and cross-country moves with a family aren't cheap… nor was the Colorado lifestyle we were going to be moving back to. We'd spent all our life savings on the farm, and then some. And, to make that blow worse, we'd spent a lot of money on stuff we knew we'd never recoup. For example, we had invested huge amounts in special soils and significant structures that made the property unique, but which would require an even more unique buyer. Selling it quickly, or for anything near what we had put into it, was a tall order. It was a blow financially that I just couldn't absorb. So, at forty-four years old, when everyone I knew my age was quite secure and established financially, I found myself having to ask for very significant personal loans so we could make the move, pay the medical bills, and get back on our feet."

"But then the move itself… wow! Once we made the decision to go, we had an incredible logistical challenge to deal with. Unwinding a farm quickly wasn't easy… finding and dealing with the right realtors for such a specialty property, selling off equipment, dealing with the gardens and livestock, getting the house and property in condition to show to buyers. Looking back on it, I don't know how the two of us made it through those stresses without ending up in strait jackets. But the worst of it was the heartache Nana and I felt as parents."

"Your Nana and I would have gnawed our own arms off if we could've spare Andy and Betsey deep heartache… any parent would. But we couldn't spare them the storm that was upon us… we could only try to help them navigate through it without suffering too much trauma. And that wasn't easy, especially since the two of us weren't on the most stable footing in our own relationship. Imagine having to explain to your precious seven-year-old daughter and nine-year-old son that within days they would have to move away from a unique and beautiful life which they were deeply attached to.

Then, imagine having to pile on by explaining they couldn't take anything with them because their clothes and toys were likely contaminated with the very molds that had been making us sick. Their soul-sobs and tears were absolutely heart-wrenching. And Nana and I had to do the same with our own stuff... clothes, furniture, and so many sentimental items we'd collected over the many years of our marriage. We just couldn't take it with us and risk contaminating our new environment, whatever that was going to be in Colorado. We were, in a very real sense, refugees... and running from an enemy that nobody understood the risks of, and most thought we were overreacting to."

"So, after we spent some time sorting out all those logistics as best we could, we handed the keys to the farm to a friend... one of the Jestroms from the compound, actually. He was wonderful... such a tremendous help, and he agreed to take care of the property we'd poured everything into while we figured out what to do with it. Then, early one morning as we cried and mourned together, we loaded up in our old truck... one of the only things we kept from the whole farm experience... and simply drove away. And just like *that*... " Pappy snapped his fingers. "... the beautiful Grand Experiment was over."

Pappy paused for about a minute while he let the emotion of the memories flow through him. And we all used the long moment to wrap our hearts around the situation he had just laid out for us, at least as much as we could, having not lived it. It was hard to imagine all that struggle, and in the context of so many other struggles. It was hard not to get a bit lost within the many layers of significant individual challenges being endured simultaneously. It did seem like a hot refining fire, and I am sure I wasn't alone in my intense curiosity about how Pappy's new way of experiencing life had sustained him through all of it. The last log collapsed into two sections, each settling deep into the glowing embers, casting off what would be the last flames of the long evening.

"So, since this is a more arid part of Colorado, we used a big chunk of the borrowed money to rent a house right here in this valley for the summer of 2016. We drove straight to it, careening headlong into an uncertain future. The idea – or, perhaps I should say gamble – was that we'd get ourselves out of a moldy environment and take a binder to detoxify the stuff our bodies wouldn't get rid of on their own. If that worked, then we'd probably stay in Colorado. If it didn't, then we'd need to figure out next steps from there. It was an informed gamble, and one we simply had to take, but a gamble nonetheless."

"So, through those summer months we followed the strict protocol our doctors had suggested. It wasn't any fun, and it required a lot of commitment and discipline, but we did it. Then we all drove a couple of hours to the city and did our labs so we could find out if things in our bodies had normalized… and, wow, was that ever a moment of truth!" Pappy put his hands to his forehead, pulled his hair back and opened his eyes wide, indicating the sort of stress he and Nana were feeling during that time.

"If all that effort and sacrifice didn't improve our health, Nana and I knew that would cause even more friction in our relationship… and we *really* didn't need any more of that. But the results indicated our efforts were working… that the chronic inflammation that had been creating so much chaos in our bodies was beginning to subside! We were elated to hear the news… knowing we were on the right track was *such* a relief! Sure, there was a lot more work ahead of us on multiple fronts, but we'd turned the big corner and were now headed in the right direction. Health was our primary concern, and the treatment and radical lifestyle-shift were having a tremendous positive impact for all of us! Nana had basically saved all of us from a lifetime of chronic illness… and likely a version of it that would have been a lot worse had she not taken care of us."

"Looking back on it, I believe all those challenges were a test, of sorts… I've been calling the time a refining fire. I have theories around the idea, though I'm pretty sure I'll never fully understand how stuff like that really works until I get to the other side. But I can say for sure that those challenges tested my new paradigm. Josh Garrels was one of my favorite singer/songwriters at the time, and he wrote a song called *Don't Wait for Me*. The last lyric in the song is *'I can't turn away from where I'm going to where I've been'*. And that really articulated my experience with my way of being during that tough season. Even though I didn't know where life was headed, had no words for what I knew to be true… I had no interest in turning back to my old paradigms of fear and anxiety, or to my old ways of relating to The One… as familiar as those paths might have been."

"During the long season of challenge after that breath, I was completely at peace though. I still felt the emotions of challenge, but like I said earlier… there was space around them. I really was living life two inches off the ground. It was a peace I couldn't explain then, and still really can't now. And it has been the same ever since. Even when the rapids of life were really scary, it's like I've just been able to relax and allow myself to be carried along in the flow of the deeper current. In the toughest circumstances, I could always pause, breathe, and recognize my connection to the stillness of being which we all are at our cores… then just put one foot in front of the other with a joyful trust that everything was precisely as it was for a reason, and that it would all work out." Pappy let out a long breath.

"The peace I maintained during that season is also a significant part of what ultimately helped me and Nana in our relationship. It wasn't just that the cats liked me. I was at peace in circumstances would have broken my old self, and Nana saw that. Others who knew me well did too, and life led me to have so many conversations with so many great folks over the years… conversations which they say helped them meaningfully on their own journeys! What a gift that has been to me!"

"And that's really all I've ever done since… all I've ever wanted to do. If I could distill my life since that breath down to its essence, I'd say all I've ultimately cared about is helping others connect with The More. I'd just wake every morning… available, ready, and willing to play some small role in anyone's coming to awareness of who and what they are."

Pappy grinned. "I know for a fact that once a person arrives at the gate of awareness, and boldly steps through it by accepting the good news, life changes profoundly for them. The moment someone tastes even a morsel of the truth that they are the very manifested energy of God, fully accepted and loved, then love, joy, peace, kindness and so many other wonderful qualities, flow into their physical experience. They have moved into 'the Kingdom', to use Jesus' words again… and life then becomes a present to unwrap… as we simply focus on the present, and ride our own rides." Pappy smiled again. The energy with which he was offering his parting words made his love and hope for all people abundantly clear, and his enthusiasm was infectious and inspiring. He couldn't help but expand beyond his own story with what he believed was such good news.

"I believe we are moving toward a time when, as the old Bible prophecy says, 'The lion will lay down with the lamb, and swords will be beaten into plowshares'. As more of us surrender to the gnosis… the deep, mystical conviction of our reality as children of God… and that we are *all* that, regardless of religion, race, gender, nationality, or any other of our silly separating notions… then peace and love will continue to flood the human experience, drowning pain and suffering. I yearn for a day when all people are simply rowing their boats gently down the stream, knowing life is but a dream!"

Andy and Betsey exchanged happy glances, with yet another fond memory prompted. A tradition had started with the four of them during the farm season, and this is one the whole extended family had ended up sharing during large family gatherings over Christmas. After setting up the Christmas tree, we'd make hot chocolate, then bake a huge cookie in a massive cast iron skillet that Pappy and Nana had purchased when they started the The Grand Experiment. Then we'd gather around the tree and sing the old hymn, *'Row, Row, Row Your Boat.'*

Pappy paused, seeming suddenly aware he had gotten carried away. He smiled wide, and looked around at his gathered family very intentionally, one last time. "Sorry… got swept into a strong current there. And yet, it's not a digression at all… all that *is* the main channel! I believe all I just said is what this story is ultimately all about, since, in a very real sense, my story is the story of us all. We're all finding our way home… each of us walking our own unique journeys."

"So, to wrap this final part of this story up… since that breath, I've never known much beyond the next step. And I've never really cared to, except on the level of being curious about what's in store. So, I just keep taking those steps, and with as much conscious awareness of my connection with The One as possible…. then just enjoy watching what unfolds. And it has been quite an unfolding! During our last months at the farm, I was practicing qigong quite a bit, and had also continued my meditation practice. So, every morning during that summer of healing in 2016, I'd go out to a spot by Brown's creek to practice. For about a week, I'd been asking God to reveal my next steps professionally, since we were of course still dealing with the reality of needing a lot of money. But I was struggling with a key question: if I stayed with my profession in financial services, how was I helping folks with the only thing I cared about? How was helping people with their financial lives helping them find peace... helping them take one step closer toward awareness of The More... helping them shine their unique Lights in the world? The reality was that I simply didn't want to do anything if it wasn't aligned with that goal."

"I wasn't a minster or spiritual teacher or anything like that, and didn't aspire to be. I was just a guy with a family who was trying to get along after some crazy life experiences. And I didn't know how I could help folks the way I wanted to with what I'd always done for a living. But wealth management was what I knew, and what I was good at... and it didn't feel prudent to throw the career away just because I couldn't see a way to fulfill my heart's desire within that money-obsessed ecosystem. So, I just kept holding the questions around all that up during prayers and meditations. It was a real tension... there were practical realities about the very real need for money, but I couldn't value how I'd always earned it without knowing I was spending my life energy helping folks with something that was about so much more!"

"Then, it all just sort of came together one morning, and I had clarity about a concept. It was laid on my heart that money was a huge stressor in people's lives, whether they have a lot or a little. And stress, of course, dims peoples' Lights. I was still with a great firm that was purpose built as the antithesis of the sales culture so rampant in the profession at the time. I was proud of our deliverable, and still had a very loyal, small client base. I felt led to rebuild my practice, but with a very different thesis... my only focus was going to be doing what I could to help lift the burdens folks were carrying about their money... and then just see how things went from there. It was a rather simple next step, but was a radical departure from my old professional motivations… and I was suddenly really excited about it. It felt right. So, I opened an office in Colorado Springs with an absolute commitment to stay true to 'my why'."

"I surprised a lot of folks in first few years when I'd have the opportunity to earn someone's business. After a few minutes of get-to-know-yous, and right when they were probably anticipating a typical financial services sales pitch, I'd just lay it on them!" Pappy laughed at the memories of what must have been some interesting conversations.

"I'd tell them I believed they had a unique light to shine in the world – and that the world needed it! Then I'd simply tell them that if they invited me and our firm into their experience with their money, and allowed us to help lift their burdens, then to the extent their burdens were lifted, they'd be incrementally that much freer to be their fullest expression of self for their families, friends and communities… to shine their lights!"

"Now, that was *out there*! But that was my pitch, if you want to call it that… and it was so sincere. Well, it was *really* well received. And I'm glad it was, or I don't know what I'd have done!" Pappy chuckled as he shook his head. "Things quickly developed into the practice philosophy that's pretty well known now… and then into the wellbeing consulting firm you're familiar with, and with all its offerings… and the rest is history. But it was always just showing up every day with one simple question on my heart: how can I help others today?"

"And your Nana… wow! What a ride she went on professionally too! You know her as the successful entrepreneur and policy-influencer. But she started with a humble desire to help folks with the same medical challenges we'd endured. She got more educated and over time became a tremendous resource to folks… the type of resource that our family had needed, but which wasn't available to us. Where I reengaged professionally by seeking to help lift financial burdens, she did so on the medical front. She was a medical professional by training, and after a few years since returning to Colorado, she started helping folks with their medical challenges."

"All either of us wanted was for folks to thrive! I don't think she'd mind my sharing that sometime around 2018, she had a powerful spiritual experience. It was rooted firmly in the evangelical Christian tradition that I'd generally moved away from, but it was beautiful and life changing for her! It's just cool how God works so mysteriously, and in such diverse ways. Our relationship healed meaningfully after Jesus showed up to her in a vision and very clearly told her to put down the burdens she was carrying… that he had them. And in the vision, he was inviting her to a great party being thrown in her honor. Well, she did drop the heavy bags right then and there, and joined the party… she entered the Kingdom! Her life flooded with peace and love too… she'd always been a wonderful woman, but there was a newness… a freshness… to her spirit since that point in her journey! I wish she was here to tell her story… it's just incredible."

"All she'd ever wanted to do with her life was to lift the burdens of others, but her commitment to doing so was renewed… and of a higher order. So, suddenly, and after so many years of intense struggle in our relationship, she and I were so aligned, and our marriage was stronger than ever… even while our spiritual paths looked different. We enjoyed a beautiful union, filled with love, respect, and a deep knowing we were meant to be together."

"And professionally, she was at the right place at the right time. The medical issues we have as a family, and which were so unknown at the time, gradually rose to the forefront of public health awareness… and your Nana was able to be a meaningful part of that. Her professional life evolved quickly, and her work as a public health consultant to both doctors and patients eventually led her to develop powerful modalities that helped many, many people. She's been a huge part of our family's longevity and vitality… and the same for lots of other folks too."

"The point in sharing what happened to the two of us professionally is that we were able to enjoy this groovy intersection of her work and mine in trying to help lift folks' burdens. It has obviously evolved a lot over time, but God honored our hearts' desires and we've been able to help so many people and do so many amazing things together. And parenting Andy and

Betsey was one of the great joys of our lives. They thrived in ways of their own, and became the amazing man and woman you all know and love." Pappy smiled at his children, as he pulled the heavy Guatemalan blanket over his shoulders. I wondered if as he wrapped it around him, it felt like a soft, warm hug from Nana. During their long lives, Pappy's and Nana's influence on the well-being of others did, in fact, make the world brighter. And they were examples of what they taught too.

It had been quite a story. Pappy knew the evening had come to an end, and was obviously ruminating on whether to say something as he looked at the large, haphazard stack beside him.

I ventured, "What is it, Pappy?"

He looked at me with familiar, bright blue eyes. We knew each other so well, and loved one another dearly. He smiled.

"Well, I just had a fun thought. It touches on a principle that I think is so important, and it doesn't feel right to not mention it somewhere in all this. So, if you'll indulge me one more minute – and I really do mean a minute this time – then I'd like to share a quick story to illustrate the reality of an important concept." Nobody moved, and all eyes stayed fixed on him.

"You remember back when things were really bleak for us… when I didn't see any way out of our really tough circumstances? I mentioned I wrote a letter to myself that said in short order I'd know God intimately and also make a crazy sum of money?" Nods were seen around the dim glow of the embers.

"Well, as you now know, the spiritual stuff happened soon after that… and that's of course most important, by a long shot. But it's fun to also point out that within the timeframe I said I would in that letter, I made the *exact* amount of money I wrote down. And we sold the farm that year, and recouped some of our investment in it. That year, I was able to pay off all our debts to friends, family and credit card companies… and even start saving! It was amazing, and so liberating. We owed so much money that it was perfectly logical to believe it would take a *very* long time to pay it off. And why do I share that?" This time Pappy answered his question.

"It's a story to illustrate something I believe is so important. And it isn't about money at all... so, don't miss the point here. You see, things just kept chugging along in an incredible way after coming out of that season. It was so simple too. All I really did was work to maintain my awareness of my connection to God every moment of every day. I'd just try to stay in this open state of submission and trust... trust that life... that God... was for me and our family. It seemed challenges would constantly come up... big challenges... that would give me the opportunity to trust, or not. And I just made the right choice time after time."

"So, then I'd inevitably get some inspiration for a general idea. First step was always to make sure it was rooted in love... in 'my why'. And, if I had clear conviction on that front, then I'd have fun dreaming up the specifics, and I'd put a lot of energy into feeling how I'd feel once the project was completed. Then I'd start taking next steps, doing the whatever work needed to be done. Then it would seemingly miraculously just come together! And watching it unfold was so much fun... like I said a moment ago, it was like unwrapping a present every day! What ultimately evolved might not have been exactly as I'd envisioned it tactically or circumstantially... but usually, whatever was created was bigger than I'd originally imagined! The Bible says we're created in God's image. Well, God isn't a man... or woman, for that matter. The One is Spirit. And the experience of my long life after taking that breath has often made me wonder if the image we're created in is the Spirit of creativity and expansion itself."

"What's so cool is that I'm not special at all with this kind of thing... not at all. Anyone can do it! It's like a birthright, or something. There's a cool Bible passage that says, 'Faith is being sure of what we hope for, and *certain* of what we do not see'. And I've experienced that as a real truth. I mean, how else do you explain the dream I've lived?"

Pappy laughed, leaned forward, and slapped his knee again. "So, how about *that*?" He smiled, and pointed playfully at each of us, knowing he might have been playing the 'old man with wisdom to share' card a little too heavily. But nobody seemed to mind, we even appreciated it. "It's about *being* first… *knowing* who you are, and grounding as deep as you can into that… and staying connected to that knowing. That's your inner purpose, as Tolle would say. But we're not here to be bumps on logs, either. We have an outer purpose, too. We're here to expand and be a part of making this world a better place. So, it's important to connect to a conviction about what The One wants to do *through* you. And then to just *do* it… from your place of *being*! That's being in-spired… *in Spirit*! And you can always trust the inspiration if you know it's rooted in love… if you feel enthusiastic – 'in Theos'… in God. If you can't know that for sure, then just have patience." Pappy paused, satisfied he'd said all he was meant to say. "I hope all that makes at least a little sense."

"The physical life in its highest form is just as scrumptious as the spiritual… in fact, on that plane, the two aren't separate. I've lived a long, long time… a really good life. And the more I see, learn, and experience, the more I realize how little I know. And I love it that way… just the pure *leela* of it all." Leela heard her name and looked up at Pappy. He looked back at her, deep into her eyes. They held each other's gaze for a long moment, then the dog laid her head back down on his feet.

Pappy sat forward and arched his spine. Then he rested back into his chair one last time, pulled the blanket around his whole torso, and lovingly hugged himself tight. He looked around at all of us with kind eyes and a gentle smile, then let go of the blanket, pressed his palms together in front of his heart, gently extended open palms out to the family, and offered what were to be his final spoken words to us.

'Thank you… each of you. Namaste."

Then he closed his eyes, bowed his head, and took a deep breath.

EPILOGUE

Thank you for your interest in this story. I hope you have enjoyed it, and that your own journey is more enjoyable having read about mine.

If you would like to follow along as the story continues, join in community with others who have a keen interest in exploring The More, and/or enjoy resources related to the story, please follow this link:

Patrick
(aspiring Pappy)

Made in the USA
Las Vegas, NV
30 May 2024

90524738R00177